Mike Huss

---

# IT MUST HAVE BEEN THE COMPO

Limited Special Edition. No. 18 of 25 Paperbacks

Mike was born in London and raised happily in Surbiton. He left the grammar school at 18 and joined the regular army straight from school. He volunteered to serve in Aden so as to join his fiancée who had been posted there. She gave him the ring back the night he arrived! He was then stuck in war zone for two years and the book is largely a summary of his time there as expressed in the person of his alter-ego hero, 'Jack'. He met his wife, Janet, in Aden.

A varied career with a N. Ireland Training Board, a group training association, being Personnel Director and Tribunal Advocate resulted in writing the *Dear Doctor* employment law column in *Sunday Times* for 10 years. This is his first venture into fiction.

To my wife, son and daughter, who, although facing many problems, have achieved much to be proud of – I know I am proud of them.

Mike Huss

# IT MUST HAVE BEEN THE COMPO

AUSTIN MACAULEY PUBLISHERS™

LONDON · CAMBRIDGE · NEW YORK · SHARJAH

A CIP catalogue record for this title is available from the British Library.

ISBN 9781528914918 (Paperback)
ISBN 9781528961059 (ePub e-book)

www.austinmacauley.com

First Published (2019)
Austin Macauley Publishers Ltd
25 Canada Square
Canary Wharf
London
E14 5LQ

I have received much invaluable help from my publishing team but most importantly, to my wife, who, hearing my stories for the umpteenth time, said, "You should write a book." So I did.

# Chapter 1

The sign said 'Welcome' but the atmosphere was anything but. Dreary, sad military buildings were everywhere apparent. The only splash of colour was the sash, bright red, worn by the Duty NCO—a Staff Sergeant, by the look of him, but it was difficult to make out the signs of rank clearly at this distance.

He had stopped some 50 yards short of the Guardroom to observe the comings and goings before subjecting himself to incarceration. As he sat in his car, a Rolls-Royce swept past and pulled to a stop at the Guardroom. Immediately, the chauffeur, very smartly dressed in a dove grey suit with accompanying cap and gloves, glided from the vehicle and held open the nearside rear passenger door. The passenger, suited in one of Savile Row's finest, cigarette on and hat tilted backwards from a slight knock against the doorframe, emerged slowly and, having eventually reached an indolent, almost vertical position, proceeded to take in the scenery.

The duty NCO, at this, exploded. "Get that bloody hat on straight, get that cigarette out and get over here NOW, sir!" erupting with a magnitude that would have put Krakatoa to shame. The immaculate apparition, for that was the only description that would do credit to the upwards of £1,000-suited target of the anger, gazed round at a loss to understand to whom this loud series of remarks could possibly be addressed. "Yes, you, you horrible little Officer Cadet, you—get over here NOW!"

With comprehension dawning that he was indeed the target of the invective, the recipient took only a split second to decide the military life was not for him, directed the chauffeur to, "Place the bags back in the boot—we are not staying," and promptly returned whence he had emerged! Seconds later, the Rolls glided away, making a U-turn in clear defiance of a sign forbidding such activities and disappeared, silently, into the distance!

*Well*, he thought, *one down already*. Would he, too, be one of the 'disappearers' or, in his case, RTU'd—returned to unit? As a serving soldier, he did not have the option of leaving the army, only returning to the unit from where he had come. Indeed, how had he come here in the first place?

His mind drifted off. Almost everything that had happened to him, he seemed to have drifted into without any conscious effort on his part to do that something, whatever it was; even the recommendation for Officer Cadet training had come from his superiors—he hadn't applied for it. He had passed the eleven plus on the second attempt, winning a place at the local boys' County Grammar; if his parents had had money, then he would have been accepted into the other grammar school with a posh name and a host of celebrity sportsmen and internationals in the sports department. Mind you, the snobs never wanted to play rugby against his school, even with their supposed superior training, because it was played by his school as a war where no rules, other than don't get caught, were recognised. They may not have been rich, posh or refined, but they did know that winning was everything.

It was his passion for shooting that had pointed him at the army very much against his Headmaster, Deputy Headmaster, Careers Master and his entire family's wishes. As with almost every other young boy of his generation, Saturday morning pictures, and the ever-playing cowboy films, was de rigueur. Hopalong Cassidy, the Lone Ranger, Roy Rogers (you could forget his girlfriend, Dale Evans, she was just a girl—ugh!), all of them were masters of the quick draw and deadly accurate shots—what young boy didn't yearn to emulate them? Unfortunately, Colt 45s were not exactly common in Surbiton!

The best he could manage was a pop out 'air' pistol which relied on the barrel springing out and the loose-fitting pellet carrying on under its own inertia once the trigger was pulled! Hopelessly inaccurate and under-powered, it was so bad that the fear of ridicule from his mates prevented him from revealing even its ownership to them! On one occasion, he had deliberately shot his sister in the back with it, and she hadn't even noticed!

The 'must have', which several of his mates had, was a genuine air-powered pistol, a Webley Junior, which fired a .177-inch pellet at high velocity and with very good accuracy. Hard hitting, it was able to hit close to what it was aimed at in the hands of a moderate shooter and even to actually hit the target, if it wasn't too small or far away, in the hands of a good one—he was.

# Chapter 2

However, it was expensive and way out of reach of his pocket money until, miracle of miracles, the news was announced that his aunt and his cousin were emigrating to America, and he was to be left the Webley pistol of his dreams and, even beyond dreams, a break barrel air rifle, also .177 calibre, as his cousin, an individual totally unsuited to weapons or any manly things—he even went dancing with girls when he didn't have to—would not be able to take them with him to America.

The three months or so before their emigration took an age, especially as his cousin, deliberately he thought, held onto the guns until the day before they departed. He experienced a terrible difficulty presenting an outward appearance of sorrow at the departure; failure to do so maybe resulting in deprivation of the promised rifle—a fate not to be contemplated so close to Nirvana.

He was about 11 at the time and leaving an 11-year-old in the back garden with an unlimited supply of ammunition, a new rifle and pistol and no end of tempting targets was not the most sensible of things to do. At first, getting a feel for the pistol and the rifle by shooting at pieces of card marked up with hand-drawn circles and spots for the centre was okay. However, the small spurts of dust behind the targets were far more interesting, and it wasn't long before the ability to penetrate, smash or otherwise destroy the target aimed at was being explored with gusto! Still, unmoving targets rapidly became uninteresting and unchallenging, so moving targets of tin lids dangling from pieces of string provided much more of a challenge—even if the shots did ricochet all over the place! Screaming ricochets off brick and other solid objects was far more difficult than the films made it seem but oh so satisfying when achieved, even if the final resting place of the pellet was somewhat problematic.

The skill to hit moving targets was to stand him in good stead later when he did join the army, but for now, his nemesis and loss of rifle was taking shape in the form of three particular garments, hanging and swinging amongst others, on the line in the neighbour's garden running across the bottom of theirs. *Would the pellets go through those*, he wondered. The world of 11-year-old boys, in those days, did not encompass bras; they were just one more of the mysteries of the world that was 'girls'. What they did represent was the opportunity to test the penetrative ability and the accuracy of his rifle against moving cloth. Indeed, a neat hole did subsequently appear in each of the cups, all at the apex except for one when the air gusted somewhat more strongly, and the hole was only halfway up the cup! The fact that he was earning himself the unique position of peep-hole bra inventor was to remain forever unknown to him!

Retribution arrived later that evening in the form of an irate neighbour banging on the door and waving around the three 'wounded' garments as irrefutable evidence of his crime. The rifle was immediately taken from him, never to reappear. Other punishments, chiefly the stopping of his pocket money for four weeks, were also handed out to convince him of the error of his ways! In fact, the main lesson he learned from this was the necessity not to get caught—something that was to serve him in far greater stead in the future. Fortunately, loss of the pistol was imposed only for the said same four weeks as loss of pocket money. Even this was to have unforeseeable benefits in developing skill with a pistol which would carry on into the distant future.

# Chapter 3

Shortly thereafter, news arrived that he had passed the eleven plus exam. Requests that the rifle be returned as a reward went unheeded. In fact, he was never to see it again or even to discover what happened to it! However, he was presented with a bicycle—shiny metallic blue with 5 Derailleur gears. This brought various woodlands lakes, rivers, ponds and other open areas within reach, enabling search and destroy missions with his three close companions, his gang, where other gangs could be hunted and shot with pistols where the only rule was that all shots had to be aimed below the waist! Most missed, a sad commentary on their skills compared to that of their Saturday morning celluloid heroes, until one day a particularly accurate shot not only hit a very special tender spot but, with Sod's law in full play, in a place where the covering trousers were very thin. Penetration of the cloth and skin was inevitable and extracting the offending pellet difficult, painful and messy! I suppose it was just luck that the damaged 'target' didn't also develop lead poisoning!

After that, the keenness of the groups to participate in gun fights was much reduced. Waiting in the wings, however, were other shooting opportunities as yet unknown and unexpected—not planned but just sitting quietly waiting.

The summer holiday that year was one of trepidation and excitement in equal measure. It was also hot. Lots of trips to the shops to buy the grammar school uniform, including white shirts with detachable collars, separate collars, a pullover with coloured stripes, house colours clearly delineated (whatever they were), plimsolls, rugby boots (didn't you get hurt playing rugby?), blazer, long scarf, again in striped house colours, long grey socks and short grey trousers (long trousers were not allowed until the second year) all needing name tags attaching. Why did underpants and socks need tags—compulsory communal showers post PT and various sports, of which there were many, were a horror yet to be discovered! All this new stuff was unattractive and expensive, so it carried dire warnings to take care.

Following the war, the make do and mend, rationing of clothes, had created a thrifty and somewhat parsimonious attitude to clothes such that to have all this lot filling up the hitherto empty shelves and drawers of his wardrobe was like a new world. What wasn't so great was having to put it all on and be paraded around in front of sundry neighbours and relatives to show off 'our Jack's success in winning a place at the grammar school'—albeit not the posh one in Kingston but the common one in Surbiton. All this much reduced his free time and limited his shooting to almost nothing.

Being a hot summer, it was ideal for playing out—if only freedom had been available. The heat meant long, hot days and uncomfortable nights, even with the windows wide open. Being semi-detached, next door's noise both through the walls and through the windows was never far away. So close in fact that one night his father farted, a real sound barrier blaster, but before his mother could administer the normal admonishment that wives and mothers normally do, the woman next door could be heard dressing down the bloke next door with, "Don't do that—they'll hear you next door!"

Little did he know that this was to initiate the (disreputable) family reputation for gaseous release, continued by Jack years later when he dropped a deadly creeper in the local library and a poor tramp, sheltering from the snow outside, was summarily ejected for being a filthy beast! He was also to let rip ear beaters at a church parade, one at the annual carol concert at Christmas and one each at two passing out parades for Officer Cadets but probably the most enjoyable was to sneak out an absolutely vile nostril gagger when acting as driver for a certain Minister of Defence to visit Hovercraft trials in Aden and being able to blame it on the rubbish lying about the dock area through which they were passing!

# Chapter 4

Arrival at the grammar school on the first day was an ordeal. None of the other new boys (easily identifiable from their brand-new uniforms and the give-away short trousers) were known to him, and all the more senior boys took evident pleasure in pushing them out of the way accompanied by various forms of verbal abuse.

Eventually, a whistle blew, and silence spread over the playground. Shouted instruction informed the new boys to follow a capped and gowned grown-up to the hall where they were subjected to a mass of information on what was about to happen to them—most of which he promptly forgot. Divided into forms and placed in rooms at desks from which they were not to move on pain of death or worse, their new lives were laid out for them. None of it interested him, only where the tuck shop was and its opening hours until, in the middle of an especially boring and wasted plea to support your House by participating in every club, sport, choir (God, not bloody hymn singing!), drama club (load of poseurs) and operatic society (loads of tenors whose balls hadn't dropped—not that his had yet!), when mention was made of the Army Cadet Force unit.

In itself, this held no interest for him until the magic words, "…and you'll learn to shoot using real .22 and .303 rifles," were uttered. The fact that the Cadet Force was regarded as particularly arduous earned treble points for the House for every parade attended went unheard and unnoticed.

He had been in the Cubs for years and recently had been welcomed into the Boy Scouts. The Cubs had been all right, the camping primitive but challenging (apart from the utterly disgusting holes in the ground overflowing with shit and shit impregnated paper blowing everywhere!) and escape from parental suspicions for a week at camp. His father, an engineer, and his mother, a clerk at the Milk Marketing Board, left home early in the morning, not returning until early evening. His upbringing, therefore, along with that of his twin sister, 45 minutes older than him, having 'pushed past' to be born first and turning him head over heels in so doing such that he presented as a breach baby—something dangerous then—meant, once he learned of it, that he decided that 'arses to the lot of them' would be his personal motto in life.

# Chapter 5

With his parents absent working each day, most of the time his upbringing devolved upon his maternal grandmother and grandfather. Grandpa had been a carter's boy, having left school at seven. At eleven, he had gone down the pit, about the only work available in the South Wales valley of his birth, and had worked underground in various roles until old enough to dig coal when he was transferred to the Pit Rescue Team, not so much because of any real skill or ability in that line, but because he was small, being no taller than 5'4", and wiry with it. He could thus squeeze into very small spaces should the need arise—none ever did. He also became the South Wales fly weight boxing champion for a number of years until the 'dust' got him.

Suspected of suffering from TB, years of tests followed, enabling him eventually to retire on a not inconsiderable pension supplemented by sickness benefit.

Silicosis, its proper description, was not to become known, and compensated for, for many years into the future. Grandpa did, however, work assiduously to ensure his health did not improve, by heavy drinking, heavier smoking and a lifestyle that encompassed everything except effort of any kind, thus continually providing ammunition for the 'Goose that laid the golden egg' in the shape of the NUM and the NCB's pension and disability funds weekly disbursements to his back pocket! The General Strike of '29—lost to the bloody bosses and their forces—only confirmed his right, in his mind, to be kept in social welfare benefits as only proper for one with 'the dust'.

His grandmother, nana, on the other hand was a sweetie. For a woman of her time, well-educated with one sister a school teacher and the other one a nursing sister, she could play the piano and even compose some music. How she had come to marry his grandpa was a matter never openly discussed. Only in later years did rumours of too much drink, a party and a surprisingly short courtship period emerge. What was certain was that they were a very ill-matched couple and probably should never have wed.

In those days, divorce was only for the rich, and so, a basic armed neutrality existed, with Grandpa leading a substantially separate life from Nana and the rest of the family. However, Mum saw it as her sacred duty to preserve the marriage and present to the neighbours and outside society an appearance of a happy family all living decently and respectably under one roof. Consequently, to all outsiders, a life of domestic bliss prevailed!

With both parents working and a grandfather constitutionally incapable of boiling an egg for himself, or even to understand that water was used in the process, Nana effectively ran the house. As far as Jack was concerned, Nana not only cooked, cleaned, washed, ironed and made his bed for him, but more

16

importantly, she was a never-ending source of pennies and protection from his twin sister who, being a head taller and far stronger built, used to bully him unmercifully if Nana was not around.

If anything, his grandpa encouraged the bullying 'as it was good for him' and was a way to ensure that he would be able to stand up for himself 'out there'! Nana could even be relied upon in times of desperate need and unfinished homework to provide a suitable note of exculpation to an increasingly suspicious band of teachers.

The only other fly in the ointment was his uncle, Mother's brother, who lived with them and who had achieved great things in the Scout movement having reached the heights of King Scout shortly before the old King's death. Jack had been bullied, cajoled and coerced into joining first the Cubs and then the Scouts. Jack did not like the Scout Master. Arkela in the Cubs had been fine but there was something decidedly odd about the 'Skipper' in the Scouts, as he liked to be called.

He was forever making physical contact with the smaller boys and stroking exposed legs and arms, even faces and necks, if such could be 'accidentally' contrived. Knowledge of, and discussions about, men who preferred men and/or little boys was a taboo subject in polite society and certainly never entered the world of eleven-year-old boys at that time. With punishment and censure being so severe, if caught, the chances of contact with, or being the target of, homosexual paedophiles were extremely unlikely. For Jack, with another one shortly to appear in the shape of a Latin master, yet to be met, who would also contrive far too much physical contact with pupils, along with a strong predilection for smacking bottoms with slippers, or canes or even his hands, young Jack was to build up an experience of life not normally expected of eleven-year-old boys!

Jack was determined to leave the Scouts. But the problem was how. His uncle's erstwhile success, combined with badges and certificates, minuscule paragraphs and photographs in two of the local papers publicising and praising this success, had created in Jack's mother and nana a desire for more of the same, but next time bigger, longer and better regarding the successes envisaged for Jack which could then be sent back to Wales, with much glee and satisfaction, as evidence of the success of their offspring and fame in the world. The fact was that his uncle was not very bright—his most notorious exploit being when he tried to emulate Tongan fire-walkers, who he had seen in the cinema, by walking barefoot over the garden bonfire and landing up in hospital for a couple of weeks. Jack believed that this meant he would be easy to manipulate, if only a plan could be devised. Jack's intended announcement of resignation from the Scouts and intention to join the Army Cadet Force, (viewed as a facet of the instrument of suppression of the working classes and the breakers of the General Strike by capitalist monsters and Tories—his grandpa's opinion, held for over 40 years) was not going to be easy. In fact, at first look, it would be bloody impossible to achieve.

# Chapter 6

What he needed was a plan. He was to discover he had an intuitive talent for planning, not deliberately and consciously carried out like most people, but effortlessly and unconsciously achieved by going to sleep on the matter—no effort required!

His eureka moment duly arrived at three o'clock in the morning, two nights later. He needed someone else to advise that he should not be in the Scouts and who better than the 'King Scout' himself? Starting a conversation with his uncle about scouting was easy, steering it towards Skipper, a natural follow on. A harmless question about touching hands during knot-tying demonstrations and how nice it was produced an immediate guarded look in his uncle's eyes. A further comment about how nice it was going to be camping with Skipper, even the possibility of sharing a tent with him, resulted in a look of sheer panic! All he had to do then was to let the seed grow and be implanted by his tale-telling, unwitting accomplice of an uncle to his parents and grandparents that Jack's continued membership of the Scout movement might not be a good thing!

A few days later, once he was sure the bait had been taken, Jack returned home from school bearing a letter listing all the clubs, societies, pastimes etc. that the school provided and which stressed in the strongest possible terms that pupils were expected to support as many as possible; earning house points was compulsory as competition between the four houses, into which the school was divided, was seen as 'a jolly good thing' and a proper preparation for life after school and university.

Earnest wishes to join some of them accompanied by immediate reasons why that wouldn't work. "Can't sing," rapidly disposed of the choir and the light operatic society and, "Don't want to dress up as a woman—it's too sissy," provided immediate relief in his parent's eyes for more than one reason when he ruled out the drama society, indicating that Uncle had done as expected and had relayed to his parents Jack's 'innocent' remarks. Having discovered early in life that parents, elders, teachers etc. did not like being presented with problems but loved being presented with a solution to the identified problem, all it needed was for a suitable solution, removing him from the suspect Scoutmaster's reach and providing a manly solution that nicely set up the statement that, "So, of course, if I joined the Army Cadet Force I would earn triple house points, uniforms would be provided free, and I will still be able to go to camp but not have to pay for it (the army provided everything), and benefit from the discipline the army would undoubtedly instil…" had neatly led to, "…but I would have to leave the Scouts because they meet on the same evening…" as a mere formality. (Years later, the Scoutmaster was to receive the proper attention of the law and a period as a guest of Her Majesty's Prison Service, but the subject was never raised at home then or ever in the future).

His uncle never entirely disappeared from Jack's life and would reappear from time to time, even once he had married, to visit family and especially to chat and swap jokes—very, very rude ones to which Jack was suitably introduced when somewhat older.

# Chapter 7

Life at the grammar school was disciplined, controlled and demanding. The teachers, for the most part, were experienced, had seen it all before, had heard all the excuses and believed none of them. The easiest path, at first, was to remain lost in the middle of the pack, never to volunteer (something useful for the army in future years) and never to be noticed until ready. Everything was manly.

Rugby, not soft football, British Bulldog and similar bruise-attracting games in the playground were not just encouraged but compulsory when certain of the masters were on playground duty. Watching who applauded what, who derided what and who could be easily diverted from the task at hand was studied assiduously but rarely to any real benefit. That was with the exception of the two Latin masters. One, an ex-councillor who could be diverted at the drop of a, "My dad says the council is not doing what it should be regarding (insert anything you like)," and carefully introduced into the lesson, ensured that he would explode into a shower of invective about the other party, voters, parents or ungrateful schoolboys depending on the mood. As these explosions very rarely lasted less than 15 minutes, and the lessons being scheduled for 40, it meant that careful timing of the time-bomb question might mean an overrun into the next lesson and a lack of time to set the homework!

Whilst such explosive diversions from him were to be enjoyed rather than feared, explosions from the other Latin master were very much to be feared. They could be set off by anything at all. With no apparent pattern, the best that could be hoped for was not to be the direct victim. He would turn and hurl with amazing accuracy the heavy blackboard duster at anyone talking behind his back whilst he wrote on the black board. To be hit meant to be hurt. He would smack errant pupils with the ruler kept for such purpose—a heavy wooden one with a thin metal strip along its edge, designed to reproduce a straight edge when used for its proper purpose, but deadly at cutting, bruising knuckles and hurting when used to chastise—and it was no use complaining to parents; their attitude was he wouldn't have done it if you didn't deserve it!

Worse yet was to be suffered. Boys reduced to tears would then be subjected to two alternate treatments. Older boys were harangued for their crying and lacking manly qualities, hurtful, even damaging, in adolescents at a sensitive stage of life and without the ability to hit back, but worse was to be handed out to those small, delicate and ever so slightly feminine boys, those always chosen for female parts in the school dramas and operettas. They would be cuddled in front of the class, their tears wiped dry and, when all snivelling had stopped, and the snot had ceased running, they would be affectionately pinched on one or sometimes even both cheeks before being sent back to their seat.

To say that he was universally despised, hated and reviled would be an understatement. However, as they say God moves in mysterious ways his wonders to perform, and one Monday, Jack arrived at school to find the playground alive with rumours to explain the evidently missing Latin master. Sorting wheat from chaff only resulted in even more improbable versions of events, all to be destroyed by a short paragraph, describing events on the previous Saturday night, in the local paper that Thursday when all became clear.

Apparently, the importuned large and violent young man (an ex-pupil!) in the notorious local public toilets was not only not a homosexual but was, in addition, homophobic to an enormous and passionate degree created in no small part by the manner in which he had been treated at school by a certain Latin master who, having made the mistake of approaching the said young man, was currently in hospital but booked for a cell in the local nick for importuning, flashing and other equally illegal activities. Needless to say, he never reappeared again at the school and nor was any action taken against the hero who had put him in hospital.

# Chapter 8

Growing up really started with the senior school. The list of subjects in the curriculum was astonishing compared to the junior school. Listed on the timetable were English, maths, chemistry, biology, physics, history, geography, music, woodworking, swimming, art and crafts, games and PT. Other subjects were offered in later years. In amongst those were odd lessons regarding the school, expected behaviour and what today might be referred to as 'citizenship' but then simply went under the heading of 'manners'.

The hypocrisy started at the same time. In rugby (played by most for the autumn and spring terms), the importance of, "It's not the winning but playing the game," was stressed ad infinitum. Rule observance and pluck were everything! But they weren't! More forcefully imparted, but never overtly or openly stated, was the absolute rule that only the winning counted and you did what you had to do to ensure that, coupled, of course, with the other absolute rule, "Thou shalt not get caught not playing the game!" Biting, punching, squeezing testicles, head butting, stamping on an opponent anywhere you could reach, hair pulling and anything else that would hurt an opponent was perfectly all right, even acceptable, and expected, providing only that you didn't get caught!

Rugby was taught by two ex-Welsh and one ex-English international rugby player. With just over 90 boys in each year, forming six teams with a few leftovers, allowing for sickness etc., meant that three matches could be played each games afternoon. Talking was not allowed. Failing to tackle hard was not allowed. Missing a tackle was not allowed. Slipping over on the wet grass was not allowed. Missing a pass was not allowed. Passing forward was not allowed (perhaps the only actual rule from the rugby rule book!). Being out of position was not allowed. Not only was it a metaphorical pain in the arse, it was an actual one since, to be caught infringing any of them meant having to bend over, clasp one's ankles with legs well spread only for the master concerned to boot a rugby ball, full belt, at the temptingly presented target!

A well-placed kick could result not only in a very sore bum but a pair of bruised knackers as well! And if they should miss with the first kick then they would take the kick again and again until a satisfactory hit had been achieved! So much for playing the game!

He was to find, as he went through life, that of all so-called sportsmen the worst were the rugby players; it was not sufficient that they enjoyed hurting and being hurt (which always happened); they were also drunken oafs with an intense Messianic determination to get others to join them!

Not only that, his grandpa was a drinking buddy (butty in Welsh terminology) of the two Welshmen, who along with others of their race, met regularly at a local public house before any rugby match, and by *any* rugby match I mean *any*; an under 12's match in Llanfairpwllgwyngyllgogerychwyrndrobwllllantysiliogo-gogoch would do! They would then reminisce, damn the English, put the world to rights, damn the English, (in)accurately forecast the outcome of the match in question, damn the English and, as the alcohol intake increased and the wit decreased in like proportion, damn the English some more. All of this bothered Jack not at all, but the passing to and fro of information between his grandpa and the teachers did.

However, his bigger problem was how to avoid joining them (i.e. rugby players)—ever! More thought and sleeping on the subject were needed. True to form, three nights later, it came to him. With always a few left over from team selection each week, the solution would have to be to always be in that group, and the way to achieve that was to sort out the selectors. As the terms progressed, the abilities of the boys would be revealed and more permanent teams developed, but at this stage, a certain selected few, creeps to a man, would be called out and they would then pick, from the crowd of boys, those to play in their team. Once realised, it was a simple matter to isolate them at school and make it clear that selection of Jack to join their team was not a good idea. Thus, within three weeks, Jack was regularly in the leftovers and destined to run round the edge of the playing fields whilst the other rugby-playing poor sods were made to suffer the outrage of the professional sadists masquerading as Games Masters.

A week or two after that, they were being sent out on the cross-country course. Three miles or so of cart track, muddy fields, paved and unpaved road, up and down, through boggy, marshy ground, provided a thorough workout, but better still, run at speed, it meant a return to the pavilion and clean water in the baths before the bruised, pummelled and bleeding warriors were released from their endeavours on the rugby battlefield!

Achieving quick times turned out not to require any great effort; there was something about his natural physiology that meant running, at quite a speed, over rough ground was not particularly taxing or tiring. More importantly, it meant escape from the pack! This ability to run distance at speed was to prove of benefit in the army in the future as it would again ensure he escaped the clutches of the rugby fanatics.

What he did not realise was that his running ability would bring him to the attention of 'authority', and he would find himself dragooned into the school cross-country team. In the sense that running was relatively effortless, this did not matter too much. But what was to upset him was the fact that interschool competitions and county competitions meant that he would have to run on Saturdays and that was a right pain, especially since he used to win and that meant announcements at school assemblies on Monday mornings, thus ruining his attempts at invisibility. He neither enjoyed nor wanted the approbation; after all, what were mere words or a minute of clapping—it would have been far more meaningful if there had been cash prizes or other tangible rewards!

In fact, throughout his first year, he and all the others of his year were being assessed for future streaming. In the second year, classes were organised on assessed ability. The brightest were selected for an academic future, which included Jack, and the not-so-bright ones went into the 'moderns' where subjects like technical drawing, economics and accounting were taught.

In Jack's case, he was to study Latin in which he had come 33rd in a class of 32! Protestations were ignored. Even his father, a technical and precision engineer, who much fancied his son following him into the engineering factory and a passionate lover of technical drawing and design, was unable to persuade the Headmaster that Jack's inclusion in the academic, rather than the Modern stream, was incorrect. Time was to show that his placement, when he was eventually thrown out of the Latin class, was wrong and, by then, his subsequent placement in the Modern stream was too late for him to catch up on the course work to stand a chance of passing GCE 'O' level in technical drawing.

# Chapter 9

It was also the second year when all sorts of things started happening. Hair started to grow in new areas of his body—a subject much discussed amongst the boys, especially following communal showers after PT. The morning stiffy did not always disappear following a pee, and at last, he started growing bigger. In fact, in that year, he grew to be a head taller than his sister and at long last was able to physically overcome her—something his grandpa was quick to stop, although when it had been his sister bullying him, no such rapid intervention had ever occurred.

The demands in school continued to grow. With the second year came more intense teaching, more homework and more pressure to get points for the House. In his first year, his House had trailed the other three by a considerable margin. The best House had duly been presented with the House Year Cup—a small, insignificant thing with most of the silver plate worn off, representing, of course, the principle and effort in winning it, not the value of it! Another lesson learned— it's hard cash that's worth everything; praise, plaudits and ribbons around tatty old cups provided no practical value whatsoever.

The first year in the school Army Cadet Force (ACF) unit had not been a great pleasure. Sure, he had left the Scouts. He had undergone a lot of drill, lots and lots of drill, some weapon training with .303 Lee Enfield rifles but no shooting. Once again, it was a con. The sales pitch "…and you get to fire .22 and .303 rifles…" had somehow seemed to forget to mention that insurance and ACF rules forbade under-13-year olds from joining the ACF. It was not, therefore, until he was well into his second year that he got to visit the range. And even then, it was only to watch older years shooting in the indoor .22 range incorporated into the stable block of one of the three enormous old houses that comprised the bulk of the school.

It wasn't until the start of the summer term that he was allowed to fire a weapon. The weapon in question was a full size .303 Lee Enfield which had been re-barrelled with a .22 barrel. The army had been left with thousands and thousands of Lee Enfields at the end of the war and downsizing some of them to .22 was cheaper than purchasing purpose built .22 rifles. It also had the advantage of introducing recruits to the proper thing in length, size and weight. Someone watching little Cadets struggling with these monsters might have formed a contrary opinion regarding the value of the introduction to full size weapons, but the army would have just ignored them if they did!

The targets were printed on thin card, a pale, off green for the top half and a pale buff for the bottom. The bulls-eye consisted of a circle about half an inch in diameter with the top half of the circle being painted dull black and the bottom half was just the pale buff matching the bottom half of the target. The problem, once he had achieved a position on the firing point and an aim at the target, was that the tip of the foresight, itself a dull black, disappeared into the black of the bull so that aiming accurately and consistently at the same point was difficult, if not damn nigh impossible. The answer to him was obvious. Leave a small gap between the tip of the foresight blade and the top half of the bull so that the contrast between the black of the foresight showed up clearly against the buff colour.

All he had to do then was to ensure consistency in the depth of the gap and heigh-ho, the bullets would all go into the same spot. The first three shots, fired for grouping, were designed to show where the bullets went when fired from that rifle by that individual shooter. In theory, once a rifle had been set up properly, any one picking it up and aiming accurately would hit the bull. Unfortunately, that theory did not take into account human beings! Some were as blind as a bat. Some had the 1000-yard stare. Some saw slightly lower or higher or to the left or to the right, so that for an individual to be really accurate with a rifle, it had to be zeroed to that individual's peculiarities.

In Jack's case, the first group fired were all touching one another, dead in line with the centre of the bull but about half an inch too low. A matter of seconds to adjust for height and the first set of five rounds (why five? No logic—just the way it was done!) were blasted into the heart of the bull, forming a beautiful cluster, some holes overlapping, giving a perfect score.

The Captain conducting the session scored the target and signed it 25 points. Expecting some comment as to his accuracy, especially since none of the other novices had managed to hit the bull more than once, and in one case had even managed to miss the entire target with all five rounds, Jack did not expect to hear, "Imagined it was a bra, did you, Private Hughes?" No smile, or hint of one, accompanied this comment. What it did tell him though was that the grapevine amongst adults must be better than he had thought!

Not soon enough his turn came around again and produced the almost identical result—five in the bull with three of them touching each other. This time the comment, 'Well shot', was far more enjoyable! He did not know it, but the scores were passed to the Major in charge of the ACF in that area with a recommendation that he be tried out for the full-bore team. Consequently, a letter arrived inviting him to shoot at a forthcoming weekend trial at the Ash Ranges near Bisley, the home of full-bore rifle shooting. Jack was delighted to accept.

# Chapter 10

Two others from his year had also been chosen for a trial, Paul Air from his class, with whom he had already been developing a closer relationship, and David Cook from another class. Come the Saturday, the three of them travelled on the train from Surbiton to Ash station and then walked the mile and a half or so to the ranges. Facilities, unless you brought your own, did not exist! Just a windswept open range with firing points set at one-hundred-yard intervals disappearing down range.

At the three-hundred-yard point were assembled a number of vehicles with a fair-sized group of uniformed individuals milling around. Introductions out of the way, they were divided into groups of four and had short safety briefings on range procedures, including what was to be the programme for the rest of the day. In essence, one half of them were taken into the butts and shown how to work and paste up the targets; Jack was in the first group into the butts, and then after lunch, the firing group were marched into the butts and swapped over with the butt party who were now to have their opportunity to place as many holes in the bullseye as they were able.

The first seven rounds were fired at 100 yards. Why seven—only the grass knew and that wasn't telling. It did mean, however, those scores were out of 35, with 5 points for a bull, 4 for an inner, 3 for a magpie (so called because the hit was signalled by twisting a black and white marker pole round and round), 2 for the next circle out and 1 for an outer. Misses were signalled delightedly by markers in the butts by vigorously waving the flagged marker pole across the face of the target!

The appearance of three white markers pointing at the centre of the bull started a drift of spectators to Jack's firing point. His seventh and final bull attracted a smattering of applause and comments such as "Beginner's luck", "Fluke" and "He'll never do that again at three hundred yards" were mixed in with "Well done", "Good for you" and similar compliments. For a first time with a .303 Lee Enfield, it was a very good performance. For a young lad, it was extraordinary. Both extremes were experienced with Jack hitting the bull with every shot and one other lad managing to miss the entire six-feet square target with every shot!

Having finished at the 100-yard point, everyone moved back to the 300 yards. This time Jack had the audience from his very first shot—a bull again! But his second and fourth shots were both inners so that he only scored 33 out of a possible 35 from his seven rounds. The wind had been gusting and Jack had not noticed the movements in the range flags flying at intervals down the range for the purpose of indicating wind strength and direction. This was a mistake he was never to make again; after all, he hadn't had problems with wind (not that sort anyway!) with an air rifle that he normally shot at 10-15 yards and which wouldn't fire much more than 30-40 yards anyway! The unfortunate who had missed all his shots at 100 yards was discovered to be closing his eyes at the moment of firing and, unable to overcome this habit, did not bother the target paster-up with his second seven rounds either! An early return home, alone, was his reward for wasting everyone's time – in the Cadet Force, as well as the Army, success was rewarded and failure punished.

Selection for the team inevitably followed, and life took a new turn. Shooting either for training or in competitions rapidly became a way of life. Outdoor range shooting took place every weekend from the weekend before Easter to the final competition of the year, the Nationals at Bisley on the second weekend in October. Indoor range shooting with .22 rifles 'to keep the eye in' took place weekly at the indoor range at the Regular Army barracks in Kingston or in the range at the school.

# Chapter 11

The weekend shoots away at Bisley, Hythe and other sites usually involved travelling away on the Friday afternoon and a meet up with the members of the team at the barracks, sometimes tents, in the evening and returning home on Sunday afternoon. As a young lad largely untutored in the ways of the world, the language and tales of derring-do in claims of ability to drink enormous amounts of beer and still walk a girl home and persuade her to perform even more extreme sex acts than the previous braggart provided an exciting and wondrous insight to the adult world he was longing to enter. It was only later that he came to realise that these tales were only that, tales, and not even nearly credible once heard by a more experienced and adult mind. Mind you, that doesn't stop most men seeking approval from their peers today from doing it!

The team captain was a lad, Wally, who worked as a Hod Carrier and was a member of the Cadet Company based in Hersham. Wally was a character. He owned an ancient pre-war Ford whose engine had long given up producing anything like the eight-horsepower claimed by its manufacturer but which had developed a gargantuan thirst for oil—more, it was rumoured, than its thirst for petrol. What was not a rumour, and not in doubt, was that when it could be persuaded to go, it left behind it a magnificent, impenetrable and lasting smoke screen; so much so that, when it could be persuaded to go and Wally to bring it, it was used in exercises to provide a smoke screen in every way superior to that provided by smoke grenades! And soot from the exhaust pipe made a fantastic face black for night exercises!

Wally claimed that it was a dead cert bird puller (with loads of fanciful tales of conquest inside it) and he loved it dearly, but not enough to spend any money on its engine or any other bit of it. Inevitably, therefore, it expired one day whilst climbing the Hog's Back, a fast (irrelevant to Wally) switchback road near Guildford later to claim the life of Mike Hawthorn, a famous racing driver. Some said the early morning mist which killed Hawthorne was in reality the ghost of Wally's smokescreen, but few believed it!

Wally had no money to retrieve it or repair it on site, so it is probably there still, mouldering and rusting away in the undergrowth at the roadside, ready for its entry into the great scrap yard in the sky.

# Chapter 12

Wally was well named. Competitions between rival teams were, of course, the raison d'être of being there, although competitions away from the ranges were actively discouraged; they still took place though, one of the favourites being to chuck buckets of water into a rival team's hut/tent in the early hours of the morning and attempt a trail of deception to lead to another team so that they would be blamed, which usually resulted in copious full buckets in return!

On one occasion when they were shooting at Bisley and staying in the Guard's Brigade barracks at Pirbright, they discovered that they were provided with the luxury of stirrup pumps, hand-operated pumps which, in theory, provided a jet of water which could be directed accurately at the heart of any fire but which, in reality, produced only a pathetic dribble—a stream less than a good pee after a good night out could produce was the common reckoning, but this did not take into account that Wally, as a Hod Carrier, was a strong, fit and powerful lad. Wally pumped, and Ted directed the stream and what a stream—enough to win any pissing competition ever devised! Unfortunately for Wally, he had upset Ted the previous weekend when he had moved in on a girl Ted had been buying drinks for all night only to see her whisked away by Wally with the promise of a lift home in his car!

"Pump, Wal', pump," screamed Ted. And Wally pumped, boy, did he pump! Wally, with head down and pumping like a good 'un, could not see where Ted was directing the flow. First, he directed it through the open window of Wally's car, and once that had been totally drenched, front and back, Ted directed the stream, from the constantly replenished bucket by others with no love for Wally, at the closed window of the other team's sleeping quarters, spray from which, in monsoon proportions, sprayed all over Wally! All Wally could gasp out, pumping even harder was, "I hope those bastards are getting as wet as I am, because I'm getting fucking soaked!"

At which Ted, taking advantage of Wally's ignorance, directed the nozzle directly at Wally's arse and let him have full measure! It was only the collapse of the bucket chain in helpless laughter which brought an end to the water supply and thus an end to Wally's pumping! Whilst the record shows that the guards were not pleased at the dampness left in their barracks, for years afterwards the cry, "Pump, Wal', pump," would act as a rallying cry to the team!

Without Jack realising it in any way, the shooting with the team, the weekends away, the competitions, especially those where they were accommodated in army establishments, gradually introduced him to the offerings of the military life and the early career route which would unfold for him when he was to eventually leave school.

# Chapter 13

Some of the competitions were just against other Army Cadet teams, but some involved the Territorial Army who really did not like to lose to Cadets, and even on occasions to teams of retired officers who still liked to shoot. Jack won prizes regularly, mainly small medals, gold, silver and bronze, some small silver spoons and, on occasions, small silver cups—Hythe near Folkestone was particularly good for these. Mind you, the best prizes of all that Jack really wanted to win were the cash prizes, £6-£10, a phenomenal sum for him at that time, for the egg pool competition; it had different names at different venues, but all, in some way, involved endeavouring to place a bullet into a one-inch diameter circle, drawn within the bullseyes—a six-inch diameter, a hard enough target to hit in itself! Competitors paid their entry fee, usually five shillings (25p in modern parlance!), for one bullet to be fired at two-hundred yards range and the pool (the competition was also sometimes called 'the pool bull' competition as a result) was shared out between those competitors who had hit the one-inch circle, not necessarily drawn around the exact centre of the bull's-eye. So often did Jack hit the inscribed egg/pool bull that mutterings started to be heard that Cadets should not be allowed to enter such competitions as they involved gambling and thus should be out of bounds to kids!

The ranges at Hythe were on the shingle beaches which made for spectacular eruptions of pebbles and sand flying everywhere when shots hit short of the butts. Not so much fun though for lying on at the firing points—they were hard, wobbly from the point of view of getting a firm firing point and managed to protrude into all the wrong places, especially those of a very private nature. It was also very tiring to run across it, especially for winning a round because of having to do it all over again in the next round.

One of the competitions, which was very visual and enjoyable to watch, was the falling plate competition—putting small holes in targets hundreds of yards away was not, in itself, an exciting event to watch. But the falling plate was. Fought between two teams of four, on a knock-out basis, it involved racing for one-hundred yards and then shooting at metal plates which, if hit, fell down, hence the falling plate competition. The plates were steel plates, a foot square, which were stood on balks of timber set in the backstop sand banks of the butts, ten for each team; normally, the right-hand man took the right-hand plate first, then the next one in. In the meantime, the left-hand man was firing at the two left-hand plates and the inside left and right shooters were firing at the fifth from the right and fifth from the left respectively. Thus, the outside ones started from the outside moving inwards, and the inside ones moved outwards. Thereby no one fired at the same plate, thereby wasting a shot—leastways, that was the theory!

31

In practice, as the target was very small, a long way away and the shooter was panting from the exertions of racing across a hundred yards of rough, sometimes very rough ground. It was hardly surprising, therefore that targets were missed and then all hell was let loose with shouts from the team captain for Smith to shoot right, Evans at the left one etc. but very rarely were the commands heard or followed since they relied on the nominated one hitting the nominated plate and they didn't, they missed and missed. Given that they each only had five rounds to start with meant, on one famous occasion in the annals of the regiment, that a team (not Jack's) missed all 10 plates, having fired the entire allocation of 20 rounds at them!

Hythe was particularly hard since the land between the firing points was largely shingle, immensely tiring and demanding to run on, with a twisted ankle potentially never far away. One particular year, Jack's team was drawn against a team of senior officers in the final. Comprising a Brigadier and three Lieutenant Colonels, their experience was formidable, and they were the favourites to win. The regular soldiers, the TA ones and the odds and sods from the Navy, Air Force and the Marines in the competition were all very aware that if you wanted to progress in your career in the forces, you did not beat senior officers; you let them win by a very narrow margin. Unfortunately for the senior officers, no one had told Jack and his team. On the shout, "Go," Jack and the team were off like rabbits. They were fortunate in having been drawn on the right-hand side of the range where grass had invaded the pebbles, firming them up and providing much better ground upon which to run.

Jack's team quickly left the senior officers way behind them so much so that they arrived at the firing point whilst the others were little more than halfway there—no Lt Colonel was going to beat the Brigadier to the firing point and the Brigadier was portly, out of condition and slow, so they were all slow—they did know the importance of letting the boss win! Quickly loading, the Cadets commenced firing. Whether it was luck, whether it was the easier running ground, whether it was whatever, the falling plates fell beautifully, almost to the tune of three bangs from each of the four rifles; ammunition checks afterwards showed that each of the team had only fired three rounds, two at each individual's own two plates and one from each of the four of them at the last two plates. The last plate fell just as the senior officers arrived at the firing point!

"Stop," called the referee and the senior officers had to stop. After whispered conversations and much to-ing and froing, it was decided that the senior officers should be allowed to shoot anyway, and they did. But even having had time to catch their breath whilst all this discussion went on, they could knock down no more than eight of the plates, not in itself a bad score and good enough on some occasions to win, but compared to Jack's team's textbook performance, a poor showing!

For that competition, Jack won a silver cup, which appeared out of a box he unpacked many years later when he moved to Ashford, only a 20-minute drive from the Hythe ranges, but many events were to occur between the two occurrences!

# Chapter 14

When he came to look back on his life, the period at the grammar school was a bit of blur, with just key events sticking out in his memory. Certainly not the best days of his life according to Jack. Very little remained in his memory of the pure schooling elements. He continued to run and win cross country races within the school and against other schools but could remember only one race against a nearby grammar school where, following the start and running second, he was staggered to see a river in front of them, getting closer at an alarming rate with no apparent bridge to carry them over it!

In fact, there wasn't one; the leading runner, familiar with the route, just kept on running, flying off the river bank and into the river which turned out to be only about two feet deep. Other than relief that he hadn't had to swim, Jack was a poor swimmer and never happy in water throughout his life, but getting socks, running shoes soaking wet and the rest of him pretty wet from splashes thrown up as he ran diagonally across the river to a low edge permitting easy egress from the river, a distance of perhaps 30 yards, and then keeping on running for a further three and half miles was not funny. You expected to get a bit wet and muddy running cross country, but this was beyond a joke, and he never forgot it but passing their leading runner twenty yards from the tape did provide some satisfaction!

He never did any training or even warming up—either no one knew about it then, or more likely none of the teachers gave a damn! Jack certainly didn't know about it; he just turned up to the event whatever it was, changed into his running or sports clothes and started running when the starter shouted, "Go."

He did discover that you should warm up when he ran in the school sports' day when he was fifteen. He was running in the 220 yards, the 100 yards was simply too fast and short for him. The 220 was also really too short but they had no one else to run for the House, so he was simply ordered to do it. As they came around the bend from the start onto the finishing straight, Jack was in the lead, somewhat to everyone's surprise, when his right leg powered forward, gave out a loud crack, which sent a shock of pain up to his brain, and simply did not come forward again. Consequently, he felt even more pain when he crashed to the ground, hard sun-baked clay, grazing arms, legs, face and bruising all of them as well. Carted off to the local A&E, he returned home on crutches to be laid up for weeks with a snapped tendon. It was simply not fair that this should happen five days before the start of the school holidays; why could it not have happened in term time when the absence would have been enjoyable?

One of the side effects of this accident went almost unrecognised at the time. Jack had always been skinny, so much so that he could have posed as the 'before' advert for Oxfam, had there been such a thing then. At thirteen, his twin sister was a good head and shoulders taller than him, and Jack made little progress in closing the gap until well into his fourteenth year. The enforced rest following his tendon damage meant that slowly but surely, he started to fill out and put on weight. At the same time, he started to shoot up, such by the time he went back to school in the autumn, shortly before his sixteenth birthday, he stood six feet tall but was still quite skeletal.

The TV star of the moment was Clint Walker, starring as 'Cheyenne Bodie' in a weekly western TV series. Much was made of the fact that Clint was a very big man, 6 ft 4 in tall and wide to match—his size and power was much to the fore in the programmes, larger than life as was (and is!) Hollywood's want when making films. One day, Jack, somewhat bothered by the excessive hero worship exhibited by fellow classmates was unwise enough to comment that 6 ft 4 in was not that tall; after all, he, Jack, at 6 ft tall, was not so much smaller! Derision immediately ensued with Jack being nicknamed 'old six foot'. Ironically, as time progressed and Jack continued to grow, the term became more a familiar, friendly term of endearment as a nickname rather than one of derision. He never did reach Cheyenne Body's height or spread though.

# Chapter 15

The approach of his sixteenth birthday raised other issues which were to lead to a further increase in his weight. Motorbikes! In those days, working men had motorbikes, cars being rare-ish and vastly too expensive. Besides, most of them were pre-war and knackered, post-war production being reserved mainly for export. Three of his mates, slightly older than he but in the same academic year, possessed motor bikes and their riding of them to school, not officially permitted but with the school having no powers to prevent them from being parked outside the school gates on the public road, meant huge, well, half a dozen or so anyway, adoring sycophants gathering around each bike immediately they arrived. Two were small two-strokes and the third, the third was a NORTON 350 cc, not quite a Manx Norton but close enough to create superhero adoration for the rider thereof.

Fast, powerful and beautiful to look at and listen to, Jack wanted one. In reality, he knew he wouldn't ever be allowed anything so powerful—his mother was dead set against him having a bike of any kind. This seemed strange and unfair to him because his father had had several bikes as a young man; indeed, he had met his mother, who had been an admiring spectator of the boys' derring-do, on the local pub car park and had had many adventures with her on the back! So it seemed very unfair that she should be so against Jack having one.

Maybe it was something to do with the things that had happened to her! On one famous or, more accurately, infamous trip, from Kingston to Maesteg—a real adventure in those days—everything possible that could go wrong had gone wrong—an epic proof of Sod's Law. It was an 'introduce your boyfriend to your family for the first time at Sunday tea' sort of visit but with a problem that Mum was a live-in Tweeny—a Between Stairs Maid—having been sent into live-in service at 14 to Surrey and her parents still living in Maesteg, an awful long way from Surrey.

Prior to leaving on the trip, his father had acquired a helmet. It was an exact replica of the one worn by George Formby in TT Racer, quite the rage at the time. The problem was the helmet was old and faded. It was also the wrong colour. His dad wanted a red one; no one knew George Formby's helmet's colour because the film was in black and white or it would have been that colour! A careful search of the garage uncovered a tin of red paint of exactly the right shade and colour to his dad's eye. So the old helmet was turned into a posing, eye-catching icon by the stroke of a brush (or two or three!). Also, as the weather was likely to be cold, he decided to wear his new, blue polo neck jumper, recently knitted for him by a great aunt, under his trench coat.

The journey was a nightmare. It rained all the way. There were no motorways or even good A roads, and travelling meant frequent stops to ask for directions. Nor was there much in the way of transport cafes in those days. As a result, on one lonely section, Mum shouted to him to stop. She needed to pee and quickly, diving behind a bush, she pulled her underwear down and squatted down, all the time watching to ensure neither Dad nor anyone coming along might see her. Consequent on her looking out for people and not looking where she was parking her nether regions, she plonked her bare bottom into a patch of nettles! The rest of the journey was spent in considerable discomfort and, of course, it was all Dad's fault!

The arrival at her home was nothing if not dramatic. Halfway along the metalled road, the metalled surface stopped and a muddy, rough, uneven road began. Realising that he was going far too fast for such a surface, Dad applied the rear brake enthusiastically—front brakes were pretty useless in those days, and anyway, you wouldn't apply a front brake on a muddy surface unless you wanted to drop the bike. The back wheel locked instantly, and the bike started slowing quite nicely. Unhappily, Mum's mum, having heard the bike approaching, opened the front door instantly, not having seen her daughter for over a year. The bike, having a mind of its own—it must be said, an evil one—decided to veer from the straight ahead and started skidding sideways, delivering a shower of wet mud and water in a beautiful tail slide which caught the exiting mother full blast. Dad did not know what to say. He did know this was not a good start!

Pulling the bike up onto its rear stand, he made his way to the front door. Standing in it was a soaking wet, mud-covered mother clasping an equally wet, if not so muddy, daughter. Looking at him dragging himself towards them, they saw a wet, muddy nightmare. In his search for red paint, it had not occurred to Jack to check if it was water soluble. It was. Consequently, the red paint had formed runnels down his face and neck. Worse, he had not checked to see if the blue wool used in his polo neck was run proof. It wasn't. As a consequence, the blue had spread across his lower face and neck and had run down his arms and out of his sleeves onto his hands. Coupled with the cold and sitting so long, he walked stiff legged and clumsily—somewhat akin to Nosferatu, more commonly known as Dracula—towards the two women.

As he walked towards the two women, he did not know what to say and was only saved by both of them turning away. He followed them into the house. Face and hands dried off first, leaving only faint patches of paint and dye across them. If that had been the end of the misfortune, that might have not been too bad but, it wasn't; it then proceeded to get rapidly worse. Struggling to take off his leather, steel-tipped, despatch rider's boots, the leather laces were swollen and hard to undo, and they proved unwilling to slide off over his wet socks. Having removed the first boot, it seemed almost inevitable that the second boot should shoot off easily and the steel tip gouge a wide, deep scratch all down the side of the upright (and expensive) piano beside him—of course, the pride and joy of the house!

Worse was to come. With profuse apologies offered and reluctantly accepted, he needed a cigarette. Thinking this would help to break the ice, he offered his cigarette case to the lady of the house first. The man of the house exploded instantly. "No woman smokes in this family or this house," he barked but did speedily accept one for himself. Jack's to-be-dad, ever the gentleman, struck a match and lit the cigarette. What no one noticed was that a piece of the burning sulphur had flown off and landed on the white keys of the open piano.

The first that anyone became aware was when the smoke and the smell started to drift across them. Hard to believe that Jack's dad and mum went on to survive 54 years of marriage, especially as most people believed that Jack's parents only met once and that briefly! Relations between them did improve over the years but Grandpa never allowed Nana to smoke to his dying day.

Following that trip, his father sold the Brough Superior, a very expensive machine, and bought instead a three-wheeler Morgan fitted with a JAP engine. The only problem with that was the roof clip on the passenger side was broken so one either travelled with the roof down or the passenger had to hold that side in place. It meant sticking one's arm out in the wind and rain with utterly foreseeable consequences. Even Jack could see that his parent's courtship and eventual marriage had been a bit of a miracle. Perhaps that did explain Mum's antipathy towards motorcycles.

# Chapter 16

Jack had his eye on a 50 cc Steyr Puch moped. The local bike shop did not have one in its stock of second-hand machines—new were out of the question, no money—but they did have a 98 cc James two stroke in superb condition, maroon in colour, saddle for one, and fitted with leg guards. It stole Jack's heart at first sight. The shop owner was not slow to spot an incipient love affair and moved in for the sale. However, Jack was made of sterner stuff, not because it was natural to him but because he knew there wasn't a hope in hell of getting his parents, specifically his mother to agree to the purchase. After explaining this to the guy, the guy said, "If you can get your mum and dad to the shop, I'll get them to buy it." Who could refuse such an offer; Jack certainly couldn't.

In the event, it proved remarkably simple. A, "Just let's have a look," got them there a week later. The sales pitch of, "He's in danger on the road on his push bike now; it would be far better if he could keep up with the traffic; one of these mopeds might be all right, but they're always being overtaken, especially on hills, and thus can be quite dangerous, so something like this little James, only 98 cc and not capable of much more than 40 mph might be just the thing," did the trick, and it was delivered the next day!

Of course, he couldn't wait to ride it. The most desirable thing in the world—he wasn't yet aware of the joys of a rampant nymphomaniac—was this gleaming little bike, a motor bike, a real motor bike, not a moped. He practised starting and stopping it all afternoon in the garage, impatient for when his father would return from work. By the time he came to get it out for real, the garage was a reeking den of partially burnt, two-stroke oil. Wheeled just around the corner into a side road he sat astride, fully rigged in his black (plastic!) motorcyclist's jacket, a white cork helmet with a peak and leather ear protectors joined together by a strap under the chin (an absolute must dictated by his mother as a condition of him having the bike), and his heavy duty leather gauntlets, he felt easily the equal of Marlon Brando in the Wild Ones although, if the truth were known, he looked more like a black Sobranie cigarette with a white tip!

This is it! Open the throttle, racing revs, too much throttle, turn the twist grip back a bit, there that seems to be just right, release the clutch, lurch, stall and stop. Not the finest of starts. Kick it back to life, clutch in, push the stubby little gear lever forward for low gear—it only had two, high and low—twist the throttle a bit, gradually let the clutch out, and this time he started moving. Christ, that's fast. In reality, it was only about ten miles per hour (no speedometer fitted or necessary) but moving without having to peddle and the crisp put-put-put of the little engine was so fantastic! He was riding a motorbike!

Time to change into high gear, his speed now having reached the dizzy heights of 15 mph or so. Close throttle, pull in clutch, move gear lever to high, slowly let the clutch out and shudder, shudder the engine having far too high a gear for the slow speed—he had taken so long to go through the process that he was down to about 5 mph, and the little engine could not cope and stalled! Start again. Gradually, through the next half hour or so, he got the hang of it and life became perfect, for now anyway; more power and more gears, more speed and more street cred were a few months away once he had become familiar and fed up with 45 mph max speed and absolutely no ability whatsoever to burn anybody else off—mopeds didn't count; they were only bicycles with small engines and big pedals!

All sorts of things started happening at the same time in Jack's life. Girls, previously dismissed as soppy drips, started to become interesting, or at least their bodies did—undoubtedly initiated by explorers returning from African and South American jungles with films of bare-breasted natives. So that's what they looked like under all their clothes—assuming white women were the same as black, that is, vague project forming to find out!

Attending camp that summer, at Fingrinhoe in Essex, also broadened Jack's knowledge of the world. Jack had volunteered for the advance party. This had meant travelling five days ahead of the main group to help set up the camp. Part tented and part permanent buildings, albeit in a pretty advanced stage of senility and disintegration, tasks involved drawing out metal bed frames and canvas bags (called palliasses in army lingo) and setting them up. The palliasses were supposed to be filled with straw to form a comfortable mattress but the army, being the army, sent them to summer camp a few weeks before the hay was harvested and thus, for most of the mattresses this meant that they were little more than canvas covers over the springs!

Travel there had been an adventure in itself. It was the first time he had travelled any real distance from home on his motorbike, and travelling right through London from one side to the other without getting lost had been a bit of a miracle. Travelling on the A roads once outside of London had been a bit of a pain because his little James with an absolute top speed of 45 mph on the flat (his mate had measured him on the speedo of his Lambretta as the James didn't have one) and much less than that if there was a strong wind against him or even the slightest slope had meant a long and uninteresting journey. However, they made it without getting lost at all—Dave Cook on the Lambretta, Paul Air on the Vespa and Jack on the James, all copious emitters of two-stroke smoke, heavily overloaded and screaming at maximum revs!

That first evening, the three of them visited the NAAFI for the first time ever—a proper one set up on a proper army camp for proper soldiers (and the odd Cadets)—and faced the barman and the decision of what to have to drink—alcohol that is! Desperately endeavouring to appear men of the world and not schoolboy Cadets (and thus well under the legal age to buy alcohol), Dave, in response to a somewhat surly, "What do you want?" answered immediately.

"Three pints of Guinness," no please since the barman's rudely posed question didn't warrant it. Three pints were duly served and they each carried their own over to a table. Sitting down, Jack immediately asked why Dave had ordered Guinness. Dave's answer was that he thought he had to think fast as to dither might allow the surly bastard to look longer at them and realise that they were only youths and too young to be in the NAAFI ordering alcohol; he'd said Guinness because there was a bloody big sign advertising it on the wall behind the barman, and he couldn't think of anything else!

Manfully drinking his pint, Jack thought the next time he'd do the ordering, and it wouldn't be this awful cat's piss. To Jack, it tasted absolutely dreadful—he could not understand how it could be so popular. Even in later years when he lived in Ireland and visited the Guinness brewery where free pints were provided at the end of the tour, he still could not understand it even though his father and grandfather swore by how good it was.

Drinking in the NAAFI was to become a regular event until the rest of the unit arrived and sneaking in there without the teachers/officers finding out became very difficult. Because they had so little money, heavy drinking was out anyway, but trying different beers, Mild, Light Ale, Cider and finally Bitter did introduce him to alcohol. Bitter, especially one called 'Directors' definitely topped his chart of favourites. Red Barrel, the subject of huge advertising programmes, came bottom of their list, just above Guinness, too fizzy and too weak. The divine pleasures of gin and tonic were still a few years away.

By Saturday, everything they were supposed to have done had been achieved, though the thickness of the palliasses would come in for criticism every morning! That day, for the main party, was spent mainly settling in and the issue of kit. Sunday started with church parade. Following the parading and roll call, those who were not of the Anglican persuasion were fallen out to attend their own services or if not Christian, dismissed altogether. The normal command initiating this was, "Fall out the RCs and others." Trevor Cocks was the Cadet Sergeant Major, and he duly shouted in his best command voice the order. Unfortunately, Trevor had spent many of his formative years living in the North of England and had only been attending the grammar school for a year or so—far too short a time to have lost his Northern accent. His 'fall out the RCs' therefore came out, shouted at the top of his voice, "Fall out the Ar Ses." Short pause and then the Company burst into hysterical laughter. The Captain, an ex-prisoner of the Japanese, feared and respected in equal portions, quickly restored order, and the parade continued in the ordained manner. At future parades, the order given became 'fall out the Roman Catholics and others' but the 'Ar Ses' went down in folklore forever more.

# Chapter 17

Camp was a mixture of drill, weapons drill, shooting on the range, map reading, Section (there were three sections to a Platoon) and platoon tactics and even some time off—most of which was organised, so they could be kept under the eyes of the staff and thus, it was hoped, out of mischief. Fingrinhoe was a few miles outside of Colchester, a garrison town, and there was little in the way of public transport to get there. However, the three of them had their bikes and thus six of them (Jack had added a saddle and foot pegs at the back of his bike) could easily access the town. Coffee bars were the in thing and haunting them for girls the de rigueur past time, all, it must be said, with no success whatsoever!

Rock and roll records filled the new jukeboxes and their contents could be listened to for the sake of a few pennies in the machine. Unfortunately, the choice of the six of them did not always—in fact, ever—suit the other squaddies in the bar and proved a fertile territory for starting fights. Still, it must be said that never did the Regular Army soldiers' choice suit them. In their minds, the girls would be so overawed by their martial prowess that they would fall into their arms like apples from the tree! It never seemed to dawn on them that being thrown out on the street, along with their rivals, and the females staying inside the coffee bar actually benefitted no one. And besides, Colchester was a garrison town, and the girls were well used to the lascivious soldiery. Just another lesson in life's journey!

By the end of the first week, the powers that be felt that the time had come to put the skills learned into practice. An exercise was planned for Thursday and Friday with night skills incorporated on the Thursday night. Jack's role in this involved leading a Recce (Reconnaissance) Patrol to find the enemy's campsite so that it could be attacked the following morning.

This meant Jack, having been given only a map square reference of the likely area of the enemy's campsite, had to lead a patrol of two riflemen, plus himself, to find it and report back. The patrol wasn't to set out until it got dark—about 22:00 hrs. Jack, as the Platoon Sergeant, was the senior Cadet of the School Platoon. He was also a devious bugger and didn't play fair; they had taught him to cheat at rugby and that winning was the only thing that mattered, and how much more important was that in war time when to lose might mean your death or at least a very unpleasant time as a prisoner?

Jack reasoned that if they were being sent out to find the enemy's position, (in reality the Cadets from the Hersham Platoon—a really rough lot) then the chances were that the others would be out looking for them. Jack, therefore, gave orders, unpopular ones, that all fires were to be doused by 21:30 and they were to move to a different position, not in the map square position they had been given in which to bivouac (camp) but two away from it in an endeavour to make it impossible for the others to find them—you couldn't rely on the others being honourable either!

There was to be no noise, sentries out and everything done to try and hide their location.

Jack chose to take with him his fellow bikers Dave and Paul. They were bigger and more experienced than most of the other Cadets and Jack knew they could be relied on in a fight, Colchester coffee bars and all. Having checked their kit was properly secure from clinking, shining and suitably blacked up under misshapen cap comforters (knitted woolly hats), they set off with Jack in the lead at 21:30; he certainly wouldn't abide by the rules, and the Captain, having experienced and lost to the Japanese who had beaten the British Army in the early stages of the war by breaking all the rules, happily waved them off!

He knew the direction of the square where he was supposed to find the enemy and had set a compass course to follow to get him there. The sun had recently set although there was still plenty of dusk light to see by. However, this did not help them a great deal since they were heading directly east, and with the sunset in the west, they would appear as silhouettes to the enemy sentries who were consequently, if they had been posted, hidden in the dark area to which they were heading.

The fields in the training areas were leased to farmers on the understanding that their crops might occasionally suffer from the activities of the soldiers. The first field seemed to be mainly grass but about 18 inches tall and pale straw in colour—not good for them because their dark shapes stood out very clearly. They were not, therefore, able to track straight across the field but had to mark where their compass bearing would have taken them in a distant hedge row and then make their way carefully around the sides of the field before they reached it.

Pausing in the hedgerow, Jack took a bearing across the next field which settled on a large tree about 100 yards away. It took Jack a while to register that he could see the tree because the moon was rising, a big full, bright moon directly behind them so that crossing this field would also be difficult. The problem was that the edges of this field were bounded to the right by a fairly substantial stream with no cover along its banks. To the left, the edge was not visible, so far away was it. The geography and the time limit he was under, he had to be back with the patrol and the information by midnight as the permanent staff wanted to go to bed at a decent time, all meant that there was no choice other than to cross this field. The only comforting factor was that the enemy's position was probably beyond the hedgerow in front of them and which would hopefully hide them from the enemy sentries, providing they hadn't posted sentries in the hedgerow—something Jack would have done.

The field they had to cross was dotted with waist-high clumps of gorse and nettles so that initially, a careful stooped walk sufficed. However, about halfway across, they started to catch murmurs of sound. Dropping to a crawl for a good 30 yards and then onto their bellies and slithering the last 20 yards or so, they approached the hedge from which the sound seemed to be coming. Something was wrong with the sounds. They did not sound like a load of lads talking, and furthermore, one of them seemed to be female. The sound seemed to be a grunting sort of noise and rhythmical somehow. Jack started to feel frightened that they were about to creep up on a wild pig; rumours of wild boar in the training area were detailed with glee by the locals, laying special emphasis on how dangerous they were, in the event, all totally untrue but seemingly very real to a young lad creeping along in the dark and armed only with blank rounds in his rifle.

Very carefully, quietly and slowly, they made for gaps in the hedge through which they could see the source of the noise. What met their collective gaze was the stuff of legend. It was a couple at it! Yes, at it! The woman was on her back, legs akimbo, and the man was between them giving it what for, for all his worth! Watching spell bound, it was a while before Jack remembered his mission. Attracting the other two by touch and signals, they pointed their rifles in the air, released their safety catches and, on Jack's signal, fired. Bang! Bang! Bang! Three rounds fired almost simultaneously and loud, loud, loud!

To their utter astonishment, the bloke leapt up and took off running at a speed an Olympic sprinter would have envied! Jack, Dave and Paul just lay there in hysterics. The woman calmly stood up, pulled her knickers up, skirt down and started walking away, tossing a heartfelt 'Bastards' over her shoulder. Paul, noticing the trousers lying on the ground, where the bloke had left them, called out, "Here, missus, what about your fella's trousers?" to which she called back, "He can get them his bleedin' self," and walked steadily away!

It was several minutes before they could gather their wits and stop laughing. Paul and Dave were for abandoning the mission and returning to base. Whilst Jack had no objection to this, in principle, he couldn't immediately think of a plausible excuse that would explain away the three missing fired, blank rounds, rounds that were jealously hoarded as the allocation was only five rounds per Cadet for the entire 14-day camp!

They didn't even know if their shots had been heard by the other platoon or even where it was located, their specific reason for the Recce Patrol. After several minutes, Jack decided that as there had been no obvious reaction to the noise, no shouting or bodies blundering around the field they thought was between them and the likely enemy camp that it was probable they had not been heard or had been mistaken for poachers or not something connected to their own Platoon. Therefore, they decided that they would make their way very, very cautiously around the edge and creep up on the other hedgerow to see if they could find the site for which they were searching.

# Chapter 18

The moon was still bright although all signs of daylight had faded from the sky, leaving a bright, clear and peaceful evening. Jack signalled for the patrol to crawl when they got about 80 yards from the hedge—unpopular but necessary. Once they got to 50 yards, they started to hear noises, too faint and jumbled to recognise but definitely noises and thus potentially dangerous. Jack signalled for them to move on their stomachs and elbows—very definitely unpopular, uncomfortable and tiring but no more complaints; they were clearly approaching potential danger as the enemy were known to be a bit free and easy with their fists and feet in any sort of a melee!

As they got closer, they started to glimpse fires through the hedgerow and started to smell wood smoke along with the tantalising smell of coffee. Inching along at ground level, it became clear that they could see between the stems of bushes and under the main foliage. Running through the bushes were animal trails, probably rabbits but for all they knew as townies they could have been made by anything up to and including lions! What they were, however, was very useful.

Signalling the other two to stay back and cover him, Jack continued inching, literally inching, forwards very slowly. Even though he was within inches of them, they could not see him. Deep in the shadows under the bushes, he was completely invisible. It was an uncomfortable feeling lying there listening to the talk, none of it of any use from the point of the enemy platoon's future actions but a clear indication that they were even bigger liars about their successes with girls than were the school platoon!

Then, casually and without looking back, one of the enemy platoon put down a mug of soup directly in front of Jack and not 18 inches away. Hardly daring to breathe, Jack lay there under the bush immobile. When nothing happened after a couple of minutes, he agonisingly slowly reached forward, grasped the mug and pulled it towards him. The owner was so lost in the story being told that he did not notice the mug's stealthy disappearance. Jack drank the soup as fast as he could—too hot, really, but needs must when the Devil drives. Once empty, he returned it from whence he had filched it.

He had only just moved his hand out of the way and vision when the erstwhile owner of the soup reached for his mug. Realising that his soup had gone, he immediately accused the Cadet next to him of taking it. He, unjustly accused, responded forcefully, and a full-scale argument ensued. Jack took advantage of the erupting chaos to start inching backwards and away from the site. As he did so, one of the Cadets in the argument propped his Lee Enfield rifle against a tree and joined in the attempts to separate the two combatants who were by now going at it hammer and tongs! Unable to resist the temptation, Jack stopped sliding backwards but reversed, slid up to the tree, slowly removed the rifle and took it with him as he disappeared backward from what was starting to be a good old ding dong of legendary proportions.

Joining up with the others, they made their way openly and quickly across the fields back to their own camp. They were late getting back and not being able to easily find their own site because of the self-imposed blackout didn't help! The school teacher, a Captain in the Army Cadet Force, Ted Hiller by name, was not pleased that the Patrol returned well after 1.00 both because he was being kept from his bed and because he had been starting to worry that something might have happened to them.

His first words demonstrated that concern with, "Where the hell have you lot been?" and the manner in which they were said indicated he was not pleased. Gradually, as the story unfolded, his grimace changed to grins at the interrupted lovers' story, and he started laughing out loud at the fight started between the two over the missing soup. "What flavour was it?"

"Tomato sir," said Jack, "and bloody hot it was!"

The Captain turned to go but stopped when Jack said, "There was one more thing, this," and produced the rifle he had removed from the other Platoon. "I thought I had better take care of this as it was just standing against a tree and just anyone could have stolen it!" Ted's face was a picture. The theft of the soup had been a good enough story to give bragging rights in the Officers' Mess for the foreseeable future, but the stolen rifle lifted that to soaring heights!

Jack said,

"One further thing, sir. Is that what they call *coitus interruptus*?"

"No Sarn't Hughes it isn't, but it might well be from now on!" With that and a cheery, "Goodnight and well done!" the Captain set off back to the Mess with the rifle secure in the boot of his car. He wasn't sure how he was going to make the most bragging points out of it—that required careful thought—but brag he certainly would.

# Chapter 19

The following morning, Captain Hiller returned to find the School platoon formed and ready to move off, their bivouac tents and other camping kit neatly piled up ready to be collected by transport later. Setting off to attack the other platoon's position, they at first travelled in a simple column with the three Sections one behind the other on alternate sides of the track. As they neared the enemy camp, they shook out into two Sections up with the third following and the Platoon HQ led by Jack in the middle of the triangle, albeit a triangle progressing with the base first and the peak following on.

As they neared the position, it became clear that something was not right. Instead of the position being defended with sentries out and the Cadets stood to, the other platoon was formed up in three ranks with all their kit turned out and some sort of altercation going on. They were further mystified to see running towards them the Captain who commanded the other Platoon, a Captain Bidmead, shouting as he approached, "Stop. Halt."

Ted Hiller, who had been following the School Platoon in his car—always needed in case of emergencies, this being long before mobile phones or radios, far too valuable to be trusted to Cadets—pulled to a stop and got out.

Careful and polite enquiries from Captain Hiller elicited the fact that there was a rifle missing from the Hersham Platoon, and none of the Cadets would own up to having lost it. Unlike the Regular Army, rifles were not issued to Cadets by recorded number, and it was, therefore, not possible easily to identify who precisely had lost it. They were about to institute a search of their camp area again, the first having failed to find it.

Before Jack could say anything, he had started to, but Jack's Captain interrupted before he could and said, "Well, good luck with that; we'll just go off and practice some platoon in attack and defence until you find it."

The loss of a fully functioning rifle with five rounds, albeit they were blank rounds with no actual projectiles fitted to them, was almost certainly a Court Martial offence.

"Right, Sarn't Hughes, get the platoon moving to that copse of trees over there," gesturing towards some trees about a hundred yards away.

After an hour or so, Captain Hiller called a halt to the exercises and ordered Jack to take the Platoon back to the other Platoon's area where they could be discerned still searching it. On arrival, Jack reported the Platoon present and correct to Captain Hiller, who had, in the meantime, driven to the site to await their arrival. Taking Jack with him, Captain Hiller approached Captain Bidmead and greeted him with a cheery, "No luck yet?"

"No," sighed Bidmead. "It looks like me for the chop."

"I wonder if I might help?"

"How so?" said Bidmead.

Walking over to the boot of his car, Hiller opened it and removed the rifle snaffled by Jack the previous evening and the subject of the extended search by the Hersham Platoon.

"My Sergeant, Sergeant Hughes here found your sentry keeping so lax that he wandered in, helped himself to a mug of soup and a rifle and wandered out again. Might this be the rifle for which you are looking?"

Bidmead's face was a picture as the import of Hiller's words sank in. Bafflement, rage and relief all chased themselves across it. Finally, bright red and purple, it settled on the look of someone who knows that their worst moment had come, that it was worse than anything he had ever imagined and that he will never ever live it down—nor did he! Hiller told the story over and over in the Officers' Mess and anywhere they gathered together which presented an opportunity to gloat. As for Jack, his reputation as the ultimate expert in how to conduct a Recce Patrol was to follow him for years to come.

# Chapter 20

Life at the camp continued with the acquisition of military skills making up the main part of the training. Some of the skills could not be practiced by all the Cadets for various reasons; some because the Cadets were simply too young and small or because there wasn't enough kit to go around. This applied especially to ammunition. The allocation of five rounds of blank ammunition per Cadet was positively generous compared to the allocation of live ball ammunition which was limited to 180 rounds for the entire two Platoons for the whole camp.

Authority had decided that simply to divide the 180 rounds by the number of Cadets, about 70, meant less than three rounds each, and as some of them were barely 13, and small with it, to allow them to shoot, besides being illegal—the theoretical minimum age being 14—the paucity of rounds would not make it a worthwhile experience. The decision was, therefore, taken to give the Cadets a fire power demonstration by the Battalion shooting team instead.

As part of their training, whether in a Section or Platoon attack, or if attacked themselves, they were taught that they had first to win the fire fight to keep the enemies' heads down, by means of the Bren gun (a light machine gun), team(s) firing bursts of bullets into the enemy's position whilst the assault section(s) moved around the flank to bayonet charge the enemy who theoretically would not be able to look up and shoot at the assaulting Section(s) because of all the bullets pouring into their position from the machine gun group(s). That, at least, was the theory which totally ignored the fact that a solid front held by the enemy could not be outflanked; in the First World War, the Allies' left flank was the North Sea and the right flank was Switzerland, so no flanking attacks there then unless you could walk on water (it was rumoured that only Staff Officers could do this!) or run up the side of vertical mountains—something only goats could do!

The firepower demonstration was, therefore, to start by showing just how many aimed (roughly!) shots a trained rifleman could send into the enemy's position and the effect of them, followed by eight riflemen demonstrating the same skill, then the Bren gun team and finally Bren gun and riflemen all letting fly together. Jack, by virtue of his deeds in hijacking the soup and the rifle, was granted the privilege of demonstrating what a trained rifleman could do. With, heavens be praised, a full magazine, 10 rounds and four more clips each of five rounds, making 30 in all, Jack, when the introduction had been completed and the order given to fire, let rip.

He was aiming at the ground just in front of the butts so that the bullets would ricochet, creating an occasional shrieking sound and an avalanche of shit (literally, given the amount of sheep shit lying around!) flying into the enemies' faces and over their heads. Keeping one's head down in such circumstances was very much to be practiced! Jack fired his first ten rounds in less than eight seconds, all of them producing explosions of sound and debris across the face of the butts.

Counting his shots as he went, having ejected the tenth round instead of closing the bolt on an empty chamber, Jack reached out for a five round clip lying only inches from his right hand, inserted it into the magazine, flicked away the clip holder with his thumb, closed the bolt, loading another round and carried on firing, the whole exercise taking less than three seconds. After five rounds, he opened the bolt, slammed in another clip of five and carried on firing. Repeating the process twice more, he fired all 30 rounds in less than a minute.

The watching Cadets knew they had seen an ace performance. Although they did not know it, regular soldiers were being retrained to handle the new semi-automatic rifle—the Self-Loading Rifle or SLR. Of 7.62 mm calibre as opposed to .303 inches and the cartridge having a groove around the head of the cartridge for the extractor to grip into rather than the cap which had an overlapping rim of the .303 round, the main differences were the very high velocity of the 7.62 round, supersonic, in fact, creating a sonic boom behind itself and thus causing a much larger and more dangerous wound. It was said to completely blow off an arm or a leg, and the fact that it had an almost flat trajectory out to 650 yds or so made it more accurate since little or no drop occurred inside that range.

Over that distance, accuracy could be seriously affected since the drop down from supersonic speed and the passage through the sound barrier, albeit in reverse, so to speak, meant that a round could potentially go anywhere—a drawback Jack was to experience years later when set upon by Arabs shooting at him from 800 yds or more in Aden and Jack being unable to do much about it with the SLR with which he was armed at the time.

The other difference, a major one, between the new SLR and the older Lee Enfield, first introduced to the British Army before the First World War, was that having attached a loaded magazine to the rifle, it could not be reloaded by feeding rounds into an empty magazine already on the rifle, as could the Lee Enfield. The SLR was cocked by pulling back sharply on the cocking lever. Thereafter, the rifle would feed a fresh round into the chamber, ready for firing every time the trigger was squeezed. It could, therefore, in theory, fire a round as fast as you could squeeze the trigger i.e. at least 100 times per minute.

In reality, the SLR could not fire anywhere near 100 rounds a minute, the first problem being that the magazine only held 20 rounds and once empty, the firer had to remove the empty one, undo a magazine pouch, remove a fresh magazine, load it onto the rifle, place the empty one into the pouch, cock the rifle, re-aim it and carry on firing. During trials of the new weapon, the army had determined that 20 rounds per minute, on the command rapid fire, represented the optimum for the new rifle.

It was hardly surprising, given its propensity to jam if not spotlessly clean and its slower rate of fire, witness Jack's 30 aimed rounds in the minute from the rifle it was replacing, that the soldiers were not quick to admire or love it. The SLR was a modified version of the Belgian FN, which could fire in semi-automatic role, as the SLR, but could also fire automatically i.e. as a machine gun. The British Army had decided not to incorporate the automatic fire ability as it firmly believed that it would encourage soldiers to spray bullets around the place rather than take carefully aimed shots; it would also generate supply problems with ammunition.

Generally, the American forces were looked down on by the British soldier who saw their practice of spraying bullets everywhere, hitting very little and missing lots and lots, as being all show and no bottom. There was also the way the

Americans looked when staggering along with mountains of ammunition given their simply enormous consumption of it.

Even with the new SLR and a standard supply of ammunition, 100 rounds per man, it meant that an infantryman in the British Army only had 100 rounds, enough ammunition for 5 minutes firing! With some engagements lasting several hours, the logistics of keeping troops supplied would be an even greater nightmare if the automatic option was adopted. Indeed, so much weight was involved in ammunition that the Americans, who had just bullied NATO forces into agreeing to standardise all of NATO's small arms to use the 7.62 round as standard, and thus make it interchangeable between the various nations making up the alliance, promptly switched to the 5.62 mm round for their own forces, thus meaning they could carry almost double the amount of ammunition for the same weight!

Jack was well aware of the capabilities of the .303 since the British Army, which had learned the savage lesson from the Boer War what aimed rapid rifle fire could do to infantry in the open, had stopped the vaunted German Army dead in 1914 by means of highly trained riflemen firing rapid fire. Indeed, so impressive and deadly was this fire that the Germans were convinced that every British soldier was armed with a machine gun!

The problem with the firepower demonstration came when the Bren gun was supposed to be demonstrated; Cadets were not issued with, and weren't allowed, to fire machine guns, light or otherwise, at all! They were issued with a Bren gun per Platoon, but it was inert and for training and pretend purposes only. It could not even fire blank rounds, no firing pin was supplied, and no blank firing attachments (a gadget fitting over the end of the barrel to 'kid' the gun that real bullets were being fired by restricting the gas flow up the barrel) were supplied to Cadet units.

Thus, whilst it was a great training aid in the classroom, lugging it around the countryside—something troubling for smaller Cadets anyway, as it weighed in excess of 23 lbs—for the dubious honour of being able to shout out loud, "Brrrrrrrr, brrrrrrrr, brrrrrr," as a pathetic imitation of a real machine gun was something no one ever wanted to do!

Captain Ripley, the officer responsible for the shooting team, surprised everyone by producing a real, proper, all singing and dancing, firing Bren gun. Taking Jack aside, he explained that there were two full magazines loaded with a mix of ball and tracer, in a ratio of four to one, which were for Jack to demonstrate, the first magazine to show how a Bren gun should be used and the second to be used in the full section and gun team in action.

Jack was like a fox let loose in a hen house. He struggled to hide his excitement. No one had been allowed to fire a Bren before and here he was, being allowed to fire two whole magazines, 32 rounds in each, with every fifth one a tracer! Jack neither knew nor cared how they had been obtained, simply that they had, and he was the one to be allowed to spray rounds down the range, making as much noise, mess and mayhem as he could!

"Remember, Sarn't Hughes, short bursts of 2–3 rounds a time, and keep the bloody thing pointing down range at all times. Now, who do you want as your number two?" The number two on the gun was responsible for loading full magazines onto the gun, once the number one had removed the empty one and for watching out for the fall of the shot and the general area to ensure the gun was being used on the best targets, the view of the number one being very restricted once looking through the sights of the gun.

The number 2 was also responsible for changing the barrel if it became too hot from prolonged firing—a spare barrel being supplied with every gun for that purpose, though not with the one Captain Ripley had obtained.

"Corporal Air, sir, please," naming Paul Air, his best mate and shooting partner in the Battalion team.

"Right, Corporal Air it is." Jack and Paul made their way to the firing point and prepared for the demonstration. Captain Ripley gave the order to load, having explained to the watching Cadets that they were very privileged to see a real Bren gun in action, demonstrated by a real marksman. Jack felt flattered by this as he certainly was a marksman with a rifle, .303 or .22 but he had never even touched a fully functioning Bren gun before, let alone fired one to qualify as a marksman! Speaking quietly, Captain Ripley spoke the sequence of actions necessary to load the magazine and cock the weapon even though Jack had gone through the actions as dry drills on the training Bren back at the school—probably to be doubly sure that nothing went wrong with two Cadets firing a machine gun to which they really should not have had access! Following the whispered instructions, Jack loaded the magazine, having first checked it, and then cocked the gun loudly.

"At your target in front, go on," shouted Captain Ripley and Jack squeezed the trigger.

Never having fired a Bren before, Jack was somewhat surprised at just how fast it fired—somewhere in the order of 550 rounds per minute—so that 7 or 8 rounds flew away in the first burst, one of them being a tracer round which none of the Cadets had ever seen fired before. As the tracer round hit the ground immediately in front of the butts, it appeared to fly straight up into the air, spectacular to the onlookers, but in reality, it was simply the burning piece of phosphorous from the tail of the bullet flying up into the air, the bullet having either buried itself in the ground or ricocheted over the butts. Either way, it was fantastic for the spectators as further rounds poured forth in more controlled bursts spraying rounds, muck and tracer over the general area in front of the butts and over and into the butt's area.

To Jack's disappointment, the gun clicked empty in what seemed like the blink of an eye. (A full magazine of 32 rounds fired in one burst could be emptied in less than 3 seconds!)

"Unload," called the Captain and the firepower of what a light machine could do on its own to keep people's heads down was over.

The full power of a section firing, light machine gun and riflemen was to follow. Before Jack could say anything, Paul Air begged to be the one to fire the Bren with Jack acting as his number two. Normally, a Sergeant and a Corporal would not act as Numbers 1 and 2 on a Bren gun, but they were the only two from the Battalion shooting team who had been on the, by now, famous Recce Patrol and this was their reward! Jack reluctantly agreed, and they swapped positions.

The full section, eight of them riflemen, each with ten rounds in the magazine, and a 32-round magazine on the Bren, on the command 'fire' let rip, and for two or three glorious minutes, all hell was let loose. Bangs, bursts, tracer tails flying everywhere, clouds and sprays of dirt, sand, shingle, shit and small rocks peppering the butts, the sky and the general view presented a graphic demonstration! As the

51

last few shots were fired, the watching Cadets burst into a round of cheering and applause. Applause was not what burst out of the civilian staff operating the butts when they emerged from their safe refuges to see the mess they had to clear up, not that that worried Jack or his fellow Cadets.

Deemed a great success, the firepower demonstration effectively wound up the camp. The following day involved handing in kit, cleaning up and generally packing for the return journey the following day. Jack had hoped to stay for the rear-guard which was the reverse of the advance party in that they dismantled all the beds, returned the palliasses etc. but the family holiday was due to start on Sunday, leaving Jack no option other than to return home on Saturday which he duly did uneventfully, if a little slowly.

# Chapter 21

Besides his mother and father, grandpa and nana, Jack's sister and her special friend S'Marlene (why did only girls have special friends?), his Uncle Joe and Aunty Winnie were also to accompany them. Jack was 'asked' if he'd like to travel with his uncle and aunty and initially showed reluctance, resulting in the offer of a bribe of a bag of sweets and a bar of chocolate for the journey. Deal! Only Jack knew that he had no wish to travel in his dad's car with three of the four adults smoking (Grandpa would still not allow Nana to smoke!) and with his sister and her dopey friend S'Marlene. Little did Jack know the horror and the delights that were to be revealed, literally, at the boarding house.

Jack's uncle and aunty were to stay at a separate boarding house in the next street which was good news as far as Jack was concerned. What wasn't good news, far from it, it was horrendous news, was that Jack discovered that he was expected to share a room with his sister and her friend. That was not on. It was bad enough to have to come on holiday with his sister and 'her special friend' and miss the delights of camp rear party but sharing a room was not on in a big way. A flat refusal to share was simply dealt with by his father saying there were no other room available. A plea to see if there was a spare room where his uncle and aunt were staying was met with a flat no.

The two girls disappeared off to the room to change and get ready for dinner. Jack, in a monumental sulk and forbidden the bedroom, took himself off to the sea front. Walking along, he considered and discarded any number of options including stealing a motorbike and going back to the camp anyway, simply stealing the bike and going home and even jumping off the end of the small pier. Each option was rejected in turn, no bikes to be seen and borrowed so option one and two out; the sea looked bloody cold, so drowning was out which only left going back for dinner—and he was very hungry.

Arriving back, it was to discover that the others were already seated at the table, with the only space the one squashed up to S'Marlene's right—the very last place he wanted to be. He took his place with much displeasure, ensuring that everyone knew he was on a sulk. He, at first, managed to ignore S'Marlene and everyone else pretty well totally. However, as the dishes of potatoes and two different vegetables were passed down the table, he had to look to his left. Watching S'Marlene ladle potatoes onto her plate, he suddenly and deliciously realised that he was looking through a gaping armhole of the T-shirt type top she was wearing at a perfectly formed, cone-like right breast in all its naked splendour! Fantastic. Stupendous. Bloody all right in three languages!

The view occurred twice more when the peas and sprouts came around and finally when the gravy boat sailed the line. After that, brief glimpses of breast appeared as she used her knife to cut the food, and Jack just wished the meal would go on forever. Needless to say, Jack was thereafter the first one at the table, sitting in the squashed seat, ensuring that S'Marlene sat next to him. The revealing T-shirt kept reappearing for three days, hygiene in those days not being quite what it is today, and for two of those days, no bra was present either, giving Jack brief glimpses of paradise each time she reached out or moved appropriately. Jack, by now, had formed the opinion that a special friend of his sister was an excellent idea.

The delight extended even to the bedroom because, although all dressing and undressing took place in the dark or the bathroom, glimpses, exciting glimpses of S'Marlene in her slightly transparent baby doll pyjamas provided much pleasure. The only problem was whether to ask her out, or not, on a date. Whilst the problem of separating her from his sister was not insurmountable, the problem of preventing her from telling his sister about how the date had gone and any moves made by Jack to kiss her, what his kissing skill was like or, heaven, whether he had touched or tried to touch any of the forbidden bits was really insoluble. In a small way, it taught Jack that not all problems were assured of a solution since he did not believe that any promises S'Marlene gave in this regard would be honoured! Hey ho, such is life, but he did very much enjoy the voyeuristic glimpses she provided that holiday. The lesson that women could not be trusted not to share secrets with all and sundry was one to prove its value again and again over the years.

# Chapter 22

That autumn was to prove busy and rewarding in equal measure. The final competition of the year was the National shot in early October. Jack had been twice before and had won his National badge for coming in the top one hundred each time. This year, the weather was awful, rain and low cloud making visibility at the longer ranges very difficult but worst of all, worse than lying out in the rain, was the wind. Constantly gusting diagonally across the range for most of the time but now and then directly across it, judging the amount to aim off was almost impossible.

Shots, seven each time, were fired from 200 and 500 yards. The first contest was at 500 yards, a long, long way especially given the poor visibility where the light green and sand coloured target merged into the sand colour of the butts and even the top half of the bull, black, could barely be made out. Adopting the prone position, with Captain Ripley spotting the fall of shot and lying to his left, Jack was thankful that he did at least have his motorcycle trousers and jacket which, being plastic, at least kept the water from soaking through his clothes. The most difficult part was trying to keep the water off the ammunition; any dampness getting onto the bullets and into the breach would cause a round to fly much higher than normal.

Having loaded and got settled, Jack indicated that he was ready. Captain Ripley was there simply to report fall of shot, not to coach, but very quietly, he whispered to use the edge of the target as your aiming point. Jack took careful aim, released half his breath and took up the first pressure on the trigger. Before he could fire, Ripley whispered, "Watch the wind." Jack glanced up at the line of flags on their poles marching down the side of the range. Some of them were only blowing a bit in the wind but some were really streaming out and flapping, but when the wind gusted strongly, they all flapped like mad. What to do? It seemed to Jack that firing when all of them were strongly blowing probably meant that the wind was consistent across the range and therefore would be the better time to fire.

Having made his decision, Jack took aim at the left-hand edge of the target and when the flags all seemed to be behaving the same, he squeezed the trigger. Coinciding with the bang came the agonised cry from Ripley, "You're aiming at the wrong target!" In raising his eyes from the sights, following the admonition from Ripley to watch the wind, Jack had shifted position very slightly, it didn't need to be very much at a target five hundred yards away, and had simply lined up on the target to his own's immediate left. Bugger, dam and blast were the first words through Jack's mind, but before he could damn himself any further, his target disappeared from view, indicating that it was being marked. Expecting to see a flag on a pole being waved across the face of the target, he was astonished to see the target pop up with a marking disc, a round black disc with a white border about six inches in diameter, sitting there smack bang in the middle of the bull! Either someone else had fired at his target and hit the bull or the wind was so strong that the bullet was being pushed three feet or so to the right in five hundred yards.

Ripley lay there saying nothing with a stupefied look on his face. Never one to look a gift horse in the mouth, Jack lined up his second shot, aiming to the left-hand edge of the target, waited for the wind to blow at full strength, and squeezed the trigger. A second bull! His third shot landed in the inner to the left of the bull and his forth in the inner to the right of the bull. As they were both absolutely right for height, it was almost certainly variations in the wind causing the shots to move from the centre of the target; certainly Jack was never going to admit it might be down to him. His final score for the round was 31 out of a possible 35.

Once all had shot at the 500-yard range, they all moved to the 200-yard point. With so much shorter range, the bullet had far less distance to travel where the wind would be able to affect it. However, the bull was now only 6 inches in diameter as opposed to the foot one it had been at 500 yards, in proportion, just as hard a target especially because the wind was varying in its speed even when gusting. The net result for Jack was another 31 out of 35 score.

He wasn't too pleased with himself until he discovered that only one other Cadet had scored a 31 at both ranges, all the others scoring less. He did feel pleased with his score when he was summoned to the OC's tent to be told that his score, along with those of three other Cadets, were to be entered into an international competition with Canada, Australia and New Zealand. He was representing his country internationally! He never did hear what the result of the shoot was—he assumed that they had not won it because they never heard another word—but Jack went home bursting with pride that he had been awarded the National Rifle Competition badge for his performance in that competition and had represented his country. His mother and grandmother's reaction on being told the news was a dismissive sniff; they still had not come to terms with him leaving the scouts and joining the Army Cadet Force even after three years!

# Chapter 23

Following the National, the school platoon was invited to take part in a weekend exercise with the Territorial Army. The East Surrey Regiment, of which the Cadet unit formed the 4/5th Battalion, had been renamed the 5th Cadet Battalion, the Queen's Surrey Regiment as part of a greater reorganisation of army regiments. In an endeavour to foster closer relationships, mainly to encourage Cadets to join the Regular Army and failing that, the TA, TA units were to foster closer relationships with their regular Battalions and the Cadets with both the regulars and the TA. The first result of this was for the School Platoon to join the TA battalion in a fairly major exercise involving travelling out from Portsmouth in landing craft, landing just along from Beachy Head and fighting their way inland from the landing site to take an enemy position some three miles inland.

Captain Hiller went off for extensive briefings and came back furious. He had been treated like an amateur school teacher instead of the Burma veteran that he was. Further, his opinion, and that of the Cadets who had seen and experienced the complete shambles that was the TA, was that it was a complete waste of space and should be shut down, so poor was it; a far different attitude to that displayed by the Cadets whose skill and professionalism had been remarked upon in unit assessments over many years—in no small part due to the work of Captain Hiller.

Hiller's briefing of the Cadets was thorough, specific as to their role and involved an aside to Jack that any opportunity to steal another mug of soup or a rifle was to be seized with alacrity—in fact, anything at all that he could do to embarrass the TA unit and especially the doozy fart of a stuck up Lt Colonel that commanded it was all right by Hiller.

The travel by 3 tonner was uneventful, if a little cold; it was, after all, the middle of October and the back of a canvas-covered lorry with no heating, little wind protection and bloody hard and uncomfortable seats was not exactly luxurious. Assembling quickly with all their kit, the School Platoon was treated to the sight of the TA battalion straggling, with half their kit still left on the lorries in which they had travelled and half of them clearly the worse for drink. Shambling rather than marching, the TA managed, just, to get itself aboard the three-landing craft waiting for them in Portsmouth harbour. With no instructions forthcoming from the TA CO, Jack surveyed the three craft before them and decided the middle one of them looked somewhat the larger with an enlarged bridge structure which seemed to offer some protection to the otherwise open space for the infantry.

Marching smartly up to the craft, Jack saluted the officer at the bow and asked permission to board. Amazed at the antics of the TA, the Army Lieutenant—landing craft were operated by the Royal Army Service Corps, not the Navy—having witnessed the difference between a rabble and a proper unit was somewhat puzzled as to who exactly was asking for permission to embark in such a markedly different and soldierly manner, asked the obvious question, "Who the hell are you lot?"

Jack explained who they were and why they were there. Saying nothing, the Lieutenant said, "Wait there," and walked off to find the CO of the TA unit. His salute to the Lt Colonel was perfunctory in the extreme at their meeting and entirely non-existent at their parting. Returning to Jack, he ordered him to get the platoon to follow him and then led the way into a small mess room in the bridge superstructure and told them to make themselves comfortable; there would be some tea and sandwiches shortly. And true to his word, a few minutes later, two crewmen arrived to hand out steaming mugs of tea and mounds of sandwiches. This treatment was not accorded to the TA who were simply provided with a Dixie (large tin can) of lukewarm tea and left to get on with it on the open boat deck.

They cast off just as the light was fading and set sail for the landing site. Just along from Beachy Head, and somewhat lower, it was still a major cliff they had to climb in the dark. It was assumed that leading assault troops had already climbed the cliffs and left ropes which they were expected to use to help them climb the steeply sloping cliff face—not something Jack was looking forward to, since he had always had a fear of heights.

As they were nearing the landing site, a narrow strip of beach at the foot of the cliffs, the landing craft seemed to speed up when Jack was expecting it to start slowing down. Cries could be heard from the TA on the cargo deck, at first indistinguishable but gradually becoming clearer, that there was water over the deck and it was rising! A rather worn out leftover from the Second World War and a hard life, the landing craft had sprung a severe leak and was making for the beach before it could sink!

Normally, infantry is more than reluctant to step into water in the certain knowledge that to do so meant wet socks, boots and feet for hours to come. This time, the exit from the craft beat all records, wet socks, feet and boots being infinitely preferable to an entire ducking or drowning!

# Chapter 24

Safely ashore, and the whole Platoon accounted for, Jack reported to the TA Lt Colonel. True to form, he was running around like a turkey with a lit match shoved up his arse and gobbling twenty to the dozen. Jack took himself off, and he and his Platoon lay down to rest. Soldiers know that you should not stand if you can sit, never sit if you can lie down and never ever be awake if you can be asleep. So, they slept with a sentry posted just in case.

It took the best part of an hour and a half for the TA to sort themselves out and start climbing the cliff. At first, it seemed to be progressing as you would expect, and Jack was a little surprised to be approached by the Adjutant of the TA battalion and asked to take his platoon up next. In the briefing, they had been briefed that they would be the last to climb, since they had been appointed the rear-guard—the furthest away from any likely action—since they were only Cadets and nothing much could be expected from them.

As they made their way to the ropes, five of them in all, one of the TA privates sidled up to Jack and whispered that there was some sort of trouble at the top, all communications with the troops who had already climbed had been lost and there was clearly something going on and the Cadets were to be sent up as sacrificial goats.

Jack thanked him and made his way over to the Platoon. Calling the three Corporal Section Commanders to him, Jack told them what he had just been told. Asked what they were going to do by one of them, Jack replied, "We know that the enemy has supposed to have been forced back by naval gunfire, but what if they're cheating bastards, like we are, and have been waiting at the top and knocking off our side as they reach the top? With only five ropes to watch it wouldn't take many to do that."

"How do we deal with that then?" asked the No 2 Section Commander.

"I want you three to climb first and when you get a few feet from the top, stop and each of you throw a thunder flash (a big banger simulating a hand grenade) over the top and then follow up as quick as you can, I will be second on the fourth rope and the platoon can be right behind us."

So that is what they did. Immediately after the three bangs, cries of 'bastards' and the like could be heard clearly. As the leading Cadets cleared the cliff top, whistles could be heard blowing. They belonged to the umpires who were calling off the six Royal Marine Commandoes who had indeed been knocking off the TA soldiers one by one as they cleared the cliff edge. Six marines had thus accounted for more than 50 of the TA and were only deemed to have been driven back by more gunfire when the Cadets threw the thunder flashes. Score one to the Cadets.

Once all the rest of the TA unit had reached the top—no word of thanks or congratulations from their CO—the combined force moved inland for about 600 yards and then stopped. The school unit was placed at the rear, as the rear-guard as planned, and because it was clear that the Marines could attack at any time, Jack had ordered that each of the Sections adopt a diamond formation which was best suited for all-round defence. An 'O' group (orders group of the various sub unit commanders) was called and Jack attended. The CO informed them that they would be moving off at 02:00 hrs and that in the meantime, they should set out their ground sheets and get what rest they could.

The plan for 02:00 was that they were to advance across the open down land until shortly before dawn when they were expected to be near the enemy position. At that time, recce patrols would be sent out to find the enemy position and the best line of approach to it. The Cadet Platoon was to remain as the rear-guard and be the reserve force if it was needed, not that it was expected to be.

When the opportunity to ask questions came around, Jack asked about the expectation of night attacks by the enemy whilst en route. The answer, brusque as was now common, was that intelligence showed that they were up against second-rate garrison troops and they were expected to stay safely ensconced in their lines. Jack started to say, "But that hardly fits with their attacks at the top of the cliffs and…" when the CO cut him off and ordered everyone to their positions.

Making his way back to the Platoon, Jack considered what he should do. The CO was clearly an idiot. Jack had also noticed the look exchanged by the two umpires when Jack was cut off by the CO. As it was dark, Jack couldn't make out the detail too well but the fact that the two of them had chosen exchange glances at that moment worried Jack.

On his return to the Platoon, Jack called his own 'O' group and passed on the details from the 'O' group he had just attended. He organised the setting out of their ground sheets to be used in rotation by those on guard and those resting; Jack was not prepared to allow everyone to sleep or doze whilst leaving the position unguarded.

All of the sentry positions were connected to their Section Commanders by lengths of string—a good tug or two being sufficient to attract the Section Commander's attention without any great noise or need for the sentry to leave their position. Jack was not too surprised when after about 40 minutes, one of the strings to him from the No 1 Section Commander jerked him into full wakefulness. Making his way across to the Section, he was told that noises, like someone falling or tripping and cursing hushed by someone else, had been heard from about 30 to 40 yards in front of the sentry position.

Jack passed the word for the Platoon to be stood to as quietly as possible. He decided he would not pass on the information to the TA unit until he was sure they were under attack; it would not be the first time nervous sentries turned restless cattle, sheep or horses into attacking enemy soldiers, and the last thing he wanted was to appear a prat in front of that supercilious wanker commanding the TA.

The shapes of men bearing rifles became gradually visible, crouching as they approached from the direction of the sea, i.e., from the rear, presumably having made their way around the perimeter of the TA position without being detected. They had been spotted because of the noise they made, because the boy sentry was alert and probably had much better eyesight than the piss artists making up the majority of the TA—not that that mattered anyway because they were all fast asleep—and because the sky was somewhat lighter over the sea, and their

60

silhouettes could be easily seen whereas the Platoon position was darker and more difficult to see.

Waiting until they were only about 15 yards away, Jack gave the order for rapid fire; it was so nice to have plenty of ammunition courtesy of the TA! Umpires' whistles blew, three of the attackers were deemed to have been killed and the rest scarpered. In fact, since Jack's action had rendered hors de combat 50% of the entire enemy force in the exercise, the umpires resurrected the dead, and they made their way off into the shadows. With a cheery, "Well done," the umpires made their way off into the dark, leaving Jack to face the enraged TA CO who now appeared, demanding to know what the hell was going on. Jack reported the events as they had happened and waited for the storm. Instead, the CO simply stalked off but from the sounds ensuing shortly afterwards, sentries were also being posted by the TA unit!

Three more probing attempts were made later that night with three TA sentries captured and abducted with no one the wiser until their reliefs arrived to find them gone. The boys were left entirely alone, not only by the Marines, which was a compliment, but also by the TA, which was not.

The Platoon stood to just as it was starting to get light and were treated to the sight of the remains of a bunch of tossers yawning, farting, scratching and generally becoming part of the world. Standing the Platoon down, but leaving sentries posted, Jack ordered the preparation of breakfast.

Composite rations, 24-hour ration packs mainly in tins, had been issued the night before, but, because of the generosity of the landing craft Captain, had hardly been touched—apart from the boiled sweets—and the tinned bacon, beans and egg powder was soon emitting enticing smells even if the hexamine blocks (a bit like firelighters) emitted odours to stun an ox but nowhere near strong enough to depress the appetite of growing boys.

Food was cleared up, not that there was much actually in the way of leftovers, waste buried and kit packed by half an hour after first light. They needn't have been so quick—it was another hour before the remainder of the TA battalion was ready to move off.

The School Platoon was again ordered to act as rear-guard for a, by now, much reduced battalion, probably not much more than a reinforced company, about 150 men, which slowly sorted itself out with two Platoons, each with two Sections in arrowhead formation leading, the Platoon HQ behind them and the third platoon following on last. With a supposed 5 yards between individuals, all in arrowhead formation, and 25 yards between Platoons, the area covered by the battalion, although much reduced in numbers, was considerable, and it was a good ten minutes before Jack gave the order to move off.

Jack decided that whilst it might be all right for the TA to move in arrowhead formation, given the professionalism of the Marines and their predilection for attacking the weakest points, which certainly in numbers was the boy platoon, he would move his Platoon in diamond formation, where each section formed into a diamond shape, still with five yards between soldiers and 25 yards between sections but with each section moving with four 'walls', two covering a wide area going forward and two covering the rear arcs, and although having to keep looking backwards made walking forwards difficult, it would provide much better scanning of the area and better firepower if attacked.

They had only progressed a few hundred yards when shots came at them from their left. Both the left lead Section and the trailing section opened fire immediately with no orders from Jack. The attack was over as quickly as it had begun with the umpires deciding that one Cadet from each of the Sections involved had been killed in the opening shots. They also decided that one of the attackers, there had been four, had also been killed. The Marine was resurrected to carry on and although the two Cadets should have been ordered to join the rest of the 'dead' who were shambling along behind the School Platoon—to watch and learn—as no such direct order was given by the umpires, Jack told them to resume their positions and carry on until someone told them otherwise. No one did.

They set off again with the TA Company leading, the Cadet Platoon behind them and following along as tail end Charlie came the walking dead. They progressed slowly with frequent ambushes being launched on the TA unit but with no one coming near the Cadet Platoon. After the third or fourth attack, Jack thought the TA would have started to get its act together but far from it, their performance got worse as their CO started to fall apart in front of their eyes. Jack thought the best thing that could happen for the TA would be for their CO to be killed in one of the ambushes, but perhaps the umpires were enjoying his discomfort too much!

About 11.00 hrs, the TA halted and went to ground. The School Platoon followed suit, again taking up all round defence—those Marines were sneaky bastards even if they did seem intelligent enough to leave the Cadets alone and concentrate on the weakest part of the force now much depleted in strength.

As a few small groups could be seen making their way forwards and away from the TA position, Jack assumed that they were Recce Patrols being sent out to find and scout the enemy position. What bothered Jack was that they all seemed to be heading in the wrong direction; they were heading off far too far to the right. Jack had been keeping constant check on the map and their route—basic stuff— and felt fairly sure that the position they were attempting to find was to their left and behind them.

After an hour or so, a runner arrived, summoning him to the TA's CO. On arrival, Jack was told that the Recce Patrols had identified the general area of the enemy but had not precisely identified it and its layout. The CO said, "As you have had it easy up to now, following us, I thought it would be a good idea if you had a chance to show what you can do and lead for a change—good experience for you what? I want you to send out a Recce Patrol to this area here," pointing to an area on the map about 600 yards to their front, "and see what you can find, if anything." Not the normal way of ordering an action but apparently the best this blowhard could do. "I shall give you a few minutes to prepare a plan and then you can tell me how you intend to carry out your orders. Everything clear?"

"Yes, sir." What else could he say?

A few minutes later, Jack was called and asked for his plan. Using the standard terminology SMEAC, standing for Situation, Mission, Execution, Administration and logistics and Command and Signals, Jack laid out his plan. The biggest problem for Jack was that he believed that the area he had been ordered to reconnoitre was wrong and he had had to think hard how he could justify heading off in the wrong direction.

Thinking quickly, he explained that he intended to head off to the east because there had been too much activity to the north which might have alerted the enemy that they were onto their position, particularly important as one of the Recce Patrols which had gone in that direction had not returned and was now overdue and might have been captured. In fact, although no one yet knew it, they had got lost and eventually, finding themselves outside a pub, had settled down for a pie and a pint before ringing for transport—much needed in view of the fact that many pints had been consumed by the time the transport got to them!

The Colonel accepted the explanation with no comment and Jack completed his plan with no reaction from the CO other than a curt, "Be as quick as you can."

Returning to his Platoon, Jack sent for the two Lance Corporals from Number 1 and 2 Sections. These were younger boys in the year following Jack and the Section Commanders, and they needed to get the experience of Recce Patrols in real time exercises. Briefing them quickly, they set off within 10 minutes with John Cox, No 1 Section 2i/c in the lead, Jack in the middle and Dave Westlands following up the rear. Keeping to cover as much as possible, they headed for the position Jack thought was the enemy location.

After about six hundred yards, they were just about to cross an area of open land when Dave hissed at them to stop. Checking with him, Jack was somewhat annoyed to discover that Dave had been taken short and needed a crap!

Staying in the edge of cover, Jack decided that they might as well spend their time scanning the woodlands across the space whilst waiting for Dave to complete his business. It was John Cox, however, who spotted the movement in the trees. At first, they could not make out what it was but a fortunate break in the clouds allowed the sun to shine obliquely under the trees to reveal two separated trenches being dug whilst two of the Marines stood guard, smoking and with their rifles leaning against the trees, their contempt for the TA was evidently obvious.

What wasn't obvious was why they were only now preparing their fairly obvious position—almost out in the open and in clear view given bright daylight. *Thank God for Dave's bowels*, thought Jack, or they would have walked out into full view in the open and been shot or captured; was it Napoleon who said give me lucky generals every time? Re-joined by the crap artist, Jack took stock.

"This lot have been very successful at ambushes. They do not seem to be making much of an attempt at hiding their trenches; the dug-up dirt has been piled at the front of the two trenches, but no attempt has been made to camouflage it; it stands out like a sore thumb. What if the TA are supposed to see it? What would they do?"

"They'd go right flanking," said John.

"Why right?" asked Jack.

"Because there is some cover from those isolated bushes," said Dave, "and there's no cover going left flanking."

"I agree," said Jack, "but given that the Marines seem to know what they are doing, why are they making it so obvious, what other surprises might they have in store for the TA? Let's just take some time and have a very good look at the area immediately to the front of the flanking route and the flanks of that route to see if anything is out of the ordinary."

For a while, they just lay there scanning the suspect areas; binoculars would have been very handy, but they were far too valuable to be issued to mere Cadets.

"Can you see 50 yards out, to the left of the flanking route, about 25 yards from it, the grass doesn't look quite even and seems to be just a tiny bit faded compared to the rest of the field; it seems to be a long trench shape, and yes, there even seems to be some smoke rising from it," said John. It took Jack a little while to identify the spot to which John was referring.

"God, I think you're right; you must have phenomenal eye sight to see that. The bastards have dug a trench and hidden it in plain sight where no one would normally have even thought to look; a couple of Bren gunners there would devastate any flanking force and I bet there's more—there must be something to the front as well; scan that area now."

The three of them scanned and watched for some five minutes but could detect nothing further. Jack ordered them away, and they made their way back to the battalion. On reporting to the CO, Jack was greeted with a sneering, "Found nothing, I suppose?"

"No, sir. I think we have found their position."

"Good God, where?"

Jack gave the map reference and described the two visible trenches at the edge of the trees. He also started to say, "But I think you should order a further recce…" when he was interrupted by the Colonel with,

"When I need advice from a mere Sergeant, and a Cadet one at that, I'll ask for it. You saw them, didn't you?"

"Yes, sir."

"Describe the ground on approach."

"Open directly to the two trenches, absolutely no cover to approach the isolated copse from the left but some scattered bushes and light vegetation to the right, the obvious route for right flanking and therefore likely to be the most defended…" Interrupting again, posturing in front of his few remaining officers, the Colonel said,

"I've told you Sergeant, that I do not want to hear your opinions, only facts. Now return to your Platoon."

*Up yours*, thought Jack as he made his way back with the two Lance Corporals. John Cox ventured a question as to why Jack hadn't told the CO about the hidden trench.

"If it was a real war, I would have, but that arrogant, insufferable, opinionated, only got-the-job-because-of-who-his-daddy-is ignorant fucking cunt full of wind and piss and making dog snot look lovely, fully deserves everything coming to him," burst out Jack with more than a little feeling!

"But what if he finds out that you knew about the hidden trench?" asked Cox.

"What trench?" said Jack. "Oh, you mean that piece of discoloured grass where the sheep had pissed all over it and changed the colour a little…didn't see anything suspicious there, after all what would I know, a mere Cadet Sergeant not fit to express an opinion to Lord High Almighty Lt Colonel shit for brains."

"But what about the smoke?" persisted Cox.

"What smoke? I saw no smoke. I only saw some mist rising from the wet ground, probably the hot sheep piss. Professionals from the Marines surely wouldn't have given their position away by smoking, would they?"

At that, Cox grinned and said, "No, Sarge, definitely not!" They arrived back at the platoon to find that, even though they were in all round defence, Paul Air had organised a brew and they had plenty of time to drink it, not always the case with the army, whilst the TA unit, such as was left of it, prepared to attack the enemy camp. Jack received a message to say that they were to remain where they were to provide a firm base in the very unlikely event that things went wrong. So, they just sat back and watched them go.

About half an hour later, they heard an enormous eruption of firing off in the direction of the enemy camp. There were obviously many machine guns firing interspersed with single shots and a dozen or so loud bangs.

"Sounds like quite a battle," said Paul.

Jack added, "Pity the Marines aren't using live ammunition."

"Naughty, naughty," laughed John Cox, "but oh so apt!"

About half an hour later, the TA returned. They had left as two Platoons, albeit slightly under strength, with the walking dead following behind. They returned as a formed unit of seven soldiers plus the CO with a whole legion of the deemed dead grinning and following on behind.

Jack was not to discover until later that the umpires had deliberately selected the 2i/c of the TA battalion, Major Soames, as one of the first casualties, thus depriving the unit of the only officer who had any idea about what he was doing and leaving the Colonel totally exposed for the idiot he was. They had also deliberately left the Colonel alive to expose him further; the debrief of the attack by the umpires had been extremely critical and included references to him shutting up Jack when Jack had tried to warn him of the route being too obvious!

Jack was sent for soon after. Approaching the Colonel, Jack made sure he was as soldierly as possible and threw up a stunner of a salute even though saluting was not normal in the field—it gave away rank to snipers. Jack waited for the bollocking he was sure was coming. Instead, wearily and in a very subdued manner, the Colonel told him that the Marines were waiting for them, probably told by the missing recce patrol that had indeed been captured, when they were coming and from which direction and had ambushed them with six Bren guns, thunder flashes both hand-thrown and fixed to trip wires on the approach to their position.

It became clear that the Marines had correctly deduced that the TA would attempt a right-flanking attack and had set out their defences accordingly just as Jack had discovered, although neither he nor the other members of the Recce Patrol had been able to spot the trip wires between the bushes or the two beautifully camouflaged trenches just within the tree line about some way to the right of the very obvious decoy trenches that Jack's patrol had spotted.

Jack was braced for some reaction to him from the Colonel including an accusation of leading them into an ambush but the umpires' debrief, which Jack did not yet know about, had already protected Jack on that score even though, in turn, the umpires didn't know the full extent of Jack's knowledge; Napoleon obviously got it right about lucky generals (even though Jack was only a Sergeant!).

Instead, the Colonel said, "I should have listened to you, Sergeant Hughes, the right flank was too obvious. However, the enemy still need to be destroyed and their position taken and as you are the only reserve I have, I need you to formulate a plan of attack as soon as possible; do you need to see their position again or do you feel you know it well enough?"

"Well enough, sir."

"Right, report back when you are ready, and if you need any kit, see the Quartermaster, and tell him he is to give you whatever you want."

"Yes, sir. Thank you, sir."

"Carry on and as quick as you can."

"Sir."

As Jack made his way back to his Platoon, he pondered on how the hell he was going to attack the position. Right flanking was clearly a no-no but the left flank or even a frontal attack over open country into the face of six Brens would simply be suicide. The Marines were also devious bastards, and there was no guarantee that they would still be occupying the same positions, or worse still, they might have further positions in the rear to withdraw to, leaving the Cadets to struggle through the woods not knowing the ground and stumbling into more trip wires and expertly camouflaged positions. What to do? How could he ambush them and attack from a direction they would not suspect?

As he was considering the problems and the options open to him, Jack thought the first thing he should do is talk to the QM and find out what kit was available. Besides ammunition, of which they had no need anyway, Jack discovered some half a dozen smoke grenades, boxes of thunder flashes and some detonator cord which was not for them, if only because, as Cadets, they did not know how to use it.

Looking at the smoke grenades and the thunder flashes, the germ of an idea began to grow in the back of Jack's mind. Turning to the QM, Jack asked, "If I was to ask very nicely, would you order your driver to drive us in your three tonner to a spot beyond the enemy position that I will point out to him?"

Slowly, a look of comprehension started to dawn on the QM's face.

"Would I be right in thinking that you would not want the Colonel to know about this until afterwards?" asked the QM.

"That would be a big help," replied Jack.

"I'll warn the driver," said the QM, "and anyway, that snotty stuck up waste of space would only try to pinch the credit, so good luck to you, lad."

Jack made his way quickly back to the Cadet Platoon and called them all together. Normally, he would have briefed his Section Commanders in an 'O' group and they then, in turn, would have briefed their Sections but there wasn't time for that so together it was; and anyway, this way he could be sure that every Cadet heard the plan in the same words with, hopefully, the same level of comprehension.

"Corporal Air, your mission is to take No 1 Section along the same route as that the TA took. Take with you these smoke grenades and a dozen thunder flashes. I want you to make some noise to alert the Marines to your presence, and show them some fleeting glimpses of your Section, but spread them well out and try to appear more than you really are. Fire a shot and then shout, you doozy idiot, wait till this is over, I'll give you accidental discharge etc and try to give the impression of a negligent discharge miscreant getting a bollocking. It's your job to keep the Marines' attention on you, hopefully falling about laughing and not paying attention to what the rest of us are doing.

"The rest of us will embark on the QM's lorry and get a lift to the back of the copse, along that lane over there, and attack them from behind; they should enjoy that, being Marines!" Jack waited for the laughter to die down and then went on, "I estimate that it will take about fifteen minutes for us to get into position so at 13.10 hours Cpl Air commence your diversion, the first action of which will be to get yourself seen and then action the negligent discharge and the shouting. Once you are sure you've got their full attention, throw all six smoke grenades as far towards their position as you can to make it look like we are going to attack behind the cover of the smoke. At that stage, fire three deliberate rounds which will be our signal to attack them from the rear; I can't be sure that we will see the smoke with the copse of trees in the way so will need the three shots as my signal. Once you hear our noise, attack yourself with fire and movement and we'll soon sort these fish soldiers," said Jack with a lot more confidence than he actually felt.

"Any questions?" Jack dealt with the two that were raised but not really necessary. He would rather someone who was not sure asked rather than they kept quiet and then made calamitous mistakes or acted at the wrong time. "Finally, Lance Corporal Cox I want you to report to the Colonel that the Cadet Platoon, in compliance with his orders, is about to launch another attack on the enemy position using smoke grenades and thunder flashes kindly provided by the QM. The attack is timed for 13.20 hours. Then, skedaddle and make your way back to No 1 Section; try to avoid answering any of his questions, but above all, do not tell him about the lorry—do your 'I'm just a dumb Lance Corporal doing as I'm told!' bit."

In the event, the Colonel listened to the message somewhat distractedly and let him go with a muttered, "Thank you, Corporal."

Meanwhile, Jack and No 2 and 3 Sections, along with the Platoon Headquarters staff had clambered aboard the three tonner and as soon as Cox joined them, they set off. Jack had them all lie down on the floor which, like all army transport in those days, was open at the back with only the tail board, about three feet high, to hide the view as to what exactly was in the lorry, and admonished the Platoon to silence on pain of death or worse. The lorry made its slow way down the lane and past the back of the copse. Fortunately, the driver had some sense about him and drove just past the probable position of the Marines and stopped where some bushes grew close to the road and at the top of a gentle slope which, once the Cadets had debarked, allowed him to roll away without having to accelerate the engine and give away the fact that he had stopped.

Just to his left, there seemed to be a narrow track. Jack signalled his fighting patrol to follow him and they set off as quietly as possible in single file. Within 30 yards, Jack started to hear some voices although he couldn't make out what was being said. By hand signals, he indicated that he wanted the two sections to spread out either side of him in an extended line. As they were still spreading out, the noise of the three distraction shots from No 1 Section was heard. So, too, could a voice calling out, "Here they come again, the silly bastards, take post."

Almost immediately afterwards, the thunder flashes from the Cadets and the Bren guns from the Marines could be heard. Signalling advance, the fighting patrol made its way through the copse. They passed three trenches, well camouflaged to the front but very visible to the Cadets advancing from the rear, and a further 30 yards or so beyond that, they could make out the camouflaged decoy trenches throughout which the six Marines were spread. All their attention was to their front where smoke, red and green, was starting to drift past. One of them even had his beret off, was firing the Bren with one hand whilst holding a cigarette in the other—so their first thoughts about the smoke had obviously been correct; the

Marines were not as professional as they made out, and it was to be hoped that the Colonel never found out about it!

Seeing that the two Sections had taken up their positions, Jack signalled the advance. They reached within 10-15 yards before anyone, ironically the smoker, noticed they were there. Before he could call out or even react—the total look of surprise on his face said it all—Jack shouted, "Charge," and the boys leapt forward screaming and yelling at the tops of their voices. Some of the younger ones weren't too loud but the shrillness of pre-pubescence more than made up for it with a penetrating high-frequency din making all attempts at action rather difficult! The boys were among the Marines in seconds firing off blanks willy nilly and the umpires blowing whistles and shouting cease fire at the tops of their voices; the Cadets were all well within the blast danger range (a minimum of 15 yards) of the blanks they were firing and headlines in the paper of 'Marines Shot Dead by Army Cadets' were only a vivid imagination away! The hubbub and chaos gradually ceased with the Marines behaving extremely crestfallen and the Cadets boisterously jubilant. The umpires quickly took charge, ordering the Marines to supervise the safe removal of their trip wires and thunder flashes and ordering forward the walking dead from the TA for them to fill in the Marines' trenches; they'd had it easy just watching the goings on and could earn their keep by a little hard labour.

The Cadets were ordered to a point further along the back lane where a 3 tonner was parked in a small car park. Set out on trestle tables were Hay boxes (large insulated metal containers in which hot food was delivered from a cookhouse to troops in the field) along with a large tea urn and mounds of bread and butter. Told to queue up and come and get it by the Army Catering Corps Sergeant-in-charge, the boys were not slow, unpacking their mess tins and enamel mugs as they went. By this time, it had gone two o'clock and having had breakfast some six hours or so ago and being pretty active in between, the boys were ready for it.

Being the army, the food was not very hot, Hay boxes being notoriously inefficient and the Catering Corps not particularly bothered at that time, but the boys didn't care; they didn't have to cook it, and there was plenty of it, although the TA soldiers at the end of the queue would not agree about its plenitude. Irish stew, mashed potato powder, processed peas were all piled into one mess tin and a runny rice pudding into the other with a dollop of strawberry jam plonked in it— the end runners in the TA didn't get any at all. The bread and butter (margarine really!) was a matter of help yourself to as much as you wanted, not an offer refused by growing lads out in the open air all night, and had to be piled on top of the stew, and holding the mug under the tap of the urn for tea was an exercise in creativity itself, nature having been a bit mean and not provided three hands or even better four! And having negotiated all this lot, there was still the problem of spooning sugar into the tea, but hey, all problems could be overcome by the School Platoon!

With the mess tin of stew on his lap and the one of rice pudding on the ground, carefully shielded from passing boots, Jack gratefully took a deep swallow of lukewarm, strong stewed tea. Swallowing was difficult since he was grinning like a Cheshire cat. Nevertheless, he felt very contented with life and his lot within it in particular. He could see the Colonel across the other side of the clearing; he was not eating and appeared to be berating the Major who was trying to eat. Jack could not hear what was being said but the body language when the Major got up and walked away said it all. Jack wondered whether the Colonel would say anything to him, but he didn't even look towards the Cadet Platoon, all scoffing and generally making lots of noise, lots and lots of noise.

After they had eaten and washed up their mess tins, the umpires called them all together and carried out their debrief meticulously describing the actions, positive and negative, of each of the three units. The Colonel did not stay to listen; if he had, he would have learnt, but not perhaps to his surprise, that his command and control of his amateurish, slack and lackadaisical unit had been marked down in virtually every respect. In fact, the Colonel had hitched a lift to the station and had caught a train home long before the debriefing had finished.

The journey back was uneventful and all of the boys, Jack included, were very happy to get home, have a hot bath and go to bed. The next day being Monday, Jack went to school as usual. He was summoned to the teachers' staff room at lunch time to be met by Ted Hiller with a stern frown on his face.

"What have you been up to, young Hughes?" he asked. Jack knew enough not to admit to anything until he knew what it was he was supposed to have done—admitting to something no one knew about was never a good idea!

"Don't know what you mean, sir."

"Well, young man, I have had two telephone calls about you and your antics over the weekend, one from the Chief Umpire and one from the 2i/c of the TA. Both told me in great detail how impressed they had been with the Platoon and especially your performance leading it. The Chief Umpire said he would be happy to see you in his Regiment, should you ever decide to join the Regulars, and asked me to give you his best wishes for the future and this paper with his Recruiting Officer's details on." At which he handed a piece of paper to Jack with the aforementioned details on it. He also said, "The 2i/c of the TA thought you might like to know that the Colonel had a meeting with the Brigadier last evening; bad news travels very fast when you are as unpopular as he was, some 'well wisher' obviously having passed on the details of the TA's lacklustre performance over the exercise, and he had been summoned to that meeting by the Brigadier at 22.00 hrs that evening! Apparently, it was quite a short meeting, and the Colonel decided that it was time for him to retire with immediate effect at the end of it. The 2i/c has been appointed in temporary command of the unit and would like to know if you would like to join them once you leave school. So, young Hughes, it would seem that everyone wants you. In addition, you are to report to Major Ravenwood tomorrow at his office in the barracks in Kingston; he wants to interview you about something or other, nothing to worry about, wear your school uniform and be there prompt for 13.55 hours. Any questions?"

"No, sir."

"On your way then."

Jack made his way back to his friends, smiling to himself and thinking, *I should really thank that little sod for wanting a shit; if he hadn't wanted to go at that moment, I would have led the patrol out into the open and we would have been shot or captured.* As Napoleon said, somewhat paraphrased, "Give me a lucky shit any day!"

# Chapter 25

The following day, he reported to the Cadet Battalion CO. He had been ordered to appear at 13.55 hours. Being the Army, Jack turned up five minutes before that time. Indeed, it was something of a fetish with the army so much so that it wasn't at all uncommon for the poor bloody soldiers to be ordered out a good hour before a major parade; the Colonel wanted them out at 09.00 hours so the Adjutant wanted them out 15 minutes before that to ensure everything was okay; the Company Commanders wanted them out 15 minutes before that for their inspections; the Company Sergeant Major 15 minutes before that and so on down to the Corporals so that they could often be parading an hour before the parade in the cold and wet because of the bloody system.

On this occasion, Jack was called for promptly at 14.00 hours; even Ted Hiller had added a safety margin! Invited to sit, Jack was asked to describe his career in the Cadet Force to date which he did in a format which wasn't much more than a list of dates and events, joined on such a date, passed drill certificates and weapon training courses, promotion dates, camps attended and, of course, his experiences with the shooting team. At various intervals, Major Ravenwood interrupted with more probing questions as to what had motivated him, what he thought about that particular event and finally, what he saw himself doing in the future.

Jack found that a more difficult question to answer, because he really didn't know. There was a general assumption that if he did well enough in his exams, he would go on to university but as to after that, that was something for another day, but he sensed that that would not be the right answer to give. So, he answered that, subject to the right results in his exams, he thought he might have a go at Sandhurst as he found himself drawn to the military life. The Major thanked him for coming and dismissed him. Nothing had been said about the purpose of the meeting and why Jack was there, not even anything about the TA exercise of the past weekend. So, Jack made his way back to school and in the fullness of time forgot all about it. He was to find out what it was all about the following summer at camp.

Jack, when he needed to fill up his petrol tank, used to use the Ace of Spades garage on the Kingston by pass, just up the top of the Hook road where Jack lived. As the bike would do a good 140 miles on a tankful, he didn't visit that often, so it was all the more fortunate that he should visit on that particular Saturday. The station was set out with one row of four pumps on the Hook road side and one row, also of four pumps on the slip road down to the bypass, the station being set in the angle of the junction. Next door, but on the same site, was the Ace of Spades nightclub—a well-known, popular, if somewhat disreputable, joint.

Jack, since there was only one attendant—in those days you were served, you didn't serve yourself—decided that he would serve himself on the two-stroke petrol pump which was hand-pumped, not powered, and had just filled up when another two-stroke motorcycle pulled up the other side of the island. At the same time, the Manager, for that was who it turned out to be, came over and instead of telling Jack off, which he expected, said, "Do you mind doing that one as well? The second and third hands have been held up and we're very short at the moment."

So Jack just did as he'd been asked. He then served a few more cars and two bikes before an old Austin tore into the station and parked up round the back. A man and woman jumped out and hurried into the office, donned their uniform coats and with a quick apology to the boss that their car had refused to start, started serving waiting cars.

Making his way to the office, set in the corner with a view down each row of pumps, Jack tendered the 4 shillings and 3 pennies for his gallon. The manager waived it away and thanked him for helping out. The icing on the cake was when he added, "And if you're ever looking for a job, give us a call."

"Funny you should say that," said Jack. "Do you have any weekend or evening hours part-time by any chance?"

"Unfortunately, we don't need anyone right this minute, despite the evidence of your eyes in the last few minutes, but I can take your number; you do have a phone number, don't you, and give you a call when I do have a job?" Jack gave him his number and drove away.

A couple of weeks later, Jack came home to find that someone had rung and wanted him to call him back. So Jack did. It turned out to be the Manager of the petrol station who wanted to know if Jack wanted to work as the third man on the Saturday, working from 1 pm until 5 pm—four hours at 3 shillings per hour plus bonus and tips. Jack jumped at it, and the following Saturday saw him start his shift. The other two on the shift were the man and woman, in fact man and wife, who had turned up late the time Jack had helped out. Stan and Olga were eastern Europeans who, having been displaced by the war, had arrived in England and had set about making a life for themselves here. They both had jobs in the week but boosted their incomes by working at the weekend in the petrol station. Jack grew to like them a lot and admire them; they certainly put his grandpa to shame who only worked hard at not working.

They also taught him the ropes as to the station operation. Petrol was sold only in whole or half gallons. If a motorist wanted his tank filling up and it became full at 4.75 gallons, the attendant had to charge to the next whole gallon—as unpopular as that made the attendant. As the pump metre counters were read at the end of each shift, so that the total number of gallons issued through that particular pump could be accounted for and more importantly paid for, the till takings were totalled at the end of the shift and if the till was short, then the shortfall was taken from the pay of those on shift, and as no attendant would accept a reading where the numbers were not exactly in line, the pumps had to be levelled at takeover.

This was done by keeping a careful note of each pump during the shift where the amount charged for was more than the amount pumped out (no one charged to the lower half gallon because they would have to pay for that themselves!) and all the estimated fractions were added up and drained from the 'over' pump(s) into cars, bikes or petrol cans shortly before the end of the shift. It was a perk of the job and a perfectly legitimate fiddle. It disappeared in later years when digital pumps started being used.

There were also some not-quite-so-legitimate fiddles adding to the attendants' take-home pay. The bottles of oil, cans had not yet been made available in varieties of oils, were counted at the start and end of the shift and the attendants were paid three pennies per pint sold as an incentive to sell oil. In those days, cars burnt quite a lot of oil, in the case of Wally's old Ford more oil than petrol, so when a customer drove up for petrol, it was quite routine (the bonus was an incentive) to ask, "Shall I check the oil, sir/madam?"—not many madams as very few women drove in those days. Any dipstick showing a level less than full resulted in the attendant suggesting that at least a pint was needed, if not two. Rarely was this refused.

The station sold two kinds of oil—Castrol, a-greenish tinged oil in glass pint and quart bottles, the market leader by a huge margin and Shell 591, which was a cheaper alternative supplied in 40-gallon drums to the station and 'served' in pint or quart jugs. Castrol was two shillings and three pennies a pint and Shell 591 was one shilling and nine pennies a pint. The problem for customers was that the three-penny bonus was only given for Castrol and not for 591, so surprise, surprise, the attendants only picked up the Castrol bottles, which were displayed on the forecourt in racks, and not the 591 which was in the oil room at the side. Not illegal or even dishonest but not necessarily moral either—still, they only had to ask!

Another almost-legal fiddle involved collecting left over oil from engine top ups. Attendants would pour the Castrol oil from the bottle into the engine. Especially in the winter, the oil, which had been left out in the open, was thickened by the cold and would be sluggish to pour, particularly the XXL oil which was a heavier, thicker grade anyway but even the XL, a 30-grade oil lighter than the 40-grade XXL, was not the best of pourers—no multigrade oils then! Attendants, therefore, made sure that, once the initial quick pour had slowed, they would stop pouring and replace the oil filler cap in the engine and hiding the bottle as best they could from the customer, would then put the bottle down by the pump, out of sight, and finish off the sale.

Once the customer had left, the bottle would be collected and placed in the warm oil room, upside down in an oil jug and left to warm up. Gradually, the oil would warm, thin, as it did in a car engine, and then it would drain into the jug. Fifteen or twenty bottles treated this way would produce up to 2 or 3 bottles worth of oil. That oil was Castrol oil anyway and therefore would not look out of place in a Castrol bottle and would better still be entirely profit for the attendant since those bottles produced from draining other bottles made from draining bottles would never show on the shift stock and therefore the money from the sale went straight into the attendants' pockets—no itemised till receipts then either which could be audited later!

The really illegal fiddle, however, was the filling of emptied Castrol bottles with 591 oil and selling it as Castrol oil which resulted in a six-penny profit straight to the attendants' pockets. To get around the colour difference, 591 being a straightforward brown oil colour with no hint of green, the 591 would be tipped into the warmed, drained Castrol bottles in the oil room and shaken vigorously in 2 or 3 bottles by which time it would have adopted a green enough colour to appear to be Castrol and to be sold 'legitimately' as such. If, of course, night had fallen, then the rigmarole of shaking was unnecessary!

A further fiddle involved upper cylinder lubricant. When pistons pump up and down, the cylinder oil gets sprayed onto the cylinder wall under the piston head, thus lubricating the walls. Each piston had at least one compression ring and one oil ring—a seal to stop the oil getting up past the piston and to act as a scraper on the downward stroke to prevent carbon build up in the cylinder bores and lots of smoke out the back. Given the amount of smoke out of Wally's old Ford, he probably didn't have any of them in his motor!

Upper cylinder lubricant, the one they sold was Redex, worked by being squirted into the petrol tank at the ratio of one squirt per gallon, where it would mix with the petrol, be atomised into the upper cylinder and oil the top areas of the cylinders not normally reached by the oil under the piston head thus reducing wear at the top of the engine and prolonging engine life. It was also claimed that it increased the miles per gallon achieved. Thus, when a customer asked for four gallons and Redex, please—please was still the norm in those days except from toffs who were invariably brusque and even downright rude. Most motorists stayed in the car whilst the attendant pumped in the petrol, something especially common if it was raining—no overhead canopies at the Ace of Spades—so as a result, they were not in a position to see if the Redex was added, but they were always charged the four pennies!

The garage was purely a petrol and oil vendor. There was no shop as there is today nor did it carry out repairs or servicing. However, when Jack revealed that he could repair punctures, something the garage did not offer, the next motorist to ask if they repaired punctures was told that they most certainly did! At five shillings a go and three or four punctures a shift, word having spread remarkably quickly that they were now offering this service, it turned out to be a nice little earner, something not possible years later with the advent of tubeless radial tyres, product liability, and strict rules relating to what punctures, where they were and how big they were that could be repaired came into force.

Occasionally, other opportunities presented themselves. One day, the three of them were gathered in the little office and watched a guy pushing his car around the roundabout, causing chaos and consternation as he did so. Reaching the start of the forecourt, he simply could not push the car up onto it, the slight slope defeated him. Reluctantly, they went out and helped him push it to the pumps. It was only when Jack asked which fuel he wanted, having assumed the bloke had run out of petrol that he discovered the car had broken down, not run out.

Stan immediately said, "We don't do repairs, mate."

To which the bloke said, "Well, can't you just have a quick look at it, it was running fine, and then it just stopped. Go on; just have a quick look, please."

Stan was obviously starting to say no when Jack said, "Okay I'll have a quick look under the bonnet but no promises mind; would you please pull the bonnet release?" The guy got into the car and pulled the release—something common to only a few, more expensive motors—and Jack lifted the bonnet. To the right side of the engine compartment, at the back, was the battery. The instant he looked at it, Jack knew what the problem was; one of the leads was hanging off!

Before Jack could do anything, the bloke was back, doing his best to look knowledgeable, making comments like I've checked the distributor and that's clearly okay; *oh no, it isn't*, thought Jack, *without power it can't possibly be okay, this guy hasn't a clue*. Sucking loudly on his teeth, the universal sign of a tradesman with the knowledge that this is going to be very difficult and expensive, Jack said to him, "Look, you go on down the road on the right there to the café, and get yourself a cup of tea, take at least an hour, and I hope I will have the opportunity to fix it between serving customers by the time you get back."

As soon as he'd gone, Jack slipped the battery cable over the terminal and tightened up the holding nut and bolt. Getting in the car, it started first pull of the starter, so Jack switched off and got Stan to move it to the side of the forecourt. The motorist, on his return, was delighted to pay the pound fee and drove off happy with the service he had received! Not many opportunities like that occurred.

The final, legitimate earning opportunity was tips. All garage proprietors made it clear that earning tips was an effective way of increasing income and, more importantly for the proprietor, a means of keeping the wages down and incentivising the staff to provide excellent service and thus earn lots of tips. As with so many things in life, Jack was to discover that there was a big gap between theory and reality.

Serving a Rolls Royce driver, who wanted his car filling up, his oil and battery checking (distilled water was provided free), upper cylinder lubricant, and his tyres checking all in the pouring rain, Jack completed the lot and was looking forward to a decent tip—the customer having remained nice and dry in the motor in the meantime. The bill came to £2-19-11d and on telling the customer, Jack was presented with three one-pound notes. Jack had expected maybe a sixpence or a shilling in addition as a tip but no, nothing. Despondently, Jack trudged to the office and rang up the sale. Picking out the penny change, Jack went to put it into the tips jar when he realised the Rolls was still there and that the customer was waiting for Jack to walk out in the rain again to return it to him! Disgusted, Jack stepped out of the office momentarily and, holding the penny up so the watching customer could see it, he placed it down on the window ledge and walked back into the office. He then had the pleasure, if somewhat disbelievingly, of watching the driver get out of the Rolls, walk over, pick up the penny and dash back to the car. *Tight sod*, thought Jack. When he related the incident to his father that evening, his father's only comment was, "Probably how he got his money in the first place!"

Four gallons of fuel cost 10d, 6d or 2d less than a pound so that motorists asking for four gallons were faced with saying, "Keep the change," or waiting whilst the attendant returned to the office with the pound note and then returned with their change. A slow return could encourage the driver to not bother and drive away—not exactly the high level of service the proprietors wanted.

Many of the customers were regulars and the attendants soon got to know who could be relied on for a tip and who were the tight bastards who could not, no matter the efficiency of the service. Since they could be recognised as they drove onto the forecourt, attendants would make a practice of immediately disappearing into the oil room or the lavatory and making the bastards wait. It probably did nothing to encourage them to tip, but it was nevertheless satisfying to the attendants.

Thus, Jack used to earn a, for him, tidy little sum each Saturday afternoon. Jack was never quite sure whether his school knew about the job nor did he care. However, in the early spring, the Saturday night man left. He worked from 11 pm until 9 am in the winter and until 8 am in the summer. As the number of customers was much lower during this time, there was only one attendant on duty. The pay was higher, 4s 4d per hour, and with no one else to share the tips or drainings from the pumps already paid for, the potential earnings were much greater. Jack thought about it, decided he could easily get a few hours' sleep on the Saturday evening before going on shift and a few on the Sunday morning after it so it would not affect his school time, and it would enable him to buy a bigger bike. So he put his hand up for it and, no one else fancying it, got the job.

To his surprise, the tips were much better, even though there were fewer of them, most coming from clients of the Ace of Spades nightclub next door. It didn't open until 11 pm and closed sometime after 4 am. Most of them leaving at that time were well under the influence—the measurement of a man in those days, long before the breathalyser, being how much he could drink and still drive meant that many were prone to show off to the young ladies, a loose term, accompanying them by dispensing large tips to anyone serving them!

After only three Saturday nights, Jack was in a position to buy an Aerial Red Hunter 350 cc single, four stroke on which he had had his eye for some time. It had a sidecar attached and was for sale by a bloke around the corner for £10. Jack already knew someone who would buy the sidecar for £3, leaving a net cost of £7. He also knew that there would be a plus for the cost of the insurance and for the paint, seat cover and fairing that Jack wanted for it.

But what to do about his parents, particularly his mum, who was likely to object absolutely to such a large increase in power and performance. In the event, when he raised the idea of a bigger bike with his dad, on the basis that the little James was proving to be a little too small for the work it was being asked to do, carrying Jack to shooting competitions, camp etc, his father readily agreed, adding that his mother was sure to be huffy about it, but she would come around. What Jack didn't know was that his dad was dying to get back on a bike and had every intention of borrowing the Aerial whenever he could, the little James being beneath his dignity!

So Jack bought it, sold the sidecar immediately and set to work stripping it down to the bare frame and started on repainting it. Along the way, he discovered that the piston, rings and bore were so worn that to reassemble them would be pointless. He had to have the cylinder rebored—something his father was able to do at the precision engineering factory where he worked and which cost him nothing—but he did have to pay for a new piston and rings.

The inlet and exhaust valves were fine in their guides, but the mushroom heads did not seat well into the head as both the head and the valves were pitted. The solution to that meant smearing grinding paste onto the seating and then pressing the valve head firmly against the seating, twisting it round and round, clockwise and anti-clockwise, to grind a nice new shiny and gas tight seating. This took ages and tested wrists, muscles and enthusiasm mightily.

Jack originally hoped to fit a full, all enveloping fairing for primarily greater speed but also for wind and weather protection and no little street cred but a full one was simply too expensive, and he couldn't find a second-hand one anywhere. So he bought a handle bar mounted one instead. Whilst this did indeed keep some of the weather off, being handle bar mounted, it also affected the steering, being not very well designed and about as aerodynamic as a barn door. Not too long after that, full fairings, nicknamed dustbins, were banned since their performance in cross winds was deemed to be dangerous in the extreme, so at least he hadn't wasted his money on one even though he felt pretty pissed off at not being able to afford one at the time!

Finally, he painted the frame black, the fairing pale blue on the top half and a light grey on the bottom, and the tank was also painted in the light blue to match the fairing upper. To finish it all off, he fitted a plastic tiger skin seat cover which was unbelievably tacky in everyone else's eye, but Jack loved it dearly.

Riding it was a world away from the little James. Far more powerful, more gears, changed by foot rather than two changed by hand and an acceleration and top speed to blow away most cars. It was, however, not the safest of bikes. Whilst it had telescopic forks on the front, there was no suspension at all at the back, the back wheel simply bolting into the frame. It meant that the back wheel would bounce off the road if it hit a bump hard enough and fast enough—something Jack did with amazing frequency. What made things even worse was that the bike still had the tyres on it from when it had pulled the sidecar. These were car tyres, cross ply, with square shoulders—fine when kept upright by the sidecar but presenting only a sharp corner to the road when leant over when ridden as a single motorcycle. Cross ply tyres had little enough grip, especially in the wet, as it only had a miniscule tyre foot print when leant over.

Jack's cornering was, therefore, something of a hit and miss affair. It did, however, have the benefit of teaching him a lot about road holding or rather the lack of it. Jack and Paul Air, by now his best mate, had taken to visiting a pub—a little back street dive in Kingston on Thames found by Paul—on a Tuesday night when it could be relied on to be pretty well empty, to play darts and drink.

They would go on Jack's bike and Paul would invariably buy the first round, two halves of Directors' bitter and two pickled eggs. Jack would buy the second round, also two halves of Directors but two bags of crisps. By the time they had consumed this lot, they would become bored with the darts and return to Paul's where they would spend the remainder of the evening listening to his latest Ray Charles record over and over and over.

One cold and frosty November evening as they were approaching Paul's, Paul sitting nonchalantly on the back, hands in pockets, Jack tried the back break gently as they came up the road to test if the wet sheen on the road was indeed ice which had been forecast or whether it was just wet. The tyre gripped without any sign of skidding, so Jack pulled across the road with the intention of stopping behind Paul's dad's brand-new Ford Anglia, his first ever new car, and his pride and joy. Unfortunately, whilst the side of the road on which Jack had tested his back brake was just wet, the side onto which they rode was not; it was frozen, and as soon as Jack touched his brakes to slow down, down went the bike. It happened so quickly that neither of them had time to do anything, so they found themselves still sitting upright on the bike which was now sliding, fallen over, along the road with them sitting on it, heading at a rate of knots towards Paul's dad's car. Above the noise of his nice new paint scraping along the road, Jack could hear Paul shouting, "Mind me dad's car, for God's sake!"

Jack could, of course, do absolutely nothing about it. Closer drew the car. Louder grew the shouting from Paul by now morphed into shrieks of, "Mind the fucking car!" Perhaps, luckily, because of Jack's initial slowing on the wet half of the road, by the time they did hit the car, they were only just moving and whilst Paul fearfully checked his dad's car for damage, Jack was doing the same for his bike. The car, in the event, had no discernable damage, but the bike had lost some of its paint but not as much as it might otherwise have done, the ice acting more as a lubricant than an abrasive, and Jack still had the leftover paint from its recent tarting up with which to repair it. After that, they walked to the pub and Jack learned that even the best actions could result in an unplanned cock-up.

# Chapter 26

That autumn term saw other changes. Jack was informed that he would not be going up to the Lower Sixth as anticipated because his GCE results were not very good. In fact, they were bloody awful! Jack had lost a lot of time through the year following an accident at school in PT when he had dislocated his left ankle. The Master in charge, new to the school and who had become a Lieutenant in the Army Cadet Force school unit in support of Captain Hiller, and having had elementary first aid training, got four of the biggest lads to hold Jack down whilst he pulled the dislocated ankle sharply to set it back into its socket. It hurt. It hurt so much that Jack had no trouble throwing the four of them off of him. His opinion of the Lieutenant, never having been too high in the first place, plummeted. That was also accompanied by a use of Anglo Saxon of which any hairy arsed Angle or Saxon would have been proud.

Somewhat shaken by the vehemence of Jack's language and a dawning that perhaps he should not have relocated the displaced ankle, the teacher sent one of the class off to phone for an ambulance which duly arrived.

The hospital, at first, were disinclined to believe Jack when he said his ankle had been dislocated, but a phone call to the school soon solicited that it had indeed been dislocated. They were not pleased that the teacher had relocated it since they were concerned that even more damage might have been done. Whether it had or had not, the fact was that it took a long time to recover and for Jack to become mobile again. At the time, Jack was not too bothered since he quite enjoyed the time off school.

No sooner had he returned to school than he was involved in another accident to the same ankle. He had been riding along on his way to school when a Bentley pulled straight out of a side road and into his path. Swerving and braking as best as he could, Jack's trouser leg caught on the bumper of the Bentley and was subjected to a savage jerk. Not realising at first that he had, in fact, been injured, Jack, having initially stopped, chased after the Bentley and caught up with it at some traffic lights. Banging on the window, Jack shouted in, once it had been opened, "You blind cunt, you nearly killed me!"

At which the posh prat inside exclaimed, "It's us cunts that make you pricks stand to attention," and drove off! Jack was never to forget that put down, and it was years before he was able to use it himself.

It came about when he was driving in Nottingham and, quite unwittingly, drove through a red traffic light. He was very lucky that he did not collide with a Volkswagen whose irate driver shouted at him, "You blind cunt."

Quick as a flash, Jack shouted back, "It's us cunts make you pricks stand to attention." It did not produce the crushing of the mouthy other driver that Jack expected. Instead of remaining silent and crushed, he retorted, in an extremely affected camp voice, "You speak for yourself, ducky!" Jack felt even more humiliated than he had done all those years before with the Bentley driver. And it was to his eternal regret that he was never able to use the retort himself.

He was able to drive home by which time his ankle had swollen to an enormous size, making it impossible for him to walk. A further time in hospital and immobilisation at home meant that, in total, Jack had lost a lot of time, almost half the school year, from school and had fallen way behind his classmates. It would also be fair to say, although Jack would never admit it, that he did not make any great effort to catch up. Hence the decision that he should not go up to the Lower Sixth but should redo the year in the Fifth Form.

# Chapter 27

Jack's interests were starting to take a different direction. The main change was Jack started to fancy the girl who worked in the sweet shop across the road—girls were very much in and running around the boondocks waving guns and shouting, "Bang, bang," were very much on the way out; Cadet camp that summer had been in Oakhampton with most of the training and exercises on Dartmoor; it had rained and rained and rained again, and Jack came to the tentative conclusion that this would be his last camp.

The girl across the road was, like Jack, a Saturday employee. She was pretty. She had long attractive blond hair. She had the most amazing blue eyes. She had discernable breasts and Jack fancied her something rotten. Unfortunately, she had a mother! Her mother did not fancy identifying her daughter at the mortuary as a result of riding on the back of Jack's high-powered (a relative term!) motorcycle—she had seen him cornering—and absolutely forbad her daughter from having anything to do with him.

Jack took to visiting the shop as often as possible, buying pathetically anything as a justification for going in (something Howard was to emulate in Last of the Summer Wine years later, but in his case, it was glue!) and tried to keep his suit alive but with no luck. He persevered, since he was no quitter, but success continued to elude him.

Other events also occupied his time. School, the Cadets, working at the weekend and occasionally filling in for other attendants during school holidays when they went on holiday or to cover for sickness absence all meant that he had little time to pursue a fair maiden even if he had a grand passion for her but, having been rebuffed so often, his pride was hurt, and he was not easily going to let go.

In addition, this term he had become a House Prefect, which gave him extra duties controlling younger boys, all of whom seemed in need of constant supervision, disciplining and even punishing—school was tougher in those days.

Towards the end of that academic year, Jack turned 17, in itself no big deal or landmark event apart from the fact that he was now old enough to drive a car. He obtained his provisional licence on the day he turned 17 and dragooned his dad into taking him out for a lesson that very evening. Learning to drive a car was not so very hard, Jack having learned all the principles of acceleration, clutch control, braking and reading the road and traffic riding his two motorbikes. Other than getting used to his hands and feet operating differently, his right foot now operated the accelerator in the car and the brake on the motorbike rather than the gear lever, and his left foot worked the clutch rather than the motorcycle gear lever. Jack's progress was swift, so much so that he applied to take his driving test three weeks later and took it some four weeks after that.

He took the test in his father's Triumph Renown—a two-litre, four-cylinder car which, as it looked angular like a Rolls Royce, was nicknamed the poor man's Rolls Royce. With a three-speed column mounted gear change and a front bench seat it could transport the six of them, Mum, Dad, Nana and Grandpa, sister and Jack. Better still, as far as Jack was concerned, the bench seats front and rear seemed to offer all sorts of possibilities of a sexual nature if he could only get a willing young lady into it!

The test was relatively uneventful other than when the Examiner prepared for the emergency stop. He had already told Jack that in the next section he would tap his clipboard on the dashboard to indicate that he wanted the emergency stop to be carried out immediately following the tap but in a safe and proper manner i.e. no skidding. Jack thought he had probably been the victim of some horrendous stops to include that level of detail in his instructions! Consequently, when the Examiner started shifting his position a couple of times to look behind, presumably to check that it would be safe for Jack to slam on the brakes, his actions indicated very obviously what was about to happen. As soon as he positioned the board above the dashboard and lifted it, Jack applied the brakes with maximum force.

There was no actual chance of locking up the brakes, because it was a dry road, because the car was inordinately heavy and the drum bakes not up to the task of locking the wheels anyway so Jack was well aware that there was no danger in skidding no matter how hard he applied them—the need was to react immediately and get the thing stopped! Unfortunately, Jack braked before the Examiner had braced himself ready for the deceleration. Consequently, he slammed into the dashboard, receiving a bit of a bump in the process.

*Shit*, thought Jack, *there goes my pass.*

The Examiner, having examined himself all over and finding nothing seriously damaged, he had bumped his head, but everyone knows you can't hurt a civil servant by banging him on his head, said to Jack, "What was all that about, why did you brake when you did?"

Facing the ignominy and no little cost in having to take the test again, Jack told himself to think fast or else. Unbidden, his mind came up with, "Anticipation. If you were driving along and saw a small child at the side of the road playing with a football you would automatically slow down, move out as far as it was safe to do so, and be ready to brake if necessary. When you lifted the board, I anticipated that you would bang it down and reacted accordingly."

"Umm," said the Examiner, "drive on please." So Jack did. The rest of the test was uneventful, the Highway Code questions easily answered, and it was with considerable relief, if not actual disbelief, that Jack heard the Examiner say, "Well, that concludes the test, Mr Hughes, and I am pleased to tell you that you have passed." With that, he handed Jack his pink pass slip, got out of the car and walked away.

How to surprise his dad? Jack wanted to play a joke on his dad and had given some thought as to how it could be done. Nothing very much had come up. Acting on his usual, let's wait and see what happens Jack tucked the pink slip pass note in his pocket and went to look for his dad. As he walked towards him, he adopted a hangdog look and immediately his father on seeing him said, "Hard luck, son, passing first time is not for most. Still, you can always take it again; let's go home. You can drive as you clearly need the practice!"

This pissed Jack off. Although he had intended to mislead his father and had clearly succeeded, he felt the last comment about needing the practice was uncalled for. Consequently, he said nothing and just drove home. Compounding his earlier error, his father jumped out of the car as soon as they got home and rushed indoors to inform all and sundry that Jack had failed. The sympathy from his mum and his nana was sort of welcome but the derision from his sister and his grandpa, albeit politely phrased, was not. But what to do?

As was to become a feature of his mind working, the answer came to him about three o'clock in the morning waking him with a 'eureka' moment with which he was to become so familiar in later years. Jack got in touch with Wally, from the Cadet Force, who had become a policeman a few months before. At first reluctant, Wally eventually agreed to Jack's plan.

So, some days later, Jack's mum and dad came home from having gone to the shops just up the road to discover that their car was missing from the driveway. A short search also discovered that Jack was also missing, as were the keys to the car which were normally kept on the hall table.

"I'll kill the little sod," and similar statements poured forth from his dad with his mother trying to placate him with, "Perhaps he's gone with Bern (Jack's uncle) or there's been an emergency with Paulina (his sister) or something…"

Sometime later, Jack swept into the drive, stopped the engine and casually got out and wandered into the house. Hardly had Jack's dad got started on him when there came a thunderous knocking at the front door. More than somewhat annoyed, both at the interruption to the interrogation and the loudness of the knocking, Dad sharply opened the door, intending to have a go at the 'knocker' only to strangle the noise in his throat on seeing a large, uniformed policeman standing there with a very, very serious look on his face—the sort of look only a policeman can deliver.

"Yes, officer."

"I understand that a Jack Hughes lives here, a Jack Hughes who recently failed his driving test but who drives without 'L' plates or a qualified driver with him, in fact, as though he had passed his test?"

His dad's face was a picture and to an experienced officer would have immediately given the game away, but Wally was new—how he had managed to pass the exams for entrance to Her Majesty's Constabulary was a complete mystery to all who knew him and especially to those who knew him in the Cadet Force (Pump Wally, pump!) but pass he had and since he was the key player in the scene unfolding, he wasn't taken in anyway.

Jack's dad answered very carefully, very, very carefully, in fact it was quite clever in that he did not lie directly but neither did he answer totally truthfully either. What he did say was, "Well, Jack certainly does live here, and he did fail his driving test recently, but what makes you think he has been driving on his own since then?"

"Because I have just seen him, and I saw him drive onto your drive, on his own, only minutes ago."

Dad was stuck, the pause was too long. What emerged was a strangulated, "Are you sure it was him?"

"Yes."

"Oh."

"Let me ask you again, sir. Has Jack Hughes failed his driving test recently and driven your vehicle unaccompanied by an experienced driver and without displaying 'L' plates?"

Defeated, Dad answered, "Yes."

"In that case, sir, I am arresting you for lying to an officer of the law and I now require you to accompany me to the police station."

Dad's face was a picture. His mother went white as a sheet instantly, and his grandpa looked ready to punch Wally. Unfortunately, both Wally's and Jack's resolve failed simultaneously, and they both broke out in hysterical laughter. Bewilderment reigned amongst those not in the know. Eventually, when both Jack and Wally had regained their composure, Wally explained that the lie was that Jack had not failed his test and had arranged this little charade to repay his dad for assuming the worst about Jack's driving ability!

They did not take it well, especially his dad, but for Jack, the look on their faces, most enjoyably his sister's, kept him warm on many a cold night in the future.

# Chapter 28

The winter came early, starting with a vengeance at the beginning of October and was well into its stride with cold days, ice, snow and bitterly cold nights by the beginning of November. Riding his motorbike in such conditions was not pleasant and Jack's thoughts increasingly turned, especially during the quiet times during the long Saturday night at the petrol station, to what it would be like to own his own car, his father not being too keen to make his car available to Jack, not least because of the Wally trick that had been played on him.

A few hundred yards or so down the road from the petrol station was a site, a cleared bomb site from the war, from which two ex-service personnel sold second-hand cars, second-hand being a very loose description in the case of most of them, which had for sale a 1938 Ford 8 which had particularly caught Jack's eye. As Jack had been born in 1944, the car was six years older than him! It appeared to be in good condition, no visible rust, good chrome and the leather seats and interior appeared to be in good condition; in fact, Jack fell in love with it at first sight. They wanted £25 for it. Perhaps not a lot of money these days but at that time a working man was lucky to earn £10-£11 for a 42-hour week so it represented more than two weeks wages and certainly more than Jack had in his possession. The problem was Jack would not be able to save up the cash, because the car was likely to be sold long before he could do so. So, the only option he had was to borrow the money. Carefully calculating how much he had, therefore how much he would need to borrow and how much it would cost to tax, insure and run the car, Jack worked out how much he would be able to repay each week. He calculated that he would need to borrow £10 from his parents and £5 from his sister.

Setting out his calculations neatly on a sheet of paper was easy to do, but Jack was not sure that evidence of such financial acumen would, in itself, be a convincing argument for the two lenders. What else to argue? Sleeping on it brought the answers. To his sister, he added the inducement he would take her out for driving lessons; she had not shown a great enthusiasm to learn to drive but could see the advantages of borrowing Dad's car on occasions. Jack was very careful not to imply that she would be able to borrow his car during the negotiations!

His parents were not likely to be persuaded by such an offer. The answer with them was to play on their, especially his mother's, fear of the motor bike. Therefore, dropping in the line, "…and it will mean me selling the bike and ending the risks associated with that…," was the clincher he needed.

The two guys running the site did not have a good reputation, rumours about sitting out the war in a cushy home posting and even more rumours about dabbling in the black market meant that Dad, a very experienced mechanical engineer, went with Jack to give the car an in-depth going over. As Dad could not find anything obviously wrong—apart from one very worn tyre which was changed straightaway for another slightly less worn one, new tyres being very hard to obtain and expensive to boot—£25 changed hands and the car was Jack's. Dad insisted on driving it home, "to ensure everything was safe and as it should be," and parked it on the drive behind his Triumph Renown.

Jack immediately set about washing and polishing it, even though it was pretty immaculate anyway. Like any kid with a new toy, Jack was all over it. Inside and out, he cleaned and polished everything. The spare wheel was mounted on the back of the car on the outside so the only way to access the boot was to pull the upright seat back of the back seat up, it hinged at the top, and half crawl, half scrabble to get to it. Clearly, it was too arduous for many of the previous owners, because the junk in there was unbelievable. Nevertheless, Jack cleared all that out, leaving it as good as the day it had come from the factory. He even gave the tyres as well as the spare tyre a coating of coal black which made them look new and shiny, if only for a few minutes!

The whole process took a good three hours. Just as he finished, his dad came out to say that the insurance company had just confirmed that the Ford had been added to his dad's policy and it was now insured for both he and Jack to drive. The little matter of driving it home uninsured seemed to be of little account! His father then added a request that Jack pop across the road to get him a packet of cigarettes, him only having his slippers on and thus being unable to do so.

Jack didn't mind fetching the fags per se, but he really didn't want to face the girl serving there especially as he had made a trip across there first thing that morning and had asked her out that evening, and he had been rebuffed again, this time with the classic, "I'm washing my hair!" Still, such a request was tantamount to a command so across the road Jack went. Jack was slow to recognise the change in her. Whilst she served him, she started asking him did his dad have another car now (the possession of even one car was regarded as posh and rich in those days) and when Jack told her that it was in fact his new (new being a loose description) car, her attitude towards him changed completely.

"My mum would not object to me going out with someone in a car like she does with someone on a motorbike," being the strongest indicator so far that invitations out would now be welcomed. When she added, "I won't be washing my hair tonight now Jenny can't come around to help me," being the absolute clincher that she was really saying 'Ask me out again and I'll say yes.'

Jack was not elated. In fact, he was devastated. From her earliest questions about 'his dad's new car' it was obvious that the attraction was not him, Jack, but having a boyfriend, any boyfriend, so long as he had a car. Jack was starting to learn about women. He had not yet learned enough and probably never would so, upset at this sudden revelation, he said to her, "That's a pity, because I'm so tired and dirty now, I think I will have a bath and wash my hair this evening," and walked out clutching the cigarettes! Of course, what the girl and her mother had not learned was that any girl was in far more danger on the back seat of that car, parked in a dark lane, than she ever was on the back seat of a motorcycle; on the motorcycle, she could only be killed; on the back seat of the car, much worse things could happen! Jack would learn that and a lot more lessons rather more quickly!

# Chapter 29

The first lesson Jack was to learn from being a car owner only three days later was that cars develop problems. Returning from showing off his new pride and joy with three mates in the car, arduously climbing the hill from Surbiton towards home, the engine revs started rising whilst the car started slowing down. Not something that was supposed to happen. Dad knew immediately, when described the symptoms, what the problem was, "Your clutch is slipping, probably knackered, and unless you've got a lot of adjustment to play with, and I doubt that very much, you're in a whole lot of shit."

A quick conversation with the local Ford garage unhappily confirmed that his dad was right. Even worse, the estimate was that it would cost about £32-£35 to fix it, more than the car had cost only three days before and certainly far more than Jack could afford to pay! Struck by the look of absolute disaster on Jack's face, the service guy added, "Of course, if you're handy with the spanners, you could do it yourself for a lot, lot less."

"How much less?"

"Just the cost of the corks, 18 of them at a penny ha'penny each; that's 2s 3d the lot."

"Nothing else?" asked Jack.

"Just the time and effort," said the guy.

"How long and how much effort?" said Jack

"Well," said the bloke, "you will either have to take the engine out or drop the back axle down to pull the prop shaft back. The problem with these old Fords is the prop shaft is not jointed so it's either the engine out or the axle down. Both involve about the same amount of work, but the back axle is probably that bit easier. It's up to you."

"Right," said Jack, "what tools do I need to remove the axle?"

"Just spanners, wheel brace to take off the wheels and probably a pair of pliers or mole grips, screwdriver and that's it."

"Okay," said Jack, "I'll buy them." The corks were solemnly counted out and the money handed over. Back home, Jack rang his best mate Paul and arranged for him to come over to help the following morning.

Anxious to be getting on with it, Jack was up early and started on the job before Paul arrived. First, he jacked the car up and placed blocks of wood under the body, lowering the body down onto them to ensure that it was firmly supported. That done, he removed the rear wheels, having loosened the wheel nuts before jacking it up. The brakes were operated by cable, no hydraulics on this old Ford! He then set about undoing the nuts holding the axle assembly to the bodywork. The first problem was he couldn't see them! According to the manual, the axle was held by the leaf springs at the outer ends and the springs were held in the centre to the car body by only four nuts. So, by undoing the four nuts, the assembly, leaf springs and axle, should part from the body and then the whole assembly should drop down and back allowing access to the clutch plate by the removal of the back of the clutch housing.

But how wrong can you be! There was so much crud and crap under there, 23 years' worth to be precise, to such an extent, that the four nuts were not immediately apparent. Getting under there with a wire brush and an old, blunt screwdriver and scraping away all crud and crap was thoroughly unpleasant with God knows what falling down all over his face, hair and eyes. Worst of all was some of it dropping into his mouth, firmly shut too late after the first unpleasant mouthful such that Jack couldn't shake from his mind the saying about stable doors, bolts and horses, given the taste of shit in his mouth, probably some of which could really be horse crap thrown up by the tyres, horses still being quite a common site on the roads.

Eventually, most of the obstructive detritus was removed, revealing not four but five nuts, four in the places the manual said they should be and a fifth, much smaller one, right in the middle of the springs. *Oh well*, thought Jack, *do the four big ones first and see what happens.* He couldn't shift the buggers; the ring spanner that fitted them tightly was only a short one, and lying awkwardly under the car, he couldn't get a good leverage, but not one of them would move at all. Back to the drawing board! His dad had a tin of easing oil in the garage; *a good spray of that should do it*, he thought. The instructions on the tin said to squirt the item and then leave it for an hour to allow the oil to penetrate (another name for it was penetrating oil). Jack crawled under the car, squirted everything in sight, including no small amount onto himself, and then waited all of two or three minutes—well, it was the end of October, and it was bloody cold lying on the hard, concrete drive—before trying again. They, not surprisingly, wouldn't shift. Not prepared to lie on the concrete for an hour, Jack crawled out and went looking for anything that might help. At first, nothing seemed suitable, but he then found a length of piping which looked as though it was big enough to fit over the spanner. The pipe was about two feet long and, although not long enough for Archimedes to lever the world out of its orbit, was probably long enough to shift those bloody nuts—and it was!

The springs wouldn't shift. Even with all four nuts totally removed, the springs and axle unit would not budge, even hitting with a hammer and trying to force the screwdriver between the springs and the mounting point didn't work. Jack's eyes kept coming back to the small nut in the middle of the springs. *I wonder does that go right through the springs and the body, locating everything in the right place, stopping slippage and holding it in place*, thought Jack. Good logical thinking but absolute proof that a little knowledge is a dangerous thing.

By this time, the penetrating oil had been working away at the fifth nut and undoing it required only the spanner and little effort. However, with the nut removed, the axle unit still sat stubbornly in place. A hammer being the tool of last resort, Jack used it to hit the springs once again. Wrong decision. With a loud noise, the leaf springs separated downwards, the only way open to them depositing themselves over Jack's upper body but more importantly and catastrophically pushing the axle down onto Jack. It happened so quickly that his rather vague plan to slip out from underneath to drop the axle down in a controlled manner could not be actioned, and there he was, trapped underneath a heavy lump of metal. He was extraordinarily lucky that it fell across his neck, the thinnest part of his upper body, and, landing on the wheel stubs, the axle itself was sufficiently far off the ground not to crush his neck but it did, very effectively, trap him against the concrete. Unable to get a purchase on the axle to be able to lift it up to enable him to slide out, Jack was effectively trapped there!

He couldn't move. No matter how he pulled or pushed, he couldn't shift the axle. He was vaguely aware of footsteps passing on the path, so he called out, "Help, help!" The footsteps paused for a moment but then carried on. This happened twice! Then it dawned on him. A couple of weeks before, Candid Camera had started to rave reviews and huge audiences and had, only that last Saturday, three days ago, featured an episode where a car had driven onto a petrol station forecourt and then, having been filled up with petrol, would not start. The petrol station attendant, the butt of the joke, was then conned into looking under the bonnet to investigate why the car would not start. Upon opening the bonnet, the dupe was faced with a completely empty engine bay—the engine had been removed and the car had simply free wheeled down the road and onto the forecourt! And now Jack was suffering the consequences, he thought, no one was prepared to help lest they be the butt of what was quite a cruel programme!

Fortunately for Jack, Paul turned up shortly after and before Jack had become too cold. More unfortunately, it was a further five minutes before Paul could stop laughing and help him. With both of them lifting, it was the matter of moments to get the axle off Jack's neck, clear the spring leaves out of the way and then pull the axle back with the prop shaft still attached and move the whole lot to the side of the drive.

Further problems were about to emerge of which Jack was blissfully unaware—as yet. Removing the back of the clutch housing was simply a matter of undoing all the nuts and lifting it off. Working out how to remove the clutch plate was just a matter of following the directions in the manual. Once removed, the corks in the clutch plate could clearly be seen to be very thin and worn and only just sitting proud of the clutch plate. It was a simple job to push them out even if a few of them did seem to be determined to stay in place.

It was when the new corks were offered up to the holes that the next problem became apparent. They were just slightly smaller than the holes, so having placed them in the holes, they promptly fell out!

"Shit," said Jack.

"Double shit," said Paul.

"What the shit do we do now?" said Jack.

"How the shit should I know?" said Paul.

"Shit," they both said together.

Besides the problem that the corks didn't fit, they also had the problem that, the Ford being off the road, literally, they had no means of transport, Paul having come on the bus because his bike had been borrowed by his dad who hadn't bothered to tell him, so they couldn't get to the garage to have a go at them for selling Jack the wrong size corks. Option two was soon forthcoming, "I'll phone the garage and see if I can get them to bring out the correct size as it's their bloody fault," said Jack.

So indoors they traipsed, oblivious to the trail of detritus they were leaving, Jack being by far the worst culprit, a fact they were only to discover when Jack's mum returned in the evening. Still, blithely unaware of that problem to come, Jack rang the garage. It took a while to be connected to 'Parts' and even longer to get hold of the bloke who'd sold Jack the corks.

"Yes, I remember," he said but his reaction to Jack's, "You sold me the wrong size," was not what was expected. The immediate comeback, with no apparent pause for thought at all, was, "You have boiled them, haven't you?" After a long while, he added, "I can tell by the silence that you haven't."

Jack's voice, feeble, faint and entirely lacking in volume just managed to squeak out, "Boil them?"

"You need to boil them, and they expand to fit," said the ever-so-helpful man from the garage whose antecedents Jack had been questioning forcibly in his mind only moments before and coming to the conclusion that the bloke's parents had only met once and that, briefly. He then added, "And when you've got them in, don't forget to flat the two sides on a piece of sandpaper, not too fine."

Forced to rapidly rethink his conclusions, Jack could only add pettiness to his performance by responding, "You could have told me that when I bought them," only to suffer the conversation winning riposte, "You didn't ask."

Conversation over, the next problem was how to boil the corks. The ever so helpful bloke had said, "…and they expand to fit." Somehow or other, this created in Jack's mind that the corks had to be in situ whilst being boiled. Not so, as things turned out, and the cause of yet another problem for Jack that he was only to discover when set about by a rather, make that a very, irate mother later.

A quick search of the saucepans on the shelf revealed none big enough to accept the clutch plate which was about eight or nine inches across. A further search turned up his mother's big puddings and boiling saucepan which was used each week to boil the best whites, a washing machine was long in the future, the weekly wash being done in a tin bath with lots of vigorous scrubbing on the scrubbing board but some whites, of a particular delicacy which could not be scrubbed, only boiled, were boiled in this pan. It was also used every Christmas to boil the Christmas puddings being the only one big enough to accommodate them.

It took ages for the pan to come to the boil. The corks, of course, being very light, kept floating out of the clutch plate and up to the surface. Putting them back as they got hotter and hotter became harder and harder. The language rapidly accelerated from shit, to more colourful and graphic Anglo Saxon. Eventually, the job was done, and the corks were all secure in their holes. The water, by this time black, oily and gungy in the extreme, was simply tipped down the sink and the saucepan upended on the draining board. The sink and the saucepan were to return later, courtesy of a vengeful mother.

Unaware of the problems to come, Jack placed the sandpaper, not too fine, on the kitchen table and proceeded to rub the surfaces of the clutch plate against it until both surfaces of the corks were flat and even. A quick few puffs of breath neatly deposited the cork dust onto the kitchen floor, and they were ready to start reassembling the clutch and axle, and Mother was going to find the dust on her kitchen floor and add that to Jack's woes in due course.

It being October, the weather intervened and started chucking it down, putting an end to work for the rest of the afternoon. When Jack's parents arrived home from work, Jack's life rapidly went from bad to very worse without passing worse on the way. First to kick off was his mother faced with a kitchen floor resembling the public bar of the worst of dives, a draining board with a trail of black, oily slime running down it and into her pristine white stoneware sink and her best boiler covered in the same black slime which was forever to remain a thick black line around it, despite Jack's best efforts to remove it notwithstanding.

Worse was to come. Dad wanted to be shown the corks and what he had been up to. Jack and Paul had, in an endeavour to protect them, slid the axle, prop shaft and leaf springs under the car. Reaching under the car, his dad pulled out one of the leaf springs and with a look of utter incredulity on his face said, "You prat, why on earth have you taken these apart, now you are totally and completely fucked." His dad did not normally swear at Jack or even in his presence, so the use of such language did give Jack a pretty good clue to the fact that he had done something awfully wrong.

Jack stammered out an explanation of how he had come to remove the fifth nut and the results of so doing. It took a while for the picture to fully materialise in his dad's mind and for him to then stop laughing. Once he had done so, he picked up two of the leaf springs and placed one on top of the other. He then pointed out that the two bars of metal did not follow the same curvature; the shortest one had a somewhat tighter radius than the next shortest so that it would not quite sit flat on the other one. His dad explained,

"These have a different curvature which, along with their different lengths, gives a variation in springing response dependent on the load in the car, the speed it's travelling and the bumpiness of the road. They are squashed together under pressure from a five-ton press and then secured together by the nut and bolt through the centre; you'll never push them together enough to get the bolt in as it's too short; it will only fit once they have been compressed together and you need the five-ton press for that—and we haven't got one. You will have to ring for a breakdown lorry with lift capability and see what you can get for it from the scrap yard, hopefully enough to cover the cost of taking it there!"

Jack was devastated. He'd only had the car a few days, and he had revelled in showing off in it to all and sundry. Now, he was going to be a universal laughing stock. His dad left him there and went indoors; it did have one silver lining, that damned great rain cloud; his dad, having told his mum what he had done resulted in her taking pity on him and ceasing the verbal tirade to which he was about to be further subjected.

It took Jack a long time to go to sleep that night; he didn't quite cry into his pillow, but it was a close-run thing. Once again, he was to experience the three o'clock wake up with an idea. He resolved not to tell his dad, in case it didn't work and to prevent any further ridicule. When Paul arrived, this time on his bike, Jack repeated what his dad had said and then explained the idea he'd had.

"It seems to me," said Jack, "that if we placed the springs carefully on top of the axle and then on top of the two car jacks and simply jacked the assembly up against the bottom of the car, we would create a one-ton or so press because the car will press down and resist the pressure of the springs and axle coming up and that could be enough pressure to compress them. Of course, we need to be careful that they don't slide apart as we start lifting—we can tie some string around the springs to prevent some movement and simply cut it off once the springs are in place. What do you think?"

"Well, so long as I don't have to go under the car while we do it, I think it's worth a try."

So try they did. Refitting the clutch plate and clutch housing took only a few minutes. Aligning the prop shaft and inserting it into the back of the clutch housing was only slightly more awkward, mainly because of the back axle attached to it, but soon, everything was ready for the big lift!

They jacked the axle and springs up slowly and carefully, pausing to readjust the alignment until the weight and pressure made that impossible and then, to their utter delight, the end of the bolt started to appear through the centre of the springs. Once a few threads were through, Jack slipped gingerly under the car and screwed the nut on a few turns to hold it in place and ensure their good work and immense good luck did not come undone. Jacking the whole assembly back into position followed and then, once the four big nuts had been screwed on and tightened up, it was a simple matter to tighten up the fifth, spring retention, nut, completing that part of the job. Reconnecting the brake cables and replacing the wheels was equally simple and quick and in what seemed to be no time at all, the car was off the blocks, standing on all four wheels and with a brand-new clutch plate in position all for 2s 3d and a lot, an enormous lot, of aggro and good luck.

To test the clutch and it must be said, to get his own back on his know-it-all dad, Jack took it for a test drive to his dad's factory and waved at him through the window before driving off. At night, when his dad came home, Jack greeted him with a great big smile and a refusal, initially, to tell him how he did it. Eventually, a desire to brag overcame his desire to keep secret his successful solution to the dismantled axle unit, so he told him. His dad thought about it for a while and then said, "Brilliant deduction; it probably wouldn't have worked if the springs were new, but after 23 years, they've probably lost a lot of their strength, and that's what let you do it, but well done nevertheless."

# Chapter 30

It took only one day for more problems of car ownership to emerge. Jack drove to Paul's to meet him and two other mates, Dave and John, with the intention that all of them would take a drive to the coast, Brighton or Worthing or Bognor as the mood took them. Having only two doors, Jack jumped out to let Paul get into the back. Paul pushed the driver's seat up and forward and started to get in. The seat, perhaps in sympathy for Jack at Paul's laughing at him trapped under the car by the axle (inanimate objects so often have their own agenda, Jack was to discover over the years) sprang back and pinched Paul's toes painfully as it dropped down. Paul's immediate response was to slam the seat forward. Wrong decision. The axle springs weren't the only part of the car to be a bit old and weak. The rim of the steering wheel was and, taking the full force of the blow, gave up the ghost and sprang off the three spokes holding it to the wheel and fell down into the foot well.

"Shit," said Paul.

"Shit," said Dave.

"Shit," said John. Fed up with the singular lack of originality in their choice of profanity, Jack joined in with, "Double shit."

Even a cursory inspection showed that there was no hope of repairing the steering wheel and the trip to the seaside was abandoned in favour of a trip to the breaker's yard. Paul, John and Dave tried to bail out, but Jack was determined Paul, at least, should accompany him as he, although he didn't know it immediately, was going to pay for the new steering wheel.

There were loads of steering wheels in the breakers, but the problem was they were all still attached to a steering column which was attached to the steering box mechanism. Cautious enquiries of the staff for just a steering wheel without all the attachments was met with, "If you can get a bugger off the steering column good luck to you, they're put on to last and are buggers to get off." As Jack had no tools with him, the only option was to buy the best one complete and take it home.

A quick examination of the handbook showed that it would be easier to detach the steering box end of the old column and push the whole length of the column through the floor and discard it. Then it was a relatively simple matter to connect the new one to the existing steering box. Getting the old one out was quite easy given that the rubber gaiter, designed to stop water, wind etc. ingressing through the gap around the column, had long gone to that rubber graveyard in the sky.

The replacement cost £3 which Jack thought was quite reasonable, but Paul didn't as he had to pay it! He did, however, some days later when Jack was stopped at some traffic lights, wind the window down, and gave the old rim of the discarded steering wheel to an old bloke standing in the bus queue with a cheery, "Here mate, this is for you," just as Jack drove off. He felt that the look on the old boy's face was sufficiently worth the £3.

# Chapter 31

The saga of the clutch and the steering wheel took up most of Monday, Tuesday and Wednesday of that half-term week. On Wednesday evening, Jack went with his dad to the Library. There on the shelf, as part of a little display on cars, was a small book, opened so that it was able to stand up on top of the shelf unit, which absolutely leapt out at him shouting, if only it could, 'Me, me, me!' In large letters right across the cover were the magic words, 'Tuning the Ford 8 Engine'. Jack felt Christmas had come early. He opened the book and the words of the very first sentence positively leapt off the page at him, 'The best way to get more power out of the 8-horsepower engine is to change it for a 10 horsepower one which slots straight in…' Jack was sold. Who wouldn't want to exchange 933 ccs for 1172 ccs anyway? He took the book to the counter and had it stamped out to him immediately; he hadn't been in the building two minutes.

Jack read it completely through that evening. Whilst it contained all sorts of very useful information, some of it was clearly way beyond Jack's abilities. Ideas like fitting higher crown and pinion gears in the back axle, fitting twin carbs, fitting close ratio gears in the gearbox followed by an overdrive were way beyond him but he kept coming back to the first sentence '…change it for a 10-horsepower.' That, he felt he could do and then fitting the cylinder head from the 8-horsepower engine onto the 10-horsepower engine to increase the compression ratio to more than 9:1 when Jaguars were only 7.5:1 was simply a temptation too far!

And he knew just the breaker's yard where they would have one. A quick phone call to Paul, "Guess what…" And arrangements were soon made for a visit to the breakers the next day. Not prone to making the same mistake twice, he took a set of spanners, screwdrivers, expanding wrenches and any anything else he thought might be needed with him.

At the yard, enquiries elicited that yes, they did have a number of engines, and one would cost £5; if he wanted more than one, a deal might be possible dependant on the exact number. Directed to a huge heap of engines, it was obvious that many, many Fords had gone to the big scrap yard in the sky! Looking at the engines, it was evident that many of them were in very poor condition, and it dawned on Jack that he had no real way of telling as they stood whether any of them were in fact any good.

Back to the shed/shop/office, in reality the back of a lorry minus wheels and suspension standing on the mud, and the somewhat troglodyte inhabitant.

"Can I take one of these apart a bit to check the engine is okay before I buy it?" asked Jack.

"Do what you like," was the useful but short reply.

"If it isn't all right, may I look at another one please?"

"Yus, and don't bovver putting the uvver one back togevver 'cause it's only being scrapped anyway."

"Thank you," said Jack and made his way back to the pile. He and Paul searched through the pile; some, at the bottom of the heap, had been there so long that not only were they rusty, far too rusty, they even had weeds growing in and around them. They identified what seemed to be a nice clean motor with no apparent mechanical damage; one they had looked at had obviously broken a conrod and rammed the piston out the side of the cylinder—Jack didn't want that one! As it was a side valve engine, it was a simple matter to undo the bolts holding the cylinder head on the one they had chosen and remove it. There was no apparent damage visible—the piston tops looked okay, the cylinder wall, those that could be seen, did not appear to be damaged and turning over the engine with the starting handle rapidly obtained from Jack's car—he hadn't thought that he would need that until he tried to turn over the engine by turning the pulley wheel at the end of the crankshaft and not being able to shift it—allowed a viewing of the cylinders where the pistons had been at the top of the bore thus hiding it. What turning over the engine did do also was allow Jack to run a finger nail along the bore at the top of the piston's stroke to feel if there was a lip at the top of the bore where the piston stopped its upward move and started its downward move to determine if there was a lip there thus indicating that the piston had been up and down many times, perhaps too many times. There was a pronounced lip in each of the four bores. Onto the next engine and the next. The fourth one seemed to be absolutely perfect with no discernable lip at all. The engine they determined on also, unlike some of the others, had some of its ancillary bits like distributor still attached. Jack expected the trog to demand extra but all he said was, "Five quid then, and I 'ope you've left it tidy up there."

Since this last was said with a smile in his eye, Jack was quite happy to say, "Yeah, as tidy as I found it!" as he walked away.

They were back home by 10.30 am and, having had to let the 8 hp engine cool down before starting on removing it, were ready to start a little after 11 am. By lunchtime, all the bits connected to the engine which needed to be removed before it could be lifted out had been released. With the plan to lift it out after lunch, disaster struck again. Paul's mum rang to say he had to return home immediately to help with a problem that had arisen at home.

Deprived of his extra set of muscles, Jack stared disconsolately into the engine bay. Having to wait for Paul's return, probably at least until the next day and maybe not even then given the unknown nature of the problem—she had been totally unforthcoming, merely imperative, in her phone call—he felt very pissed off. The longer he looked, the more he thought, *that doesn't look very big, that engine*, and it wasn't very long before he started thinking, *maybe I could try and lift it a bit to see how heavy it is.* Thought being the master of the deed—or something like that—Jack soon found himself precariously perched on the chassis members either side of the engine with his hands hooked under the engine. The first tentative tug produced no reaction. A harder tug produced a lurch from the engine and its resettling into a slightly different position. *At least it's free*, he thought. Now, how to get it out? It was patently heavy but, perhaps, not too heavy. A straight forward lift was out as he couldn't get a proper purchase on it; he knew that from the effort he had already made.

94

Looking around the garage, this time he was working inside, having discovered how cold and unpleasant it was two days ago working on the clutch outside, he espied, hanging on the wall, the tow rope used for all sorts of emergencies in addition to that of towing other cars. Further examination showed a piece of timber, about 2" x 2" which looked more than strong enough to support the weight of the engine, so it was a matter of moments to wind the rope around the engine, front and back, such that the engine was properly balanced once the rope was tied to the timber. Standing as close to the front of the car as he could, grasping the wood as hard as he could, he started to lift. Modern day practitioners of 'elf 'n safety would have had a conniption fit at attempting such a lift with a bent back and leaning forward, but it worked and slowly, the engine emerged from the engine bay and was balanced precariously on the front of the car whilst he discarded the rope and timber and got a better grip underneath it. It was only a matter of moments to lift it onto the bench and set it down safely. It took a bit longer for him to get his breath back and for the blood infusing his face to disperse! In fact, it wasn't until he had had a cup of tea that he felt sufficiently rested to recommence work on the engine.

Revived and refreshed, the first job was to take the cylinder heads off the 8 and 10 engines so that he could fit the 8 head to the 10 engine in due course; this wouldn't be until the engine had been fitted into the engine bay thus making the weight of the 10 engine that much lighter by virtue of it having no head.

On examination, once the head was off, the 8 engine revealed considerable wear in the bores, as evidenced by the ubiquitous fingernail test, and heavy deposits of carbon in the head and the manifold leading to the side valves. *Good job I am doing all this work*, thought Jack, *as I would have been forced to carry out a decoke soon anyway. Looking at that little lot and the amount of wear in the bores, I bet it wasn't producing anywhere near the 23.5 horses it was supposed to be.*

He left the distributor and the other ancillary bits that were still on the 10 engine on it as they weighed very little and it seemed a bit pointless to remove them only to have to put them back on once it was in the engine bay. The 8 head had to be decoked ready to be placed on the 10 engine and the areas around the valves on the 10 engine had also to be cleaned up.

Jack started a search through his father's tools, looking for a screwdriver or similar with which to scrape off the encrusted carbon. In amongst them was the old screwdriver, old in the sense that the two edges of the flat head were rounded off and so it must be old to be so worn. Looking at it, it dawned on Jack that it wasn't old at all, at least not very, the corners had been deliberately rounded off so that, when scraping off crusty carbon, they would not gouge the cylinder head—just the tool, and so it proved. He even had the wit to stuff old rags into the cylinders to prevent debris falling into the bores and creating wear and mayhem.

Scraping off all the old carbon, bits of the head gasket still sticking to the head and other undesirable gunge took most of the afternoon. He also removed everything from the 8 engine that would be needed on the 10 engine as spares in the future, thus removing the distributor from the 8 even though the 10 already had one because who knew what the future held. There was no oil pump to remove, as such refinements were only fitted to much later engines but every conceivable bit possible was kept as spares should they ever be needed. He finished off the preparations necessary to be ready to fit the 10 engine into the engine bay and then rang to see if Paul would be able to help the following morning—he would—so, content with himself and what he had achieved, he called it a day.

Paul turned up early the next day and fitting commenced. The new, new to Jack that is, engine did indeed fit straight into the engine bay although getting it to fit into place with all the splines lining up to slide it into the clutch was a fiddly, swearing-a-lot type of job. Once it was in, the rest was relatively simple. The head from the 8 engine nicely cleaned up, fitted straight on as the book stated and connecting up the water hoses and spark plug leads dead simple. Connecting all the other bits, choke cable, battery leads and filling up the radiator matters of simplicity itself, and by midday, they were ready to try the starter. It had to turn over a few times for the fuel mixture to feed through the carburettor and into the cylinders but once it had, it burst into life and sat there throbbing away. Several prods of the accelerator pedal produced lovely healthy roars. Jack left it to tick over for a few minutes to check for leaks, of which there were none, and then it was off down the road.

The car was only fitted with a three-speed gearbox and all of them of quite low ratio, with a nominal 23.5 hp at best, and Jack knew from what he found in the 8 engine when he took the head off that his motor had not been producing anything like 23.5 hp, probably not much more than 15 hp or so, it meant that the gearing had to be low, even with 23.5 hp, for the engine to be able to produce enough grunt to get the thing moving at all or to cope with hills with a full load aboard. It also meant that changing up had to happen quickly to prevent too much loss of road speed.

Now the world was a different place! With bags of revs, the thing took off like a rocket, squealing tyres, clouds of smoke and a rapidly approaching horizon meant joy, excitement and grins all round. Now he had to change gear quickly not to maintain road speed but because he was running out of revs, so quickly did they build up. Jack would never know exactly how much power the new setup produced but he did think he must have doubled it at least—not double the nominal 23.5 hp but double the more actual 15 hp so that he now had 30 real horse power on the road, not so very far off the 25% increase promised for the 10 hp swap and the increased compression ration created by swapping the 8 head onto the 10 engine. He enjoyed his little run out, but all good things come to an end, and he had to turn for home. That's when further problems decided to shit on his parade.

As they returned home, in a more sedate manner it must be said, Jack discovered that not all was quite right. He slowed right down in top gear as they approached some red traffic lights and as they changed to green before they had come to a stop, Jack, being a bit lazy, instead of changing down simply pressed the accelerator to be greeted with a noise like a tin of nuts and bolts being violently shaken but three times as loud. This was accompanied by a considerable juddering, bad enough to shake the whole car and occupants. Jack immediately changed down, and the juddering and the rattling immediately disappeared.

Dad knew what the problem was almost as soon as Jack described the symptoms.

"It's pre-ignition or pinking," he said. "There's three main causes, pre-ignition caused by the built-up carbon deposits glowing red hot, so hot that they ignite the petrol/air mix before the piston reaches the top of its stroke, causing the cylinder to fire too early so that the ignited gas is trying to push down whilst the piston is still trying to push up—not something you want, as it will eventually destroy the engine.

"The second cause is the timing of the spark plug igniting, which should be as the piston gets to the top of its stroke, but for some reason the timing has been altered or slipped in some way and the third most common cause is running an engine on low, or too low octane petrol for that engine. Of course, if you're really unlucky, it could be all three at the same time. It could also be a problem with the petrol gas/air mix, too weak or more likely too rich, but your carburettor is so basic, you'll not be able to do too much with that but weakening the mix might be worth a try!"

"Well," said Jack, "I know it's not carbon build up because I decoked the engine, and it was pristine. I didn't do anything to change the timing of the engine, but I suppose that could have been wrong in the 10 engine when I bought it, and I never thought to look at the timing marks and the petrol, as it is a mix of Shell Mex (very low octane), Shell (moderate octane) and Shell Super, all mixed together as I had levelled the pumps at the end of my shift, might be anything. I will need to check the timing and weaken off the mixture."

Checks of the timing revealed no apparent problem. Jack weakened off the mixture as much as he dared but knew he would have to revisit the tuning once he had run the current petrol out of the tank and refilled it with Super. *A good enough excuse for a run*, he thought and thought being master of the deed, it was only moment to ring his three mates and arrange a trip to Brighton for the following day.

# Chapter 32

The fact that it rained mattered not a whit on the journey to Brighton although it did reveal that the windscreen wiper, only one, slowed to a virtual stop when climbing up hills, something to do with pressure, or lack of it, in the inlet manifold, and almost beat itself to death with its rapidity when going downhill when there was more than adequate pressure available; it was to be years before Ford swapped to electric wipers and cured this problem. Also noticeable was an improvement in that there was less obvious pinking going on, partly because of weakening of the mixture and the more frequent use of the gearbox to change down to prevent the engine labouring. What wasn't a problem was the weight of the four of them in the car—the new, high-compression engine easily dealt with that.

Brighton turned out to be a disappointment. Almost everything was shut, being Sunday and out of season probably didn't help, and none of them fancied a walk out onto either Pier in the pouring rain. So a quick confab ended in the decision to drive along the coast to Worthing or even Bognor. But the problem was, the car wouldn't start. Three pulls of the starter resulted in the engine turning over okay but not starting. *Funny*, thought Jack, *it can't be cold because we've only been stopped for five minutes.* Pulling out the choke entailed risk since there was the danger of flooding the engine, but if he kept churning it over and it didn't fire, there was that risk anyway, so he pulled out the choke and the engine fired immediately. So off they set. They got about halfway between Brighton and Worthing and the engine slowly died; no dead stop, no coughing or missing, the power slowly faded away and the car came to a stop on the coast road in the middle of nowhere. Even jiggling the choke made no difference.

Jack's first thought was that he hadn't a clue. If it was petrol, which the use of the choke seemed to indicate that it might be, it didn't seem likely as an engine running out of petrol usually spluttered before coming to a stop and besides, the petrol gauge was showing half full. Electrical problems usually presented with misfires or a clean dead stop, and this hadn't seemed like that so where to start? At the beginning, of course, so he checked the fuel gauge to ensure it was actually showing the right level of fuel.

A visual and smell check of the carburettor revealed no obvious leaks and the tick over screw and the mixture screw both seemed to be in the proper position. The choke cable was still firmly in place and the starting cable had not broken. He knew that the starter motor was okay because he heard and felt it turning over the engine; no need to try the starting handle yet, too much like hard work, until he could find out what the problem was.

Basic petrol problems checked, now for the electrics. All the instruments appeared to be working when he turned the ignition on, so the basic connections seemed to be okay. So next was to remove one of the spark plug leads and, by getting Paul to pull the starter, to check for a spark. Nothing. So, replace the plug and disconnect the lead at the top of the plug and place it near the cylinder head, close enough that the spark could jump the gap if there was one. There wasn't. Move to the other end of the lead and check at the distributor. Again nothing. Check the low-tension lead (the spark plug leads are high tension) at the top of the distributor and lo and behold, a small spark when it was shorted across the top of the engine. Therefore, electricity was going into the distributor as low voltage, as it should, but somewhere in the gubbins (a technical word!) of the distributor, something wasn't working but what?

Just at that moment, an AA Patrolman on a motor bike and side car approached them from the other side of the road. Seeing the broken-down car, he slowed down past them, turned round and came back and stopped. Dismounting and walking back to them somewhat ponderously in his heavy duty long weatherproof coat and pulling off huge gauntlets, he opened the conversation with the immortal words, "Broken down then, have we, lads?"

Knowing that he was not a member and more importantly that he did not have the money to join, Jack responded, "Yes, we have, but I am not a member and I don't have the money to join, so thank you for stopping but I can't afford your help."

The AA man looked at him for a moment and then said, "Well, at least I can give you an idea of what is wrong which might be of help. What happened?" As soon as Jack got to the bit about there being current into the distributor but none coming out, the guy immediately said, "I've got just the thing to test for that," and, before Jack could say anything, walked away to his combination and started ferreting around in the sidecar which was full of tools and bits. In moments, he returned with some form of voltmeter and proceeded to touch the two wires attached to it to various points on the distributor. "Thought so," he said, "your condenser has packed up and you will need to get a new one, unless you happen to have a spare one in your back pocket. Ho. Ho. Ho." At that, he turned away and started back to his combination saying over his shoulder as he went, "But I think I have something which will act as a temporary fix." Jack kept trying to speak to him, but he was not listening, convinced he had the answer to the problem.

Whilst he was bent over delving into his sidecar, Jack reached into the tool/odds and ends box attached to the engine bay bulkhead and lifted out the complete distributor unit from the 8 engine which he had removed from it 'just in case' and placed in the box. Quickly jamming it into his back pocket, he waited until the guy was close back to him and with exaggerated motions pulled the distributor from his back pocket and said, "Like this?"

The guy looked at him absolutely astounded. "You had one in your back pocket! Where on earth did that come from?"

"Back pocket," said Jack with a straight face. The bloke looked completely bewildered and dumbfounded so much so that Jack felt he had no option other than to take pity on him and explain where the distributor had really come from. The bloke broke into laughter. It was only a matter of minutes to check the settings on the new one and then replace the old one with it. The engine started with the first pull of the starter.

Jack was sure the guy was going to ask for payment for his assistance but all he said was, "Just wait till I get back to the depot and I tell the lads, 'So I said to him you'll have to get a new one unless you've got one in your back pocket,' and blow me, didn't he just reach round and pull a complete distributor out of his back pocket and say, 'Like this?' They'll never believe it!" And on that note, off he went chuckling to himself.

Jack and the lads carried on to Worthing but if anything, that was worse than Brighton, but it was, nevertheless a happy group that made its way back to Surbiton at the end of an adventurous day.

That ended Jack's first week of ownership of a car—an expensive and expansive week to be sure and one he would never forget. Just as he would never forget the impression he created driving up the school drive and parking alongside the cars of the only three teachers to own one, the Head, the Deputy Head and Ted Hiller's the Cadet Force Captains. It wasn't long before the word had spread around the school with many younger boys crowding round to look. His peers affected disdain, but the green pallor of their complexions gave the game away. It also wasn't long for an imperious note to arrive from the Headmaster ordering its removal from the school grounds instanter. Jack had expected this, seeing that pupils' motor bikes were banned, and there was a clear rule about this, but there wasn't one about cars because no pupil had ever arrived in one. Still, it enabled Jack to enhance his notoriety even further, as well as to demonstrate the power of his car, when he took off down the drive with a scream of tyres and huge amounts of acrid rubber smoke. Champion!

# Chapter 33

It snowed on Christmas that year and then froze solid until March time. With no heater in the car and the bitterly cold wind whistling in around the brake and clutch pedals, driving was not exactly pleasant. Jack had to tuck his trouser legs into his socks and place a small travel rug over his legs even to stay less than frozen. He even wore his motorbike gauntlets to drive, so cold was it. But none of that could dampen his excitement and enjoyment of owning a car.

He especially enjoyed the opportunity to practice controlling skidding and handbrake turns on the icy back streets—a skill that would last a lifetime.

Life progressed. Halfway through the summer term, he was called to the Staff Room to see Ted Hiller, who told him that in recognition of his contribution to the School Cadet Platoon and his efforts in representing England against Canada, Australia and New Zealand and his command of the Queen's Guard, he was to be promoted to Cadet Under Officer. There hadn't been a Cadet holding such a senior position for many years, and he was very much to be congratulated. It would mean that he would mess with the officers at camp and not with the boys. Jack wasn't at all sure that he thought that was a good thing but, heigh ho, what will be will be.

# Chapter 34

Before that summer, he had had an interesting Easter. At Easter, Jack drove over to the hairdresser's where his sister worked to collect her from work and get her home quickly as she had something special on that night and had lots to do getting ready. Jack was a bit mystified by it all; after all, her face was already made up and her hair, of course, working where she did, was an armoured mass of bouffant glory, but she still had to change her clothes and, of course, re-do her makeup and hair!

Having completed all this, she announced that she was now ready to be taken to where she was going! Jack was more than pissed off since nothing had been said about being a taxi driver. Still, she offered to pay some money for petrol over and above the cost if Jack was prepared to wait for her or to come back and collect her. Jack elected to come back, waiting with an unknown time commitment was not an option he was prepared to consider.

The address he delivered her to was another hairdresser's. It did not even require putting two and two together to work out that she was going for a job interview.

On collection, nearly an hour later, his sister was bubbling over with excitement and couldn't resist blurting out, "They want me to start next Monday and its £5 per week more, plus I get to keep all my tips and don't have to share them with the Manager!" Five pounds, when the average for a 44-hour week was only about £11, plus all the tips, did indeed represent a significant increase; no wonder she was so excited.

What Jack didn't realise was that this was to change his life quite nicely too. Jack was inveigled into collecting Paula from work on the Friday night when she finished 'as she would have all her personal stuff to carry as well as all the presents she expected to be given!' As she again offered petrol (which he didn't really need, having the ability to access free petrol from the petrol station when he worked on a Saturday night, but it was always nice to put a little extra in the tank midweek if someone else was paying!), he agreed to meet her.

On the Friday night when he arrived she wasn't, of course, anywhere near ready to go, so Jack was invited into the staff room to wait. It was really a little pokey with lots of the available space taken up with washing machine, drier and racks for airing the towels and with an enormous boiler and hot water tank taking up a huge amount of space. With a sink and draining board, kettle and small work top, there was hardly space for all the staff, five of them, to be in there at the same time.

Jack perched somewhat precariously on a rickety chair to wait. The owner/manager came and sat next to him and started the conversation with the usual banal comments, "We're all going to miss Paula…" etc, and Jack could not help but think he wished he was going to be able to miss her as well, but no such luck. He was somewhat jerked back from his reverie of how nice life could be if his sister did not exist when he realised he was being asked a question which required an answer.

The owner/manager, Carmen by name, (in reality Daisy!) was saying, "I couldn't help noticing that last week, when you collected Paula, you had paint spots and blotches on you; are you a qualified painter, then?"

Jack's immediate thought was, *did I?* But he didn't ask it. Instead he said, "Ah yes, I had been decorating the outside lavvy and the garage at home. The lavvy suffers a bit from the damp because there is no heating, and in the winter, it can get very damp and unpleasant with mould in patches and that's to say nothing about some of the smells in there! The garage was a bit the same although built on to the house it had no heating so the walls which had been plastered and painted in the past needed cleaning and refreshing from time to time."

She looked at him for a moment and then said, "What would you suggest to fix this place up, how long would it take, and how much would it cost?"

Jack thought about it for a moment.

"Well," he said, "it obviously suffers from damp, a bit like the garage and lavvy, but caused more by the drying towels than cold." He stood up and moved to look behind the hot water tank. Behind it and in other places, the original plaster was breaking off in places and there were various cracks, wear marks and normal chips and dents only to be expected in such a confined environment.

He said, "It depends on what you want doing. At one extreme, all the fittings should be removed, the old plaster stripped off, new plaster which would need to be painted and the fittings stripped down to bare metal, properly re-painted and then replaced. I have no idea what that would cost. I would not have the skill to remove all the plumbing stuff, and it would clearly take quite some time. I have no idea what that would cost or even if it would be worth doing.

"What I could suggest is scraping out all the loose bits of plaster and filling the pits to create a more or less flat surface. We could, I would need my mate Paul to help me, paper onto the now smooth wall either a lining wall paper or some sort of patterned embossed paper and then paint over it with a gloss paint to seal it so that any areas of damp from condensation could simple be dried with a cloth or I might be able to find a waterproof paper, something like an oilcloth which would do the same job. I am not sure we could paint over that, I'd have to check and let you know, and if we can't, could you live with whatever colour or pattern it was?

"The ceiling needs lining paper and then painting with a white emulsion—something with a shiny surface, again to fight the damp. It would take the best part of a day to rub down, fill in, prime and generally prepare for the new papering and painting gloss for the wood areas, and I would suggest gloss also for the hot water tank and other metal pipes etc. The second day would be for the painting of the walls, ceiling and any other bits and bobs. It would help if we could access the shop the night before we start work proper to empty out as much as possible to let us hit the ground running the day we start on the main work. It is possible that the wall and ceiling surfaces will require additional coats to give full cover, so we would try to get as much as possible done the first day, including getting a first coat on, if we could, to allow it to dry for an additional coat or two. If we run into problems, then it is possible we would need a third day.

103

"The problem is you work on Saturdays and are only closed for one day normally at the weekend; I'm thinking that there might be an opportunity with Easter coming up to do the work on the Good Friday, Easter Sunday and Monday when you will be closed. As far as the cost is concerned, I would estimate, and it is a bit of a guess because I don't know how bad the plaster is and therefore how much repairing we will have to do, so that would be £10 per day for the two of us and between two and three days. That won't include materials which will be extra." As he said all this Jack was hoping it sounded like he knew what the hell he was talking about and that Paul would be available to help!

Carmen, she was a dolled-up looker but somehow very hard, didn't even blink. She said, "As it happens, though the girls don't know it yet, I am going to close for the whole of the Easter weekend because my boyfriend is taking me to Rome from Thursday night until late Monday night, so you can have the four days. I'll be finishing at lunchtime on Thursday, but I'll arrange for the girls to clear out everything before they go home in the evening, five o'clock, and you can come over and check they've done it before you let them go home."

The idea that Jack would be in charge, so to speak, of a load of females was somewhat daunting, but at least it did mean he could be sure the room was emptied out. It would also mean that he could bring over the pasting table, ladders, sugar soap for washing down the paintwork, lining wall paper, tools, plaster, filler and the various paints/sealers he would need. He would need to borrow his dad's Triumph Renown as it had a roof rack for the step ladders and planks he would need as well as a large boot. In the event, Jack had to put some of the stuff in the back on the floor.

Paul helped him load, his mother apparently having got over her hissy fit. The last job was to tie the ladders to the roof rack with strong string. Jack, without realising it, left his penknife, a rather fancy folding knife with a slightly curved end to the handle to protect the tip of the knife, on the roof of the car once he had cut the last bit of the string. Because he was none too sure of the security of the ladders on the roof rack or the stuff piled in the boot—paint spilling all over the boot of his dad's car could not be contemplated—Jack drove very carefully the three miles or so to the shop. Once there, he reached into his pocket for his knife to discover it was gone. Shock. Horror. *Oh shit.* Just some of the words flooding through his mind. *Where did I use it last? Oh fuck, I left it on the roof.* A swift walk around to the nearside rear corner, the last one he had tied down and what should be sitting there but the knife! Instant relief and some instant disbelief from Paul.

"Bloody hell," he said, "that's not possible!" But it was. Years later, Jack was to watch a programme on the TV where drivers competing in the programme were required to drive a 100 yards on a smooth runway with a half-full glass of water balanced on the bonnet. Most failed. *Easy peasy*, thought Jack, *what a bunch of prone to self-abuse buggers they were; bet they couldn't drive three miles with a knife balanced on the roof.*

# Chapter 35

On entering the shop, they were stared at as some kind of microbiological low life by both staff and the few customers. In turn, Jack and Paul stared at these over-haired specimens and the shocking aliens with slanted eyes from the tightness of their hair in rollers and other funny things all covered over with plastic capes and even funnier spells.

No one spoke, they just stared at one another. I suppose Jack and Paul didn't look too prepossessing either in their roughest old clothes, in Jack's case, covered in paint spots and slicks. *Surely, that should indicate who we were*, thought Jack. They were both to discover that this lot were so wrapped up in themselves and their looks that logical thought was a very alien concept. Indeed, the single brain cell they shared between them all was overstressed to deal with haircuts, perms, romantic magazines and astrological forecasts.

As they stared at one another, the door to the staff room opened and into view walked a young woman, heavily made up and coiffured but wearing a darker blue overall than the lighter blue worn by the four other assistants. On spying Jack, she immediately walked over and introduced herself as Helja, the Assistant Manager and said, "Hi, Jack," and turning to Paul said, "And you must be Paul. I've heard a lot about you both from Paula—all of it good, I must say." Jack doubted that, but he wasn't going to contradict her.

Jack responded, "Dead on. I don't remember seeing you here before?"

"No, I only started the week Paula left, but I did see you when you came to collect her on her last day." They were then shown through to the staff room and shown the work that had already been done to empty it. Helja said, pointing to some piles of towels and shoulder capes, "We'll shift all that lot out into the salon once the last customer has gone and then it's all yours. They are just finishing off the last two customers, probably about 10 minutes; would you like a cup of tea while you're waiting?"

"Yes, please," Jack and Paul responded in unison. Whist she made the tea, Jack asked how she liked working at the salon. She responded enthusiastically, dropping out along the way that she was quite young to have got the Assistant Manager's job but that might have been something to do with Carmen being her aunty! Tea made, she bustled off back into the salon to see how they were progressing. She reappeared almost immediately to announce the two customers had gone and could the girls come in to finish off. Jack agreed.

He had been somewhat surprised at the initial reception he received on arrival in the shop because he had been there a few times before, collecting Paula, and had spoken to them all several times. It was only later through the grapevine that he learned they had not been told it would be him, they would not have recognised

Paul since he had never been there before, and they had only been told to expect 'workmen'.

The work progressed rapidly; the girls were all keen to get away and it was not too long before Jack and Paul had unloaded all the kit, the Staff Room had been emptied of hairdressing paraphernalia and filled up with paint etc. The pasting table and the rolls of paper, packets of paste and the pasting brush and larges decorator's scissors were all left in the salon on an old sheet as there wasn't room to set it up in the staff room. Helja stayed with them, even though Jack said there was no need for her to stay. Jack had been given a key by Carmen and the code to the burglar alarm and told to let themselves in to come and go as they pleased. She made a point of saying that no money was left in the shop, but they should make sure they locked it properly and set the alarm properly even if they only went to the café over the road.

They all left at the same time and Jack and Paul drove off to drop Paul at home. Jack's sister wanted to know all about how they had got on when he arrived home. As soon as he mentioned Helja, his sister reacted like a bee stung horse, "That stuck up cow she really thinks she's so clever, but she doesn't even know how to…" Jack stopped listening at that point, but he did note that there were obviously issues between them.

They had arranged for Jack to call for Paul the following morning at 7.45 am, and they arrived at the shop at 8 am. They were bemused to find Helja already there and the tea made. She casually informed them that she had heard them discussing their start time for the morning and she thought she'd just pop in to see they had everything they needed. Assuring her that they had, she then disappeared.

"She's got the hots for you," Paul said. Jack looked at him absolutely astounded.

"Bollocks," he said. "I only met her yesterday, and I've only had business type conversations with her, nothing personal at all."

"Nevertheless," said Paul, "she's never taken her eyes off you; when you were bringing things in, setting up the table and all the other stuff, she was watching you like a hawk and only took her eyes off you to look away when you turned to look at her."

"Nah, you've got it wrong; you're just trying to wind me up. Come on, let's get started." And on that, work commenced. Work progressed steadily and at about 9.45 who should reappear but Helja.

"Anyone for a cup of tea?" was her opening remark, to be gladly accepted by both boys. This time, Jack kept looking away and then looking back and sure enough, every time she was looking at him. Once she had gone on her way, Paul said immediately, "See, I saw you looking at her and catching her looking at you; I told you she fancies you like a cat fancies a kipper."

"You might be right," said Jack, but he had no idea of how to progress from there. Helja kept popping in during the three days it took them to finish the job; they also spruced up the toilet, although not requested to, simply because it was easy to do, could be fitted in between other jobs while they were waiting for filler to dry (they tied up one of the hand-held hairdryers so that it directed a warm stream of air to help the filler dry—not too close or strong to cause it to dry too quickly and crack; it was under the lining wall paper and thus subject to damp paste landing on top of it!) and it used up what was left of the white emulsion, saving them the trouble of taking it back.

Jack awoke on the Monday morning at 3 am with the answer of how to proceed with this potentially nascent relationship with Helja. When she turned up to make tea in the afternoon, in fact just as they were tidying up and loading the car, Jack said to her, "You really have been spoiling us, and we both feel guilty; what about me taking you out for a drink one evening in return?"

She said, "Yes, I'd like that although you don't have to. I thought how hard you were working, and men are so useless at making the tea that I was glad to help out." Jack thought, *men, she said men!* The first time that Jack could ever remember being called that or referred to as such. He was even more pleased that she had said yes and not put him down in front of Paul—that would have hurt! She gave him her phone number at home, she didn't want him to ring her at work; something Jack was pleased about since it lessened the chance of their going out getting back to his sister and it seemed unlikely that, given his sister's comments about Helja, that they would be likely to exchange any intimacies whatsoever.

# Chapter 36

Jack left it two nights, on Paul's advice not to appear too keen though his experience of girls/women matched Jack's i.e. none. Jack rang her on Wednesday evening and asked her, after some rather perfunctory small talk, if she would like to have dinner (such grand talk) on the following Saturday. She accepted with alacrity and then suggested they could perhaps go to the restaurant, and named what Jack knew to be a very expensive eatery on an island in the Thames just upstream of Hampton Court. That should have told Jack what sort of relationship this was going to be, but at that stage, he was too innocent to recognise the signs. What he did counter with, knowing that he simply could not afford her suggested location, said was, "Well, actually I have booked a table at the Crooked House in Molsey," which he had visited with his parents and various visitors. It was very old, very crooked, having sunk down on its foundations unevenly over the years, and specialised in good, home cooked pub grub long before it became fashionable and widespread. It was also cheap!

Helja paused for an uncomfortably long period and then said, "Yes, that would be lovely." Jack then had to ring the Crooked House and seek to book a table for two! Fortunately, he was able to do so. He duly collected Helja from her home, a rather posh detached property in Hersham, and drove her to the pub. Jack was still only seventeen and hoped that no one would question his age. No one did.

Helja chose just about the most expensive items on the menu and Jack the cheapest. She wanted a bottle of wine, but Jack headed this off with the fact that he was driving so she had to settle for, in the event, three individual glasses of wine. Jack, conscious of the bill that was racking up and starting to feel a little resentful of it, only had two halves of shandy.

The conversation did not flow particularly well. Jack felt this was probably due to the fact that they did not really know one another at all and therefore much of the talk involved exploring one another's likes, dislikes, pastimes and hobbies. Helja seemed only to talk about ballroom dancing and made much of gaining a gold medal. Jack hated dancing; he had two left feet and both of them were severely disabled. He was pretty tone deaf as far as music was concerned too although he did enjoy rock and roll, Rock Around the Clock by Bill Hayley and the new wave of rock singers starting to emerge, Elvis, Cliff, Eddy Cochrane and Marty Wilde who were just starting to make names for themselves with the younger generation, but he did not like waltzes, quick steps, foxtrots and the Charleston—all popular with ballroom dancers. Helja was to try to teach him these steps in the future but with absolutely no success whatsoever, not even how to waltz which was only three steps at its simplest.

Every time Jack tried to steer the conversation to things that interested him, Helja steered it back to dancing or sometimes about film stars' latest fashions.

Although Jack did not know it, that was to form the pattern for all their future dates, even double dating with Paul and his girlfriend a month or so later when he found one.

Driving Helja back to her home, Jack started to worry. The perennial problem for men—should he attempt to kiss her good night or not on a first date? If she did respond to the kiss and kissed him back, should he attempt to go further or not? If he didn't try, would she be upset? The swinging 60s, the permissive society was starting to dominate the press and, of course, combined with Jack's raging teenage hormones, Jack was hoping for a serious session on the back seat. In the event, as soon as he pulled up, some yards back from her home and in the darkest part of the street, she leaned over, gave him the briefest peck on the cheek, thanked him for a lovely evening and hopped out. She was gone quicker than greased lightning, but it did at least solve his dilemma, although not in the way he was hoping!

The relationship followed much the same pattern over the next few months. She continued to suggest meals out when Jack only wanted to go for drinks. Gradually, Jack realised he was being used. Although she did progress to kissing him on the lips when saying good night, that was it. To try to touch her breast resulted in a stinging slap to the errant hand. He once, when she was wearing a lowish top, placed a single finger on the upper slope of one breast which resulted in two slaps. Even when, as the summer came, and he took her to the seaside for the day, Brighton was her favourite, she always expected Jack to pay for the food, drinks and amusements which, along with extra petrol used, meant he found his finances were increasingly under strain. Enough was enough; he was getting fed up with the cost, she was clearly high maintenance for a very poor return—there was clearly no evidence of the permissive society allowed here! He wasn't sure how to break off the relationship, so he simply stopped asking her out at the start of May. When she rang him and asked why he hadn't rung her, he explained that he was having to build up money for summer camp (although he wasn't sure that he would be going this year) so he couldn't afford to take her out until after camp. Although not pleased with this, Helja had no choice other than to accept; she could have offered to pay, but that was clearly not something she was prepared to do. So there the relationship rested.

# Chapter 37

One day, Jack was sent for and given the news that the Queen was visiting Kingston for some anniversary or other; Jack wasn't really interested until he was told that the School Platoon was to provide the Guard of Honour! That grabbed Jack's attention all right. It was to be in three weeks' time and that meant rehearsals every night to make sure they put on a proper show. How much of a show, Jack didn't know.

The rehearsals went off fine. However, a bit of a wobbler was thrown into their drill, with only five nights left before the big day when Captain Hiller announced that they were to parade with bayonets, something not normally issued to Cadets. The Mk4 Lee Enfields that the boys possessed were normally fitted with spike type bayonets which had been universally disliked by the troops issued with them in the war because they only had one use i.e. to poke holes in things, people especially, but really had no other use. Sword-type bayonets, short or long, could be used for poking holes in people just as well or better, far more damaging holes than the spikes, and could be used for a myriad of other uses such as cutting up wood for the fire, tent pegs, tent poles, opening tins of food etc. They also looked much more warlike, smart and impressive, than the spikes.

The problem was that sword bayonets would not fit on the Mk4. Captain Hiller, however, had the answer. 30 Mk3 Lee Enfields were to be delivered on loan the following day along with 30 short sword bayonets. Given that bayonets are primarily designed for sticking into people and knowing that boys will be boys and thus likely to play at stabbing with the bayonets, it was a sure-fire certainty that someone would get stuck before, during or after the drills! Consequently, all drill was to be done with the scabbards left on the bayonets—they were only to be removed for the big day.

The big day duly arrived. Most of the parents of the boys were there to see their little darlings perform in front of the Queen, even including Jack's mum, nana and grandpa; his father could not get the time off work, and his sister simply didn't care.

They were shown to their positions by a harassed looking Major from the Scots Guards. They had been standing at ease for only a few minutes when a band came marching down the street. It was only as they got closer that Jack could make out that they were, in fact, an American Air Force band. They marched down with a single drummer beating the step—something standard in the army as well. However, as they neared their position, the band burst into music. It was a matter of moments to realise what they were playing—it was the St Louis Blues, not particularly a military march. However, then to Jack's horror, instead of continuing marching, they burst into some sort of dance routine in time to the music, with

110

prominent soloists appearing out from the front of the band whilst they marked time and presented the crowd with their party pieces!

Jack was absolutely horrified. This wasn't what the military was about at all. These clowns, despite their perfect playing and presentation, were simply making a mockery of what it was to be a soldier. Worse was to come, once the parade was over, all the girls in the crowd made a beeline for the Americans, completely ignoring the boy soldiers.

Not even the success of the Guard, presenting arms perfectly for the Queen and indeed even exchanging a few words with Her, the content of which he could never remember in the future, could not calm the anger he felt at the non-professional, non-military show put on by the bloody Yanks. And the fact that the crowd had loved it only made it the worse for Jack. Still, they did manage to carry out their Guard without anyone stabbing themselves with a bayonet, and Jack did receive a commendation from the CO for the manner in which the boys had performed once back at the school. The cutie, effeminate prancing around by the American Air force band, however, was to disgust Jack for many years to come.

# Chapter 38

When the subject of the summer camp came up, that year it was to be in Shorncliffe camp near Folkestone, Jack took a long time before he decided he would not go. The reaction that generated at school and home surprised him. Initially, the pressure to change his mind was quite light, "You've always enjoyed it in the past," sort of thing. Only as he maintained his position did the pressure become more severe until in the end he said he would go, but this would definitely be the last one.

Word came down that all Cadets had to make sure they had their cleaning and blancoing kits (blanco was a caked light green/khaki chalk which was used to colour belts and anklets) with them at camp as there was to be an important inspection by a VIP on the middle Sunday. Jack suspected nothing.

Sunday dawned bright and clear. The three Platoons comprising A Company were formed up as three sides of a square with a small raised dais in the middle of the fourth side. Once the Cadet Sergeants had got the three platoons lined up correctly, Jack, as the Cadet Under Officer, was responsible for quickly inspecting them before taking up his position dead centre and in front of the Sergeant of the Platoon facing the dais which, by coincidence, happened to be the School Platoon.

Soon, the Company Commander could be seen approaching with a tall figure wearing the uniform of a Lieutenant General, followed by the adult officers and NCOs of the unit; completely surprising Jack, his mum and dad were accompanying them. Major Ravenwood stepped onto the dais and in a loud, clear voice said, "I should like to welcome here the Lord Lieutenant of Surrey, Lieutenant General Sir Rupert Smythe who has come here today to inspect you and to make a very special award."

At that, he stepped down from the dais and proceeded to lead the Lord Lieutenant around the ranks for a very thorough and diligent inspection. He inspected Jack and then had a few words with him about his shooting before proceeding with the inspection. Inspection over, he made his way to the dais and stepped up on to it.

"Good morning," he said. "It is a great pleasure for me to be here today and to have the pleasure in inspecting you all, and what a fine turnout it is, and to make an award to one Cadet who has been judged to be the best Cadet NCO in the county of Surrey this year. More than 1500 Cadets' names were submitted to me, and the one who came out on top was Cadet Under Officer Hughes. Of course, he was a Sergeant then and has subsequently been promoted in recognition of his achievements." He then proceeded to list a number of those, including the battle with the Royal Marine Commandos for which even the Commandos admitted he had defeated them, his shooting exploits having represented England three years running, his having come in the top five of the National for five years, and his command of the Cadet Guard when the Queen had visited Kingston a few months ago.

Jack had found himself drifting off in the warm sunshine but was brought back to the present with a shock when the Lord Lieutenant finished his speech with, "So, without further ado, I should like to present the award to him. Please step forward, Cadet Under Officer." With a start, Jack pulled himself to and marched stiffly forward to meet the Lord Lieutenant as he stepped down from the dais. He crashed to a halt with a lovely sound of steel-capped boots. The Lord Lieutenant took from his pocket a gold and red badge about 3"x2" in the shape of a shield and handed it to Jack. He then shook Jack's hand whilst calling out, "Well done. Well done."

Much more quietly, he whispered, "Perhaps you could give me a salute on the way back, old man, as you completely failed to do so on the way forward!"

Jack was mortified. Here he was, supposedly the best Cadet NCO in the county, and he couldn't even salute the General! Shit! He felt a right tit, and it was with a very red face that he smartly stepped back a pace, threw up a salute that would have done credit to a Grenadier Guard and marched smartly back to his position to the cheers and applause of all the Cadets.

Following the parade, in the Officers' Mess—a posh tent—the General came over to speak to Jack and his parents. Opening with some general remarks, the General then said, "You're going to Sandhurst, of course." To this, Jack replied that he couldn't because of his age; he was too old. Following a conversation as to why Jack was too old (that year he had had several injuries and had missed so much schooling that he had had to redo the Fifth Form Year) the General said, "Load of damn nonsense, the army needs bright lads like you; leave it with me."

The rest of the camp passed quickly. The main event that Jack enjoyed most in the last week was a visit from a Corporal from the Light Infantry Regiment in the camp next door to spend two days teaching the senior Cadet NCOs the SLR and the Stirling Sub Machine Gun and, quite unofficially, some training with the Browning Hi Power 9 mm pistol which was just being introduced to the army.

The SLR, standing for Self-Loading Rifle, was being introduced to the Regular Army to replace the ageing Lee Enfields which had changed very little since before the First World War. Experience had shown the need for more fire power and although the Americans had been issuing automatic rifles, i.e. ones which fired bursts like machine guns, the British Army bigwigs thought this would just encourage soldiers to blaze away their ammunition in minutes flat without taking aim at all so, not to be trusted, they were to be issued with self-loading rifles which meant that having cocked the rifle for the first bullet, the rifle would fire when the trigger was pulled and then it would eject the empty case and reload a new round each time the trigger was pulled. It would continue to do this until the twenty rounds in the magazine, only ten in the magazine of a Lee Enfield, had all been fired. Thus, firepower would be more than doubled without the risk of the soldier taking un-aimed shots. It would also mean less ammunition would need to be carried and ferried up to replace stock used up wildly. Leastways, that was the theory; in practice, soldiers, especially un-blooded rookies, would blaze away and keep squeezing the trigger on an empty magazine in blind panic, but that also happened with the Lee Enfields where soldiers would keep working the bolt on an empty magazine.

They spent a full day learning to strip, clean and re-assemble the SLR before taking it down to the range to fire. Jack found it a very different beast to fire compared to the Lee Enfield with which he was so familiar. Where he customarily 'hooked' his right cheek bone over the butt of the Lee Enfield ensuring the same sight picture through the sites every time he fired, he found that so doing on the SLR resulted in a very sore cheek bone within minutes.

When Jack complained about this, the Corporal pointed out that the Lee Enfield tended to kick straight back when the trigger was squeezed whereas the SLR tended to kick upwards, twisting to the right as it did so, thus causing the bruising on the cheek. The answer was to hold the SLR much tighter to prevent it from twisting and kicking upwards rather than letting it kick into the shoulder and let the body absorb the recoil as had been the practice with the Lee Enfield. Jack tried this, but as his cheek was already sore, he didn't feel it helped very much. He much preferred using the Lee Enfield with which he was so accurate. Still, his accuracy was repeated with the SLR, sufficient that the Corporal spent a little time trying to persuade him to volunteer to join his Regiment when he left school on the promise of a place in the Battalion shooting team!

The following day, they were trained on the Stirling Sub Machine Gun. The replacement for the old Sten gun, which had seen such sterling service (no pun intended) with the army, the Stirling was the same basic design but modernised and better made. It was not issued to Army Cadet Force units and Jack never did find out how Captain Hiller had pulled it off, but Jack fell in love with it on sight.

It could fire single shots or bursts, indeed a whole magazine of 32 rounds in one go if desired, simply by selecting the position of the firing lever. Normally the SMG would be carried with the working parts forward, with an empty chamber and a loaded magazine on the weapon. To fire, the bolt was pulled back and the trigger squeezed, and it would fire singly or in bursts as desired. Simple as that! It worked by, when the trigger was squeezed, carrying a round forward into the breech; having seated home the round the breech block still moving forward would drive the firing pin into the base of the round and detonate it. The explosion would drive the bullet up the barrel, but the force of the explosion would also push back on the breech block, which was only held in place by a spring so that the resulting explosion drove the breech block backwards, extracting the fired casing from the breech and throwing it clear of the gun. Having been driven back as far as it would go, and the power of the explosion having dissipated, the spring then drove the breech block forward again scooping a round from the magazine and driving it into the chamber where the whole firing process would start all over again.

The SLR fired a 7.62 mm round which was very high velocity so that it flew pretty well flat over the first three hundred yards and only dropped slightly by 600 yards. At that point, the velocity dropped to below that of the speed of sound and the passing through the sound barrier could cause the round to wobble and go off course. It was the power of this round which caused such a kick which bothered Jack. The SMG, on the other hand, fired a 9 mm pistol bullet which had almost no kick to it since the backward explosive force of the bullet and the weight of the breech block cancelled one another out just as the block reached its rearward travel. The pistol bullet had lost most of its killing power by 75 yards and wasn't much use over this distance but, in reality, this did not matter since it was designed for clearing trenches, buildings and other close quarter work where it was very effective. Jack loved firing it and his accuracy with it was superb. For the SLR, they were using the new imitation figure of a man, and at 200 yards, Jack put nine rounds into the rectangular bull and one just outside it. With the SMG, he put all ten rounds into a smaller head and shoulders target at 25 yards. He loved the SMG but could take it or leave it as far as the SLR was concerned. What he did not know was just how useful the knowledge and skill obtained during these two days would be in the future.

The training on the Browning pistol took place in gaps in the other training, but by the end of the two days, he was quite competent in all three weapons.

On the return from camp, there were just under four weeks left of the summer holidays. The next two were taken up with a family holiday to South Wales to make contact with all of his mum's relatives—the annual ordeal, as Jack thought of it. Jack had to undergo the story of his winning the Lord Lieutenant's Award over and over again at each new set of relatives in turn who had to be regaled with it, lots of one-upmanship and points scoring going on; his mum was at last showing some pride at his Cadet Force membership!

Eventually, it came to an end and they returned home to find a letter from the Lord Lieutenant waiting on the mat. Jack had thought that the comment about seeing what he could do was just politeness and had expected to hear nothing more about it. Also waiting were his GCE O level results—eight passes—and a letter from the Headmaster of his school. The Headmaster's letter, the first one he opened, asked Jack to get in touch as he was to be appointed School Captain from the autumn term, and there were matters that needed to be discussed. His mum's reaction to the letter was to go off in a fit of ecstasy and to start planning how they could go back to Wales to get in some real class bragging.

Jack also, on the afternoon, in fact only ten minutes after they all got home and before he had opened the rest of the mail on his return from Wales, received a telephone call from Helja.

"Where have you been? I have been calling every day and nobody has answered. There's a special dinner at the Marquis of Granby tonight and I want you to take me; there's to be awards presented for dancing and I think I might be in for one. It's only ten pounds per head and I've ordered two tickets." Jack was stunned. Twenty pounds was a relatively huge sum of money and even if he had any after camp and the holiday with the family, he was buggered if he was going to spend twenty quid, sit through stuff on dancing for hours and quite frankly, he couldn't care less whether she had won something or not. Twenty quid for a meal and a kiss on the cheek was definitely not good value. So, he said, "I've only just got back from holiday ten minutes ago, I'm very tired, I'm very broke and I don't like the assumption that I will pay out £20 quid just like that." Whilst they were talking, Jack had opened a letter which, among other things, said that a provisional place had been awarded to him at the Army Outward Bound School, starting in a week's time. Adjusting the date slightly, he didn't after all want to go with her, he said, "And I've just found a letter inviting me to attend the Army Outward Bound School in Towyn, Mid Wales, starting tomorrow. That means I have a ton of kit to get ready, I have to go into school to draw some more, (Jack was a key holder for the stores), so I simply don't have time to come out with you. These places are very rare, and it has been arranged for me by the Lord Lieutenant of Surrey himself. It is a very great honour for me as well as the fact that I was awarded his badge for the best Cadet NCO in the county at camp. So there really is no chance of me coming."

There was a very long silence at the end of the phone but then, in a very small and injured voice, she said, "But I've told all my friends that we would be going."

Jack replied, "Well, you can still go but not with me." The phone line went dead. *Well, that's that*, thought Jack, *no more of her.*

However, the rest of the Lord Lieutenant's letter really put the cat among the pigeons. It explained that the Royal Army Service Corps had a scheme for Potential Officer Cadets, who had to be serving soldiers and who could be, because they were serving soldiers, one year older when applying to go to Sandhurst.

It went on to suggest, as he had already told Helja, that he would benefit by attending the Army Outward Bound School at Towyn in Mid Wales and he had been provisionally booked for the course starting on the 1st September and finishing on the 21st. To aid him in this, a travel warrant was included for the train for a return Surbiton to Towyn which was to be returned if he declined the offer of the place. Further, he was to apply to join the Army, in the RASC, as a Potential Officer Cadet before the end of September. He would also need to take and pass the Civil Service exam for entrance to the Royal Military Academy Sandhurst. He should also confirm to the General that he was attending the outward bound school, taking the exam and joining the RASC so that the necessary arrangements to take the exam, attend the outward bound school and join the army could be made as the first of these, the exam, was to be held the following week! *Bloody hell*, thought Jack, *that's a programme and a half!*

Jack paused for a moment to consider the implications and then handed the letter to his father. He, in turn, having read it, handed it to his mother. His mother was the first to speak.

"Does this mean that you would be joining as an Officer Cadet?"

"No," said Jack, "I would be a Potential Officer Cadet candidate; I would still have to pass the Regular Commissions Board."

"But if you didn't pass, what would happen?"

Jack, who had been scanning a leaflet about the scheme included with the letter, said, "It seems like I would have the choice to either stay in the Army as a Private Soldier, and perhaps try again for a Quartermaster's Commission years down the line or resign and come out of the army."

Mother, desperately trying to balance the bragging rights between a Private Soldier, albeit a Potential Office Cadet, and a definite School Captain, and firmly of the opinion that a bird in the hand is worth any number in the bush, had no trouble in saying, "Well, there's no choice to be made there; School Captain it is."

Jack, now within only a few weeks of his eighteenth birthday, simply bridled at his mother taking so abrupt a decision without him having any say at all in the matter and, reacting just as quickly, said, "It's my decision to make, and I'm going to think about it overnight."

This was not greeted well by his mother, but before she could say anything further, his father stepped in and said firmly, an unusual event for him, "I think you should take some time and think about this very carefully as it's your whole future you're deciding." Mother, with a glower and very strong sniff, stormed off to the kitchen.

His father then, very quietly, said, "Think about it very carefully, son, and I will stand by whatever decision you take."

Jack's mind was in a whirl. Returning to school would mean a further year as a schoolboy, but with the responsibilities of School Captain which would inevitably mean working with the Head teacher which Jack was sure he would hate—returning and refusing the Captain's role was certainly not an option so that left the Outward Bound School, the exam and the army. There were two big hurdles there, passing the Regular Commissions' Board and passing the exam for Sandhurst. Of these, the exam was only just over a week away. Failure would mean the end to his becoming an Officer Cadet. A pass would mean joining the army and attendance at the RCB at some indeterminate date in the future but certainly long after the start of the autumn term. Failure would mean no chance, realistically, of going back to school and taking up the Captain's position as he would have been in the army for some time, certainly long after the start of the term

Which did he want—school or army? A no brainer really. Jack had been at school for a long time, it seemed like his whole lifetime, before going to school at four being a forgotten memory. He was being offered a fantastic opportunity, Outward Bound School, which was generally regarded as fantastic thing, and a route into a scheme which developed men for Sandhurst and all he had to do (at the moment) was to pass an exam. Decision made. Jack went to sleep with the worry of his mother's reaction to his decision downgraded by knowing that his father would support his decision.

As expected, Jack announced that he was going to take the exam and then, if he passed, join the army in the RASC as the General had suggested and arranged. His mother looked at him in stunned silence—all bragging rights over her son's success in life disappearing out of the window in an instant. Before she could say anything, his dad spoke. He asked, "If you fail the exam, what then?"

Jack, realising the opportunity his father was offering, replied, "Well, I'll just go back to school. I won't respond to the Head's letter yet; if he should ring in the next week, would you tell him I stayed in Wales for an extra week and will contact him when I return?"

His dad replied, "I think that's a wise decision, because at this moment, you are keeping all your options open. Let's wait until we know the results of the exam and we can then sit down and discuss your future." Mother was clearly not happy but simply left the room, leaving a distinct chill in the air as she did so.

# Chapter 39

The following week, Jack duly made his way to Piccadilly and Burlington House where the exam was to take place. Jack knew it was made up of five subjects and he had to pass all five—a bit like the old matriculation exams which had only recently been replaced by GCEs. Each subject was set for an hour and there was a half hour break at lunch time between the first three subjects and the last two. There were about 35 young men present, some chatting in groups who obviously knew each other.

The first subject was Maths which was Jack's greatest worry. He was all right with direct numbers but once algebra, full as it was of mysterious 'x's and 'y's of no known value entered into the paper, he knew he would be lost. Fortunately, as the Maths paper covered all aspects, numerical sums, geometry, and trigonometry (another subject with which he struggled) and algebra, it meant that only a few of each could be present. Years later, when Jack was 70 years old, he thought back over his life and reminisced that even after all these years, never once, not once, had he ever had a use for Algebra, Trigonometry, Geometry or those bloody quadratic equations! As it was, the ones he worried about were relatively straightforward so that he was able to answer them with some degree of confidence.

Maths was followed by English which was probably Jack's strongest subject and then History, another subject which Jack enjoyed. After a quick hamburger and bottle of Coke, it was back to French and a General Science paper, in both of which Jack felt he had done well.

On the train back to Surbiton, Jack considered his next move. The start of the Outward Bound School was next Sunday and this was Monday; he needed to check his kit and obtain whatever he was short from the list of kit needed which accompanied the letter. In the event, it was only a couple of items he didn't already own, a compass and a whistle which he could easily afford without having to tip off his mother that he was heading for the army. He could probably have drawn them from the stores at school but that would have let Hiller know something was up, and although Jack felt he would probably be on Jack's side, the fewer people that knew for the time being, the better, as far as Jack was concerned.

The result of the Sandhurst entry exam came through in the post on Thursday; he had passed in all five subjects, the scores ranging from 64% for Maths to 87% for English. Mother was not best pleased; indeed, it would be true to say that she was bitterly, bitterly disappointed at Jack's success, but his dad stood by him when Jack said he was going to go to the Outward Bound School, but the atmosphere for the rest of the week was rank and his mother did not say goodbye when his dad drove him off to the station early on the Sunday morning.

# Chapter 40

Changing trains in London was a doddle, as was getting into the correct part of the train as it divided for the run along the Cambrian coast. It was only as the train was reduced to two carriages that the other passengers for the course could be identified. As to be expected, tentative conversations were struck, and friendships started. Some of the scare stories started almost immediately. Tales involving stories of horrendous heights, long marches, heavy weights, cold nights, awful food—that would indeed turn out to be true—and tales of horrendous injuries— which would also turn out to be true within one day!

On arrival at Towyn station, they were met by a loud, vociferous and pompous Sergeant who fussed around them whilst ordering them to put their kit on the 3 tonner in the car park and then to form up into three ranks, ready to march off.

The Sergeant made the mistake of shouting, "Get a move on, you horrible idle little man," at Jack. Jack took exception to this especially as he had paused to secure the back of the three tonner which would otherwise have deposited half the kit on the road.

Instead of doubling up, he stopped and said, in his loudest voice, "I am an Under Officer and as such, I outrank you; you will address me as 'sir', and I shall neither get a move on nor fall in."

The Sergeant went bright red and stood there, clearly struggling to get his brain, all two cells of it, to work. As Jack gave no indication of any intention of obeying and the Sergeant, being unable to think of any other action to take, called the parade to attention, turned them to the right and gave the order to march off. As they stepped off, a previously unseen piper blew up his pipes and set off in front of the parade. Jack simply followed on behind. They marched up through the town and about two miles to the Outward Bound School. Jack did not know what would happen, given his run in with the Sergeant, but nothing at all was said by authority, perhaps because the Sergeant didn't want to draw attention to his failure to control the situation or because he had transgressed by his shouting and treatment of the attendees, some of whom were civilians as it turned out and not subject directly to military law anyway.

The camp was a sprawl of wooden huts with a more substantial building containing the offices and the cookhouse. It was this latter building to which the squad was marched, halted, turned to the front and stood at ease. Jack simply sauntered up and joined them on the left flank.

The Sergeant disappeared into the building as the piper finished strangling the cat and marched off. Shortly, they were called to attention by a different Sergeant who then saluted a Major who emerged from the building. The Major stood them at ease and then started in on his welcome speech; it wasn't very long but it did not bode well for the future.

"Welcome to the AOBS," he said. "My name is Major Brazil, as in nut, and you will find that I am. Our aim here, by a series of tasks, difficult tasks, some of them extremely dangerous and demanding tasks, is to break you into the smallest possible pieces and then to put you back together again as much better men than you were when you first arrived here. We normally have about a 20 percent dropout rate, not counting the injured drop outs.

"You will now be split up into your respective teams (every bloody thing they did was as 'teams') and shown where you are to bunk. Dinner will be available from 1700 hours and the cookhouse entrance doors will be closed at 1705 hours. The timetable of all meals, and the training programmes are pinned up in your huts. Just one thing that is very important; you must make sure you move your bowels every morning without fail. If you don't, you will suffer for it. Carry on, Sergeant." At which the Major turned about and disappeared into the offices.

The Sergeant then proceeded to allocate them to huts and gestured in the general direction of where they were to go. The huts were not clearly marked, the numbers succumbing to the weather and the apparent lack of interest in doing anything to repaint them.

There were ten of them in Jack's section, three civvies, in fact public school boys with no experience of the army at all, a Corporal from the Regular Army who was attending the course as part of his training to become an instructor at the School, an Officer Cadet from Sandhurst and two boy soldiers who were also Regulars. The remaining six were all Army Cadet Force Cadets like Jack.

They had only been in the hut for less than 10 minutes when the Sergeant appeared, ordering them to fall in outside immediately. When they did so, they were greeted by a Lieutenant from the Parachute Regiment. He announced his name, which Jack immediately forgot, and that he was to be their training officer.

He said, "I am just going to give you a quick tour of the camp and its facilities before tea," (To the army, there was only breakfast, dinner—at lunch time—and tea, a somewhat early dinner), indicating that he was far more familiar with the correct terminology than the Training major.

At that, they were doubled off around the camp with the Lieutenant calling out designations of the various buildings as they passed them. They eventually arrived at an assault course. Here, instead of just explaining the various obstacles, he called out individuals to attempt them. Since they were wearing, for the most part, their best uniforms or civvies, it created a very bad start as each obstacle, walls swing, narrow plank over water, monkey ladder over water that had to be traversed by hanging from one's arms and swinging from bar to bar, left unpleasant deposits of filth on their clothes.

They had been given the designation Team Bravo; in front of them on the tour was Team Alpha and following behind was Team Charlie. In front of them was an enormous structure of scaffolding and ladders reaching up at least 40 to 50 feet in the air. From the top of it stretched a rope angling down to the ground, which with the ground sloping away from them gave a long length of rope before it finally was secured to a tree. The last few feet of the run in were a morass of mud where the feet of users hit the ground.

They watched the penultimate member of Team Alpha slide down and splosh into the mud. Whilst this was happening, the Lieutenant introduced this apparatus as the Death Slide, called that, he said, for obvious reasons! He picked up a hoop of rope, twisted it to form a figure of 8 and then slid his hands through to grasp either side of the crossover. "When you get to the top, throw the loop over the rope, twist, grip either side of the crossover, lower yourself so that you are just hanging at arm's length and then step off just like that guy is doing now." At that, the last member of Team Alpha stepped off the platform, swung violently forward and fell, screaming, 50 feet or so, to land on his back with an ear cringing thud, whereupon the screaming stopped. Jack was to hear that scream in his sleep for years to come.

Jack's team was hurried away from the scene but were very aware of the sound of the bell on an ambulance when it arrived about ten minutes later. The word eventually spread that he had broken his spine in the fall and would probably be paralysed for life. It was a very subdued team that went for tea that evening.

# Chapter 41

The following morning, the team were woken at 6 am and told to parade outside in swimming costume, jumper and canvas shoes immediately. They were then doubled down to the beach, about half a mile, and told to immerse themselves fully in the sea. It was bloody freezing—it was, after all, September. In response to the general mutterings, Jack included, it was made quite clear that they should think themselves lucky they were not on the course in January when the sea was really cold. This was rich coming from a Lieutenant in a warm track suit who did not, of course, deign to enter the sea himself.

They were dismissed to breakfast with a curt, "And make sure you move your bowels!"

In the event, the weather for most of the three weeks was sunny and hot although the sea was bloody freezing each time they entered it—most days, in fact. Jack hated, loathed and detested almost every single thing they did in the three weeks. The few classroom lessons, for first aid, map reading, especially—the lessons related to the areas over which they would have to trek during the 50 mile, three day test at the end of the course—were useful but as to the physical exercises, they were a nightmare. The lessons relating to knot tying were undoubtedly useful but augured badly for the amount of rope work they were to undertake.

They were taken to the Assault Course as the first exercise on the Monday morning. Wearing fatigue uniforms was fine since they were designed for dirty work, but the Death Slide was not just daunting, it was fucking terrifying! The tower now appeared to be a thousand feet high and the speed coming to the end in excess of a million miles an hour! In reality, it had not grown an inch, of course, but Sunday's accident was still too raw in their memories. The army's attitude was simply to get on with it in such circumstances; in war, people got killed as par for the course, so a little thing like a broken back was nothing to worry about. In the event, they all completed it successfully even if it was somewhat slowly and carefully; by the third week they were romping round the whole course with very little caution, such are young men.

# Chapter 42

They were taken to some high rocks on the beach and taught how to abseil. Involving as it did one individual belaying themselves to a rock and holding the rope so that another poor sod could 'walk' down the rock face with the body more or less perpendicular to the rock face, and with their back horizontal to the ground, it was not for the faint hearted. There were no fancy metal carabineers or other equipment common place in mountaineering circles today; the army just did it with ropes on the basis that that would probably be all that was available in the field.

The rope work meant forming figure of eights of rope in which to place one leg into each of the loops so formed to act as a support. It cut in to legs, rapidly cutting off circulation. Worse, if it was really incorrectly positioned or slipped, it could get the wearer screaming falsetto with no effort at all. There was a 'lowering' rope held and pulled in or fed out by the climber above as necessary, who was belayed onto a rock, or piton hammered into the rock, as the lower climber or descender moved up or down the rocks. The person lowering themselves, or abseiling, did so by feeding the rope anchoring them to the rock above through a friction loop and thus controlling their descent speed. Any imbalance between the higher anchor-man letting out the safety rope and lower climber lowering themselves resulted in high screeches from the lowered!

As Jack was climbing, the Lieutenant shouted, "Let go and fall that man." It took a while for Jack to realise that it was he who was being addressed!

"Me?"

"Yes, you let go and fall," shouted the prat again.

"I don't understand," yelled Jack whilst hanging on for grim death.

"You need to let go so that you can see how well your anchor-man is holding you and build confidence in him. Once you get up there, you will swap over and catch him, and he will trust you." Jack looked at him for a moment in sheer disbelief and then, feeling a distinct hatred for all things Parachute Regiment, let go. He fell only a foot or so before being cut to the quick by the figure eight loop in his groin. Agony wasn't the word for it. It did not instil confidence; after all, the man above was waiting for the let go; would he be so alert during a real, long climb or lower?

As if this weren't enough, as they started abseiling, it was to discover that as they descended the rock face they were descending directly over a triangular cave mouth! Since their position on top of the rocks had been dictated by their Trainer, he must have known that they would be descending into this danger. It meant that the feet became further and further apart as the cave widened out until it became impossible to progress further. Shouted instructions made it clear that the only way to progress was to bring the legs together whilst at the same time letting out sufficient rope so that the individual could drop some feet and swing into the cave, missing splattering their head on the rock at the top of the cave whilst so doing. The army's position was that you might just come upon such a situation 'in the field' and therefore the training was to cover that.

Jack's position was that they were the rawest climbers you could find, Jack hadn't even ever stepped off a high kerb, and to subject them to such advanced climbing from the word go was inappropriate in the extreme! It wasn't helped by the fact that when Jack swung forward, he wasn't far enough down to entirely miss the peak of the cave and he smashed both wrists into the rock. The right one was the worst with a cut and sprain making it difficult to hold anything. It was examined at the Medical Centre and firmly strapped up. Two Aspirins completed the treatment—no X-ray or examination by a Doctor, just an Other Rank Medic to provide the treatment.

Unfortunately, then it got worse! They were taken after only a couple of days training to Snowdonia—Jack never did find out exactly where—but they were taken to a massive, vertical rock face rising hundreds of feet in the air. The prat of a Lieutenant announced that they were to climb that. Jack, craning his neck right back, looked up at it incredulously and then to the Lieutenant. He, ignoring the looks of the entire team, then announced that this was classified as extremely severe, in the mountaineering text book, but given their performance on the beach, he was sure they would have no problems completing it!

The climb for Jack was an absolute nightmare—the incident on the Death Slide paled away to nothing compared to the fear generated by it. Initially, Jack climbed last of three in his particular sub-section of the team, made up of one of the public schoolboys, Algernon by name, you couldn't make it up, and a boy soldier, inevitably, Dusty, based on his surname of Miller. Climbing first was Algernon (he flatly refused to answer to Algy) then Dusty and finally Jack. Jack was still suffering with his wrist and found grasping for a handhold with his right hand extremely painful and difficult; effectively, he was having to climb with only three strong points, both feet and his left hand and a severely limited right hand. This injury was in fact to bother him from time to time throughout the rest of his life.

There was no way to avoid it without showing craven, so off they started. The Mad Major made a dramatic entrance leaping around the rocks and calling out to Jack when he, Jack, was about two hundred feet up. They had been taught that they should always have three points of stable anchor whilst the remaining unanchored limb moved upwards to seek another point to grasp or stand on depending whether it was a leg or an arm which was moving. They were also supposed to be pushed out from the rock face with clear daylight between their body and the rock face.

Jack drew the line at this; he wanted to hug the rock and even grip it with his teeth if the opportunity presented. This would not do for the Mad Major.

He appeared a few feet to the side of Jack to announce, "That man there with the purple jumper, push yourself off from the wall and adopt the posture you have been told." Jack couldn't pretend that he hadn't heard, and he couldn't avoid the fact that he had a very purple jumper tied around his waist. Up until then, he had loved that jumper but how quickly love turns to hate! It was a sunny, hot day, as it was to be for almost all of the course, and, although he should have been wearing an army pullover, the issue one he had been given was thin, worn and tatty in the extreme and expecting it to be cold in the mountains, he had worn his thick purple one.

Now that decision came back to haunt him, both because with the exertion of climbing he was boiling hot and had had to cling on precariously whilst removing it and tying it around his waist and because it had drawn the Mad Major to him like a fly to shit.

Once he had adopted the position, the Major called out, "That's it, perfect, that jumper shows up lovely against the green grey of the rocks; all the others don't stand out with their green uniforms, but we'll use this one for training at the camp as an example of the correct stance to adopt whilst climbing. You did move your bowels this morning, didn't you?" and, without waiting for an answer and having taken his photos, off he bounded across the rocks like a mountain goat with no ropes, no support just driven by insanity, as far as Jack was concerned. Jack obtained copies of the photos taken of him, but only black and white ones as coloured ones cost too much. He was therefore unable to show the purple jumper, but he was able to point to the bandage on his right wrist which showed up clearly in the photos.

Then it got worse! Hundreds of feet up, clinging to the rock face as hard as he could, it was to hear the prat, by this time Jack was thinking of him as the Great Prat when considering him in polite language—when he lapsed into Anglo Saxon, it was to think of him as a right cunt whose parents had obviously only met once and that briefly in a back alley—ordered them to change their order of climbing, with Algernon to drop down to climbing number three, Dusty to move up to lead and Jack to number two.

Whilst the element of being brought up by the climber above was still the same, having someone below to bring up added two further problems. The first, obvious, was that you had to belay to somewhere secure to bring up the lower climber. The second was that you had to look down to see how he was climbing and to be ready to take his weight should he fall. So far, Jack had managed to avoid looking down—wasn't that one of the primary rules, 'don't look down', one to which Jack was very happy to adhere. Now, he couldn't avoid it and keeping from succumbing to the instant dizziness it created took every last ounce of his being to carry on. Jack didn't think it could possibly get any worse, but it did!

After they had climbed for a further half hour or so, the Great Cunt—Jack was running out of expletives to describe the Lieutenant, the course and the army—called to them to change order again so that Jack was now the lead climber. It was only as he started in the lead that he realised that things were very much worse. As the lead, he had no one above him to reel in the rope and hold him if he fell! Merde, merde and double merde. Once he had climbed some 10 feet or so, he was told to hammer in a piton and loop his rope down to the second climber through that. The idea being that, with a piton every 10 feet or so, should he fall, the most he would fall would be 10 feet with the rope through the piton being secured from below by the second climber. It was a very big trust that the piton would not be jerked out of the rock by the sudden pull on it caused by the falling lead climber. Jack made sure that each piton was really, really hammered home!

In the event, Jack reached the top and crawled, literally, over the rim and lay there trembling and shaking in every limb. He was covered in sweat, panting and very grateful to all supernatural entities out there that he had made it. He didn't know if any of them had had any influence on his arriving safely at the top but he wasn't prepared to take the risk of offending any of them by not thanking them profusely. Roused from his reverie by a voice from below calling out, "Climbing now," Jack had to call, "No," as he had not, as yet, belayed to anything to allow him to bring up the next climber safely. This he did by belaying around a large boulder, and shortly, Algernon appeared over the rim. He in turn belayed on and brought up Dusty and the three of them lay there panting with their muscles afire. The total climb had taken over four hours and the unnatural stances involved in the climb had taken a severe toll of their muscles.

As Jack recovered his breath, he started to become more aware of his surroundings. The cliff face they had climbed was sharply curved. Further around the curve was parked a Morris Minor. Sitting by it, obviously having a picnic, were a little old couple at a collapsible table with primus stove, kettle and teapot much in evidence. The lady called out, "We've been watching you climbing all morning and were absolutely amazed at how brave you are."

With neither Algernon nor Dusty replying, it was left to Jack to make a suitably modest response. Before the conversation could progress further and perhaps result in a scrounged cup of tea, the Lieutenant appeared, "Well done, you chaps. There's some food laid on back down at the car park. You can either climb back down the face or make your way back down this track. The choice is yours."

Jack's response was instantaneous; climbing down would clearly take immense effort again, be bloody dangerous and take hours in time so it was a no brainer to say, "We'll go down the track, sir, thank you." And at that, Jack set off before the easy choice was removed, that being the army way. As they strolled, an easy stroll down the dirt road, it was a dead cert that it was easy, a little Morris Minor had driven up it! From this episode, Jack was to adopt an attitude that was to last the rest of his life. Climbing up had taken just over four hours; walking back down took less than 15 minutes. Why do things the hard way if there was an easy one? Surely, we had been given a brain, so we should use it. If you wanted to get to the top of a bloody mountain, 'because it was there' why not go by helicopter? People who chose to do things the hard way were clearly lacking in grey matter. They had risked life and limb for four fucking hours when they could have strolled to the top in 15 minutes at no risk whatsoever. Yes, yes, he knew all about Monte Casino and all the other mountain battles involving the troops having to climb all over the place but that was done then because there was no alternative—if there was one, take it!

After dinner, stale sandwiches and cold tea, of course, the Lieutenant announced that they had actually completed the climb quicker than expected so that there were four hours to fill before the arrival of the truck to take them back to the camp; so those who wanted to could come with him for more climbing practice, an easy one, just along the valley, or they could repeat the morning's climb again. Those who didn't want to could stay there and be idle. An army way of saying, stay here at your peril, you idle soldier you!

Jack didn't care. He knew that there was no more rock climbing scheduled in the programme allied to which the complete fatuousness of doing things the hard way, and the sheer terror in so doing meant that Jack was not going to climb even a high kerb ever again unless he could not avoid it. The Regular Corporal leapt to his feet and cried, "I will, sir, I will." If he wanted to be an instructor there, he had no option, of course. Jack was dismayed to see all the others of the team, one by one, stand up and join him. Jack didn't move, annoyed at the lack of courage of his team

126

mates to resist the moral blackmail, and the stupidity of effort wasted and fear engendered by that four-hour climb.

"You're not frightened are you Hughes," asked the Great Cunt (GC).

"Sir, I have just climbed for four hours, a climb that is described as extremely severe in the mountaineers' handbook; I have nothing to prove to you or to myself. I have done it, so well in fact that the Training Major has taken photos of my climbing posture. So I am merely taking up your offer to stay here. As I am sure you know, the army says never to stand when you can sit, never to sit when you can lie down and never be awake if you can be asleep. Further, it is a maxim never to volunteer. Given what you are putting us through, I consider it merely prudent to store up some energy, sir."

The GC looked at him astounded. Those of the team behind him and thus outside his sight grinned broadly. The Corporal on the other hand looked daggers at him. This bothered Jack not a jot; he might be Regular Army, but he was only a Corporal and Jack had been a Sergeant and was now a Cadet Under Officer. Further, as a Sergeant, he had commanded a platoon in a major exercise with the TA and against the Royal Marines; a Corporal who had, at the most, commanded a Section, was not something to be bothered about. Shouting loudly to the rest of the team, the GC lead them off without a word or further glance at Jack. Jack considered what to do, should he wander up the track and try to scrounge that cup of tea or should he just take his own advice and lie down and have a zzz? Zzz won.

# Chapter 43

They returned to Towyn in time for tea—not much better than the dinner. The improved quality of army messing for a regular army had clearly not made it to the AOBS, although it would be fair to say that there was ample food; it was just so overcooked, tasteless and unpleasant.

They spent the next couple of days mainly in classroom work, punctuated by excursions to the assault course just in case they were getting too idle. Being the army, some of the time was spent learning first aid—days after they might have needed it!

They also spent quite a lot of time on map reading. As the lessons progressed, it became apparent that one of their number was never going to make a map reader. He was one of the other Army Cadets with no rank even though he was at least 17 years old. As he gave answers to the problems set, the extent of his incompetence was exposed. Where the task had been to work out the bearing needed to be followed to get from point A to point B, all of his bearings were reversed, that is he quoted bearings from B to A rather than towards B, meaning that anyone attempting to follow the bearings would disappear in the exact opposite direction!

Both Jack and the regular Corporal offered him extra lessons from themselves in the evening, but the offers were curtly refused. No one could pronounce his name, it being made up almost entirely of consonants without a vowel to be seen. Consequently, he became the wnk—pronounced 'wunk'.

He was also showing poor performances on all the physical activities, especially the assault course, seemingly being unable to cross any high obstacle, the eight-foot wall, the monkey ladder over water, all were all impossible for him. He wasn't overweight, he didn't seem to be weak, he seemed to be able but just didn't seem to be able to summon up the effort so that he simply failed at everything. As for his ability to pack and carry a knapsack, he took no notice of the instruction from the staff as to how to make best use of the space but bunged everything in and then, lacking space, tied his mess tins and enamel mug to the outside of the knapsack with his spare socks so that his progression was marked by a doleful clanking and flapping at every step.

Jack was more and more concerned. He knew that the culmination of the course was a 50-mile hike through the mountains in Mid Wales which had to be completed within 60 hours or any team not achieving it would have to repeat the distance. The Wunk would be a liability. Jack determined to make sure that the Wunk would not be in his section.

Three days after their return from Snowdonia, it was announced that there was a change to the programme and that they were going to be taken to the Llanberis Pass the next day so that they could walk the Snowdon Horseshoe. This was to be regarded as a reward for their hard work so far and would be just a pleasant walk of about seven or eight miles along the top of the world, or at least Wales.

They all discovered the hard way that they were being lied to again. Dropped off at a car park, the GC led off on a path that curved out of sight. Within only a few yards, they found themselves ascending a steep climb. Within minutes, they were panting. The pace was remorseless, and it wasn't long before the weaker team members were starting to lag. Jack thought it was quite a relief to hear the clanking Wunk gradually fade away. The GC didn't! He turned to Jack and the Corporal and said, "Get back there and chase them up; no one is allowed to lag, we've a full day ahead of us, and we've only just got started."

Alternately shouting, dragging and pushing, the two of them harassed the Wunk and the other laggards so that they gradually caught up with the rest of the team. Although the GC lowered the pace slightly, the climbs were a torture and the descents even worse, punishing the fronts of the thighs which were not used to downhill walking.

The Snowdon Horseshoe was so called because if you looked at an Ordnance Survey map of the Snowdon range from above the mountains making up the range curved like a horseshoe. In years to come, walking the Horseshoe was to become a popular mountain walk but most doing it would ride the steam train to the summit of Snowdon and then walk down the easier half. They were scheduled to walk the complete horseshoe.

Jack was soon asking himself, why walk—they were scrambling up and down slopes of loose rock, they were having to use hands and feet to climb with quite severe drops threatening the life of anyone who slipped. Jack was sweating profusely, not from the effort which was nevertheless considerable, but from fear of the heights they were scrabbling at. Then it got worse.

They had been climbing solidly for more than two hours with very little forward visibility as the ground they were climbing kept curving away from them. However, eventually, the GC stopped at a small open spot and waited for the team to catch up with him. Jack, the Corporal and the Wunk were inevitably the last to arrive.

"There we have Crib Goch. The peak is just over 3000 feet high, and it is no more than 5 inches wide along the ridge, or arête as it is technically called. We are going to walk across it."

Jack couldn't believe what he was looking at. The top of Crib Goch stretched away before them. The ridge, running in roughly a straight line away from them, was about 150 yards long. It wasn't completely even but undulated by perhaps as much as 10 feet. He could see a footpath of sorts running right along the top. The sides of the mountain fell away steeply, one side being officially described as a precipice, so that if one looked down, there was no ground beneath the path until the precipice swelled out nearly 2000 feet below. A fall would mean death. Jack was looking at it and thinking this cannot be true, I'm dreaming and having the mother of all nightmares. Please, please let it be a nightmare.

At that, he was brought back to reality when the GC started talking again.

"You may be able to see on the side of the ridge a foot path about three feet from the summit. Most walkers walk along that and hold the top of the ridge as a hand hold as they traverse the ridge. They are a bunch of softies. We are not softies; we are the army. We are going to prove we are real men and walk across the top of the ridge. We will not be roped together because we didn't bring a rope, and we didn't bring a rope because there is nowhere to belay to anyway. I will go first to show how easy it is and will be watching for any wimp who does not walk the top. Just think the bragging rights you will have to say, 'I walked the crest of Crib Goch.' Last course, a pupil fell, and an instructor tried to catch up with him to prevent him falling to his death. He failed, and they both died. You had better take great care because, if you fall, I have no intention of trying to catch you." At that, he took off across the top of the ridge. Quick to follow was the Corporal and then far more slowly and reluctantly, the rest of them, with the Wunk clanking on last of all.

What followed was the most terrifying, most awful, most frightening few minutes of Jack's life including being shot at and the target of grenades in Aden and various serious incidents to come in Northern Ireland. It took probably less than ten minutes to cross the ridge, but every fibre of his being was shaking and cringing during it. Once started, there was no way back and so uneven was the ridge that it was impossible to traverse it without looking down to see where to place one's feet. So, looking down meant one could not avoid seeing the precipice on one side and the very, very steep fall away on the other side. Sweating, shaking and trembling, Jack eventually made it across. The small area in which they congregated was only just sufficient to hold the team as it assembled. Watching the Wunk cross was almost as frightening as crossing oneself; he was constantly teetering from side to side and recovering with much waving of his arms and clanking of his kit. He arrived looking as white as a sheet with sweat pouring from his brow and, on leaving the ridge, a great big smile on his face.

Jack thought, *God, I hope I don't look as frightened as that.* The GC then spoke, "Well done, everyone. I bet you all enjoyed that." Jack looked at him in sheer disbelief. His thoughts must have shown clearly on his face because the GC then said, "What's the matter, Cadet Under Officer? You don't look as though you agree with me."

Jack thought very carefully of the Lord Lieutenant who had arranged for him to be there, his school Cadet Force Captain and not least his mum who had not wanted him to come on the course and he said, "Sir, at each stage as I have progressed through the NCO ranks and especially as a Cadet Under Officer, I have had it stressed to me that one day, I might have to send men into battle knowing that some of them would die, and I should only do this having taken the greatest care to ensure that the fewest number were killed. Taking care of them was my primary duty. Could you please explain to me why we were made to cross that arête in the most dangerous way possible when there was a far safer path, just a few feet from the top, where we could have used the arête as a guiding hand rail; that seems to me to have been an utterly unnecessary risk but perhaps you can explain it, sir?"

As he said it and watched the colour mount from the GC's collar to suffuse his whole face, Jack thought perhaps I should not have said that, but I did enjoy it and there goes any hope I might have had of passing the course but fuck him, he isn't just the Great Cunt, he's the Fucking Great Cunt and FGC was his designation thereafter. Jack stood there waiting for the explosion, but it did not come. Instead, the FGC turned to the Corporal and said, "You lead, Corporal, just follow the path until we reach the railway line, then someone else can take the lead."

# Chapter 44

As he had predicted, they arrived at the railway line after a few hundred yards of quite hard going but with nothing like the terror of Crib Goch. Running alongside the rack and pinion railway line of the Snowdon Railway was the normal walkers' footpath to the summit. As they walked along, the FGC took the lead again and after a short walk, led them on as the space between the railway line and the apparent edge to the left of the ground could be seen getting closer to them. In fact, they were approaching another cliff edge with the distance between the railway line and the cliff edge not being much more than 15 to 20 yards—a terribly narrow and inadequate gap to Jack's way of thinking. This time, looking down, they could see the road through Llanberis Pass twisting away into the distance.

"Isn't that a fantastic view," he said. "You are very lucky; it's not normally as clear as this; normally, we are in cloud at this point and you can't see a hand in front of your face. In fact, it is sometimes so bad you can't see the edge and are in very great danger of walking off the edge."

Jack did think it was a very fantastic view but would very much have preferred to have looked at it from the train rather than the very edge!

They continued toiling upwards towards the train station and café at the top of Snowdon. They were not, however, allowed into the café until they had scrambled up past the cafe for the final 30 or 40 feet to the very summit.

"You must reach every summit of the Horseshoe to have completed the walk properly; you have 30 minutes to get a drink or whatever before we leave for the second half of the Horseshoe," called out the FGC as he disappeared into the café.

By the time they had made it to the top, squeezing between all the tourists, and made it back down to the café, another train had disgorged its passengers who had formed such a long queue that it took 25 minutes for Jack to be served, meaning he had to take his cup of tea and pie with him when they set off.

The rest of the Horseshoe passed in a blur of toiling upwards and scrambling down from the remaining peaks until, utterly shagged, he staggered into the car park and the end of the Horseshoe where the three tonner was waiting to take them back to the School. As the team rode in the back, the FGC, of course, rode up front in the cab with the driver; they discussed the day. All of the team, bar the Corporal, commented favourably on Jack's comment about officers taking care of their soldiers. The Corporal insisted that they should all feel very proud of the fact that they had completed it the hard way. Jack said, "I'm not proud; I'm ashamed I didn't have the courage to tell him to get stuffed and walk across the lower path. In fact, if I had known what we were going to face I wish I would have had the guts to."

The next few days were spent in the classroom being taught map-reading; something Jack didn't need, from the point of view of how to do it, but as they were using maps of the Brecon Beacons, which Jack knew would be where they would be carrying out their 50-mile trek, any tips which could be picked up were worth having.

The names of the Sections, three to each of two Sections and one of four, were posted up two days before the trek. As Jack had dreaded, he was teamed up with the Wank (the name had evolved naturally to describe him, so useless was he) and two boy soldiers. Jack could not think of how to get rid of the Wank without drawing attention to the fact that he wanted to get rid of him and did not want him in the team—sacrilege, as the team was all. The day before the trek, the Wank's name was crossed off the list. Enquiries elicited nothing of use but the fact that his bed space was empty seemed to indicate that he had gone completely from the course.

It wasn't until the second day of trekking that the boy soldiers let out that they had cornered him in the latrines and suggested that if he didn't want to fall off one of the mountains he would be climbing, he would be better off resigning from the course and going home! Since neither of them would be the sort of lad you would want your teenage daughter to bring home as her new boyfriend, Jack could well understand that a threat with menaces from them would be taken very seriously!

The trek, equivalent to the Duke of Edinburgh's Gold Award, which had recently been introduced but done in much less time and designed to be as hard as possible, proved to be as unpleasant as they expected. They had to check into map reference points, sign their names to prove that they had all been there—previous course members had taken it in turns to send one of the team up to the checkpoint, all on the tops of mountains, of course, to sign them in. This was definitely not allowed; everyone had to suffer the pain.

Climbing up to each point, carrying as they were all their camping kit and three days' food, was tiring in the extreme. Worse, however, was coming down. The thigh muscles particularly suffered with the strain of balance and taking the full weight as they took each step downwards.

The second day involved climbing to the top of Cader Idris, the highest mountain in the Beacons. Forming a horseshoe shape, as in the Snowdon Horseshoe range, but made up of just the one mountain, Cader was softer than Crib Goch but still contained a mass of scree slopes, boggy areas, sheer faces and lots and lots of hard going. They reached the point on the summit for which they were aiming about noon and, having signed in and obtained the reference grid for the next check-in point, they stopped for a hurriedly snatched lunch and a long drink. As they set off down, they came to a very steep grassy slope. With Jack leading, they had only gone a few paces when there was a crash and a cry behind him. He turned around to see Jim, the smaller of the two boy soldiers, come zooming past him sliding on his arse on the damp grass slope. Within seconds, he was miles ahead down the slope and it only took moments for Jack and Ted to drop onto their arses and slide after him.

Jack supposed that they were lucky that Cader Idris was, for the main part, a rocky and scree covered mountain; had there been any of those rocks protruding through the grass, then the three of them would have been singing soprano for the rest of their lives. As it was, they arrived breathless and laughing several hundred feet lower with simply a sore arse each for a few days.

132

When they checked in at the next checkpoint, a Land Rover with a permanent staff member sat in its shade, they showed their check sheet which clearly showed them as having booked in at the point on top of Cader Idris only 20 minutes before. This drew extreme suspicion as the time from top to bottom should have been about an hour and a half. As there was never a staff member at any of the points on the various mountain tops, it was sufficient for someone to place the blank record sheet at the commencement of the exercise and collect them at the end; that way, they only had to climb to the top twice saving climbing twice a day for the three days; it was the poor sods on the course who had to climb up and down every bloody mountain in sight and some of them twice!

Subsequent checks showed them checking into the valley bottom prior to the Cader Idris checkpoint with a time verified by another member of staff; although their time at the top was unverifiable, their presence there was verifiable by their three signatures on the record sheet at the top and their time at the valley bottom, following the bottom slide, was equally verifiable. However the staff looked at it, they could not challenge the time from valley bottom to valley bottom and their time was to remain a record until the AOBS closed years later.

As they were ahead of schedule, they decided to carry on to the next checkpoint, on top of a mountain, of course, giving them a head start on the final leg to the finish the next morning. Unfortunately, the next check-in point was back on the top of Cader but way along the crest from the previous way point. Making their way back up, at an angle to their previous descent, was a relentless struggle of effort, effort and effort to climb the never-ending mountain. Not for them the use of the walkers' footpaths, they had to follow the compass bearing they had been given as to the location of the next check-in point and that bearing took them over some of the worst terrain possible; some of it so vertical or boggy that they simply had to detour and then, having passed the obstacle, do their best to pick up the bearing line on the other side of the obstacle.

Eventually, they found the checkpoint, a post driven into the ground with an upturned empty tin tied to it with the record log stuck up inside it. The ground around it was reasonably flat, certainly flat enough to pitch their two bivouac tents and with what must have been one of the most fantastic views one could ever find. The air was crystal clear, and they could see for miles down into the valleys and away to the sea in one direction and the Snowdon range in another.

That night, the weather broke, or rather, the world was split asunder. Torrential rain, blowing more horizontally than vertically, with thunder and lightning crashing all around woke them and kept them awake for the rest of the night. The thunder eventually passed but the rain obviously had a duty to make up for the previous almost three weeks when there had been none, and it just bucketed down.

Like all experienced campers, they had dug water run-off channels around their tents, but these were simply overwhelmed, and the water flooded into the tents. Jack, at least, on his own, was able to avoid touching the roof of his tent for to do so meant water then made its way through the very old and very thin canvas where it had been touched. The two boy soldiers were not so lucky as, although designed to be two-man tents, they were very small and avoiding touching the canvas was almost impossible. Consequently, they had water dripping down from the roof and water flooding in from underneath; Jack only had it flooding in from underneath, but in reality, he was just as soaked as the other two. The only consolation was that at least they did not blow away, a wonder given the wind strength, and they did have at least some shelter from the driving rain.

Breakfast was cold food and a small mug of hot tea. A hot breakfast was impossible to produce in the prevailing conditions and all three of them were only too pleased to pack up and get off the mountain top as quick as possible. There was, however, a problem. Whereas the evening before they had benefitted from the most fantastic visibility, now they were in cloud in a world of murk and very, very poor visibility. Literally, they could not see more than five or six feet. Travelling in such conditions would be hazardous in the extreme but they had no option, they had to get off the mountain and quickly, to finish the trek in time and thus pass the course.

Jack arranged for Jim to walk alongside him as he had to concentrate on reading the compass to ensure they didn't deviate from the bearing whilst Jim watched out for the ground ahead of them for any dangers. As it happened, Jack and Jim both spotted that the ground immediately ahead of them disappeared, not into the mirk, but literally, it wasn't there anymore; careful exploration showed they were teetering on the top of a precipice with no view of the bottom. They could not climb down so their only choices were to follow the top to the left or the right until they found a passable route down. Careful scrutinising of the map was of no help. They could not identify any such precipice on the line of the bearing they were to follow on the map. This could be because the map was faulty, their map reading was faulty, their following of the bearing shown by the compass was faulty or all three! What they could not assume was that the compass itself was faulty as there had been strong emphasis, during the map-reading classes, that they should always trust their compass and the map; that left them with that they had somehow, despite their care, wandered off the correct bearing. It could be, of course, that they were intended to have to deal with the precipice—it could certainly be assumed where the FGC was responsible for setting the routes.

Since they did not know where they were, they could not identify properly on the map the precipice. Two bunchings of the contour lines on the map showed the possibility of two precipices but as one was to the left of their bearing line and one was to the right, that was no great help! As far as they could tell, the ground to the left seemed to be sloping downwards slightly whilst that to the right seemed to be sloping ever so slightly upwards and it was that that settled it. They wanted to get down so to the left it was.

The slope increased markedly as they walked, and they were soon having to proceed with extreme caution as the ground was very steep, so much so that they had to clutch at protruding rocks while they carefully sought footholds for their feet. Soon they were descending almost vertically, and Jack started to become very frightened. Cursing inwardly at the bloody school, the bloody staff and especially the bloody Training Major, Jack was about to suggest that they really ought to climb back up since this was becoming bloody dangerous when the visibility cleared for just an instant and enough for Jack to see that they were only about 10 to 15 feet above a scree slope. They had done some scree running in the early days of the course, dangerous but exhilarating, and it was infinitely preferable to the wall they were climbing down even if they were carrying substantial packs rather than unencumbered as on their earlier foray.

Sliding and scrambling, they eventually made their way off the scree slope into a valley bottom, no scree running this time with a 40+ lb rucksacks on their backs, only too ready to pitch them forward into oblivion. Running along the valley bottom was a track way made up of cart tracks in the grass and rocks which showed little recent usage; in some places, it was almost entirely overgrown. Following downwards as their best policy, they turned left and followed the track downhill; they had only followed it for a couple of hundred yards when they came to a huddle of ruined cottages. Clearly, this had been some sort of habitation for people whose work was somewhere up the track they had just come down. By now, Jack was so wet and cold that he couldn't care less what it was so long as they could identify it on the map. They couldn't. But this old track had to come out somewhere, so they simply followed it. As they walked steadily downwards so they emerged from the cloud and although they were still in rain they could now start to make out some of the scenery but not enough for it to provide a clear idea of where they were. After about a mile, they reached a metalled road but there were no road signs to indicate which road it was or where it went to or came from. Once again, they decided to follow the road to the left as this seemed to slope downwards; they hoped desperately that this was not the wrong way because if it was, it would mean trogging all the way back uphill to get to their destination. After something over two miles, they reached a road with a number and a sign post indicating Dolgellau in one direction. That was sufficient for them to locate themselves fairly accurately as being something over four miles from where their compass bearing crossed the main road where a car park was indicated on the map and likely to be the final check point. They had exactly an hour to make it before their completion time was up. Normal walking pace is about three miles per hour and fast walking about four, depending on the freshness of the walkers and the terrain which had to be traversed. They set off smartly enough, but their wet clothes, heavy packs and insufficient breakfast soon started to take their toll. After two miles, Jack was having to cajole and drive the two boy soldiers in turn. The last mile was nothing but agony of muscles and will to reach the finish which was, of course, uphill. But make it they did, only by five minutes and they were only one of three patrols to do so. The other six teams failed by as much as six hours and worried permanent staff had started to think in terms of search parties when the last team staggered down from the mountains. Fortunately, those who had finished were taken back to camp after waiting around, cold and shivering in the back of a three tonner, for only about an hour; any longer and, as they were all wet through, they would all have been going down with pneumonia or worse.

Back at camp, it was all just a sorting out and cleaning of kit and then placing it in the drying rooms ready to hand it all back in the next day, their penultimate one at the School. That day was a leisurely one, handing in the kit and swapping yarns with the other patrols as to what had happened to them with each retelling of the yarns increasing the exaggerations of difficulties overcome and heroic actions carried out.

In the midst of it all, Jack was a little surprised to be approached, a bit bashfully, by the two boy soldiers. Jim, prodded by his confrere, cleared his throat and said, "Sir, we just want to say thanks for your leadership on the hike and for pushing and carrying us the last few miles on the trek. We know that without you, we would not have made it; we would have been lost in the mountains and failed to reach the final RV in time. Because we did, we can expect automatic promotion back at the Apprentices' College and this will go with us into man service. So, thanks a lot."

Jack was more than nonplussed at this. He had not expected that. All he could think of to say immediately was, "Well, thanks. All I did was shout at you a bit, you carried the kit and yourselves to the finish, so well done both of you. Good luck with your careers in the army, and who knows we might meet up again some time." They never did meet but, ironically, Jack was to spend a period of time as a Platoon Commander in a Boys' Regiment some years later.

At 1600 hours, they were all assembled in the main lecture hall to be debriefed by the Mad Major. He opened by congratulating them for completing the course, they had suffered slightly less than a 10% drop out which was better than average, but only three patrols had reached the RV in time and passed the course. This was a much lower average than normal or expected and could probably be put down to the appalling weather on the last day, but this was no excuse because, in war, you had to succeed whatever the weather. The members of the three successful patrols were called forward and handed their certificates and reports. The remaining reports were just left by the door for their recipients to claim them.

It was proof positive, if it were needed, that success was rewarded and failure punished. His final words were to remain with Jack for a long time, "…and finally, remember to move your bowels every day; it will always stand you in good stead." *How fucking stupid*, thought Jack, setting him on the road to conviction that the army valued muscle and stupidity rather than mind and efficiency. For the rest of his days, Jack could not value the stupidity of climbing to the tops of mountains by the most difficult and arduous routes when their existed perfectly good foot paths which could have been used. And as for taking unacceptable risks like those on Crib Goch, that was for the mentally challenged. Yes, of course, there might be times when risks had to be taken, especially in war, but taking risks for the sake of risks and hazarding the lives of soldiers for some sort of ephemeral, 'I did it' was just plain stupid when lives were unnecessarily put at risk. And as for climbing a mountain, 'because it was there' when a helicopter was the obvious solution if it was actually necessary to get to the top was simply an illustration that those so doing were seriously challenged in the brain cells department.

Their Patrol Leader, the FGC, had a brief chat and shook hands with them all, wishing them successful careers in the future. Whilst he had a brief conversation with each of them, Jack was omitted, receiving only the briefest of handshakes before he moved on to speak to the next man.

The following morning, they were fell in expecting to have to march to the station even though the rain was still sheeting down. Just as the rain was starting to seep through their clothing, a three tonner turned up and they were all ordered aboard, much to their relief. The station was only a few minutes away in the three-tonner, but even so, it was a relief to jump off and crowd into the waiting room.

Much as on their way there, but in reverse, numbers left the train at various junctions to disperse to various destinations all over the country. Once Jack was on his own, he opened the report they had each been handed by the Mad Major and read it. It didn't say anything bad in the sense of no direct criticisms but neither did it say anything very good, despite the two boy soldiers stressing to the Lieutenant that their success had been all down to Jack. It was to be years before Jack became familiar with the expression damning with faint praise, for this is what the Para Lieutenant had done. In fact, it never had any effect on Jack, because, although they had been told to hand their reports to their commanding officers, Jack's was the School Platoon Captain, Captain Hiller, and as he never knew the report existed, he never missed it when Jack simply destroyed it.

The Training Major, at the start of the course, had said that their aim was to break each course member down to their smallest parts and then rebuild them into much better men than they had been at the start of the course. Jack reflected on this. Some had been so broken down that they had elected to leave. The aim with them had clearly not been achieved. Only a small percentage of the course had actually achieved a pass. Did that mean that those who had not completed the 50 miles in the time set were failures? Not in Jack's opinion. To describe them as failures when their whole lives were before them, when many of them would go on to achieve success in their lives either in the army or out of it, was considerably lacking in acumen. To describe those who had achieved the target as succeeders was only to measure physical fitness, mental fitness, map-reading ability and luck. Success in life was so very much more than that, the measure was largely meaningless. The one item that Jack took forward and practiced mercilessly in the future was not the concept of the importance of team work but the importance of identifying weak links and getting rid of them at the first opportunity. Had the two boy soldiers not 'persuaded' the Wank to leave the course, they would have failed the trek. He was too weak physically, he lacked the mental stamina to push himself and the nature of the task being what it was, Jack and the other two would not have been able to get him to the finish on time whatever they did. Was this the real lesson they were supposed to learn? Jack didn't think so; too much of the emphasis had been on team spirit, team working and team success. Nothing whatsoever had been said about what if a team member wasn't up to it. Although nothing had been said, in actual practice, when someone was failing, it was very evident they disappeared from the course. It seemed that they preached one thing but practiced another. Allied to their preference for muscle over brain, Jack came away mightily unimpressed with the AOBS, its staff and its operation. The only lesson he took from it, if lesson it was, was the one to get rid of any weak link, a policy he was to follow for the rest of his life.

# Chapter 45

His parents were astonished by what he had done. He took back with him a handful of photos of him climbing, abseiling and canoeing. He did nothing to diminish the reputation of the AOBS' reputation for toughness but he did, on occasions over the years, do as much as he could to denigrate its claims to build better team players—particularly when a number of civilian schools were set up, mainly by ex-service personnel, making extraordinary claims for the value of their courses.

He returned on the 21st and was due to join the army before the 30th September, so his time was limited but extremely busy. He returned to school on the 22nd to return all his Cadet Force kit and say his good byes. He was very surprised and hurt to be refused an opportunity to speak to the Head Master. His request was answered by the School Secretary whose words, "He feels ashamed that a boy from this school should join the army as a Private Soldier and so will not speak to you," were to rankle with Jack for years until he was able to take revenge in an entirely unexpected fashion. It was also an entirely stupid thing to say as his was very much a run-of-the-mill county grammar school with no particular claim to fame or prestige.

The reception from fellow pupils was also unpleasant, surprising him far more than that of the Headmaster, they seemed to be taking their lead from the Head, either that, or they were simply sycophantic. The only ones who seemed to be genuinely pleased were Paul and Captain Hiller who wished him every success and bade him keep in touch.

On the 23rd, he had to attend for a medical at the Milbank Army Hospital in London. His appointment was for 1000 hrs, so he arrived at 0945. He wasn't seen and started on until 1030 hours; he was already familiar with the army passion for hurry up and wait. They finished the various tests just before 1300 hrs, and he was told to return at 1400 hrs when he would receive the results. He sat around the waiting room until 1445 hrs when he was called in to see a Medical Corps full Colonel. It became apparent quite quickly that the Colonel had imbibed more than freely of a liquid lunch. His words, blurred and disjointed, seemed to say, once he had found Jack's file which was on his desk right in front of him, "Yes, excellent results. A1. Fit for paratroops; I'm sure they'll be very glad to get you."

Jack was horrified. There was no way on God's earth that he was going to join that lot of idiots even if it meant no commission. As he exited the room, he was met by a Sergeant who handed him a sealed letter. He told Jack he was to hand it in at the Recruiting Office when he signed on. He also asked, "Did he say you were fit for paratroops?"

"Yes," said Jack, "he did."

"Don't worry about that," said the Sergeant, "he says that to everyone once he's had a few, even those who've failed the tests." Jack thanked him and left.

He went into the Army Recruiting Office in Surbiton the following morning, introduced himself and explained he wanted to arrange to sign on as a Potential Officer Cadet the following Monday, the 29th. The Recruiting Sergeant to whom he spoke had never heard of the scheme and, taking Jack's letter from the Surrey Lord Lieutenant from him, disappeared into an inner office. It was a good 20 minutes before he reappeared with a Captain from the Royal Engineers who turned out to be the Commanding Officer of the shop, for that is what it was.

He introduced himself and explained that they were not familiar with this particular enlistment, but they would be by the time he returned on the following Monday. He explained that Jack would have to fill in some paper work and take an oath to serve Her Majesty, the Queen—this was referred to as attestation, and his parents could be present when he took the oath if he wished. Jack's father would also have to sign that he agreed to Jack enlisting.

He also said that they could make a start now getting basic information and administering the tests, basic intelligence tests, necessary for Jack to pass before the army would accept him; he was sure that, as a grammar school boy, he would have no trouble with these. Jack agreed and then found himself filling in reams of forms. He was even asked to sign a provisional signing-on form. Jack was a bit cautious about this; he had visions of finding himself in the Parachute Regiment the next day, especially as he had handed over the medical assessment forms and still had in his mind the Colonel's comments about being A1 fit for paratroops!

He also took the tests for joining the army which were made up of a maths test, an English test and a reasoning test. They were all timed so that, after a period of time, he was simply told to stop what he was doing at that point. He, therefore, had no idea whether he had done well or not.

Later that afternoon, Jack answered the telephone at home to discover that it was the Royal Engineer Captain who asked him a lot of probing questions regarding his GCE 'O' level results and the Civil Service exam at 'A' level which he had taken four weeks before. The conversation ended with the Captain ordering him to bring his 'O' level certificates and the written results of the Civil Service one with him the following Monday at 1100 hrs.

On Tuesday evening, Paul telephoned him to invite him to a dance. Jack was not keen, but Paul was very persuasive, explaining that it was at the girls' grammar school, and they had a reputation for embracing the permissive society with some gusto. So they arranged for Jack to pick up Paul at 7.30 pm on Saturday.

The dance was being held in their school hall with refreshments being served in a classroom off of it—non-alcoholic of course—but it took only a sip of the punch to discover that it had been liberally spiked with vodka. Jack was not a willing dancer and sat in a chair at the edge of the room whilst Paul found himself a partner for a waltz. A few glasses of punch later and Jack was ready to have a go at dancing to a rock and roll number, Rock Around the Clock, then all the rage, with a friend of Paul's pick up. Her name was Fianna, short, only reaching to Jack's shoulder with dark hair cut with a fringe and bob, nothing like the exaggerated beehive styles adopted by the majority of the girls present. She had just started her second year of 'A' levels which made her a direct contemporary of Jack.

She seemed neither too keen nor too put off by Jack but when Paul revealed, accidentally on purpose, that Jack had his own car in which they had come to the dance, she suddenly became very attentive. Jack struggled through two more dances and then the final dance, a waltz, was announced. Jack clumped his way through and was delighted that Fianna snuggled up to him far more closely than he expected. She even put her face up and pulled him down for a passionate kiss—*so that's what a French kiss is*, thought Jack; *I like, I like, I like and she's definitely getting a lift home!*

An offer of a lift was quickly accepted by both Fianna and her friend, much to Paul's delight. Having determined where they both lived produced a problem. Fianna lived very close to the school and her friend lived just a few doors down from Paul so that the obvious route was to drop Fianna first, then Paul and his girl but that would not give an opportunity for Jack to explore limits with Fianna. As they neared Fianna's, she suddenly said, "If you drive past my house and take that turning on the left, it's very dark down there and no one can see into the car." Jack, delightedly and in great expectation, did exactly that.

It seemed somewhat surreal, with Paul and his girl in the back and Jack and Fianna in the front, to settle down for a snogging session but that's exactly what they did. French kissing started immediately for Jack and, nothing ventured nothing gained, Jack put his right arm around her so that his arm lay across her left breast. Such action with Helja used to immediately result in his arm being pushed roughly away. With Fianna, no such action occurred. Indeed, after a few moments, she turned so that his hand naturally slid onto her breast. He waited for the slap. Instead, she whispered in his ear, "Not while they're in the back." He carried on kissing her for a while longer and then nudged her hand down into his lap. She removed it after a little squeeze of his todger, again murmuring, "Not while they're in the back." And with that, he had to be content. He did, not letting an opportunity escape, walk her to her door and set up a date with her for the following evening.

The following evening, he took her to the first Chinese restaurant to open in Kingston. A converted shop, it was quite small but cosy although the garish red flock wall paper did little to provide a romantic atmosphere. Jack discovered that Fianna was hoping to become a doctor and was very focussed to that end. Jack stressed his Officer Cadet training, 'forgetting' to mention the potential bit.

Jack ordered Chinese tea to finish the meal and amused Fianna by telling her what had happened the first time they had come as a family to the restaurant. Jack's dad had been for a business lunch and, impressed with the meal, had brought Jack, his mum and sister to have a meal in the evening. When the waiter asked them would they like tea, Indian or Chinese, his dad had said, "Chinese, of course." When the cups had been distributed, his mum had picked up the tea pot and started to pour the tea. What came out was an almost clear, slightly green in colour but completely transparent liquid with just one large tea leaf floating in the cup. His mum, to a waiter who happened to be passing, said, "You've forgotten to put any tea leaves in this pot, and you haven't brought any milk."

The waiter looked at the poured cup, picked it up and took a sip and said in very poor English, "No, it fine no milk," and walked away.

Jack's dad was laughing his head off. "No," he said, "Chinese tea is supposed to be like that; you drink it without milk."

"Why didn't you tell me? Why did you let me make a fool of myself like that?"

"Because you spoke so quickly; if the waiter hadn't been there I could have told you, but you were too quick for me." It was clear from Mother's look that Dad was not going to be forgiven any time soon. The telling of the tale was to be told many times over the coming years, mainly at family gatherings, but not least when Jack recounted it to Fianna at the restaurant.

Jack parked up in the same dark lane as before, but this time suggested that they move to the back seats as there was more room and comfort there. Fianna agreed, and the move was quickly accomplished. After kissing for a while, Jack moved his right hand to her left breast. She did not remove it this time, so emboldened, after a short while of gentle squeezing and caressing, he moved to unbutton her blouse—no resistance, so he carried on. Reaching inside, he stroked her breast over her bra at first and then slid one finger under the bra searching for her nipple. He couldn't reach it. So he reached around to her back and undid the clasp. He was quite proud of his ability to undo it with one hand! Bringing his hand around to the front, he slid it under the now loose bra and clasped a naked female breast for the very first time. It was very pleasant. It was even more pleasant when he leaned forward and gently kissed the nipple before taking it into his mouth and sucking it gently. *What a pity I didn't meet Fianna all those months ago which I wasted with Helja*, passed through his mind.

He wondered whether he should attempt to move his hand lower and slip it between her legs; perhaps the ultimate goal was within his grasp? Nothing ventured, nothing gained. He removed his hand, which had been clasped around the base of her breast while he pleasured her nipple with his lips and placed it on her knee before starting to slide it upwards. She immediately clasped his hand and moved it back to her breast at the same time whispering in his ear, "Wrong time." It took a moment for Jack to understand what time meant; it didn't mean the first time they had been together on a date with perhaps the liberty to be allowed in the future, but the wrong time of the month for her. It augured well for the future, but Jack didn't have much time; he was due to enlist in the army the following day!

He replaced his hand on her breast before pulling her bra right up and exposing both breasts so that he could kiss and nuzzle the left one while holding and squeezing her right one. Absolute heaven!

She moved a little and he realised that her hand was now in his lap. She whispered in his ear, "I don't see any reason why you should have all the fun," and using two hands, fumbled around his trousers until she had undone his zip and could free his rampant erection which she proceeded to stroke and squeeze alternately. The tingling sensation built up and up until he knew an explosion was imminent. Starting to moan softly as a warning of what was about to happen, he hoped she would not stop and she did not disappoint him.

"Aaaaarrrrrghh!" He exploded. Once he had come down off his high, she sat up and said, "It sounded like you were ready for that. You can return the compliment next time, if you like."

Even though he wanted to, he had no option other than to say, "I like," anyway.

All that was left then was to tidy up their dishevelled appearance and say their good nights with several prolonged kisses. As he was due to enlist in the army the next day, and from then his time would not be his own, he could not make a firm date for the next weekend, she having said she would not go out in the week as she had too much studying to do, so it was agreed that he would ring her when he knew his availability.

# Chapter 46

On Monday morning, Jack dressed in his best suit, bought for his sister's wedding which was two weekends away but deemed suitable for the situation, Jack having decided his school uniform was a sad remnant of his past and definitely not for parading around in. His mother, ever prudent, removed the badge from the pocket and the gold cord braid from the lapels and collar thus handing him a navy blue, double-breasted blazer for smart casual wear; the school tie and cap went straight into the dustbin.

His father, also suited, arrived at the Recruiting Office at five minutes before 1100 hrs and they were shown straight into the Captain's office.

After rather brief pleasantries, the Captain asked to see Jack's 'O' level certificates and the 'A' level Civil Service exam pass letter. Jack produced them and handed them over. The Captain read them twice and then said, "Well, this is most peculiar. According to these documents, you are a highly educated and, therefore, intelligent young man but you have failed the army intelligence test."

Jack looked at him in utter astonishment. His dad was the first to react and said, "That can't be; surely there must be an error in the marking or something."

"There is no error in the marking," said the Captain and opened a folder in front of him. "Your Maths and English answers are absolutely fine. You have scored highly in each and in line with what I would have expected. However, in the logic and reasoning paper your score was a fail." At that point, he extracted Jack's completed paper from the folder and turned it around so that his father and Jack could see it. "For question one you marked up the shape at C as being the odd one out; why did you choose that one?" The one he pointed to was question one on the paper and showed three shapes, a square, a circle and a triangle. All three shapes had two lines crossing one another inside them. Jack looked at them for a moment and said, "Well, the lines in the square and the circle cross at right angles and the ones in the triangle don't so that's the odd one out."

Jack's father looked at the question and said, "I would give the same answer, and I think it's correct. What do you say is the correct answer?"

The Captain didn't answer; instead, he pointed to the second question and said, "Why did you go for B in this answer?"

Jack looked at the question and said, "Well, the square and the pentagon have their two lines crossing at acute angles but the rectangles are at right angles." Jack's dad looked and again said that he would have given that answer.

"You didn't think that it was the pentagon because it had five sides and the square and the rectangle only had four?"

"No, too easy," said Jack.

The Captain sat back.

"I, too, think that when I send these results up the line, there is going to be a bit of a stink, because I think you are right. That will be for them to sort out because I think you are easily intelligent enough to join the army. So now I am going to get you to sign a few more papers, and you Mr Hughes, and then I'll administer the oath and pay you your bounty. I'll then answer any questions both of you might have and send you on your leave. I can't give you joining instructions or a travel warrant because you and I will have to wait to see what the army has to say about your reasoning answers. I can't imagine for a moment that they will refuse you, so you will hear in due course what they are going to do about you. Until then, you are on paid leave, and I do have some money for you."

Jack and his dad signed the various papers with which they were presented and then, standing, Jack took the oath to serve the Queen. He was handed a day's pay for 'taking the Queen's shilling' and a leave slip; pay for the paid leave would be posted to him. The Captain wished him every success in the army and sent them on their way.

"Well, that was a turn up for the books," said his dad. "No wonder he was so keen to see your GCE results; you clearly weren't fit material for the army!" At that, they both burst out laughing, and still chuckling, made their way home. In fact, Jack never heard another word about the issue, but he did have some work years later in Aden marking personality tests for the Parachute Regiment where there were different tests for several different degrees of intelligence. His mother seemed quite pleased that there was a chance Jack might be refused by the army, and Jack was quite pleased that with any luck, he would still be at home for the forthcoming weekend to be able to ask Fianna out.

Unlikely as it had seemed, Jack had totally forgotten that his sister was due to move into her new house that weekend and to get married the weekend after that. As a strong back and a driving licence holder, Jack was roped in to fetch and carry ready for the move and for the move itself. Protests that he wanted to go out on Saturday night were ignored. Jack had reached the stage in his life when being ignored, unless he wanted to be, was not something he was prepared to tolerate. So when his dad's car—his dad had taken Jack's car because it really had little boot space and thus little carrying capacity and his dad's had a bigger one—was fully loaded for another trip Jack refused to drive it. Words were said, lots of words were said and it was reluctantly agreed that Jack could bring Fianna with him to the new house on the Saturday for the small house warming party that had been planned. In the event, Fianna had had an accident playing hockey and was able only to hobble around and did not want him to see her in that state. Jack was a little disconcerted by this, especially as it was not her ankle he was interested in! No amount of cajolery worked so the telephone conversation had to end with him agreeing to ring her the following week. Although he didn't discover it immediately, he was being dumped; he only found out through Paul who was still seeing Fianna's mate who they had met at the school dance. Clearly, being a Private Soldier did not have much pulling power!

The week following his attestation went quickly as did the weekend of the move into the new house by his sister. Worse than not hearing from the army was selling his car to a colleague of his dad's from work as he couldn't leave it on the drive as he didn't know what would be happening to him in the army. He did sell it on the understanding he could buy it back for the same price if the army refused him but that was little compensation for its loss.

On the Thursday of the second week, he received a letter containing instructions to report to the RASC Recruitment Depot in Bordon in Hampshire the following day! It also contained a train travel warrant and a money order for his first week's pay. Talk about rush and wait; just how much training could be started on a Friday? Surely it would have been far more sensible to report on the Monday as it was highly unlikely that much would happen on Saturday and Sunday, but that's the army way of doing things, as he was to find out on other occasions in the future. Still, it did mean he didn't have to attend his sister's wedding nor do all the running around they had planned for him to do.

To his surprise, as he was sorting out the items he needed to take with him, not a lot as the joining instructions letter made clear there would be little space to store, or opportunity to wear, civvies, his mother appeared at the door to his bedroom with a brand-new, all-leather suitcase she had bought for him to use. He was surprised and very touched at this gesture, and he gave her a big hug for it.

His father dropped him off at the station the following morning following goodbyes to all the family with a special goodbye, at his mother's insistence, to his grandpa as 'might not be there' when he returned. In fact, he was to have to say a special goodbye to his grandpa for the next 10 years!

On the train, a stopper at every station, he shared a compartment with two Geordie lads, by their accents, who spent a lot of time talking about the girlfriend of one of them who had not commented favourably on the new suede shoes her boyfriend had just bought. When asked by the other what he had done about it, he replied, "Why, I blacked her eye for it." Jack was stunned by this statement and was not even sure as to whether it was true since over-colourful bragging was quite common among young men.

Gradually, the conversation between them turned to the army and what their reception was likely to be like. Jack hoped they would get off before him because he couldn't imagine going through Potential Officer Cadet training with these two. However, his wish was to be disappointed. As he prepared to leave the train, they also started getting their kit together. Realising what was happening, Tommy, the eye blacker, asked Jack if he, too, was joining the RASC. When Jack said yes, introductions all around took place with Tommy and Jimmy announcing they were both hoping to become drivers.

Bordon station was not much more than a rural halt and it took only moments for Jack to see that there was no transport waiting to pick him up. Examinations of the joining instructions for Tommy and Jimmy made no mention of transport, implying it would be for them to make their own way to the Depot. Jack's letter further contained the information that if there was no transport there, he was to ring a number to inform them of his arrival. Jack told the others about his letter and said, "I can tell them about you as well if you like." They liked, so Jack said, "We'd better give it a few minutes just in case there is transport on the way," and that they did. No transport appeared, so Jack rang the number.

The phone was answered, "RASC Depot Corporal Hobson speaking, sir." Jack told him who he was, that there were three of them in total and, according to the orders in his joining instructions, he was telephoning for transport to collect them. To say the Corporal was upset was an understatement. Gradually, it became clear among the expletives that new recruits did not have transport provided, and anyway, they weren't expecting any recruits that day!

What was said did not surprise Jack, either as to no transport or the fact that none of the three of them was expected—typical army—but they did still have the problem of what they were supposed to do. Using his knowledge of the army to the full, Jack said, "Well, Corporal Hobson, are you saying we should go home and wait for more instructions as to when we are supposed to report for recruit training?" There was something in the manner of the way that he phrased his question that gave Corporal Hobson pause for thought. Jack's phraseology was that of an officer addressing an NCO, something Jack was used to doing, not that of a new, raw recruit.

There was a long silence then, "Read me your letter in full," he instructed. Jack started at the top, reading out the heading and references, then when he read out Potential Officer Cadet, Corporal Hobson interjected, "Oh, so you're one of those, are you? Right, wait there, and I'll arrange for transport," and he then rang off.

Tommy and Jimmy were looking at him in amazement when he put the phone down.

"Officer Cadet?" said Tommy.

"No," said Jack, "I'm a Private Soldier, like you, but I am on an engagement which, if I am successful, means that I will have to go to the Regular Commissions Board and only if I pass that will I go to Sandhurst and only if I pass that will I be commissioned, so there's a load of ifs in there before I see the inside of an Officers' Mess."

Tommy and Jimmy looked at one another for a short while and then Jimmy said, "I think it might be a good idea to stick with this man as he knows how to deal with the army." Tommy agreed with him, and they started asking Jack about this special thingy he was on. Jack explained that it was just a variation which gave him a chance at a commission because he was too old to go for it straight from civvy life. He didn't tell them anything about his Army Cadet Force experience, having decided that it might count against him, drawing the attention of NCOs who would select out 'different' recruits for ridicule or even bullying if the fancy took them. The last National Serviceman had been demobbed only two years before and many NCOs were having trouble adjusting to the fact that any soldiers joining the army now were volunteers and were not willing to be bullied in the way that had become common during National Service. So, Jack reasoned, keep your head down and avoid attention. Unfortunately, he had already drawn attention to himself by revealing his Potential Officer Cadet status, but as that was bound to have come out sooner or later, he wasn't too concerned about revealing it, but he would still not be volunteering for anything because he knew the cardinal rule, NEVER VOLUNTEER.

A few minutes later, an old and well-worn Bedford Army coach pulled into the station yard. The three of them made their way over to it and identities being confirmed that they were for the RASC Depot, they climbed aboard. The depot was less than ten minutes away. The driver dropped them at the Guardroom and told them to report in. A huge Regimental Police Sergeant behind a desk looked at them for a moment and then, looking directly at Jack, said, "You'll be the clown that phoned then." Jack said nothing. "What have you got to say for yourself?"

"I just followed the orders in my letter, Sergeant." At that, Jack took his joining instructions out of his blazer jacket and handed it to the Sergeant. "Should I have done something else?"

The Sergeant was not pleased. He took the letter from Jack and read it through slowly and then read it through again. He was obviously looking for a fault but unable to do so, fell back on the old army faithful and said, "But this doesn't mean you can join this man's army with hair down to your arse; get it cut." As Jack had had his hair cut quite short in preparation for joining the army, he knew he had won this battle even if he did have to get a haircut.

A Lance Corporal was summoned to take them to the Admin Offices where their joining instructions were taken from them and they were issued with 'welcome' letters which gave all relevant details that they needed to know like meal times, which barrack block they were billeted in, even down to their bed number. They were then taken to the QM stores to be issued with a mattress, sheets, blankets, pillows and pillow cases—luxuries for a National Service Man but normal kit for Regulars. It turned out that Jack's bed was between Tommy and Jimmy's.

Immediately, Jack started making up his bed. The two of them looked at what he was doing and started taking the mickey. Jack responded with,

"If you survive long enough, you'll discover that old soldiers always make sure their beds are made so that when they stagger in with a skin full their bed is ready made; no struggling with pillows and pillow cases when pissed and ending up sleeping without. Also, it keeps NCOs off your back as an unmade mess is just the sort of ammunition that they look for to give you fatigues and other pleasantries."

Tommy and Jimmy looked at one another, then nodded and started making up their beds. Just as they finished and started putting their bits and bobs in the steel wardrobes by their respective beds, the Lance Corporal came back in with a Sergeant and immediately started screaming, "Stand by your beds. Come on, you're too slow like a load of old women!" all in the same breath. Looking at him, Jack took in an older man who had reached the dizzy heights of the bottom step on the ladder after years of service and knew that he was looking at a substantial failure who would be likely to be a bully and tyrant—someone to be given as wide a birth as possible.

Once they were standing at the bottom of their beds, the Sergeant introduced himself.

"My name is Sergeant Ellis. They call me Bullshit Charlie and you will find out why in due course. I am the Platoon Sergeant of a platoon which you three are the first members of. Once enough idiots have joined this man's army, you will be formed into a proper platoon and transferred to Buller Barracks in Aldershot where you will undergo proper recruit training. I'm going to start on your training here and the more effort you put in here and the more you learn, the easier it will be in training proper. Tea is at 1700 hours and Lance Corporal Coggins here will march you to the cookhouse at that time. Reveille is at 0630 hours and you will be ready to be marched to breakfast at 0700 hours at which time you will have completed your ablutions and made your beds in a smart and soldierly fashion. Any questions?"

This announcement was met by total silence.

"Any questions, the Sergeant asked," screamed L/Cpl Coggins.

146

"No, Sarge," was the answer from Tommy. Nothing from Jimmy and "No, Sergeant" from Jack. Coggins now had his target and started in on Tommy and Jimmy.

"You idle soldiers, you," at full volume erupted from his mouth. "You will answer 'Yes Sergeant' in a loud, clear and soldierly voice or you will shout 'No Sergeant' as necessary. You, you horrible little man will not call a Sergeant Sarge, you will answer Sergeant and you, you silent oaf will answer any question asked in a loud and clear voice, is that clear?"

"IS THAT CLEAR?" in an absolute scream elicited, "Yes, Lance Corporal," from Tommy and Jimmy. Clearly that was not loud enough so he screamed again, "I CAN'T HEAR YOU AND YOU ADDRESS ME AS SERGEANT BECAUSE THERE IS A SERGEANT IN THE ROOM 'CAUSE YOU'RE ANSWERING HIM. GOT THAT?"

Both of them screamed out, "Yes, Sergeant." Coggins was about to start in on them again, but Bullshit Charlie intervened and said, "Well done for making up your beds," and marched out. Coggins had no choice but to go with him.

Jack was a little perturbed by this. As far as authority was concerned, the three of them were brand-new Regular Army recruits; Jack had not put down on any of his paperwork that he had been in the Army Cadet Force for five years because none of the questions had asked about the Cadet Force; they only asked about previous service in the Navy, Air Force, Army or the Territorial Army. The treatment was more in accordance with that meted out to National Serviceman. As Regulars, they could, if they didn't like the army, buy themselves out in the first six weeks for £25. In addition, Jack could, if he failed the Regular Commissions Board, simply ask to be demobbed and that would be his army career at an end; given that, he wondered at their treatment. He suspected that their problem would be Lance Corporal Coggins. Jack put him down as a failure relatively speaking, having only reached the rank of L/Cpl, probably after long service and someone who was probably bitter and twisted as a result. He also had a red-veined nose and the high colour of a heavy drinker. Based on the little they had experienced of him, Jack knew he would be a bully and pick fault with everything they did. Praise for effort or success was likely to be entirely absent and for Jack personally, he was likely to be a target for spite once Coggins found out that he was destined for Potential Officer Cadet training. To avoid him entirely was not going to be possible as not only did he seem to be the junior NCO in charge of them for the next two or three weeks, but he lived in a separate room set in the corner of their barrack block.

The three of them, under Jack's coaching, were waiting outside the barrack block a good five minutes before 1700 hours for Coggins to appear. When he did turn up, nearly 10 minutes after 1700 hours, he immediately started shouting for them to get in line, they already were, and then he turned them to the right when the direction they needed to go was to the left. Giving them the order, "By the right quick march," when the correct order would have been, 'In single file, by the front quick march,' they set off for the cookhouse, not in step as that was as yet beyond Tommy and Jimmy, and not the shortest route but all around the camp until they got there. Jack thought, *this bastard is going to make our lives an absolute misery.* All the army recruiting emphasised professional army, no bullshit, just necessary cleanliness and smartness. But the signs were that this was all bullshit, and the army had not changed at all.

While they ate their first tea choices from four or five meat meals, loads of vegetables and plenty of bread and margarine and mugs of tea strong enough to re-float the Titanic, Jack gave Tommy and Jimmy his assessment of Coggins and the need to give him nothing to justify him picking on them if it was at all possible.

They made their way to the NAAFI after their meal and Jack was introduced to the pleasures of Newkie brown, (Newcastle Brown Ale), by Tommy when Jack revealed he'd never heard of it. Once he'd sampled it, he wished that had still been the case! As they sat at a table, Coggins staggered past, heading for a row of three tables at the side of the room labelled 'For Junior NCOs only' in prominent letters. Normally, junior NCOs, Corporals and Lance Corporals had their own Corporals' Club totally separate from the other ranks in the NAAFI but the depot was too small to warrant a separate Corporals' Club and they had to be content with their roped off section. Coggins bought a pint at the bar and weaved his way to a seat and slumped in it.

Coggins quickly drank the pint and then started holding up the glass in their direction with gestures that one of them should buy him a pint. Tommy and Jimmy's reaction was to tell him to fuck off; Jack turned his back to Coggins and said quietly to them, "Trust me, I know exactly how to get rid of this bastard," and he stood up and walked over to Coggins. "A pint of Mild, is it, Corporal?" As a Lance Corporal, Coggins should have been addressed as 'Lance Corporal', but having weighed him up, Jack thought a bit of toadying might not go amiss.

Clearly, Coggins accepted it because he did not correct Jack, merely saying, "Yes, that's right, lad," and handed him the glass.

Jack made his way to the bar and ordered a pint of Mild and three double vodkas which, when the barmaid had turned away, he quickly emptied into Coggins's beer. Fortunately, the glass was one of those with a line around it just below the top of the glass to show the proper level for a pint leaving enough space for the vodka to be poured in without spilling any over the top. He then walked over to Coggins and handed him the pint saying, "There's plenty more where that came from Corporal," to which Coggins replied, "I could tell you were a good lad the moment I set eyes on you; stick with me and you could have a very easy time of training."

Jack walked back to Tommy and Jimmy. From their position, they had been able to see what Jack had done. Jack said, "Two or three more of them, and he'll be legless. With any luck, the Guardroom might receive a message of a 'body' lying on the ground and in need of attention." Tommy and Jimmy broke out in broad grins. As soon as Coggins had drunk half of his pint, Tommy leapt up and called, "Same again Corp?" which should have elicited a telling off for the abbreviation and over familiarity of a Private to a Lance Corporal, but with free beer in the offing, Coggins was prepared to overlook it on this occasion. Simply emptying the glass in one huge swallow, he handed it over whilst wiping his hand over his mouth. Tommy took the empty glass to the bar and ordered another pint of Mild and three double vodkas. While the barmaid was getting the vodkas, Tommy quickly took the three empty vodka glasses which Jack had left on the bar over to their table and said, "We'd better build them up here to make it look like we've been drinking them." Jack was impressed and said so.

Jimmy kept careful watch for his turn and repeated the process as soon as Coggins was halfway through his pint, obviously making him drink his spiked drinks quite quickly. Coggins must have thought he'd won the football pools to have three such simple recruits to keep him in beer. *He would almost certainly,* thought Jack, *have started borrowing ten bob notes from them to be repaid at some non-specific date in the future i.e. never but, in that, Coggins was to be unlucky.*

When Jack approached him for the next drink, he was showing clear signs of being three sheets to the wind, his speech was slurred, and he spilled most of the last half pint when trying to swallow it quickly. He took only a couple of sips of the new pint before getting up and announcing to all and sundry that he was going for a slash. The Gents led off the foyer into the NAAFI which meant Coggins had to go through a door to a corridor where the Gents was first on the right. When he hadn't returned after ten minutes, Jack went to look for him because the last thing he wanted was for Coggins to have staggered off to bed.

He found him slumped over the urinal, kneeling in a pool of pee and totally out of it. Returning to the door to the NAAFI, Jack gestured for Tommy and Jimmy to join him. Between them, they half dragged, half carried him outside without anyone seeing them. They moved him to the side of the main road running through the camp and dropped him so that his head hit the kerb with a satisfying thump about 30 yards from the Guardroom. They then returned to the NAAFI and acted as though they were just returning from the Gents. Being Friday evening, the camp was very empty, and there had been no one about to see them when they dumped him.

They stayed in the NAAFI for another half hour and then Jack advised them to buy some of the staples they would need like yellow dusters, boot polish, Brasso, blanco and spare boot laces. Jack assured the other two that they would need all of these items, and more, and they might need them from the following day depending on what happened in the morning.

As they walked out of the NAAFI, they could see some activity where they had dumped Coggins. Leading the way, Jack led them over to see what was happening as to walk on by ignoring it would appear very peculiar indeed. There were three or four people clustered around Coggins and as they got closer, they were just in time to see the Sergeant of the Guard slapping his face none too gently whilst at the same time calling out, "Come on. Can you hear me? Wake up, you bugger." Coggins sat up, projectile vomited all over the Sergeant's beautifully polished boots and ankles and trouser bottoms and collapsed again. If it had only been in daylight, all and sundry would have been able to enjoy the startling Technicolour as well but the dark spoiled that. The Sergeant went berserk, screaming at the others, who turned out to be members of the Guard; he let fly with, "Get that drunken sod into the cells now, DO IT NOW AND LOCK HIM UP!" Jack and the other two never saw Coggins again.

The following morning, they were woken at 0630 hours by Bullshit Charlie, immaculately uniformed, with orders to stand by their beds. Looking at Jack, Charlie started musing out loud about how, in the good old days of National Service, it hadn't been unknown for junior NCOs to encourage new recruits to buy them beer on the promise of getting an easy time of it in training; then looking Jack straight in the eye, he said, "You wouldn't think about bribing an NCO like that, Private Hughes, would you?"

"No money, Sergeant, not on the engagement I'm on." Jack's enlistment, allowing as it did for him to walk out anytime he liked without having to buy himself out, where Tommy and Jimmy would have to pay £25, received a lower rate of pay than the other two.

"Good answer," said Charlie and that was the last time Coggins was ever mentioned even obliquely.

Bullshit Charlie proceeded to tell them that they were to fall in at 0800 hours, having completed their ablutions, made their beds and tidied their room beforehand, ready to be marched to the QM Stores where a start would be made on issuing their kit. Charlie then left them to it. Jimmy said, "I'll not bother shaving this morning; it's Saturday and I never shave at the weekends,"

Jack said, "You're in the army now, and if you don't shave, Charlie will have your arse." Jimmy ignored him and started making up his bed while Jack and Tommy went off to wash and shave. Showering, unless following PT or sports, took place in the evenings when hot water was available from 1800 hours until 1930 hours; it was always best to be there prompt at 1800 hours because the hot water soon ran out! Shades of National Service. It was to be some years before hot water was available for most of the day.

After breakfast, which was plentiful if not wonderful—scrambled eggs were one lump or two, and the bacon was a game of spot the meat in the fat but the bread and marge, covered in lashings of jam and with as much tea as they wanted even if the sugar ran out very quickly, was all calculated to provide loads of energy for active bodies—they returned to their room to finish cleaning it up. Jack tried to persuade Jimmy to shave and make his bed properly rather than just pulling it together which was patently obvious, what he had done. Jimmy was having none of it even though Tommy was saying to him to listen to Jack because this man knew his way around the army.

They were standing by their beds ready when Bullshit Charlie returned. He took one look at Jimmy and his bed, grabbed it at the side and turned it over, tipping mattress, sheets, blankets and pillow onto the floor. He then proceeded to kick them all over the room. He then turned on Jimmy and ordered him to get down and 'give him' 20 press ups there and then and once he'd done that to double over to the Ablutions and get a shave or he would be spending the rest of his army time on jankers. Once Jimmy had completed them, struggling for the last five or so, and had returned from shaving, Charlie shouted in Jimmy's face, "I told you I was called Bullshit Charlie, you horrible little man, and I meant it. Anyone who annoys me regrets it, you filthy maggot, you; you are bone idle, and I will not tolerate an idle soldier. When you are dismissed at dinner time, you will report to the Cookhouse for fatigues. Have you got that?"

"Yes, Sergeant."

"I CAN'T HEAR YOU."

"YES, SERGEANT."

"And I will check up that you did report, you horrible, idle soldier. If you ever present me with idle again, I'll make sure you wish your mother had never had you."

At that, Charlie told them to fall in outside. Once they had done so, they were marched over to the QM Stores where they moved along a counter being asked by the Storemen behind it, "Hat size?" "Boot size?" "Chest size?" "Collar size?" "Waist size?" and then being handed berets, hats, two pairs of boots, one with steel tips to the heels and toes and one pair with rubber soles, combat trousers and jackets, two worsted shirts (horrible, rough things to wear), a set of denim overalls, PT kit, plimsolls, three pairs of woollen socks, three pairs of olive green under shorts, two pairs of Long Johns, a woollen jersey, a woollen, slim-jim tie, a huge one-pint china mug, a knife, fork and spoon, a housewife (a sewing kit containing needles, darning wool, buttons of different sorts—not a real housewife!), a button stick, webbing anklets, web belt, two webbing straps, two ammunition pouches, a small pack and a large pack, a kit bag, a suitcase, a jack knife, two poplin collarless shirts and three separate collars, front and back collar studs, striped pyjamas that, when worn, made them look like convicts and so it went on. Jack stuffed as much as he could into the suitcase and then followed that by shoving stuff into the kit bag before using the large pack and then the small one. Seeing what he was doing, Tommy followed suit, but Jimmy continued trying to get his arms all round it and dropping stuff all over the place including the pint mug which promptly shattered on the stone floor! All the time, Bullshit Charlie was hectoring them to get a move on, he hadn't got all day, and he was missing doing far more important things than nurse-maiding a bunch of wet-behind-the-ears recruits. However, interestingly, when the Storeman said to Jimmy that he would have to pay for the mug, Charlie interrupted and said, "Can you show me that soldier's signature for the mug, soldier?"

"Well no, Sarge, but you saw him break it."

"No, I didn't, soldier, what I saw was a Storeman pushing so much kit at a new recruit that he had no chance to keep up, so you were the cause of the breakage, not the recruit. Anyway, you can put it down to handling breakages which means it will be written off and not charged to anybody. That's what's going to happen, isn't it?" That last said in an ever increasingly loud voice. Recognising the inevitable, the Storeman replied, "Yes Sergeant."

"Good lad; I knew you'd see it my way," at which point Charlie told the three of them to take their nice new expensive paid-for-by-the-tax-payer kit back to their room where he would join them shortly. He joined them a few minutes later, handing Jimmy a new mug as he did so.

"Say 'thank you, Sergeant' to the nice man." Jimmy said thank you with alacrity.

Taking off his beret and belt, Charlie sat on one of the empty beds and said, "Right, listen up. For the rest of today and tomorrow, you will make a start on getting your uniforms in a fit state to be worn. In a few minutes, I will demonstrate some of the skills you will need to master and the more you pick up now, the easier will be your training. On Monday, we will start with some basic training to give you a head start for when you transfer to Buller Barracks in Aldershot in two or three weeks' time when enough recruits have been mustered to make a reasonably sized platoon. You will also be measured for your SD uniforms (the army had just started changing from the old Battledress, a blouse and trousers, to Service Dress which was made of a much nicer and smarter material which was styled very much like an officer's uniform and, so unlike the 'old' army, this uniform would be tailored to fit them.)" Charlie continued, "We'll fit in some PT to start getting you fit and a few press ups for idle soldiers," this last said with a grin in Jimmy's direction. "We'll teach you a bit of drill and interior economy, the army's new word for Bull since we don't do Bull anymore, leastways no more than we need to, to keep the barracks in a fit state for modern soldiers and you've got some medicals and jabs to come."

He walked into what had been Lance Corporal Coggins's room and reappeared almost immediately with a large colour photograph which showed kit laid out in a locker and on a bed. Holding it up for them to see, he said, "Now, this is how I will expect to see all your kit laid out on Monday morning when I come in at 0800 hours. The floor will be highly polished," he showed them the bumper which was a large metal block at the end of a broom handle with brushes on the underside which was used with polish and then a duster over the brushes to polish the floor to a high shine. Using it was bloody hard work; it was much easier to get down on hands and knees and to polish the floor with a small amount of polish on one duster and to shine it with another one, which Jack pointed out once Charlie had gone.

Bullshit then carried out a series of demonstrations of how the studs, a bit like large drawing pins, should be driven in to the soles of their ammunition boots (the ones with steel plates like horseshoes on the heel and toe) thus creating the proper pattern and ensuring that they would never wear out and so that they would make a satisfying crunch when driven into the tarmac during drill! He showed them how to shine the toe and heel caps when polishing their boots using water and polish, his demonstration did not actually involve polishing a boot but just mimed the actions of so doing; he didn't comment on the fact that they all had several yellow dusters each and tins of black polish already. What he didn't show them how to do was to get rid of the 'dimples' in the leather surface of the boots. During the manufacturing process, the leather surface was quite smooth and would have polished up beautifully and easily, but the army had the surface 'roughed up' with a sort of dimpling which meant that no amount of spit and polish, (although the term spit and polish was used, anyone using spit from a mouth that still contained remnants of a meal soon discovered how detritus in the mouth in the spit gummed up the polish, making a thick, unworkable gunge which was impossible to shine or set), no—the best tool to use was water in the polish tin lid, and this would produce a shine, but even then, only after multiple applications. Jack wondered why Charlie didn't emphasise that the leather on the toe and heel caps had to be smoothed first before attempting to polish them. The traditional term for this was to 'bone' the boots first, derived from soldiers using rib bones from horsemeat or cows, scrounged from the cookhouse which were suitably strong and curved to press down on the leather and 'iron' out the dimples. Jack was aware of Cadets who had tried to literally iron out the surface using their mum's electric irons only to discover that the iron burnt and charred the leather, ruining it from ever taking a polish whilst at the same time ruining the iron with black dirty deposits left all over the ironing plate of the iron! Jack knew an easier way to bone boots, but he wasn't about to reveal it to Bullshit Charlie, especially not when Charlie seemed to be setting them up for a fall.

Charlie also put together one set of the 1938 Pattern Webbing, including showing them how to adjust the belt size. He then sent them off to the NAAFI for their tea break with instructions to be back sharp in 15 minutes. They had to double there, ask for their tea to be topped up with cold water to make it cool enough to drink and then double back to do so within the time allotted only to have Charlie turn up 30 minutes later; the Sergeants' Mess was a fair bit further than the NAAFI and Charlie wasn't hurrying for any bunch of recruits!

While they were waiting for him, Jack started in on studding his boots, and the other two soon followed.

When he arrived, with no apology for where he had been, of course, Charlie explained a bit more about their training for the following weeks and what to expect once they transferred to training proper in Aldershot and their trade training after that assuming that they all passed their basic training. He then asked if they had any questions and Tommy immediately asked, "When do we get paid, Sergeant?" Charlie explained that pay day was Thursday in the army and they would attend a pay parade on that day and he would explain the parade to them if they lasted that long, this last with a hard look at Jimmy.

Since the others did not ask, Jack had no option other than to ask, "Are we allowed out of camp, Sergeant?"

Charlie looked at him, "Wanting to go home already then, Hughes?"

"No, Sergeant, but there is some stuff I need to buy to see me through training which the NAAFI doesn't sell." Jack prayed Charlie didn't ask what because he hadn't a clue what he would say since he certainly didn't want to tell Charlie what it was. Charlie had been making his way to the door and clearly had other things he wanted to do so he called over his shoulder,

"Be at the Guardroom at 1300 hours, smartly dressed and a credit to this unit, civvy clothes mind, you're not fit to wear uniform yet, and if you are good enough, you can have a leave pass for two hours only. If you are late back, you'll be on fatigues for a week with your mate here." At that he was gone before Jack could say thank you Sergeant.

Come the appointed time, Jack turned up at the Guardroom and asked for his leave pass. The Guard Sergeant looked him up and down. Jack had his blazer on, white shirt and Regimental tie that he had bought in the NAAFI the night before and well-pressed grey flannels. His shoes were gleaming as they should be. The Sergeant inspected him very carefully but unable to find any fault, handed Jack his pass. Jack was off out of the depot like a shot. He was lucky to catch a bus immediately and minutes later, was at the station. The journey each way was just over half an hour, so he was going to be pushed. While waiting for the train, he telephoned home and when his dad answered, he explained what he needed and asked his dad to meet him at the station with the items so that Jack could jump on to the next train going back. Grumbling at the awkwardness, given the wedding that was going on, he nevertheless agreed to comply with Jack's requests. Grabbing what his dad had brought, with a quick, "Thanks, Dad," he was back on the next train to Bordon and into the depot with 10 minutes to spare.

In the barrack room, Tommy and Jimmy were lying around doing not very much. On Jack's return, they both wanted to know what he had been up to. Without saying anything Jack pulled from his bag a soldering iron. The main shaft tapered to an end a bit like a chisel but blunt and about three quarters of an inch wide. The soldering arm was just a small cross bar which Jack proceeded to remove. Switching on the iron, he placed the hot end on the lid of a tin of polish to warm up while he liberally smeared polish on the toe and heel caps of his rubber, DMS boots. Once the soldering iron was hot enough, Jack started to 'iron' first the toe cap using the wide blunt end until it was nice and smooth and then moved to the heel cap. He did this for both boots and within less than 10 minutes, they were done to his satisfaction. Tommy and Jimmy looked on astounded.

"You canny lad," said Tommy and Jimmy joined in with a long, "Yeah." Jack then started in on his Ammunition boots, but these took quite a while longer as the whole of the boot had to be ironed since they were expected to get them gleaming all over for their passing-out parade. Jack then produced from his bag another two pairs of boots, one DMS which already had polished toe and heel caps and a pair of Ammunition boots which were all over gleaming. Jack placed these in the lidded part of his locker, which they had been told was their private area, and which the permanent staff would not search or inspect on normal inspections providing they had no reason to do so caused by the soldier himself.

Tommy excelled himself this time with, "You canny bugger, where did you get them?"

"From home," said Jack and refused to elaborate further. His issue boots having cooled, Jack reached into his bag and took out a bottle. When he unscrewed the cap and took it off, it revealed a length of wire with a square brush at the end. The brush was pitch black in colour and full of a black liquid from which he proceeded to scrape the excess liquid before painting it on the toe cap of the first DMS boot. He was careful to paint the edge of the liquid as a line around the toe cap, leaving a narrow gap between the toe cap and the welt of the boot. Jack had learnt years before that bulling boots to a shine right up to the welt was impossible because the thickness of a finger prevented it. If he had painted right up to the edge, which he could have done with the brush, it would have given the game away to a discerning eye that some sort of fiddle was being practiced.

Once he had finished the DMS boots, he replaced that cap and put the bottle of Luton Hat Straw dye, for that was what it was, something the School Platoon had used for years, back in his bag. He then said to the two of them, "That bottle is my secret, and I won't share it as there is only half a bottle left, and I won't be able to get any more once it's gone. Providing you keep stum about it, I'll iron your boots for you because there is a skill to it and if you get it wrong it'll burn the leather and you'll be buying new ones as well as being in deep shit for destroying army property. Deal?" Tommy and Jimmy were happy to agree. By the time Jack had finished their boots, it was time for tea.

There was no sign of Bullshit Charlie and knowing how quickly the other vultures in the depot polished off the food on offer, Jack said, "Come on, let's go, but to make sure we're not in the shit if spotted, we'll march in a file of three the same way as Bullshit Charlie marched us before." The others agreed and at Jack's, "By the front quick march," they shambled off as best as they could seeing as Tommy and Jimmy had no idea yet of how to march, let alone march in step. Jack was careful not to march as smartly as he could, because he didn't want to reveal yet just how qualified he was. So the three of them made more or less soldierly progress to the Cookhouse and then back again after their tea.

Once back in the room, Jimmy was all for going to the NAAFI for a pint or two, but Jack said he was going to make a start on his issue boots to get a bit of a shine on them ready for Monday, and he would join them later. Tommy said that he, too, would stay and, not fancying going on his own, Jimmy, grumbling, said that so long as he got a pint before bed, he'd stay with them.

They both watched as Jack placed some water in the polish tin lid and wrapped a yellow duster round one finger. He then rubbed a thin smear of polish onto his finger tip and started to rub it in small circles onto the toe cap of his DMS boot which was already quite shiny from the hat dye. He explained to them that the dye was fragile and needed polishing anyway to build up a shine but only a small amount of polish should be used at a time, because if you put too much on, it would take hours of rubbing to get it to almost dry. As he had now reached that stage with his thin smear, he dipped the cloth into the water in the tin lid and transferred a small drop onto the polished area. Working in small circles with frequent additions of water, the polish soon started to take on a shine. Tommy and Jimmy were amazed to see the shine appearing. Bullshit Charlie had only talked them through the spit and polish system, although he had said about using small amounts of polish, polishing in small circles and using lots of water, but hadn't actually demonstrated it so there was nothing like seeing the process actually happening to understand it properly.

Tommy started in on one of his boots and copied more or less exactly the way Jack had demonstrated. Jimmy, on the other hand, took a large scoop of polish onto his duster and started to rub it in with great sweeps. Jack leaned across and, using Jimmy's duster, rubbed off as much of the polish as he could and said, "Too much polish, just use water on it now and in a while, it might come up all right. However, I think it may be too much, and we'll have to burn it off with the soldering iron and start again." From that, having just clearly demonstrated the correct method and emphasised only a little polish, and Jimmy's performance so far not shaving etc, Jack had already formed the opinion that Jimmy was going to be the one the NCOs picked on because he was clearly a poor learner whereas Tommy was soaking up what Jack had said like a sponge.

It took a good hour for Jack to polish his DMS boots to a reasonable standard for now. Putting down his boots, he reached into his 'magic' bag again and pulled out some pieces of cardboard from a shoe box. He then proceeded to cut it into a number of strips about half an inch wide and about 8 inches long. Tommy and Jimmy were again watching him, wondering what he was going to get up to next. Carefully looking at the kit layout photo, Jack started folding up items of kit as shown in it. As he folded each one, he placed a strip of the cardboard into it so that the fold became a long rectangle with a nice straight appearance. As each piece was completed, he placed it on top of the previous item and built up a pile of straight, even and equally sized items, exactly as shown in the photo. He said, "You'll never get cloth to form square edges on its own; it needs something to help it like cardboard; that's how it's been done in the picture."

"How do you know all this, canny lad?" asked Tommy.

"Ask me no questions, and I'll tell you no lies," replied Jack.

He then hung up his kit which was shown as being hung up in the photo barring kit with which they had not yet been issued. Within just a few minutes, the lockers, in effect steel wardrobes, were starting to look smart and soldierly as in the photo. Returning to the bag he had brought back with him that afternoon, Jack removed an enamel mug and a knife, fork and spoon set which clipped together in a neat group and said, "You might want to think about getting a spare mug; enamel is best as it doesn't break; I saw some in the NAAFI, so you can keep the china issue one just for inspections and just put it out for that, because they start to stain in no time at all and they'll be buggers to clean up to white again; they are also very vulnerable to breakage and chipping, which if Bullshit finds even one small chip, I bet it will result in it being thrown across the room. And replacements will cost you a fortune. But that's up to you. Anyway, that'll do for now," said Jack. "I think it's about time you two bought me a pint or two." In the NAAFI, sitting down with his pint, Jack was subjected to more questioning from Tommy especially as to how he knew as much as he did about the army and how it worked. All Jack would say was that he had read a lot in preparation for enlisting. Questions about had his father been in the army were met with, "None of my family have been in the forces; my dad was in a reserved occupation in the war as a technical engineer working on powered turrets for tanks and Lancaster bombers to name just two. My uncle was in the Airforce but that doesn't count."

The Sunday was spent working on their kit. Jack started off by working at his webbing belt. Looking at his own and those belonging to the other two, it was clear that they had been issued with belts that had been horrendously over-blancoed. It was caked so thickly on the belts that the material of which they were made could not be seen. Even careful handling resulted in dustings of blanco everywhere.

"The first thing we need to do is brush off most of this old blanco," said Jack. Matching words to deeds, he made his way, followed by the others, to the Ablutions where he applied water to his blancoing brush and started to scrub off the thick coat of blanco. When it was sufficiently reduced so that the webbing pattern material could be seen, he set it aside and did the same for the straps and anklets they had also been issued with that also were too heavily blancoed. The army was in the process of introducing a new pattern of dark green webbing kit, modelled after the American pattern where most of the kit was carried in pouches attached to the waist belt and supported by a yoke over the shoulder, which did not need blancoing but that was slow filtering down to the support arms who had to rely on the 1938 pattern for a while yet.

He returned to the webbing later in the day and applied a thin layer of fresh blanco by wetting the blanco brush with a little water and scrubbing up some blanco from the block with which they had been issued from the Stores and spreading it evenly over the surface of the outside of the whole belt, straps and anklets. He just applied a new, thin layer of blanco to the ammunition pouches as they were not thickly coated. Jack then showed them how to use the button stick to protect the freshly blancoed belt while they cleaned the belt buckles on the back of the belt.

He also showed them how to shrink berets by alternately placing the beret in sinks of hot and cold water to make the woollen part of the beret shrink; as they were issued, they looked like huge sails on the top of their heads and needed to be shrunk and moulded to shape before they could look anything like a proper soldier. The final step was to stretch the hat band, put the beret on the head, shape the body pulled down over the right ear and then carefully remove and leave it to dry in the preformed shape—something Bullshit hadn't shown them or told them about. Feeling they had really made some progress, they took a quick break to the NAAFI and then last thing on Sunday night finished off by polishing the bit of the floor they had been walking on and then laying down paper on the floor to protect it for the morning.

They were woken at 0630 hours by a Lance Corporal, who having woken them, left them with an order to be standing by their beds at 0800 hours, ready for inspection. At 0800 hours promptly, he returned and called them to attention as Bullshit walked into the room. Bullshit said, "I see you've met Lance Corporal

Hobson; he is going to be responsible for you to me for the rest of your time here. Clear?"

"Yes, Sergeant," they yelled in unison. Charlie then made his way down the room, starting with Tommy who was closest to the door and then Jack and finally Jimmy. Turning to face the three of them, he said, "Okay, who's ex-army then?" No one answered. Zeroing in on Jack, he repeated again, "Who's ex-army then?" Again, no reply. "Have you been in the army before, Private Hughes?"

"No, Sergeant."

"What about the Navy then?"

"No, Sergeant."

"Not a Brylcream Nancy-boy; tell me not that?"

"No, Sergeant."

"Not ex-TA?"

"No, Sergeant. I was in school until only a week ago," said Jack. Not technically true; it had been nearly three weeks but what's a week or two between friends, he thought. Interestingly, Bullshit didn't ask the same questions of the two Geordies. Although they were all dressed identically in their denims, belts and anklets, Jack looked like he had been wearing them for years while Tommy and Jimmy looked as though they had just been taken out of the box.

Charlie found faults with all their kit layouts, throwing one or two items of Jimmy's kit on the floor and then said, "There is lots of room for improvement, but for a first inspection, not too bad." Jack took that as a compliment as even perfection would not have been good enough at this stage of their training. They were then marched over to the MI room to see the doctor. Being the army, they then went through, all over again, the same tests as Jack had had in London and the two Geordies had had in Newcastle. Pronounced fit, they were sent off for a cup of tea in the NAAFI.

When they returned to their barracks, it was to discover two new faces sitting on two bed frames and looking very lost. One, Cliff Polisey, turned out to be a potential Staff Clerk, which was the trade Jack was to learn, and the other, a short 5-feet 2-inch Scotsman, who introduced himself as Andy McKay, was hoping to be a driver. Before much more could be said, Sergeant Ellis and Lance Corporal Hobson arrived. Hobson, brother as it turned out of the Corporal Hobson who had taken Jack's original phone call, took the two newcomers off to the QM Stores while Bullshit examined their kit layout again. He picked up Jack's Ammunition boots and gave them a very thorough inspection. Looking Jack straight in the eye, he said, "How did you get these boots so smooth so quickly, soldier?"

Jack answered, "Boned them with a spoon, Sergeant, and then polished them."

Bullshit looked him up and down then took another long look at the boots and said, "Bullshit. No recruit has ever boned a pair of boots that quickly. When I find out what you have been up to, and I will, I'll give you boned with a spoon indeed. I never said on Saturday how to smooth leather, so how come you knew how to do it?"

"Read it in a book, Sergeant."

"Bullshit," said Charlie again, indicating quite clearly how he had got the nickname. "I will find out; just you wait and see." With that, he told them to report to the gym as soon as the new two returned from the Stores with Lance Corporal

Hobson. Hobson was not prepared to let them wander off to the gym on their own, so they were formed into two ranks and marched, sort of, to the gym.

Inside, they changed into their PT kit and were introduced to the pleasures of an army PT Instructor whose only purpose in life was to make theirs a misery – and they were very good at it. Jack was to have trouble with PTIs for the rest of his service. He could see the need to be fit but to raise fitness to a fetish, as a means in itself, seemed to him to be a waste of valuable time which could far better be spent doing useful things.

They then spent a very unpleasant 30 minutes being hounded towards fitness as was proper for a soldier for they were soldiers first and tradesmen second. They were then sent for a shower, cold, and formed up outside to be marched back to the barrack block ready for dinner. Tuesday and Wednesday followed a similar pattern of mixed military, medical inspections and jabs and PT training. Three more recruits joined on Tuesday and two more on Wednesday at which point they were 'closed off' to newcomers and were told that they were now to be known as Number 1 Section. Although their barrack room held 16 beds, the 'powers that be' had decided that once 10 recruits had been 'welcomed' any arriving after that should start forming the second section because adding new recruits constantly to an ever-expanding group interrupted the first recruits' training too much by having them go over the same things again and again or simply left them idle while the latest ones had kit issued, medicals etc.

One of the Wednesday newcomers was Keith Voisey, a tall skinny kid, who had worked in an office since leaving school two years before and thought it would be much better to push paper around in Singapore or Malaya or indeed anywhere other than Yeovil where he had been brought up by a widowed mother, his father having been killed during National Service in Korea. Voisey, Polisey and Jack were to naturally gravitate together for clerk training as all the others were hoping to become drivers.

# Chapter 47

On the Wednesday afternoon just before being fell out for tea, Bullshit arrived to speak to them.

"Why," he opened with, "are soldiers taller in the morning and shorter in the evening?" Silence. Bullshit repeated the question in a very loud voice.

"Don't know Sergeant," they all screamed out except Jack who had started to scream out something else and chopped it off but not quickly enough for Bullshit not to notice it.

"Well," said Bullshit, "why, Private Hughes, are soldiers taller in the morning and shorter in the afternoon?"

"Well," screamed Jack, "because the discs between the vertebrae get compressed during the day, especially if the soldiers have been carrying a lot of kit, and that would make them a bit shorter, Sergeant."

"Go on," said Bullshit.

"Well," screamed Jack, "there are about 33 vertebrae in the human body and if each disc was to be squashed by 1/33rd of an inch, which isn't very much, that would mean the soldiers would be a lot shorter by the end of the day, Sergeant."

"Smartarse," said Bullshit, "but quite right, if you say so Private Hughes. The problem we have, Private Hughes, is that Private McKay is too short to be a driver—he isn't 5 feet 2 inches tall, he is 5 feet one and a half inches tall—so how are we going to make him tall enough to qualify?"

Jack thought of the options and then screamed, "If we could borrow a stretcher from somewhere, we could carry him first thing in the morning, before he gets out of bed and loses any height, and carry him to the MI Room to be measured, Sergeant."

Bullshit looked at him for a full minute which seemed like eternity to Jack before saying, "I knew a smartarse like you would know the answer to a little problem like that, Private Hughes, well done. Now that you have volunteered to carry him, who else do you think should volunteer to carry the other end of the stretcher?"

"Don't know, Sergeant."

"Louder," shouted Bullshit.

"Don't know, Sergeant," screamed Jack.

"Yes, you do," shouted Bullshit.

"Private Smith, Sergeant," screamed Jack.

"Two good answers, Private Hughes," said Bullshit in a normal voice. "Arrange to get him there for 0830 hours prompt and ensure he passes." Tommy looked daggers at Jack for he was Private Smith and did not fancy this duty at all; as his was the only surname Jack could remember at the moment Bullshit was shouting at him, Tommy got volunteered! Bullshit looked at Jimmy for long enough for Jimmy to start squirming and then said, "And you, Private Thomson, can report to the MI Room at 0800 hours and persuade them to lend you a stretcher. Dismiss," and at that, they were dismissed for the night.

The following morning, Jimmy came back from the MI Room without the stretcher. All he could say was that the Corporal had simply told him to fuck off. Jack knew that Bullshit would not accept that.

"Right," he said. "We'll have to carry him on his mattress. Tommy, Jimmy and Cliff each grab a corner and we'll move him that way." Which is what they did. As they neared the MI Room, they spotted Bullshit heading in their direction. There was nothing they could do about that, so they kept going. Bullshit watched them struggling to get the mattress with Andy on it through the door but continued to say nothing; he simply accompanied them into the building. The Corporal who had refused Jimmy the stretcher, perhaps because Bullshit was standing there, simply stood by the measuring strip. Andy stood up and was measured at 5 feet 2 and a ½ inches. Result! As they started to make their way out of the MI Room, Bullshit stopped them and asked Jimmy why he hadn't gotten a stretcher like Bullshit had told him to. Jimmy said, in all innocence, "Because he," pointing to the Corporal, "because he told me to fuck off when I asked to borrow one."

"Whose idea was it to use the mattress?" asked Bullshit.

"Private Hughes," said Jimmy.

"Carry on," said Bullshit. So they did. They could still hear Bullshit having a go at the Corporal when they were a 100 yards away. Jack said to Jimmy, "If I were you, I would make sure I stay well away from that Corporal if you can."

Unfortunately for Jimmy, later that morning they were marched to the MI Room again for more injections. When the Corporal saw Jimmy, his eyes lit up. Everyone else had a jab in each arm; Jimmy received his as one in each cheek of his arse and had difficulty sitting for several days!

# Chapter 48

Wednesday afternoon was designated for sport virtually throughout the entire army. The problem for Bullshit was that with only 13 of them in the platoon, there weren't enough to make two full teams for any of the common sports such as football. But sport said the training programme, and so sport there would be. Bullshit devised a cross-country run except they didn't really have any countryside to run over. What he did was to tell them to run down the road outside the camp for 2 miles to the Royal Engineer's Camp at Longmoore where they were to make a mental note of the unit designation number. They were then to follow the signpost to an ancient site and note the date of it before returning on a B road from that site to the camp. Bullshit told them that the reason they were sent on this route was to prevent cheating; "I know you lot. If I sent you down to the REs and back you'd all stop halfway there, you horrible, idle lot you, and send just one of you to the RE Camp to get the number then you'd all run in here panting and wheezing like a lot of old women, that you are, and pretend you'd all run all the way. Well, I won't have it. They don't call me Bullshit for nothing. The first one back is excused parade in the morning and the last one will be parading in the cookhouse to wash up after tea. On your marks, get set, go!"

Jack returned first by a good ten minutes. Bullshit was suspicious but as Jack could answer the set questions and a couple Bullshit threw in for good measure, he reluctantly accepted that Jack had indeed run the full five miles of the route. Last in by quite a margin were Tommy and Jimmy. They hit on the idea that if they crossed the finishing line together, then no one person would be last, and Bullshit would be defeated! Bullshit was not defeated; he called it a draw for last and sentenced both of them to the cookhouse fatigues. He also sent them both back to the RE Depot because they both obviously needed the training. Having come from a life of boozing, smoking and very little physical exercise, Tommy and Jimmy struggled to get fit, but this was not a problem for the army; they were used to having very unfit recruits joining them. For Jack, straight from school where fitness, PT and manly sports were a mantra, the run hardly broke a sweat.

What did break a sweat was to discover that the first parade in the morning was Pay Parade and he had been excused it! Bullshit thought it was hilariously funny. Jack didn't. It also taught him that being the best didn't always pay and he resolved from then on to make sure that he didn't shine at anything unless he had to. The resolve didn't actually last very long.

At the Pay Parade, they were lined up in two ranks facing the pay table at which sat an officer, a Lieutenant, without a hat on, and a Royal Army Pay Corps Sergeant. Bullshit instructed them that once their name was called, they were to march forward to one pace away from the officer, halt, salute, and hand him their pay book with which they had just been issued. The Pay Sergeant would call out

161

the amount they were due. Once the officer had handed them the book back, duly signed with their money sitting on it, they were to count their money, ensure the money amount matched the amount written in the book and then in a loud voice they were to shout out 'pay and pay book correct, sir'. They were then to salute again, turn to their right and march back to their position.

Since two of the recruits had only joined the army the day before and none of them had had any instruction in how to salute, Jack thought *this is going to be good*. The first three recruits were awful, and Bullshit made each of them march out twice. He would probably continue doing this, but the Lieutenant realised that this was going to take all day and told Bullshit to stop making them do it again and to take them away afterwards and make sure they could present themselves properly next week.

There was one more recruit before Jack and then his name was called. Jack, perhaps in shame at his failure to salute the Lord Lieutenant of Surrey, marched forwards, swinging his arms shoulder high, crashed to a halt, saluted with a salute that would have put a Guardsman to shame, and handed his pay book to the Lieutenant. Having had his book and pay handed back to him, he counted the pay and then called out loudly and clearly, "Pay and pay book correct, sir," saluted, again a cracker, took a step back, turned to his right with a crash of boots and marched off back to his place.

As he returned, he could see the looks on the faces of the Platoon, but best of all was the look on Bullshit's face. Bullshit marched them from the Pay Parade to a classroom where they were to be indoctrinated into the Corps' history, so Bullshit didn't have a chance to have a go at Jack until the end of the day when they had returned to their barrack room.

Bullshit ordered Jack outside and then ordered him to quick march, slow march and incorporate left turns, right turns, halts, saluting to the front, breaking ranks and then made Jack do them all again at the double, all of which Jack executed impeccably!

"Right, smartarse," said Bullshit. "You didn't learn that lot by reading a fucking book, SO HOW DID YOU LEARN IT?"

"In the Army Cadet Force, Sergeant," replied Jack, realising that the game was over.

"What rank did you hold?" asked Bullshit in a more normal voice.

"Lance Corporal, then Corporal, then Sergeant and finally Cadet Under Officer, Sergeant." Bullshit continued to stare at him. He then asked why Jack hadn't said anything before. Jack answered, "Because you didn't ask me about the Cadet Force, Sergeant." Bullshit continued to stare.

"What unit were you in?"

"The School Cadet Platoon of the 4/5th East Surreys, which became the-"

"And how long were you in?"

"Just over five years, sergeant."

"What courses/qualifications did you get?"

"Passed Certificate A, parts one and two, qualified as a Marksman five years running, won an NRA Cadet 100 badge five years running, shot for England two years running and won the Surrey Lord Lieutenant's Badge as the best Cadet NCO in the county this summer, Sergeant." Bullshit looked at him for a long time.

"I knew you were a smartarse," said Bullshit, "but not a fucking smartarse," and at that he walked away.

# Chapter 49

By the end of their second week at Bordon, they had increased to 23 recruits which was just enough to form a Platoon. Although new recruits continued to trickle in, they were now a formed Platoon and new arrivals formed the next one, in another barrack block, to follow them to Buller Barracks in Aldershot at some time in the future. They were to spend the third week at Bordon receiving final fittings for their new Service Dress, quite a lot of drill and PT and final medical assessments.

On the morning of that last week, Bullshit came along their ranks when they fell in outside at 0830 hours and inspected them. When he got to Jack, he took a long time examining every detail of Jack's appearance. He ended up standing behind Jack and then asked, "Am I hurting you, soldier?" *Oh no*, thought Jack, *not that hoary old one*.

"NO, SERGEANT," he screamed.

"AM I HURTING YOU, PRIVATE HUGHES?"

"NO, SERGEANT," screamed Jack.

"WELL, I SHOULD BE; I'M STANDING ON YOUR FUCKING HAIR. GET IT CUT. YOU'RE A FUCKING DISCRACE, A FUCKING, DISGUSTING CRAWLING SHIT HOUSE; WHAT ARE YOU?"

Jack was annoyed and upset at this. He knew, because he had done it for years, that the 'am I hurting you…' was the standard result of an inspecting NCO not being able to find anything wrong with the individual's turn out, thus the 'am I' etc and the order to 'get your haircut.' He knew that Bullshit was going to do something, because he was clearly pissed off at Jack's failure to reveal his Cadet Force history soon enough, but he hadn't expected the swearing, especially as swearing at recruits was specifically forbidden under Army Rules and Regulations. Of course, a degree of it always went on, it was just something you expected, but Bullshit's tirade was over the top in Jack's view, especially as his turn out was excellent, so instead of repeating the language as he was expected to do Jack shouted, "I'M A FORNICATING DISCREDIT, AN UNACCEPTABLE, LIKELY TO CAUSE DISGUST, MOVING ON MY KNEES, ROOM OF EASEMENT, SERGEANT."

Bullshit looked at him, getting redder and redder by the second. *Oh, oh*, thought Jack, *he's going to kill me*. He didn't. What he did do was march Jack at the double straight in to the Adjutant's Office. The Adjutant, a Captain, looked up, startled by their sudden appearance with Bullshit calling out the step and Jack crashing to a halt and saluting when ordered to do so. Bullshit was virtually incoherent. He managed to blurt out, "This is Private Hughes, sir. I had reason to chastise him for his appearance, and he used unsoldierly language to me. He said…" and at that, Bullshit came to a stop. He paused and then said, "Tell the officer what you said."

Jack said, "Sergeant Ellis was unable to find any fault with my turnout, so he made the old joke about hurting me by standing on my hair. He then, contrary to Army Rules and Regulations, started swearing at me. He used language I do not use, and then he ordered me to repeat it. This I could not do, so I changed it to," and at that, Jack repeated what he had said.

The Adjutant said, "All right, Sergeant, I will deal with this." Bullshit saluted smartly, about turned, and marched out.

"Stand at ease, stand easy," ordered the Adjutant. "You are quite right about swearing, and it is discouraged in the modern Army, but NCOs used to so many years in National Service are finding it hard to adjust to the new rules. Sergeant Ellis is a very good senior NCO, and he is extremely good with recruits. Consider how well the other recruits in your platoon have come on, and I am sure that you will agree with me what a good job he has done. I don't believe for one minute that you haven't used that language or indeed used it to recruits at the school platoon where you did so well.

"Yes, I know all about that. Sergeant Ellis came to see me last night and told me what you had told him about your career in the Cadet Force; so this morning, first thing, I telephoned the school and spoke to Captain Hiller who not only confirmed what you had told Sergeant Ellis but told me several other things about you including that you would have been School Captain had you not joined the army which he said was their loss and our gain.

"I do not propose to take any action against you for what you said to Sergeant Ellis, nor do I intend to take any against him. What I will do is give you some advice; never show up an NCO in front of more junior ranks, it's terribly bad form and likely to lead to a loss of prestige and authority for the NCO and grief for the insulter when the NCO gets his own back. I don't believe that Sergeant Ellis will try to get his own back, by the way, that's how good an NCO he is. The other thing I will say to you is always bollock in private and praise in public. March out." And at that, Jack came to attention, saluted, about turned and marched out.

# Chapter 50

The following day, a Friday of course, they were transferred to Buller Barracks in Aldershot—home of the British Army. The barracks had been built in 1890 and very little had been done to update them; they were told that there were plans to replace them with new, modern blocks but that would be in a few years' time. As it was, the blocks consisted of two rooms upstairs and two down with the ablutions situated in the centre of the blocks between the rooms. The good news was that there was a good supply of hot water and a heated drying room for wet kit; the bad news was that the only heating in the rooms was a pot-bellied, cast iron stove. Set in the middle of the room with a small coke holder alongside it, the stove and the holder were highly polished. This meant they hadn't been used for heating for quite some time. As they were now heading for the end of October, the nights were becoming markedly colder.

Each of the Sections was allocated a room. The bed spaces were not pre-allocated so Jack lost no time in grabbing a space near the stove, but he only realised, having examined it carefully, that it was highly unlikely that he would ever benefit from any heat from it. It was so clean that it was obvious that it had not been lit in a long time. However, they were told where to fetch their allocation of coke each week so perhaps it was possible to fire it up now that the winter was fast approaching—they'd soon see.

They were told that they were confined to barracks until otherwise informed. This was peculiar since the camp was quite spread out with a number of roads running around and through it and there was no perimeter wall as such. There was a Guardroom, with which they were all to become familiar in various ways, and besides the normal offices there was a NAAFI attached to the Cookhouse and nearby the Jock Club, as it was known. Properly, the St Andrew's Club, it served food, drinks and bits and bobs, very much like the NAAFI, but cheaper and a better quality; it was run by a church of Scotland set-up and was mainly intended for homesick Scott's soldiers, but with National Service having finished there were nowhere near as many soldiers coming through the training system so the Jock Club was open to all and very welcoming it was. Also, nearby was a church and canteen run by the Salvation Army, known to all squaddies as the 'Sally Bash'. The Jock Club and the Sally Bash were preferred by the soldiers to the NAAFI. The NAAFI was run by paid staff of a not-so-wonderful enthusiasm; you bought things there because you couldn't get them elsewhere, a case of buying something despite the staff, not because of them which was not the case in the other two. Run by volunteers, committed individuals determined to do good, it was a pleasure to attend them. They would both send a mobile tea shop out to the ranges, if requested to do so. Strictly, the platoons were supposed to order the tea van from the NAAFI, but the NAAFI was universally disliked as its service was poor, the tea or coffee cold, the buns and sandwiches stale and the costs much higher than the Jock Club or the Sally Bash ones; the NAAFI was also unreliable, often not turning up on time or at all, just because it was raining or cold whereas the others always turned up, on time, and in every weather. They could only request the Jock Club or Sally Bash to come out if the NAAFI were unavailable, so the log book showed a lot of 'NAAFI unavailable' to justify the Jock Club or Sally Bash booking! Initially, they were not to get much time to visit any of the establishments as their basic training was to take up so much of their time. The basic military training was planned for six weeks to be followed by trade training of various lengths dependent on the trade, in Jack's case, a further six weeks.

Monday started with the usual room inspection and kit was thrown about willy-nilly. The day was to become the usual mix of drill, PT and visits to the MI Room for more injections. On Tuesday, they were being hounded in the gym as usual and then they were formed into two lines and doubled to the MI Room where they had a vaccine—for smallpox—dabbed onto their left arms which were then scratched all over by the Medic with what looked like a needle stuck in a cork. As soon as the platoon had been vaccinated, they were doubled back to the gym to carry on being put through the normal hazing by the PTIs.

Jack was to develop a hatred of all PTIs throughout his service. Soldiers had to be fit, but the PTIs were for the most part sadistic bullies, Narcissists who couldn't walk past a mirror without admiring themselves in it and who, of course, were never to face danger in the line, they were always nice and safely tucked away in training depots.

Having suffered the rigours of PT, they then showered, always under the eyes of the PTIs before being hustled to the next lesson. However, the showering was to have an unusual result as virtually the entire platoon was to wake up the following morning with enormously swollen left arms which were very painful to the touch and to move. Marched to the MI Room en masse, the cause was deemed to be the vaccine spread down their arms by the showers and so they were then all put on light duties for a couple of days—it was worth the pain!

What it did mean was a rapid change to the training programme to put back the more energetic lessons and bring forward those of a less strenuous nature. The following morning, the timetable had listed drill to be followed by PT, both from which they were now excused. Consequently, they were split up into three Sections, two of which were taken off in one direction, and the one of which Jack was a member were marched to the Armoury, more a stroll really since they couldn't swing their left arms properly, to collect an SMG, Stirling Sub-Machine Gun, each, it being much smaller, lighter and easier to handle than the SLR rifle which would normally have been taught first. They were then 'marched' to the Weapons' Training Wing and placed in a room. The NCO then left them saying the Weapons' Instructor would be with them immediately, and in the meantime, they were to sit still on the chairs provided and not, under any circumstances, to play with the SMGs.

As soon as he had gone, there were the ones who just had to 'machine gun' everyone else with 'rat-tat-tat' in various forms ruling the sound waves! Jack, after about ten minutes, started to feel uncomfortable not so much by the imitation war going on all around him but by the absence of the Instructor and sure-fire knowledge that authority would take a dim view of a squad skiving and doing nothing when they should have been undergoing training. Consequently, Jack made his feeling known which was not greeted too well at first by the other seven members of the Section but when he explained that they would maybe enjoy the relaxation now, but they would certainly pay for it in the future, and anyway, even if they sat there unaccompanied for the lesson, they had no idea where to go for the next one or even if this was supposed to now be a double lesson given the changes that had had to be made to the programme. Sense prevailed, and little Andy McKay was sent off to the Headquarters to report their situation.

Once he had gone, Jack stripped his SMG to its component parts and laid them out on the floor—the day's training at Shorncliffe Summer Camp now paying dividends. He swiftly reassembled it and looked up to find all the others looking at him in sheer amazement. Tommy was the first to ask to be shown how to do that. Jack was reluctant. None of the safety protocols had been gone through and it was obvious that all the others would be into 'me too' as soon as he started. Jack reluctantly agreed to show all of them but only on the condition that it was done properly.

Consequently, he lined them up, standing, and stood to the side but enough in front of them that they could all clearly see him but such that he was not directly in the line of fire if one of the SMGs should be loaded. Just as Jack started into his spiel, they heard footsteps outside the door. There were obviously at least two persons which Jack assumed were Andy and the missing Instructor. But it wasn't. In strode the Commanding Officer, a Lieutenant Colonel, accompanied by the Regimental Sergeant Major. It is commonly believed that when someone is about to die, their whole life passes before their eyes at that moment; in Jack's case, as he was a young man, that didn't take very long, but pass it did!

"Where is your NCO?" asked the Colonel. Since he was looking straight at Jack, Jack felt he had no choice other than to answer.

"We don't know, sir."

"What have you done about it?"

"Private McKay has gone to HQ to report, sir."

"You are?"

"412 Private Hughes, sir."

"It looks to me, Private Hughes, that you were in some way instructing this class?"

"Well, sir, I…"

"The answer to that question, Private Hughes, is 'Yes, sir' or 'No, sir'. Which is it?"

Jack had no choice other than to answer, "Yes, sir," as he had clearly been doing just that, albeit he had hardly started.

"Carry on, then," said the Colonel before walking to the back of the room and sitting down, the RSM following suit.

Jack swallowed. Jack closed his sphincter muscle as tight as he could. Again, faced with no choice, he started. "The first and most important thing when handed any weapon or during weapon training is to ensure that the weapon is safe. At least one soldier per month is killed by an empty weapon." He hoped to God that the NCO at summer camp had been right with that statistic! "That is, the soldier concerned thought it was unloaded, but it wasn't. So, keep your fingers well away

168

from the trigger and point the weapon towards the ground. Why towards the ground, Private Smith?"

After a pause Tommy answered, "To be safe."

"Good answer, but why not point it towards the ceiling?" Silence all round. "Well, I'll tell you. There is a floor above this one and you can hear people moving around if you listen. So unless you know exactly where the Sergeant Major is and you purposely intend to give him another fundamental orifice, you point the weapon at the ground." It took a moment for what Jack had said to register before laughs erupted from the squad.

"Settle down, it wasn't that funny. Had there been no room upstairs, we would point the weapon at the ceiling as the floor could be hard, something like concrete and a negligently discharged round could ricochet up and injure someone. In our circumstances, pointing at the floor is the least dangerous option so that is what we do. Now see this button on top of the magazine," and Jack pointed to the button he was talking about and demonstrated how to press it and remove the magazine.

As the Colonel showed no signs of leaving, Jack had no option other than to continue the lesson covering how to ensure the weapon was unloaded and then how to strip it down to its component parts and then reassemble them again. Just as he had them carrying out the exercise quickly for the third time, footsteps could be heard outside. The door flew open and in marched a Corporal followed by Andy McKay. Not seeing the Colonel and the RSM, the Corporal barked at Jack, "And what do you think you're doing, sunshine?"

The Colonel interrupted and said, "I've already had that conversation, and I don't think we need to go there again. What I do think you need to do is to take this squad to their next lesson and then explain to the RSM exactly why you were not here to give the instruction that Private Hughes so ably did. Carry on." At which he got up and left the room followed by the RSM who paused long enough to give the Corporal a look that indicated that he was not going to enjoy giving his explanation to the RSM.

# Chapter 51

The rest of the day passed fairly uneventfully on the rearranged light duties programme. But on Part I Orders that night, the admin programme published in the afternoon to let everyone know the events for the next day, especially things like defaulters' parades, compassionate interviews etc to be carried out by the OC, a Major commanding a Company, and that by the CO, the Colonel, for more weighty matters. Jack was more than somewhat dismayed to find that he was listed for CO's Orders at 10.30 hours the following morning.

The others thought it was hilarious with various suggestions from that he was to be shot by firing squad to the Sergeant Major was going to tear him an additional fundamental orifice. In the event, he presented himself to the RSM's office 10 minutes before the appointed time to be minutely inspected by the RSM. His comment, having completed the inspection, that Jack's hair was too long and needed to be cut again was a clear indicator that there was nothing wrong with Jack's turnout. At the appointed time, the RSM knocked on the Colonel's door and went inside, leaving Jack outside. In moments, he reappeared, called Jack to attention and then marched him in to a halt in front of the Colonel's desk. He was ordered to salute and then stand at ease.

"Private Hughes, I have looked into your record following our meeting yesterday. The demonstration you put on was quite exceptional, especially as you had no handbook or notes to guide you. Army Cadets are not normally trained in the Sub Machine Gun, it being generally regarded as too dangerous for them. Just how did you come by your knowledge of it?"

Jack explained the special training the Battalion Shooting Team had received as a reward for their performance and Jack being chosen to shoot for England against Australia and Canada.

"That was back in the summer?"

"Yes, sir."

"And no refresher training of any kind since?"

"No, sir."

"And only the one lesson on it?"

"Yes, sir."

The Colonel paused and then said, "Is your knowledge of the SLR as good as your knowledge of the Stirling?"

"Yes, sir," said Jack although he was very glad he had been caught with the SMG, the SLR being quite a bit more complicated with more parts and more knowledge required and he was damn certain a presentation on the SLR would not have been as good as the SMG.

"Tell me about the other training you underwent in the ACF?"

Jack wasn't at all sure where to start so he described the requirements to pass Certificate A Parts I and II, including drilling a squad, map reading, camping, shooting, including representing England and the Battalion for five years and brief details of the exercise with the TA.

"Hmm," he paused for a while.

"Your presentation was positively excellent, quite the best I have seen, and the RSM agrees with me that it would embarrass the NCOs here who would be training you if you continued in basic training; given what you have just described it would be a complete waste of time for you to complete basic training with your current squad, and therefore, I intend to transfer you with immediate effect to the Potential Officer Cadet Wing. Your move will appear in Orders tonight. I shall be keeping an eye on your progress, Private Hughes, and I am assured the Company Sergeant Major bears you no ill will for planning a second fundamental orifice for him. Any questions?"

"No, sir," said Jack with a smile on his face at which the RSM called him to attention, had him salute and then march out.

Jack returned to the barrack room and packed his kit. There was no sign of the lads, so he took his kit over to the POC Wing, in the event, another barrack block two rows over. The other POCs, seven of them, were gathered around a Sergeant who broke off to greet Jack with, "You'll be Private Hughes, yes?"

"Yes, Sergeant."

"I'm Sergeant Williams," and before anything else could be said, the door opened and in strode the Platoon Sergeant from the Platoon that Jack had just left. Having gained permission from Sgt Williams to speak to Jack, he took Jack aside and told him he had volunteered to box for his old recruit platoon as he was the only one big enough to fight the heaviest guy in the Platoon two weeks in front of them. Jack tried to protest but his efforts were in vain.

The contest was to be two nights hence, and Jack was not looking forward to it. When he got his first look at his opponent as he climbed into the ring, his heart fell. He was a good two inches taller than Jack and probably five or six stones heavier—a veritable giant if a bit podgy. As he sat on his stool waiting for the bell, Jack tried to remember everything his grandfather had said about his boxing days. As Jack had tried to avoid everything to do with his grandad's would-be lessons, there wasn't very much to remember. The only item that stuck in his mind was his grandad's statement that no one liked to be hit in the face, so they always made sure that was covered. They also covered their face and head well so that they could only rarely be reached by a blow to the face or head.

Grandad had also explained that a good body punch, delivered with sufficient force into the solar plexus, could result in the end of the fight. Jack only had a vague idea of where the solar plexus was. He knew it was a concentration of nerves and somewhere in the stomach, just under the rib cage. So that was it, that was the plan, because Jack had no intention of going three rounds being battered by the brute in the opposite corner.

As soon as the bell rang, Jack shot out of his corner and faced his opponent just as he came clear of his stool; jabbing two straight lefts at his face resulted in Goliath raising his gloves to cover his face from the jabs as he expected and intended. Doing so left his stomach exposed, and it was quite a big flabby one, evidence of an unfit lifestyle which the army had yet to rid him of, and Jack let rip with a straight right into the point, dead centre and just at the base of the rib cage where he believed the solar plexus was situated. He was right, as was his grandad. By luck, Jack had delivered a perfect punch with his whole weight behind it. The other thing he remembered just in time was to try and punch completely through your opponent when delivering what you hope would be a knockout blow. As he had never boxed, Jack had never practiced the proper placement of his feet or getting his shoulder behind a punch but somehow he got it just right, and the result was an enormous woof of expelled air and an anguished cry as his opponent collapsed onto the canvas. He was still gasping, trying to breathe and giving out loud moaning sounds when the referee counted him out. At first, the audience sat stunned, then the cheers from his ex-fellow platoon members erupted.

Jack wasn't to know it but word of his prowess, a bout that lasted only 13 seconds from beginning to end, spread far and wide throughout the Corps, perhaps the explanation for why he never experienced much in the way of bullying or hazing from other soldiers. As his victory meant victory for his platoon, the other matches being tied three each, Jack was quite the hero of the day but as far as he was concerned, that was the last time he would ever box, solar plexus or no solar plexus!

# Chapter 52

Jack, by now 6 ft 1 ½ inches tall, was used to being one of the tallest in any gathering but amongst this lot of POCs, bar one, he felt like a dwarf. Ranging between 6 ft 4 inches and 6 ft 7 inches, they all towered over him bar one who was, as it turned out, 5 ft 6 inches tall. Skinny with it, Charles Wilson, he refused to answer to Charlie, turned out to be a right little shit. It very rapidly became clear that the others all hated him and routinely called him Charlie as a sign of disrespect and to annoy him.

As it turned out, they were being briefed for an exercise to start the following day where they were to be attached to two-man teams, one driver and one signaller, who, as part of their training, were to drive to various map reference points, set up signal stations and send and receive signals to a central command. These teams were to provide communication links to higher echelon during convoy movements in peacetime and in war; thus, the driver needed proficiency in map reading and driving and the signaller in keeping radio contact, mostly coded, with HQ.

The POCs, supposedly more intelligent and more experienced, were attached to the teams to provide whatever support was needed. Lasting three days, they were a bit of a skive and, so long as the weather was good, a pleasant way to while away time. Jack enjoyed the exercise, but he couldn't really say he learned anything from it.

As his time went on in the POC wing, it became apparent that what they did not do was provide anything in the way of training or experience which would be useful in passing the Regular Commission's Board, the first vital step on the route to Sandhurst. In fact, as Jack was to discover, the POC Wing wasn't much more than a handy source of more-intelligent-than-normal soldiers who could be used for any task the depot needed doing.

Shortly after joining the Wing, Jack found himself volunteered with Charlie Wilson to be the enemy during a night exercise involving Jack's old platoon. They were briefed to recce the platoon at night who were on a five-day exercise. The briefing included finding their position, learning what they could about what they were doing and if possible, to take a prisoner. Since this last could be quite physical, Charlie was not at all keen to take part. The most he would do was hide in bushes near to their campsite and wait for Jack whilst he went off on the recce.

Jack wasn't bothered about being on his own; in fact, he preferred that as there were no others to make noises, blunder around and generally cock things up. The fact that Charlie was shit scared that the recruits might catch him and give him a good going over didn't bother Jack at all—he knew that if they were chased, he could easily outrun Charlie, leaving him to be caught and done over!

Jack found their position quite easily as they had a good fire going and were making plenty of noise. Jack approached carefully and slowly, making sure he always had trees or bushes behind him which meant that he would not be outlined against a light background. Exactly as he had done when he had crept up on the enemy platoon when he had been in the Cadets, Jack reached just a few feet from their position. Lying still for some ten minutes or so, he was able to pick out the outlying trenches dug around the position, and carefully skirting them as he slid on his belly, he was able to slide under some undergrowth and ensconce himself within a few feet of the fire knowing that the recruits would have no night vision as they were all looking into the fire.

He was able to listen to the briefing for the following day, including who would be acting as the Section Commanders etc. As he prepared to slide away, he heard Andy McKay's voice declaring that 'he was going for a slash.' Recognising the opportunity this represented, Jack slid back behind a bush, stood up and simply walked after him. To anyone who noticed, he was simply another member of the platoon, identity being impossible to determine as it was so dark. He followed Andy and let him finish his slash before grabbing him from behind, with his hand firmly clamped over Andy's mouth Jack whispered in his ear, "If you make a sound, I'll cut your throat." At which Jack laid the back of his bayonet against Andy's throat to ensure he was thoroughly cowed. It was then a simple matter to march him away from the position and back to base, collecting Charlie on the way.

Back at base, on reporting in, Charlie immediately claimed credit for the capture of the prisoner. Jack was not surprised since he had seen enough of Charlie's fawning and creeping around Sergeant Williams back at the wing. So Jack interjected, "Why don't you tell Sergeant Williams how and where you captured him and what the recruit Platoon's plans are for tomorrow while you're at it?"

Charlie stuttered nothing of coherence, because, obviously, he had no idea of how it had been accomplished. Sergeant Williams then turned to Jack and said, "So why don't you tell me what happened?"

Normally, soldiers stick together in the face of authority, so Jack very carefully explained that Private Wilson had thought it prudent to secrete himself in some bushes and thus be able to run back for help if he, Jack, should be captured. He then described how he had approached the recruit Platoon's position, listened to their plans for tomorrow and had then seen the opportunity, when Private McKay had announced his attention to relieve himself, to take him prisoner.

Sergeant Williams then turned to Pte McKay and asked him if Jack's version of events was correct, which he did. He then turned to Jack and asked exactly where Pte Wilson had hid. Jack pointed to some bushes just visible about 20 yards away.

"There, Sarge," pointing.

"And where did you find their position?"

"About three quarters of a mile that way, pointing. I have the map reference position if you want it."

At that they were dismissed for now. Andy was given a place to sleep and was returned to his platoon in the morning.

Nothing was ever said to Jack about his efforts in capturing Andy, but Charles Wilson found life far less pleasant than it had thereto been. And although he didn't know it, he carried a reputation with him throughout his service of being a daffodil, i.e. yellow.

Life passed by in a series of military drills, fatigues and odd jobbing until one day Jack's name appeared on Orders, instructing him to attend a Company Commander's interview the following day.

Duly scrubbed, polished and ironed, Jack paraded at the appointed time. What he was told came as a bit of a bombshell. He was told that he was to return to his platoon on the forthcoming Friday, it was Wednesday today, and travel with them to Yeovil to undergo trade training; he had nominated Staff Clerk as a choice when signing on but had been assured this was just a formality to 'fill in the form'; he would never actually become a Staff Clerk as he would obviously exercise his option to leave the army if he was not selected for Officer Cadet training. The real ball breaker was to be informed that a decision had been taken to aim him at Mons Officer Cadet School rather than Sandhurst. Mons training lasted about six months whereas Sandhurst was two years, so in theory, he would be commissioned much sooner by going to Mons rather than Sandhurst. He was not to worry that the commission from Mons was a Short Service one as he would always be able to apply for a Regular Commission at any time once he had been commissioned—this last remark was to come back and haunt him in the future. In fact, he had been lied to in this regard and would be again. There was, however, just a slight problem with the Regular Commission's Board in that the next Board he could attend was not until September next year, in other words, just about ten months away and there was the problem of what to do with him in the meantime. He was, therefore, being sent to re-join his original Platoon and accompany them to Yeovil where his trade training would take place. Following the completion of his course, he was being posted to 1 Company, RASC in Colchester which was part of the new Air Portable Brigade which was just being formed.

It was explained to Jack that the army was moving away from large numbers of big overseas garrisons which were to be closed and in the event of troops being needed in any particular part of the world, they could be flown in at very short notice. Much of their equipment could also be flown in but the very heavy kit, tanks, major artillery pieces etc. would be stored in much smaller and cheaper bases, strategically placed to service flown in troops anywhere in the world.

Jack marched out of that interview in a very mixed frame of mind. There was the uncomfortable feeling that he should have been told all this when he was in the process of joining but on the other hand, he would be an officer, provided he completed the selection and training process, much sooner than if he went to Sandhurst.

He made his way over to the old Platoon to find out the travel details etc. He discovered that Tommy had won the Best Recruit Award and Jimmy was packing to go home, having decided the army was not for him—something which did not surprise Jack as Jimmy's attitude had been completely wrong from the very beginning for someone joining the Regular Army, more in keeping with an unwilling conscript during National Service times.

# Chapter 53

They left Buller Barracks at lunchtime the following day, each of them clutching a paper bag containing a sandwich and an apple; why could they not have had a proper meal early enough so that they could at least be properly fortified for the journey ahead of them? They were rapidly becoming convinced that there existed in the army a highly secret department whose job was to ensure that the most difficult, inappropriate and buggeration factor was to happen to troops at every opportunity!

They eventually arrived in Houndstone Camp in Yeovil at 16.30 hrs on Friday evening when the next day was Christmas Eve. There was no sane reason why they could not have left Buller Barracks after breakfast and arrived comfortably for lunch with the whole afternoon to settle in. Instead, they arrived at just about the worst time possible. They were formed up on the parade ground in freezing, pouring rain and addressed by a Lieutenant Colonel. His welcoming address, for that was what it was, amounted to, "Welcome to Houndstone. Do your best, and I am sure you will pass your trade training. Keep away from the local Scrumpy; it is far too strong for young lads like you. The Company Sergeant Major will get you settled in. Happy Christmas to you," and he was gone!

Then the news got really bad. The CSM informed them, with some glee, that they had been chosen to provide the Camp Guard over the whole Christmas period! It worked out that they would form two details of 13, each of which would provide the Guard alternatively for 24 hours each for the next nine days.

Worse was to come. They were billeted in wooden 'spider' huts in 14-man capacity rooms. The good news was that they were centrally heated. The bad news was that the heating for the whole camp had been turned off for the entire Christmas period. The only places that were heated were the NAAFI, operating with a skeleton staff and reduced hours, and the Guardroom which was independently heated by the ubiquitous cast iron stove.

Jack was in the group to provide the Guard from 1800 hours on Christmas Eve. It meant he was free to come and go as he pleased, subject only to an inspection at the gate to ensure that he was clean, neat and tidy. The problem was the cold. They had each been issued with three blankets but although of wool, they were quite thin and worn and completely lacking in warmth. It was only the work of moments to remove the blankets from the other Guards' room giving them six blankets each and some small degree of warmth especially with four of them folded in half and sandwiched between the two remaining blankets tightly tucked in to retain them on the bed.

During their days off, Jack, along with Keith Voisey and Cliff Polisey, took a bus into Yeovil to explore, so they only did it once! There wasn't much. True, the Christmas decorations and atmosphere lifted the place, but it would take briefings from the full-time staff at the Camp to brief them on the decent and not-so-decent, pubs, bars, and cafes. The main thing that drove them back to the camp was the cold. It struck through their clothes and knifed them to the bone in seconds flat. It was to stay that way over the whole of Christmas and well into the New Year. For the first time, Jack wore his army-issue Long Johns. He had always regarded them with disdain as his grandfather's Long Johns on the washing line at home had forever painted a picture of such horror that he had vowed he would never wear such things even when he was old. However, so bad was the cold that not only did he wear them under his uniform on guard, but he wore them under his civvies when off duty!

When the 13 of them did parade for duty at 1800 hrs on the Christmas Eve for inspection, in their service dress and greatcoat, it was to discover that only 12 were actually required for the Guard; the best turned out soldier was chosen to be Stick Man. The Stick Man stayed in the Guardroom until midnight and was then released so that he could return to his bed. Up until that time, he kept the stove well stoked up and a never-ending supply of tea for the Guard Commander. The rest of the Guard were allocated 'stags'. Stags were the periods when they would patrol their allocated beats on the basis of two hours on and four off. Since they were ordered for a 24-hour Guard, it meant they would each do four periods on stag and four of four hours on rest. In reality, rarely did they get four hours of uninterrupted rest with sentries coming and going every two hours and preparation for going on guard, noise and disturbance from others, it was an extremely lucky soldier who got an hour's uninterrupted sleep, let alone four. 24 hrs on and 24 hrs off was scheduled for the following nine days! Many times during those days did Jack consider his option under his POC engagement that he could say, 'That's it, I've had enough' and walk away from the army but the main thing to prevent it was Jack was invariably selected as the Stickman. Just on one occasion was he not selected, and Jack was sure that was because the Guard Commander decided he should experience the pleasures of being on guard and not because he wasn't the smartest on parade.

It was every bit as bad as expected. Freezingly, bitingly cold. Within minutes, his hands, enclosed in plain woollen gloves, and his feet were like blocks of ice. The turned-up collar of his Greatcoat did little to protect his neck from the wind, and his nose dripped two icicles of frozen snot like stalactites. And at the end of his two hours' patrolling, the Guardroom was barely warm enough to reduce his extremities from frozen blocks before he had to once more venture out into the cold for a further two hours. The stags during daylight hours were little better as regards the cold but, at least there was less fear of the bogeyman or other nasties leaping out from dark corners, a common fear to all sentries especially during the darkest hours before dawn.

The one thing the cold did prove was the efficacy of Scrumpy in fighting it. Little Andy McKay was listed for Guard the first night there. Released from duty at 1800 hrs the next evening, he was in a taxi into the town by 1830 hrs. He returned at 2230 hrs pie eyed and legless. As a true Scott, he had gone out to show these Sassenach Colonels that no southern puffter Scrumpy could compare to the Water of Life turned out by the Scots for centuries which he was able to down in copious quantities before feeling even the slightest bit merry. His first pint of Scrumpy, flat and lacking any strong flavour to hint at its alcoholic content, had gone down like cordial and so, too, did the second and third. Navigating to the Gents mid-way through the fourth pint had proved mightily difficult as his left leg had wanted to go one way and his right leg, the opposite. It hadn't helped when one step forward had been followed by two back and his ending up further away from the bogs after three steps than he was when he started. Assistance from the Landlord, very familiar with such incapability of young soldiers imbibing more than a couple of pints of his best rough Scrumpy, rapidly, smoothly and with evidently much experience had Andy in a taxi and on his way back to camp within five minutes.

Back at camp, Andy somehow made it to his room but on arrival at the door, fell onto his knees and crawled into the room roaring like a lion. Amusing at first, it soon became very boring, especially the noise, and when he started to bite the waste bin, an old tin which had once contained the wax polish with which they polished the floor and which was in an absolutely disgusting state both visually and hygienically, it became enough is enough, so that several of the others grabbed him and forcibly tied him in his bed. Whilst this stopped his crawling and biting, it unfortunately did nothing to stop the roaring noise which continued unabated. Threats did nothing to stop it and with it by now being well past midnight and sympathy for Andy being at an all-time low, the suggestion by one of them to undo the large doors at the end of the room and carry him outside still in his bed was seized with alacrity and pleasure; so outside he went. Unfortunately, he could still be heard so it was only the work of moments to carry him, still strapped in his bed, way down the camp and onto the square where he could no longer be heard. He was fortunate that, everyone being on leave apart from the Guard, he was not discovered in his bed on the square. Having sobered up and with the monster of all hangovers, he managed eventually to free himself and find one of the off-duty guard to help him carry his bed back to the barrack room before anyone in authority discovered him or the bed. It was a surprise to discover the lethality of the local Scrumpy, the accuracy of the Colonel's warning and above all the efficacy of Scrumpy in helping the drinker sleep in sub-zero temperatures and come to no harm—apart from a three-day hangover!

# Chapter 54

Christmas was not a success that year; there weren't even any officers around to serve the Christmas lunch and worse, there wasn't even a Christmas lunch, just an unappetising gloop served up by a disgruntled Army Catering Corps' oik who made his displeasure at having to cook on Christmas as clear as he could.

The army being the army, all the permanent staff and trainee drivers and clerks, other than the few unlucky ones on duty over the Christmas period, had to return from leave by the Saturday lunchtime. The heating came on and the camp came alive on the Monday morning. That evening, Jack, Cliff Polisey and Keith Voisey decided to give the camp cinema the once over. Warm, cheap and comfortable was the decision. The film didn't matter too much; they were warm at last.

They occupied the end three aisle seats in the backrow. Just as the lights went out, three latecomers, women, otherwise indistinguishable in the dark, pushed past them to occupy the three seats starting next to Jack. Quite why they were there was a mystery since their chatting and laughing clearly indicated that they had no interest in the B movie and were not watching it. Jack started to get annoyed and was about to speak up when a man in the row in front of them turned around and told them in clear, precise, Anglo Saxon to be quiet and blessedly, they were.

At the interval, they then launched into a discussion about ices, drinks and nuts which culminated in the one sitting next to Jack standing up and squeezing past the three of them on her way to buy the required items from the ice-cream lady slowly moving up the aisle with her tray of goodies. As the woman squeezed past Jack, he couldn't resist saying to her, "And I'll have an Orange Maid, please."

Lo and behold, when she returned, fully laden, she handed Jack an Orange Maid lolly and said, "That'll be nine pence." Jack hadn't really wanted one but had said it in jest, but it had opened a door, and little did he know what going through it would cost him.

In the dark, even when the cinema lights were on during the interval, it wasn't very easy to distinguish features, but he could see well enough to realise that she was quite a beauty. Long dark hair and a southern-European complexion with a figure to die for, Jack decided there and then that he would try to further the conversation. With the cinema lights dimming and the start of the main feature that wasn't easy, but he did manage to extract her first name, Sylva, and that she was due to start a clerk's course on the Monday. A suggestion that they meet in the NAAFI on the Sunday was cut off when the Anglo-Saxon speaker interrupted again with the same threats, bringing their conversation to an end.

On Tuesday, they fell in outside their billet to be told that Jack was to be regarded as the Senior Soldier and thus, responsible for them for the next six weeks. It meant, for instance, that Jack marched the other two, Keith and Cliff, to the Trade Training School across at the other side of the camp when all the others who were to be trained as Drivers marched off in the opposite direction.

At the Trade Training School, they were to discover that there were 37 Women's Royal Army Corps soldiers and the three of them to be trained as Clerks. As it happened, 17 of the WRAC were complete beginners, like Jack and his mates, in that none of them could type while the remaining 20 women could. It thus made two even groups of 20.

The training itself was divided into two halves, learning to touch type taking up about half the six weeks and all the admin details of how to compose letters, create files, filing, the handling of documents of varying classifications from Restricted to Top Secret UK Eyes Only, signals and all the other bits and bobs necessary to become a properly trained Staff Clerk took up the other half.

The typing training commenced with an older WRAC Corporal producing several pairs of nail scissors which she handed out so that all the women could cut their finger nails—none of the three lads had finger nails long enough to worry about but many of the women did, and they were not pleased at losing their pride and joy grown and developed fastidiously over several years. But as the Corporal explained, it was impossible to learn to touch type with long finger nails. Upset was spread around when the two classes met in passing at the NAAFI, the other class taking their break before Jack's class, when the shorn sheep discovered that all the ones who could type had been allowed to keep their nails long. No explanation was forthcoming other than an enigmatic smile and an order to get on with it.

Pay day turned out to be a hoot. Pay parade was held in one of the huts large enough to hold both classes at the same time. Pay parade was conducted by a WRAC 2nd Lieutenant who sat at a table in front of the parade along with a civilian clerk who called out the amount to be paid to each soldier and ticked off the amount paid as each soldier took his or her pay. The lads were told to fall in at the back of the parade as they were to be paid last. Bad idea. It meant they stood there as each of the female soldiers were called forward to receive their pay. As was standard at every pay parade Jack attended, even when he was to conduct them himself years later, each soldier marched forward when their name was called, halted, saluted even though it would not be returned as the officer conducting removed their hat thus meaning they could not return the salute—done to prevent saluting dozens of times as each soldier was paid. The amount was called out, the pay book was signed, and the soldier called out, "Pay and pay book correct, ma'am."

It was the marching forward that caused immense merriment to the three lads. Most of the females could not march in a soldierly fashion at all. Some were too fat so that they wobbled forward and crashed to a halt like a jelly hitting a wall. Some of their arms were pushed so far from their proper up and down position that salutes looked like someone with knock knees except it was their arms and almost none could salute with a straight wrist with the hand ending up anywhere from their foreheads to their chins.

As this woeful display unfolded, it led to sniggers and muttered comments among the lads which did not really subside even though the female CSM, present at the parade, was loud and threatening in her demands for silence on parade.

The second pay parade was even worse with the girls' performances deteriorating as the parade went on, and the laughter from the lads got louder.

At the third pay parade, the three lads were told to parade at the front of the parade and it was, therefore, evident that they were to be paid first and then dismissed so that they would not be present when the women were paid. As they stood there watching the table being set up and the money laid out, they were able to see clearly the money being piled up in neat little columns on the table— something they had not been able to see from the back of the parade—and, of course, the piles of money had diminished to almost nothing by the time the lads were paid.

Seeing the piles gave Jack an idea. Whispering to the others, he outlined the idea. As it happened, Jack was called first as he appeared in the alphabet before Polisey and Voisey, so he was the one to try out his idea. Jack really dug in his heels as he marched forward and really crashed his boots in as he came to a halt before saluting. The hut had a wooden floor, raised above the ground, of considerable age. The springiness of the floor was very evident, sagging and rebounding, even when someone just walked across it. So, his heavy marching and crashing halt set up such a rebounding in the floor that the table was vibrated so much, considerable damage was done to the neat piles of two-shilling pieces and half a crowns forming the bulk of the pay laid out; the coins spread everywhere including on the floor.

The army being the army, all the coins had to be recounted and restacked while Jack stood there, the picture of martial innocence! Having received his pay and called out, "Pay and pay book correct, ma'am," Jack took a crashing step backwards, crashed a left turn and marched off, leaving another heap of fallen coins spread over the table and the floor. Authority was not amused. Both the 2nd Lieutenant and the CSM made it clear to Polisey and Voisey that so much rigidity would result in a considerable sojourn in the Guardhouse and weekend fatigues in the Cookhouse that both of them chickened out and almost tip toed through their payments.

Outside, all three smirked at their success which was to be short-lived. The following week, they were ordered to parade at the Driver Centre for their pay, and since this meant marching almost quarter of a mile each way in the bad weather that blighted the whole of the course, it would probably be true to say that it was a draw at best and they were deprived of the weekly entertainment that was the females' pay parade.

# Chapter 55

Jack and Sylva's relationship developed nicely. Sylva had been blessed with a long name, Sylva Anne, Connie Brodhead, and Jack used to tease her by calling her a different name each time they met. There wasn't a great deal of time for them to meet; being in different classes, they could not even meet during NAAFI breaks as Sylva's was ending as Jack's started. Still, it was quite soon before Sylva would buy him a tea and hand it to him as she left, enabling him to savour it—if that is the right word to use to describe NAAFI tea—since it was by that time cool enough to drink. Most drinks had either to be swallowed scalding hot or left almost untouched as the break was nowhere near long enough to get to the NAAFI, order a drink and drink it before having to rush back to the classroom. The Driver trainees were much luckier in this regard as they used to stop at the Instructor's, civilians for the most part, favourite truck stop, and they were only too willing to take a leisurely break in comfort before hazarding themselves to the learner drivers in their charge especially as it might be the last mug of tea they ever had, and so it always seemed entirely fitting that the trainees should pay for the Instructor's tea!

He and Sylva spent as much time together as possible, but this was not much. On camp, there was nowhere to go except the NAAFI, and it was impossible to be alone there. Saying goodnight never amounted to more than a quick kiss at the gate to the women's compound—the weather was awful and standing around in the cold and wet was distinctly unpleasant and even though Jack would have tolerated it, Sylva wouldn't. The back row of the cinema offered some privacy but that functioned only on Saturday and Sunday nights, and even then, there was always the problem of the staff flashing torches along the row.

They did one night find the TV room in the NAAFI deserted, deserted only because the TV was broken. Switching off the light and settling down in the darkest corner they could find, they settled down for a serious bit of snogging. After a few minutes, Jack thought, now is the time to start taking liberties; after all, it is always left to the man to make the first move and to risk his face being slapped, and his hormones were racing and well in the lead of any race, so he slid his right hand onto Sylva's left breast. He had anticipated a number of reactions from a slapped face at worst to her opening her blouse and bra at the best; what he got stunned him; she burst into tears and started sobbing her heart out. *Christ*, he thought, *I am glad I didn't attempt to put my hand on her leg she'd have had a conniption fit*; he didn't actually know what that was but his dad used the expression a lot, and he knew it meant extreme action somehow. Once she had stopped turning Jack's hanky into a sodden rag along the way, she explained between sobs and sniffs that she had been the victim of bullying and molestation at home by both her father and her brothers, two of them, and had secretly joined the army to get away from them. She had not told them what she planned to do and as

182

far as she was concerned, they were dead to her and she never intended to return to Mosside ever again.

Jack had no idea what to say, so after a while, he simply took her in his arms in a comforting cuddle and kissed the top of her head. They stayed there in the dark until she was ready to leave, and Jack then walked her back to her barracks. No goodnight kiss just a squeeze of her hands and a soft good night. The following day was a Sunday, and they walked to the transport café a few hundred yards from the camp and had a cup of tea and a sticky bun each with their relationship apparently back to normal although it was to be a long time before Jack made any passes again.

The course passed quickly. Jack found the typing quite easy, he had long and supple fingers and more by chance than judgement, had been allocated an Imperial typewriter which fitted him perfectly. To reach a B3 standard pass, the lowest one acceptable to qualify as a Clerk, meant being able to type 150 words in ten minutes with three or fewer errors. Jack was achieving more than 200 words with less than 5 errors regularly by four weeks into the course. This was B2 standard and entitled him to a pay increase but unfortunately, both because he was on the POC engagement and because he wasn't being taught the other B2 clerical skills, he could not benefit from it. Unusually, the average speed of the three lads on the course, at 175 words per minute, bettered the 17 girls on the course whose average was only 169 and this quite upset the female Instructors who were used to belittling any males on the previous courses who on every occasion had been beaten by the girls.

They all knew that the final Thursday would be taken up with written and typing tests; failure of which would result in back-squadding. It came as a surprise, therefore, to see in Part One Orders (the written instructions for the admin of the unit) on Wednesday night that the three lads were to parade for Adjutant's parade at 0900 hrs the following morning dressed in their best Service Dress.

Promptly at 0855 hrs, the three of them paraded as ordered. Unusually for the army, they were not kept waiting but were subjected to a cursory inspection by the RSM before being marched in before the Adjutant. Told to stand at ease and then stand easy, the Captain immediately addressed them. "I don't know how much you all know about the situation in Cyprus but EOKA, the terrorist organisation there which has been waging a mini war against us, seeking freedom to unite with Greece, has now started threatening to attack British families on the island. Since there is no way that we can protect them all, spread about as they are, the Government has decided to bring them all home. As I speak, they are all being brought out in little more than the clothes they are standing up in. They will be flown into various RAF stations around the country. Why am I telling you this? Because the RAF needs administration help at RAF Lyneham, which isn't very far from here. You will provide assistance by issuing travel warrants, money, helping by making telephone calls or anything else that the families need. Needless to say, you will be smart, soldierly and show these Brylcream lot how things should be done. Private Hughes, you will be appointed Senior Soldier as from now and are responsible for ensuring all three of you report back here at 1030 hrs dressed as you are and with sufficient kit to last you for five days. The rest of your kit is to be packed up and handed into the QM's Store to be kept safely for you until you return. You are also to hand in all your bedding and other kit with which you were issued when you arrived here. Transport will be here waiting at 1030 hrs, and I will inspect you before you go. Any questions?"

The three of them were stunned at the unexpected news. Jack was the first to speak.

"What's going to happen to our trade tests and qualifications, sir? Will we have to return to take them, will we be back-squadded or what?"

The Adjutant turned to a WRAC Captain sitting in the corner who Jack had not noticed until she spoke.

"I am in charge of the clerical training here, and I can tell you that you have all passed. Last night, Corporal Smythson spent her time examining the dummy test papers you took and the typing tests you took, and I am pleased to tell you that all achieved the necessary standards and you in particular, Private Hughes, obtained the highest scores ever achieved on these courses. Well done."

"Any other question?"

"No, sir."

"Fucking typical," said Jack once they were outside, "they knew yesterday that we would have to go because they had Corporal Smythson sorting through our work last night. They could have told us last night so that we could have prepared our kit, handed in the excess and been ready this morning. Instead, we are having to rush around like blue-arsed flies. Fucking typical."

# Chapter 56

And rush they did, only to then wait—the standard army system, hurry up and wait. Eventually, a mini-bus turned up and deposited them at the Guardroom at Lyneham at 1400 hrs—just too late for dinner. Eventually, an RAF Pilot Officer arrived to welcome them with the welcoming expression, "I don't know quite why you lot are here; we can perfectly manage without the army."

Not prepared to take any crap from the Brylcream boys, Jack responded with, "Does that mean we should return to Yeovil, sir? If I hurry, I am sure I could catch the mini-bus which has gone to fill up with fuel and get him to take us back?"

The Pilot Officer looked at Jack. Officer he might be, but he was no match for a squaddie feeling very pissed off at having to go and help the useless RAF and miss his last two days with his girlfriend. Eventually he said, "Well, as you're here now, we might as well use you. Corporal Wright, take these three soldiers to the temporary offices in the reception hangar and hand them over to Flight Sergeant Williamson. See they are issued with the necessary passes before you take them over there. Carry on." And at that, he strode away in that terribly important way that junior officers attempt, with little success, to adopt to impress lesser ranks. Unfortunately, lesser ranks didn't regard them as important enough to take any notice of them whatsoever.

Having been issued their passes, they then strolled over to the reception hangar offices led by Corporal Wright who proved to be their direct 'boss' in the role they were to carry out. It turned out that they were to be billeted in the room directly above hers in an accommodation block—nothing so common as barrack blocks in the RAF; even the Cookhouse was referred to as the Airmen's Restaurant. Snobby it might be, but the food was out of this world compared to the slop the army was still serving up, not quite having woken up to the fact that regulars, volunteers all, were not prepared to put up with the crap that was regularly served up to National Servicemen. It was to take several years for the army to extract its fundamental digit from its fundament and serve up decent food.

In the porta cabins that had been set up in the hangar, obviously of long standing, not just set up for this exercise, they chose a desk each and then were told about what they were expected to do. As it happened, filling in travel warrants and the supporting documents had formed part of their course only days before, and if anything, they were more au fait with what to do than were the mixed crew of airmen and airwomen, about 25 in all, who made up the team designated to do this work.

As it was just about 1700 hrs by the time they were 'inducted', Corporal Wright announced that it was time for food and led them off to the Airmen's Restaurant. There was no marching in a smart and soldierly manner, as they had been ordered to, to ensure they showed up the Airforce, by the RSM just before leaving Yeovil. Instead, they just joined in the mob shamble over to the restaurant.

As they walked, Cpl Wright chatted to Jack asking how long he had been in the army and what had made him join up etc. Jack reciprocated in kind and as happens occasionally, by the time they got to the restaurant they were chatting comfortably like old friends. Given that she was attractive and had a good figure, Jack was very happy at the way things were working out; hopefully she would be pleasant to work with.

The choice of food was enormous, the quality excellent and the amounts they could help themselves to prodigious. Once they had finished, Corporal Wright led them to their allotted accommodation in her block. She told Voisey and Polisey to make themselves comfortable, make their beds etc.—the necessary sheets, blankets and pillows were neatly stacked on the mattresses—and she told them to sort out Jack's as well since she had further issues to discuss with him.

Leading Jack upstairs, they came to double doors across the start of the upstairs corridor festooned with notices about this area being out of bounds to male airmen, female airwomen only allowed on penalty of death or worse.

"Don't worry about them," said she. "No one takes any notice of them, they are just for show for any visiting big wigs concerned with liaisons between the sexes leading to moral turpitude," she laughed. Jack was a little uncomfortable at being in an out-of-bounds area but comforted himself that he had been ordered to be there by a more senior rank and that would be his defence if he ever needed one!

Once inside her room, nicely feminised and entirely demilitarised, she closed and locked the door. Jack looked and thought, *that's a bit unusual*. Her next action astounded him. She unbuttoned her uniform dress and stepped out of it. Underneath, she wore only bra, pants and a garter belt holding up a pair of black stockings.

Smiling, she said, "We haven't got enough time for anything now as I was handed a note while we were eating that the first flight is due to land in half an hour, but I just wanted to show you what will be coming later." She laid extra stress on the 'coming', leaving no doubt as to what meaning she was attaching to the word. At that, she picked up a uniform blouse and invited Jack to do up the buttons. This he did with lots of 'clumsy on purpose' touching of her breasts through her bra. Stepping into a uniform skirt laid ready on a chair, she zipped it up and said, "Go and collect your other two, make sure they've made your bed up and get them and yourself over to the hangar 'toot sweet',"—least that's what it sounded like—and then spoiled her impeccable military order by brushing her right hand over the bulging front of Jack's trousers.

The work was hectic and extremely demanding. The children were the most difficult. Grabbed at a moment's notice, hustled into military transports of lorries, old coaches with little more than they were stood up, having had to abandon favourite toys and only allowed to bring one small toy that they themselves could carry and escorted by heavily armed soldiers, grim and warlike, deprived of sleep on the military transport aircraft, noisy and uncomfortable they then had to wait in slow moving queues whilst clerks, Jack included, dealt with their onward movement whether that was to be by railway travel warrant, laid on coaches or waiting for friends or loved ones to come and get them. It was harrowing for Jack and the others but absolutely devastating for the families, especially the kids, but they weren't service families for nothing and the stronger comforted the weak and amidst all this strode several airwomen, organised by one of the SNCOs from the Airmen's Restaurant with drinks and sweets which had a remarkable and calming effect on troubled, screaming, little children.

Starting at 1800 hrs, their shift lasted until 1000 hrs the next morning when they were released for three hours before the next batch of planes were expected. Jack and the others were totally fucked and could only fall into their pits only to be woken two and a half hours later, just time enough to shower, shave and snatch a hasty breakfast before it started all over again.

This pattern repeated itself over and over again for the next four and a half days. Towards the end of this time, feeling well and truly fucked off that he wasn't actually fucked—Corporal Wright had only been glimpsed in passing and Jack, was reasonably certain that she did not have the energy or time to engage in any of the promised frolics—Jack got fed up with nookie being so near and so far that he spent a lot of time trying to see a way that Nirvana could be achieved. He could not think of anything for nookie, but he did come up with an idea that he thought could ease the pressures on the clerical function and the families. The thought occurred to him that if teams of clerks flew out on the empty planes, they could then fly back with the families and get a lot of the admin done on the way back, easing life for the families and the resources back at Lyneham. Nothing ventured, nothing gained; Jack put forward the idea to a Flight Sergeant in the section who seemed mightily unimpressed by the idea, especially as it came from an almost brand-new Private soldier in the army. He nevertheless agreed to pass it on. On what turned out to be the last day at Lyneham, an RAF Wing Commander appeared among them, looking for Jack. Addressing himself to Jack, he said, "This idea of yours, Private Hughes, to travel out on the empty aircraft and then back with the families and get a lot of the work done on the way is a capital idea, but why did you not come up with it sooner?"

Jack had been in the army for long enough to know that praise rarely travelled downwards, only shit, and was stunned by the unfairness of it; after all, he was only a Private and all the scrambled eggs on their hats and shit for brains had come up with nothing. Before he could stutter a reply, the Wing Co carried on, "Still, the last aircraft is on its way back now, and you will be returning to your unit sometime late this evening." And they did in the same minivan that had delivered them there a few days before.

Corporal Wright did find them just as they were about to get into the bus and she pulled Jack into a passionate embrace and kissed him long and hard full on the lips. With that, she tossed a quick 'Good bye' to the other two and was gone. Both of them looked at him in amazement.

"How did you manage that?" asked Keith.

"Never you mind," said Jack and with that the two of them had to be content.

# Chapter 57

They arrived back in Houndstone Camp just in time for tea on Tuesday afternoon. The Guard Commander was all for sending them on to their next postings immediately, but the three of them did not know to where they were posted, and the offices had by this time closed so no travel warrants or flight documents could be forthcoming. They, therefore, drew bedding, mattresses and bedded down in one of the empty spiders.

The following morning, they reported to the Adjutant and were given their postings. Keith Voisey was posted to HQ 1 British Corp in Bielefeld in Germany, Cliff Polisey was posted to Singapore and Jack was posted to 1 Company RASC Air Portable Brigade in Colchester. They were never to meet again, and the erratic correspondence of letters and post cards between them gradually ceased as time went by.

Worse, as far as Jack was concerned, was the fact that he was totally unable to find out to where Sylva had been posted. Enquiries hastily made before they were bussed to the station elicited nothing although Corporal Smythson, their typing instructor, suggested that if Jack wrote to Army Records, they might forward a letter to Sylva although they probably would not tell him her address. Jack duly wrote off, and four weeks later, he received a reply from Sylva. She had been posted to Army Legal Services in London and was resident at a WRAC camp in Richmond Park. Jack actually knew the camp from running cross country competitions in the Park. The only problem in seeing her was he was bloody miles away in Colchester—right across the other side of London and then some. Still, over the next few months they managed to meet, either by Jack spending the weekend at his parent's house in Surbiton and borrowing his dad's car at every opportunity or by her travelling to Colchester and spending Friday and Saturday nights in a B&B.

The trouble with both situations was the lack of places of privacy. No visitors in bedrooms was the totally enforced policy in the B&Bs, and his mother was little better! The only place there was some privacy was his dad's car parked down a quiet cul-de-sac. And it was on one of those occasions that whilst they were cuddling, Sylva moved his right hand and placed it on her left breast. Jack was elated not just by the pleasure involved but also by the fact that it seemed to signal that he was different and was being allowed a special privilege following her appalling treatment by men earlier in her life.

Such intimacy developed slowly until one evening when Jack's parents had gone with his grandparents and sister to visit his Uncle Bern as he was celebrating his engagement to Patricia who he later married. Jack had promised to follow along when he had collected Sylva, but his route involved picking her up and then returning to his parent's house to collect the present he had conveniently forgotten.

Although time was short, it was long enough for them to enjoy a brief session of the ultimate. He was so surprised at the warmth inside her as he entered, and the excitement of the act meant that it did not last very long! But still, he had done it, and it was as good as it was rumoured to be!

# Chapter 58

They were not to have too many opportunities to meet, let alone enjoy moments of intimacy, during that summer. Jack's life at 1 Company was quite hectic, ranging from the most incredibly stupid to the most exciting events.

Jack had arrived at Colchester only just before knocking off time and had only just managed to acquire a bed space and bedding before the Stores closed. They were not on warning for call out, so at 1700 hours, the camp emptied like the exodus from Egypt. Jack spent the evening quietly in the NAAFI being, for most of the evening, the only one there. At least he was able to watch what he wanted on the TV in the television room, something which had been utterly impossible in the densely populated training depots where most of the time only football would be watched, it being the most mentally challenging that most recruits could manage.

On Saturday morning, he carried out normal laundry activities and then in the afternoon, he went into Colchester to explore the town although he knew it a bit from visits there when he had been at camp in Fingrinhoe. He could see the walls of the castle sticking up over other buildings and decided that he would wander over that way and take a look. He made several false starts with the roads and alleys he strolled along not leading to the castle. The final alleyway was a dead end, blocked by a building which looked a bit like a village hall of some kind. Outside was a notice board which announced that it was a Spiritualist Church. Jack knew very little about spiritualism other than a media generated picture of groups of people sitting in a circle, holding hands in the dark and asking, "Is there anybody there? One knock for no and two for yes!"

Having noticed that a service was shortly due to start, Jack turned away to retrace his steps. However, blocking the alleyway were three women obviously headed for the Church. Seeing Jack turn away one of the women spoke up and said, "Don't be frightened, love, everyone is welcome, and it isn't like they show on the telly; come in, you might like it." These sentiments were echoed by the other two women, and together, they ushered him into the building. As Jack had nothing else to do, and if the truth were known, he was a little daunted by the three, he went along with them. The Church was laid out like a pretty traditional one and Jack took a seat in the second row—no one ever sits in the first row.

Shortly, the service started just like most churches with hymns, prayers and a moment of quiet for personal prayer. The woman who was acting as leader then introduced the second woman who was to demonstrate clairvoyance. Everyone was asked, if the medium came to them, to respond by voice rather than a nod of the head. The leader explained that this was so that spirit could tune in to the individual—a bit like trying to tune a radio to a particular frequency when there was no music being played at that particular moment. That figured, thought Jack. She further explained that clairvoyance was to provide evidence of life after death, not to predict the future, we all have free choice, so the future is not yet decided since someone could decide to go against their conscience and off the route mapped out for them. That took a bit more thinking about, and Jack was still thinking about that when the Medium said, "Hello, Jack, we've waited a long time for you." Jack was astonished. How could she know his name? She continued, "They are showing me two round things on your shoulders, I don't know their proper name, but they are the things that show you are an officer in the army. Are you an officer then?"

"No," said Jack.

"Well, in that case, that is something that is to look out for in the future. They are also showing you in Ireland."

"In an island?" asked Jack.

"No, Ireland, the country of Ireland. Have you any plans to go there?"

"No," said Jack.

"Well, remember this because you will be going there. You are surrounded by much love and power. God bless you," and at that she moved on to the next person in the congregation.

Jack sat there stunned. How could she know his name? How could she know he was in the army, although she had got his rank wrong? And what was all this about Ireland? Jack thought that there must be army barracks and regiments in Ireland, but he had no knowledge of them. The service lasted for another 30 minutes or so and then, declining to stay for a cup of tea to which everyone was invited, Jack left. Still wondering, he made his way back to camp in time for tea. He was to think back to that service quite frequently over the years, but he never did actually get to visit Colchester Castle, only by proxy many years later when Time Team carried out a dig there.

On Monday, Jack was allocated his duties which involved a pretty mundane mix of filing, typing and general gophering, him being the most junior rank and the newest recruit. One thing he did discover was that Company Sergeant Majors were all slightly mental—in the case of some of them, totally mental with a capacity for malice which was truly amazing. This one had a foible about toilet paper. When Jack entered a cubicle of the toilets nearest the offices, it was to discover that none of them contained any toilet paper. Returning to the offices, Jack asked one of the Privates where you get toilet paper.

"From the CSM," was the answer he got. So, approaching the CSM's office, by now with some urgency, Jack knocked and entered.

"What do you want?"

"I've been told I must ask you for toilet paper, sir," answered Jack.

"Toilet paper. Toilet paper. Toilet paper," he roared. "Have I nothing better to do than give out toilet paper to Private soldiers?" he roared. Jack, thinking he had been set up as the newbie, turned to go away only to be told, "Wait." At that, the CSM got up from behind his desk and walked over to a steel cabinet in the corner of his office, pulling out a large bunch of keys as he did so. Besides the standard padlock there was an additional, huge padlock attached to the door as well as the locking mechanism built into the door as standard. Jack was squirming by this time and wondering what the penalty for a newbie crapping on the Sergeant Major's office floor might be—castration at the very least was his starting point—when the CSM finished unlocking the cupboard. Opening both doors, the cupboard was filled with toilet rolls from floor to ceiling! Jack had never seen so many in one place before.

Picking up one roll, the hard, shiny stuff sold as St something or other and pretty useless at the job, nowhere near as efficient as the new, soft toilet rolls flooding on to the market, but more expensive and, therefore, never to be issued to the army. The CSM tore off one sheet and handed it to Jack. Jack stood there dumbfounded. How are you supposed to get your arse clean with one, small, shiny-sided piece of toilet paper?

"Well," thundered the CSM.

"I need more than one sheet, sir," said Jack.

"Do you think I'm made of paper? Do you think I have nothing better to do than hand out multiple sheets of paper to newbie recruits still wet behind the ears? Do you? Do you?"

Jack meant to say 'no, sir', but struggling not to shit on the CSM's floor it came out as, "Yes, sir." It, however, stopped the CSM in full flow. Glowering, he carefully tore off two more sheets, one at a time, and handed them to Jack.

"Now get out and don't come back for at least a week." Jack went at a rate of knots sufficient to let him keep his knees crossed whilst at the same time letting him make maximum speed back to the bogs in time to avert a catastrophe. Returning to his room that night, the three other Privates there all solemnly stood up and opened their locker doors. On the top shelf of each was a roll of soft toilet paper.

"Get yourself one in the NAAFI," said one of them before all three collapsed howling at Jack's look. Jack never did discover why the CSM behaved in the way he did; it was just one of those things in the army.

# Chapter 59

So ended Jack's first day at 1 Coy. Tuesday promised more typing, filing and gophering until mid-morning when a Corporal appeared in front of Jack's desk. Starting to rise to recognise the senior rank, Jack was told to sit down. "Is it true," said the Corporal, "that you are a qualified Marksman?" he asked.

"Yes," said Jack.

"When and how," asked the Corporal, "as you have only been in the army for five minutes?" Jack laid out his history of shooting for the past eight years, listing the weapons he had fired, some of the prizes he had won and finished with his description of representing England against Canada, New Zealand and Australia. "Be dressed ready in combat kit tomorrow at 0800 hrs ready for a day on the ranges; we'll give you a trial for the Company team," said the Corporal and at that, he turned and walked away.

Jack was tested on the SLR and the SMG, proving himself a master of both, beating all the other four members of the team by some margin. As with most units in the army, if you were 'in the team', whatever the team might be, you were excused all sorts of duties so that you could practice for the next competition coming up. Throughout the summer, they competed in various inter-unit competitions, in the Air Portable Brigade, only ever winning two but as they were prestigious ones beating The Rifles and the Parachute Regiment in both with Jack achieving the highest scores in each, Jack's summer passed pleasurably enough apart from the crash out exercises.

As an air portable company, 1 Company had to be ready to move at a moment's notice if required to do so. The Company spent periods where they had to be ready to move at one hours' notice, or four hours or 24. Each call out, one occurred just as Jack got to the Guardroom gate on a Friday night at 1600 hrs, on one occasion, when the Adjutant opened his window and shouted at Jack, "Close the gate; we're on crash out." One minute earlier and Jack would have been out and away, but he wasn't, and his weekend planned in Colchester with Sylva went down the Swanny! The crash outs could be for just an hour or so, or for several days, where their abilities to function to the limit were tested. The one where Jack had just reached the gate lasted for four days. So his intended weekend with Sylva was totally wrecked—something Jack was to learn was part and parcel of army life.

One of the exercises was mega big. The exercise was to test the Brigade in as realistic as possible war-like conditions. The RAF were to see if it could supply a Brigade from the air and 1 Co was to see if it could collect, store and issue all the stores needed by a Brigade fighting a war. The exercise took part mainly in the Thetford training area (an area he was to get to know very well watching Dad's Army some years in the future). This was an area of mainly heath with scattered copses of trees bounded in the south by the main A11, London Norwich, road and to the north, about half a mile away, by the main London-Norwich railway line. It was not a very large area for such a major exercise, but Britain did not have sufficient space to devote to army use—much of the land previously commandeered for use during the war having been returned to its pre-war owners.

Come the day, Jack's role was to man a telephone point just off the A11 and record all the messages he heard. It was linked by radio to the frequency the RAF were using and would enable contact to be made with them, if necessary. Jack was told it was highly unlikely that contact would need to be made, but he was there just in case. An officer would send any messages that needed to be sent.

It was a very windy day, on the margin of what would be safe, but with so much planning, so many units, including the RAF, involved, it would have been difficult and costly to have abandoned the exercise. So it went ahead. Jack had a grandstand seat of everything happening. The RAF were having to fly quite a distance north of the railway line so that the dropped items would be driven by the wind to land safely (!) south of the railway line in the designated landing area. At least, that was the plan. And initially, it worked well. First to drop was a squadron of Beverleys whose drops all landed inside the designated area even if they were quite widely separated across it. Following them was a squadron of Argosies, the modern replacement for the ageing Beverleys.

Jack saw all of it. A huge load dropped out of the back of the Argosy, second in the flight to drop. Almost immediately, one parachute opened but could not support the weight, so it tore to shreds. Two more parachutes opened but in turn were torn to shreds. The forth parachute opened just before the one-ton ammunition platform hit the ground. The good news was that it did not blow up; one-ton of explosive would have made quite a noise and hole. The bad news was that it had not drifted as far south as was intended but had come down almost straight, right onto the London-Norwich railway line! The fact that it had not detonated was good news but one-ton of weight dropping at high speed from a great height does an awful lot of damage to a railway line and leaves a bloody big hole, which was not good news.

Jack's radio telephone crackled into life with a posh RAF voice saying, "By God, you've dropped a clanger there, George, old son." Jack duly wrote it into his log which was otherwise completely blank.

"Fuck off, Julian," duly followed onto the page.

Elsewhere, panic was gradually developing as the realisation that the main line was completely destroyed in both directions and expresses were due imminently as far as anyone knew. Soldiers were despatched with scraps of anything red, much like the Railway Children were to do years later, to try to flag down any approaching trains. The first soldier to encounter a London-bound express found that as he was waving to the train driver, so the driver was waving back!

This was happening at high speed and the soldier waving the red rag started a high-speed shit until he heard the engine noise reduce and the grinding hissing of the brakes being applied. He ran down the track after the train which eventually came to a stop more than a mile away from the red flag waving site and only 200 yards from the 'bomb' site! Luck, not only in the ammunition not detonating but also in the soldier waving the flag being sufficiently far away from the damaged rail tracks for the warning being in time to let the express, all 80 mph of it, stop in time.

The exercise was suspended to allow thought about what had happened and what should be done next. Clearly, the air dropping had to be cancelled to allow examination of the parachute mechanism on the damaged platform which meant the remaining platforms could not be dropped until their mechanisms had also been inspected.

After several hours, it was decided to carry on with the exercise without the RAF airdropping and 1 Company's role changing to the extent that all supplies would be collected by road and delivered to the Brigade units by road. Jack was pissed off with this; if the exercise had been cancelled totally, then there would have been just enough time for him to meet Sylva for a slightly truncated weekend, but no such luck.

Worse, some weeks later, Jack received orders to appear at the official investigation to give evidence about what he had seen and what he had heard on the radio telephone. Conducted by a full Colonel with more brass around him than a brass foundry, Jack had to appear immaculate in his full Service Dress and be a 'credit to his unit'. In the event, giving his evidence was a non-event since he was simply asked, on oath, was his statement describing what he had seen and heard accurate? When he answered, "Yes," the great Panjandrum, addressing the rest of the enquiry team by asking, "I don't think we have any further questions for this witness, do we?" was answered a unanimous "No". After all, who was going to question such seniority when a leading question was posed. Certainly, Jack was glad that was it, but it did seem a terrible waste of time and money for him to attend not least because it pissed him off having to prepare his kit just so he could say, 'Yes' as his total contribution to the proceedings.

Jack's time at 1 Coy went quickly, most of it spent on the range. It was all to the lead up to the Corps' annual competition in early October shot over the Ash ranges which Jack knew well. Every other weekend, Jack managed to meet Sylva either by travelling home and seeing her for the weekend, something his parents did not enjoy since to them he seemed to be using them as a hotel, and other weekends when Sylva travelled to Colchester. The problem with that was the various B&Bs they used were much against male visitors in a female resident's bedroom; the permissive society hadn't yet reached Colchester Landladies and probably never would! Nevertheless, their sex life progressed even if it had to be snatched whenever the opportunity occurred. Then, in August, the bombshell exploded. Sylva was posted to HQ Middle East Command in Aden with just seven days' notice. Fortunately, the seven days included a weekend, so Jack travelled home and managed to see her for most of the Saturday. There seemed to be no opportunity in the future for them to meet again. Jack, however, was determined to keep her as his one and only, having fallen deeply in love with her which love she declared she reciprocated. So, he proposed and was accepted. All in a rush they drove to Kingston, it having more and better shops than Surbiton, and searched the jewellers for a suitable engagement ring. They settled on a three ruby and gold ring which cost £3-15-6, more than a week's pay for Jack. Their farewell that night at the camp in Richmond Park was liberally sprinkled with declarations of undying and everlasting love. As it happened, they were to be reunited much sooner than they could ever have imagined or wished—at least on Jack's part.

# Chapter 60

Lovelorn, Jack returned to Colchester on the Sunday evening. Still, the time passed quickly, and the Corps' shoot rushed upon them. Jack was the only Private Soldier in the team, all the others being junior NCOs. When the travel arrangements were being planned, the other five divided naturally into their friendships and cars, leaving Jack as the odd one out who, it initially appeared, would have to make his own way to Aldershot—something he didn't fancy at all. Fortunately, Corporal Jewson, the Corporal who had originally interrogated Jack about his shooting record, offered to squeeze Jack into the back of his Mini if Jack could manage there; normally, there would be plenty of space for two adults but Cpl Jewson was carrying a lot of the team kit which not only filled the boot but most of the back as well. Given the two alternatives, Jack had no problem in choosing a bit of discomfort against British Rail.

Being part of a small team, Jack's rank, or lack of it, did not ostracise him as much as would have been the case normally—a very junior Private would not have been welcomed into a 'club' of NCOs. But Jack was welcomed even to the extent that he wasn't expected to buy tea and wads at the various cafes they stopped at on route, it being recognised that Jack's pay simply wasn't up to doing so.

The shooting did not go well. The team had fired all their allocated ammunition practising for the event and had had to supplement their stock with ammunition bought privately. Keen to save money, they committed the cardinal error—you get what you pay for in this world—they paid for crap, and they got a dump of it.

The 7.62 mm rounds for the SLR's miss fired often. In the deliberate shoots this was not too serious as there was plenty of time to load another round but in the timed shoots, snap shooting for the main part, there simply wasn't time to clear the dud round which had not ejected itself and that meant missed shots.

With the 9 mm rounds for the Stirling SMGs, the situation was worse. Not only did some of the rounds not detonate and have to be cleared, some of them detonated sufficiently to drive the bullet up and out of the barrel but there wasn't sufficient power in the detonation to drive the working parts far enough back to hook up on the trigger. The empty case of the fired round was ejected from the barrel, but as the breech mechanism did not latch onto the trigger, it shot forward and fired another round and in some cases two or three rounds. Having expected to fire only one aimed round, the unexpected subsequent rounds shot all over the place, near to where they were aimed but not near enough! Jack particularly suffered with a runaway gun and scored very badly. He did better with the SLR and came second in the Young Recruit category. Had the ammunition not been crap, the whole team would have done much better, but they learned a lesson.

As they were packing up at Friday lunchtime, one of the Regimental Police from the Training Regiment at Buller Barracks came around seeking Jack. On this occasion, Jack had a clear conscience so he had no worries when Cpl Jewson told him the police were looking for him and to report to the RP at the Range Control Centre. Presenting himself to the only RP there, easily identifiable by the RP Armband and the complete lack of any intelligence in his eyes, Jack was astounded at the message he received. He was instructed not to return to 1 Co in Colchester but to report to the Adjutant at the Training Regiment at 0800 hrs on the Monday morning. The RP knew no more and cared less, his duty having been completed with the delivery of the message. The note he handed Jack had little other information other than he was posted to the Training Regiment and to whom, and the time, he was to report. Jack made his way back to the team very slowly; what bothered him was the word posted. This implied a permanency in the move but all his kit, other than that with him, was locked in his locker in Colchester, and he could see no way that he would ever get it back if he didn't return there and collect it himself. The order he had received said not to return to Colchester but was completely silent regarding what he was to do between that Friday afternoon and reporting on the Monday morning.

Arriving back at the team, his mind was made up. He told Cpl Jewson that he was posted to the Training Regiment in Buller Barracks with effect from the Monday morning and made no mention of the instruction not to return to Colchester.

"Well," said the Cpl, "I'm glad that order didn't come through before you shot for us," and that was it. They travelled back to Colchester in the afternoon, returning early in the evening, having been slowed down by weekend traffic all through London and out on the A12 with people heading for the coast for the weekend.

Jack said his good byes to the few lads who were left in the barracks, most having gone home/away for the weekend before Jack arrived back. With postings to the RASC units being for mainly periods of two or three years, rather than in the infantry regiments where joining the regiment was for life, farewells were never a big deal as you could expect to meet again in a year or two.

Jack had planned during his walk back to the team that he could pack leisurely on the Friday night, then travel home by train on the Saturday morning and spend the rest of the weekend with his parents. He briefly toyed with the idea of travelling to the barracks on the Sunday afternoon, but with minimal staffing over the weekend, he had no confidence that any one there would know anything about him, and he didn't fancy a night in the cells as the only place where there was a bed! That left only the option of an early train Monday morning and that was what he did, walking into the Adjutant's Office at 0745 hrs and reporting in.

What came then was a shock. The Adjutant informed him that as someone had dropped out of the Regular Commissions Board interviews that week, he was being awarded the honour of standing in at the last minute and he was to catch the 1000 hrs train to Westbury and attend the interview—and good luck. He was handed a return warrant and ordered to return on Friday afternoon. And less than five minutes after reporting in, he was on his way again.

# Chapter 61

Jack had no idea what to expect at the RCB. Whilst some rumour rubbish, like they watch to see if you eat your peas off your knife, the assault course is a killer, loads of lads get injured, paper exams are killers—*that's two killers*, thought Jack, *so it's a wonder anyone survives the Board*—were just a few of the rumours that Jack had heard.

The start was very informal. Although a Board staffed by military personnel, most of the candidates were civilians so for the most part, serving soldiers like Jack were treated as civilians; the dress for all the physical activity stuff was army fatigues—denim type material, olive green in colour, quite comfortable to wear and, as it turned out, quick to dry out.

They were gathered together on arrival and given a detailed talk of what to expect over the next few days. The Major addressing them even went so far as to say they could happily eat their peas off their knives, as nobody would be spying on them!

They were directed to collect the kit they would need from the QM Stores, the most significant bit of which was a bib-like tunic which had large, prominent numbers on the front and back. They were then divided up into teams of eight, the first group being numbered 1 to 8, the second 11 to 18, the third 21 to 28 and the fourth 31 to 38, making 32 of them in total. From then on, they were only ever referred to by the staff as number 21, 37 etc. Very inhuman, Jack thought, but it made for easy identification when they were taking part in group activities. The use of numbers for identity even made its way into their private time on tea breaks, meal breaks and the evening time in what effectively was a NAAFI-run café.

The following few days were a mix of exams, personality profiles—although Jack did not know what they were—a general knowledge test and physical tests, these last being particularly unpleasant. Working in their teams of eight, one of them would be selected and taken away by the RCB Staff. They would be taken to a problem. This could be quite complicated scaffolding or the stream running through the grounds. There would be a burden of some kind, most commonly a large oil barrel half full of fluid so that it was not only heavy but difficult to handle because the liquid surged inside it, changing the point of balance and causing problems when trying to wheel it across the obstacle which might be the stream, the scaffolding or a made-by-the-group bridge. It was only when they started the task that they discovered the planks, scaffold poles etc. were all too short or inadequate for the purpose.

The team member who had been taken away would have the task explained to them and be given two or three minutes to come up with a plan that had then to be explained to the Staff member, most of them Majors. Having explained the plan to the Staffer, they would then call over the team and explain to them their plan. They would then start with a target time to complete the task.

The barriers to be overcome would be painted variously in green and red—anything green could be touched but anything red could not. Each of the eight team members had a task to lead in, in turn. In Jack's team, none of the tasks were completed within the time and some were not completed at all. Even years later, Jack could not make up his mind if the ones that could not be completed were ones that no one could complete or whether it was just that they could not find the right solution to the problem. Certainly, they found out very easily how to fall into the stream, fall off scaffold poles and get entangled in the wire on some of the obstacles.

As each of the plans of the selected team member fell apart, some lost complete control of the group with stronger, natural leaders emerging who, when they spoke, would be listened to and those who, when they spoke, would be totally ignored. Of the team, three men seemed to be particularly conversant with all aspects of the RCB procedures; they banded together as a team within a team and worked to support each other to the extent of putting down the remaining five team members. They ridiculed, in whispers intended to be heard, the plans, never volunteered to be the first across a pole bridge and were particularly clumsy in building apparatus intended to span water or a fence of all the team members who were not one of the three. Recognising what was going on, Jack manoeuvred so that he was working with the one who was leading the three and when the Major was unsighted, took the opportunity to kick him in the ankle. The guy rolled around the ground and whilst tenderly helping him to his feet, Jack whispered in his ear, "Next time it'll be in the balls if you try any of your fancy games when it comes my turn to lead." That worked; the three of them tried no tricks, however, Jack had an especially difficult command task and although he retained command throughout, his first plan did not work and the changes to it extemporised as he went along didn't either, and he eventually ran out of time.

Jack returned to Buller Barracks on Thursday afternoon. On Friday, he was told to parade at 10.00 hrs for an interview with the Colonel. The only reason for that, thought Jack, was the Colonel had the result of his RCB appearance and indeed he had. His first words, once Jack had been marched in, were, "I'm very sorry to tell you that you failed the RCB. I have only received a telephone call as yet; the confirmation paperwork will not get here until next week, but we like to let applicants know their result as soon as possible. It means that we can start your termination paperwork straight away and with any luck, you will be walking out the gate as a civilian again by 16.00 hrs this afternoon."

Jack was devastated; he felt he had done well enough to pass and he had an outstanding record in the Army Cadet Force to back up his application. Further, although he was on a contract that would let him leave the army if he failed the RCB, should he wish to do so, Jack had long ago decided that he would not exercise this option because he liked the army life and if he couldn't get a commission directly now, he could work his way up through the ranks and earn a QM Commission in due course. Consequently, he spoke out, "Sir, I do not wish to be demobbed; I want to stay in and make my way up through the ranks to a QM Commission in due course. I have said that in a number of interviews that I would stay in." The Colonel looked stunned and it was a while before he spoke.

"Yes, indeed you said it, you have said it to me but I thought you were just handing out the standard, proper answer to that question that all Potential Officer Cadets give."

"Well, I wasn't," said Jack.

"Please wait outside for a moment, Private Hughes." Jack left the room of a senior officer for the only time in his army service without being marched out by a bellowing NCO or Warrant Officer. He was, however, marched back in by the RSM after about 10 minutes.

"Well Private Hughes," said the Colonel once Jack was back again, "I am delighted to hear that you wish to remain in the army, and I feel I should offer you a posting choice, but I would like you to consider electing to remain here in the Training Battalion, and if you do, I will guarantee you three stripes in 18 months. What do you say?"

"Sir, I appreciate your offer very much, but I would like to go to HQ Middle East Command in Aden." If the Colonel looked stunned last time, this time he looked absolutely gobsmacked.

"Wait outside, please." This time, the RSM was quick enough to march Jack out.

Marched back in again after a few minutes, the Colonel asked, "Is your wanting to go there anything to do with the fact that your fiancé is there?" Now it was Jack's turn to be stunned. The Colonel could only have found out about Sylva from the RSM—Jack's first experience of the amount a good RSM knew about the soldiers under his command.

The only answer was, of course, "Yes, sir."

"Right," said the Colonel, "I'll see what I can do. March out please, RSM."

Jack was never to see or speak to the Colonel again, but the RSM did have a word with him outside.

"Prat," he said and gestured for Jack to go. Amazing the amount such a short, single word can convey.

A few days later, appearing on Part 1 Orders was the detail, '412 Pte Hughes JM posted to HQ Middle East Command Tuesday 1st November 1964. To report to QM at 10.00 hrs 16 October 1964 for kitting.' Jack immediately wrote to Sylva with the good news. The rest of the time passed in a blur but nevertheless, nowhere quick enough for Jack.

Jack travelled to Gatwick, there was a convenient cross-country rail line from Farnborough station, arriving hours ahead of the check-in time—typical army hurry up and wait. Still, if Jack had known what was to come, he probably would have wished for the time to go slower still.

# Chapter 62

The flight, in a Britannia—known as the whispering giant—took just over 12 hours, landing at RAF Khormaksar at just after 08.00 and before the sun had started to really heat up. Passage through Customs and Immigration was pretty simple for Jack as a serviceman and by just after 10.30 hrs, he was standing in front of a Captain Robertson who was responsible for the Clerks in HQ MEC. Told to sit, Jack was then made aware that pretty well everyone on the clerical side knew who he was and how he'd got there—his introduction to just what a small community he was joining. There were about 350 Clerks in total, spread across Privates like himself rising through all the non-commissioned and warrant ranks. There were only two Captains, Robertson who was the Superintending Clerk and a Captain in the Cheshire Regiment who Jack was to have numerous contacts with, but Jack never really did discover what he did other than the Duty Officer Roster for cover once the HQ had finished for the day. All the other officers were senior ranks, that is, Majors or above rising to the GOC in C who at the time was a full General. Command of the HQ alternated between the Army, Navy and Air Force. Jack was initially over awed at so much brass. True, he had seen the Lt Col commanding the Training Regiment a few times, but contact with such senior figures was extremely rare for lowly Privates. As time progressed and the awe gradually disappeared into the past progressing to downright contempt for some of them, ignorant, thick, stuck up and dependent almost entirely for their position and promotions on their family connections, Jack was to discover that as the wartime experienced officers retired, so they were reverting to the peacetime standard of Hooray Henrys with a God-given knowledge of their superiority over lesser mortals and their superiority over the ranks and rankers created a loathing of each group by the other. Officers from the ranks, who had earned their commissions on the battlefield, looked down on by these Hooray Henrys, were being pensioned off as quickly as possible, because they weren't really gentleman and the peacetime army was to revert to being staffed by the right sort of chap; like the ones before the war where everyone knew everyone else, came from the right schools and background and who, when faced with an utterly professional army of Germans, proved their complete and utter ineptitude for the positions they held. This was all to become clear to Jack in the next two years.

The interview with Captain Robertson was relatively short and not what Jack or Captain Robertson expected. After some jocular comment or other about knowing how Jack came to be in Aden, Robertson said, "As you have arrived here before your documents, you weren't given them to bring with you by any chance?" eliciting a shake of the head from Jack, Robertson said, "I'd better get some details from you and then fill in the rest on your docket when your documents arrive. So, what's your date of birth?" followed by standard questions about where and when he joined the army before moving into questions regarding his army qualifications. He was surprised that Jack had his Number 2 Drill Certificate—gained whilst a POC—and then utterly astounded when, in answer to the question do you have any army education qualifications, Jack answered, "I am excused army education, sir."

Robertson asked the obvious question, "Why?"

"Because I have eight GCE 'O' levels and the equivalent of five GCE 'A' levels," he answered.

Robertson looked at him with his mouth agape and it was a while before he asked, "What the hell are you doing in this man's army as a Private Soldier?" Jack gave a potted history of his service and had just finished when the door to the office smashed open and in burst a long, lankly piece of piss of a Private who, in a loud Scott's accent, demanded, "Has ma replacement no arrived yet?"

Jack expected Robertson to explode and rip him a new fundamental orifice but instead, he looked at Private Reece, for that Jack found out very quickly was his name, turned to Jack and asked, "You can't by any chance drive, can you?" Jack had had a number of lessons with the Territorial Army driving three tonners and had learnt to drive mainly and had passed his test in his dad's Triumph Renown before purchasing his own Ford 8 and of course his experience on motor bikes. Jack, therefore, simply said, "Yes."

"Right," said Robertson. "Private Reece, meet Private Hughes. He's your replacement; I was going to put you in the Registry, Hughes, but with your qualifications, you would be wasted there. You'll enjoy G Tech, I hope; if you have any problems, come and see me at any time. Good luck; now get out, the both of you."

Jack wasn't to realise it for a while but Reece's arrival at that precise moment was to prove a major, if not the major, turning point in his life. Reece took Jack into the wooden hut to which Robertson's little office was attached. They entered through a door set in the middle of the hut; to the right were two desks and beyond them a wall with a door set in the middle through which two desks could be seen. To the left were a number of desks and a huge pigeon-hole structure into which a couple of Privates were sorting letters. There was also a wall to the left through the door of which stationery stocks and machines could be seen. In fact, a couple of weeks later, Robertson moved into that end office when a violent wind storm blew his little office away! The whole of the wooden huts making up part of the HQ were ancient and decrepit and riddled with bugs; it was a miracle that any of them had the strength to stand up.

Turning to the right, Reece walked over to a Corporal and in his loud voice said, "This here's ma replacement," picked up a beret and belt from the other desk and walked off. The Corporal introduced himself as Corporal Graham Pectin, as in jam, and asked Jack to tell him who he was. When Jack told him his name, Pectin interjected and said, "Ah, I know all about you, you're the prat that volunteered to be posted to the arsehole of the empire; you'd better hope you're never sent up to Bahrain because then you'd be 350 miles up it!" At which he burst into peals of laughter. Settling down eventually, he picked up the telephone and asked for a number. When connected, he spoke to someone on the other end of the line saying, "There's someone here who wants to speak to you," upon which he handed the phone to Jack and said, "It's Sylva."

"Sylva, hello, it's me, Jack." The silence was deafening.

After what seemed like hours, but couldn't have been longer than a second or two, she said, "I'm at work now and can't talk. I'll meet you tonight at 1800 hrs at the Wrackery; Pectin can give you directions," and rang off. Not quite what he was expecting, but at least he was going to see her that night. Queries of Cpl Pectin revealed that the Wrackery was a block of civvy flats which had been taken over by the army for the women of the WRAC, was heavily wired and guarded to prevent the ingress of any randy soldiery and was only at the other end of the area where Jack was to be billeted.

The rest of the morning passed in a blitz of introductions, to the QM Stores to hand in all his normal uniforms, greatcoat etc. to be cleaned and sealed in heavy plastic bags from which all the air had been vacuumed out, to be handed back at the end of his two year posting; to the RASC Company at RAF Khormaksar to get him an army driving licence, arranged by Cpl Pectin without the formality of a driving licence test or any silly bureaucratic nonsense like that; the dropping of his kit in the four-bedded room that was to be his 'pit' for his time in Aden and, finally, the most important, an introduction to the room cleaner who would look after Jack during his time there. The cleaner, Mo, would make Jack's and the other three beds in the morning, change the sheets three times per week and put out the used sheets for the Dhobi Wallah who, besides washing would be starching and pressing Jack's uniform every day. Aden was so hot, humid, dusty that it was perfectly possible to get through three uniforms a day. Coming in from work—normally, working days were 0700 hrs to 1300 hrs for the Clerks and Officers in the HQ although this was about to change although no one knew that yet—soldiers would strip out of their uniforms, throw them in a heap on the floor at the foot of their bed along with belt, beret and boots all of which would be collected up by the room wallah who would sort the kit for washing into a bundle and place it outside the room for the dhobi wallah to collect early in the morning. That kit would be taken away, washed, starched and ironed and returned every evening about 1700 hrs. Army kit was done free of charge, the army paid for that, but if a soldier wanted any civvy clothes' laundering, that would cost five East African shillings per week—at that time, equivalent to five shillings Stirling per week. The room wallah, Mo, cost the same five shillings per week so, for the magnificent sum of ten shillings per week, Jack would have two servants to wait on him hand and foot. Mo would even pop over to the local shop and purchase food and drinks! Jack had changed to a nine-year enlistment following his failure at the RCB and his pay had gone up to a magnificent £8-10 shillings a week. What he was still to learn was the problem Mo had with drink every pay day. A Christian and thus not forbidden alcohol, Ethiopian and Arab-hating, Mo would drink solidly until all his money was gone, and since he was an aggressive drunk, then pick a fight with all and sundry. It meant, the morning after, someone would have to arm up and turn up at the local nick, more a mud hut than a steel jail, and bully the jailers to get him out. Their opening ploy was always a demand for a huge sum of *baksheesh* and only the placing of a loaded magazine onto the weapon and cocking it would mean that he would be instantly released with the most blood-curdling threats if there was to be another occasion. Still, that was something for the future.

The two Majors making up the small team in G Tech were both away in Little Aden, and Jack was not to meet them until the following day. As they were in the desert, it meant that the other G Tech vehicle, a Hillman Husky Station Wagon, was left there for Pectin and Jack to use visiting the RASC Company and the QM. Jack felt quite grand and once ordered to drive by Cpl Pectin, this feeling multiplied tenfold. Although painted the normal shitty army green, it was still an almost brand-new car, with only something over 1200 miles on the clock. Powered by a 1.4 litre, four-cylinder engine, it was reputedly good for just over 70 mph although officially there was a blanket maximum speed of 40 mph throughout Aden State; it was exceeded so often that the MPs had declared speeding 'a prevalent offence' which meant the punishment for those caught speeding would be much increased— prevalence also applied to drunkenness, virtually compulsory in Aden.

Nevertheless, Jack would have the, slightly fiddled, use of the car for which he could see many advantages when it came to taking Sylva out. The rest of the day seemed to drag, but eventually, there he was walking nervously up and down outside the Wrackery shortly before 1800 hrs. Promptly on time, Sylva appeared. When he went to embrace her, she pushed him away with a "Not here". Leading him to what appeared to be a Groundsman's hut in a small group of shed/gazebos sheltering various bits of junk, she indicated he should sit down on an old garden bench under one of the lean-tos. As soon as he sat, remaining standing, she said, "Jack, I'm sorry, but I have met someone else." At that, she handed him the engagement ring he had given her and, as she walked away, said, "I hope you will find someone else," and at that, she was gone. The whole time with her had lasted less than 30 seconds. Jack sat there stunned with a whole slew of thoughts piling through his mind. Here he was in a war zone, stuck for two years, all because of her. He had turned down the opportunity of a guaranteed three stripes in 18 months to be with her, and the time with her had turned out to be less than a minute! He was heartbroken; at least, he felt like he was. His first inclination was to strike out at something, preferably the cause of his unhappiness, but he couldn't hit a woman, so his upbringing had inculcated into him and anyway, she wasn't there to give a good lathering to, nor was the bastard that had stolen her away. After all, she was the innocent one stolen away by some opportunistic bastard, wasn't she? Wasn't she? Here Jack became a bit unstuck because he didn't know who he was and whether he was small enough to beat the shit out of him, thus earning her return to being his or if he was a big bastard, then a solution would have to wait until he, Jack, was armed and able to take him out. Would he get away with it? After all, he would be the first one suspected and he certainly wasn't going to do time for that bastard. Jack was thoroughly confused, and had no one to talk to, no best mate; in fact, apart from Cpl Pectin, he knew no one in Aden, and he couldn't confide in him, he represented authority, albeit very lowly authority, and anyway, Jack didn't want anyone knowing what a prick he had been to volunteer to serve in the arsehole of the Empire for a tart who'd given him the heave ho the minute he arrived up it! Without being aware of it, Jack was already consigning her to the dustbin of history, but it was to be many years before she would be totally loaded on the bin lorry and carted away.

In fact, Aden being such a small place and the HQ community being such a small one, Jack's dumping became common knowledge to everyone within days. Jack, however, was functioning in a daze and was oblivious to events around him. His mind was occupied with increasingly wild plans to kill her and 'the him', whoever he was, but all of them ended in Jack being caught—he was, of course, the most obvious suspect. Then, just before finishing at 1300 hrs on a Saturday, they worked a six-day week in Aden, all hell was let loose. MPs and Snow Drops appeared, summoning all the soldiers and airmen to parade at which they were divided into Sections.

The war currently being brought to a victorious conclusion up country in the Radfan Mountains was to take a very different course, one much more dangerous to the Brit community in Aden State. A rag tag and bobtail outfit, thousands strong, calling itself the National Liberation Front had crossed the border from Yemen with the intention of liberating the Arab population being held in servitude by the Imperialist aggressors of the United Kingdom and at the same time seizing the harbour and its facilities which, through the coming and going of ocean going liners, brought great prosperity to the possessors of it. In fact, without the British 'occupation forces', the harbour would have reverted to a lot of water and a few Arab villagers scraping a bare living from the desert. Although the retail community looked forward eagerly to the arrival of a liner, the continued prosperity of the port relied on the presence of the British, their families and the purchases they made.

# Chapter 63

The invading NLF, even though numbering a few thousand, had been held in the passes up country by a scratch force hastily assembled from troops on exercise in the area, about a Company and a half of men, supported by a squadron of armoured cars hastily scraped together from Cavalry Troopers scattered throughout the command HQ, numbering no more than 250 all told and supported by Hawker Hunter ground attack fighters flying from RAF Khormaksar. But they couldn't hold them indefinitely as the NLF could infiltrate around their road blocks using footpaths through the mountains unknown to the British. Authority was looking at using the four RAF Shackleton, maritime reconnaissance aircraft, in a bombing role, on the assumption that it would carry 10 tons of bombs like its Lancaster predecessor and do the insurgents a whole lot of grief, but by the time the problems of changing it from a maritime to a conventional bomber could even be considered, the war was over. In fact, it only lasted four weeks altogether, two before Jack got to Aden and two weeks after. Since he wasn't there for the four weeks, he didn't qualify for the Radfan General Service Medal which also pissed him off more than somewhat.

The war up country having been brought to a sudden end by the appearance on the scene of a Para Battalion and the disappearance of the enemy, it was assumed that the war was over. But it wasn't. It was to take a different and nastier form. The day before they were all called to parade, an incident occurred in the market place in Tawahi, the closest town to the barracks. An Arab threw a hand grenade under a bus taking schoolchildren home from school. The bus drove off without the grenade detonating so the terrorist picked it up and shook it. Then it detonated, killing him and three Arabs nearby. Intelligence identified that there was a box of grenades in the market place in Crater, an Arab town in the crater of an old volcano which wasn't yet out of bounds to UK personnel but soon would be, where people were being encouraged to take a grenade and, on returning with the pin as proof of having thrown it, were given 500 East African Shillings, equivalent to five UK pounds, and worth about two to three weeks' average wage. A lot of money for little work! The problem, for the thrower, was the thrower was given no training in the safe and proper use of a grenade and the death of the bus thrower was to be the first of many.

From the following day, the HQ Clerks were to provide patrols and roadblocks around the immediate area of the HQ and the town of Tawahi. Jack's first patrol was as a member of an eight-man Section patrolling in Tawahi. In theory, all soldiers were soldiers first and tradesmen/specialists second. The Corporal commanding the section and the Lance Corporal second in command had completed their military training years before, the Corporal before the SLR rifle had been introduced and had no idea of how it worked; he had qualified on the range each year firing a .303 Lee Enfield.

In the event, that wasn't a problem as they were not to be issued with ammunition; a certain Labour Minister of Defence was far too frightened of upsetting the Arab oil barons so he had issued the order, no ammunition. They were, however, issued with bayonets; not because anyone had thought about it, but simply because the rifles were stored with a magazine, empty, and a bayonet attached. So they were issued that way, rifle, empty magazine and bayonet on the rifle.

The troops prayed fervently that the terrorists would not know their magazines were empty. To enforce the appearance of fierceness, the bayonet sheath was removed from the bayonet and attached to the soldiers' waist belts, giving a sufficiently war-like figure to deter the terrorists—they hoped! This hope was not to last long. A resulting uproar from the Arab states produced, from the said Labour Defence Minister, assurances that the bayonets would be instantly withdrawn and the statement that the troops had not been issued with ammunition anyway! Looking back years later, it still seemed incredible to Jack that troops could be sent into harm's way unarmed but that is exactly what that Labour politician did—far better a few soldiers should be lost than our Arab oil masters should turn the price screw. Years later, Jack was to be sent onto the streets of Northern Ireland effectively unarmed, this time under the orders of a Tory Defence Minister—troops were always expendable to bastard politicians.

Jack's first patrol was progressing with four of them on the right-hand side of the road and the other four slightly further back on the other side of the road when they came to a corner. The first three turned the corner and the fourth man stopped at it. This stop went on for ages, long enough to indicate that the first three had encountered something around the corner. After about half an hour, they were beckoned forward and the patrol continued. It was only when they got back to Fort Morbut, an old French Legion style fort, at the mouth of Aden Harbour, surrounded with a moat mainly filled with blown in sand, that Jack found out the cause of the delay. The first part of the patrol had turned the corner to discover a screaming new-born baby girl deposited on a rubbish heap. The local Arabs were simply walking past, ignoring the situation. The Corporal, with no means of communicating with base, had had to go into one of the shops and get them to allow him to use their telephone to ring the HQ for instructions. Eventually, the MPs turned up with an ambulance and the baby was taken away. Over the next two years, Jack was to learn how different Arab society was compared to European, to the extent that he used to explode with anger when some liberal left loony expounded that the two societies were equal. The abandonment of a new-born girl to die simply because she was female and the treatment of women as possessions, and not very important ones at that, the failure to educate them and the isolation of them in the home except on the occasions when they were allowed out but only if escorted by a male family member was not a social model for society which was equal to the UK's. It was self-evident, except for those who were determined not to see, that the Arab society was positively medieval and not to be seen as in any way equal to the western model.

The pattern of guard duties intermingled with their normal work continued for a few days, but it was clearly unsatisfactory, not because the Clerks weren't very good soldiers—they weren't—but because their clerical duties were not being carried out and were piling up, some of it a fairly urgent nature but typing whilst patrolling was not possible! Indeed, some typewriters were situated in the Guardroom but expecting soldiers patrolling on a two hours on, four off schedule to carry out clerical work when they should be sleeping was pushing it too far. Inevitably, all sorts of rumours were flying around, some hilarious like the terrorist who was transporting plastic explosives moulded into the underside of his seat, not having anywhere to hide the detonator pencils, glass tubes of explosive containing acid, which once the glass was broken would detonate the main explosive into which they had been inserted. They were horribly unsafe and had been known to detonate just by being shaken too much or simply by getting too hot. Hiding the tubes, by pushing them completely into the plastic explosive, turned out to be a poor idea as, whether by shaking, heat or some other reason, the detonator did its job admirably, if a little too soon, and blew the small truck and the terrorist to kingdom come. Unfortunately for the Governor, the terrorist's head was blown through the window of the bathroom in the Governor's Residency, knocking out the Governor who was shaving at the time. The story ran around Aden like wildfire but was not true. It was one of the headlights that knocked the Governor out, not the terrorist's head. In fact, he was blown into so many bits, his head was never found.

The powers to be decided that one of the worst enemies of morale in this situation were incorrect and exaggerated rumours. Consequently, an intelligence summary was added on at the end of Part One Orders published at the end of work every day and compulsory reading for all service personnel. It worked very well and when the HQ Clerks read that an infantry battalion was on its way from the UK to take over their military patrolling in 10 days' time, morale amongst the HQ staff rose considerably.

Jack was to earn considerable notoriety on what turned out to be his last duty guarding the HQ. The approach road to the HQ from the main road was barricaded by two barricades placed so that any vehicle was forced to slow right down and zig through the obstruction. At about 3 am, Jack had taken the opportunity to pee in the bushes at the right-hand side of the road. His fellow sentry was standing by the end of the left barricade with his hands in his pockets because he was cold. His rifle was resting against the other end of the barricade. Walking back and forwards from one end of the barricade to the other, a matter of eight feet of so, kept his legs from locking up and meant that he was never more than eight feet from his rifle which was a considerable lump to hold and carry around but not exactly proper military practice even though he had no ammunition.

Jack whispered to his mate that the Duty Officer was creeping up the road. The Duty Officer that night was a Pilot Officer in the RAF and like a lot of them, had creased down both sides of his hat to make it look like he wore headphones when flying when in reality he worked in the MU (Maintenance Unit) in some sort of admin role—not one to attract the few free females in Aden. What he didn't realise was that a light in a house at the end of the street behind him clearly outlined him creeping up the street and enabled Jack to identify him from quite a way away. As it happened, Jack's oppo was at the opposite end of the barricade to his rifle when the Duty Officer arrived at the barricade. His first words were, "What would you do, soldier, if I snatched your rifle and aimed it at you?"

Jack's first words, from behind him, were, "I'd blow your bleedin 'ead off, sir." Spinning round to face Jack, the Pilot Officer looked down the barrel of something that must have seemed bigger than the Mersey Tunnel and aimed directly, as the voice had said, at his head. Jack said nothing but remained with the SLR aimed directly at the Duty Officer.

He took a while to speak before saying, "Jolly good show. You are obviously prepared and ready." And at that, he departed, if not at a run, at the very best next thing to it. Jack and Bill, his roommate and fellow sentry, watched him go and once he was safely out of hearing, burst out laughing.

"I'll blow your bleedin 'ead off, sir," burst from Bill and continued to do so throughout the rest of the stag. Within minutes of the two of them returning to the Guardroom the, 'I'll blow your bleedin 'ead off, sir', was echoing throughout the Guard, even those sleeping between stags so tickled were they by a stuck up, pansy officer, especially an RAF one, being shown up for a prat.

The following morning, it was echoing around HQ MEC and continued to do so for some time. The Clerks were delighted when the Battalion of the 3rd Royal Anglians arrived to take over the main guarding duties.

HQ MEC was concentrated mainly in two buildings, apart from the wooden hut Jack occupied. A big, colonial style building grand enough for all the commanders of the Army, Navy and Air Force sat high above the Arab village, and Fort Morbut, the Beau Geste look-alike built during Napoleonic times, about a mile away, to protect the harbour and more recently the coaling station for steamers and even later still, the oil refinery. As they were still very short of infantry, it was decided that the fort would be guarded 24 hours a day by HQ Clerks but the HQ, full of working soldiers, did not need extra protection; there was no point in arming them since a rifle without bullets is only a club at best. Every four or five days, Jack's name would appear on the guard duty roster which meant finishing early on the day job i.e. at 12 noon so that he could get his lunch and change into a long-sleeved shirt and long trousers ready for guard at 1300 hrs until 0700 hrs the next day. There was no Stick Man exemption in Aden; every able-bodied man was needed. Duties involved being on guard at the gate to the fort or patrolling the ground area including the road up to the HQ. The limits of the fort were easy to identify; it was the moat around it. It had never had water in it, being on the high ground at the harbour mouth and was dug out originally to provide a ditch with walls 20 feet high. Unfortunately, over the centuries, sand had blown in and virtually filled the moat and no one had ever felt the need to maintain it by digging it out so that a formidable barrier to the fort was now nothing more than a low wall no more than 18 inches high in places. It meant patrolling the area was serious business as no real obstruction to entry existed. The one serious change to the original guarding and patrolling was that they were now being issued with live ammunition whilst on guard. 10 rounds were counted out to each member of the Guard, signed for and counted back in and signed for by the Armourer at the end of the stag—each two-hour shift; what an administrative bollocks it was. Jack comforted himself with the thought that he could defend himself and the fort for all of the seven seconds it would take him to fire 10 rounds!

Wandering around his allotted section of the fort was extraordinarily peaceful after about midnight and the stars in the sky were stupendous with the quite frequent meteors flashing across and burning up. Looking back in his seventies,

Jack regretted not paying more attention to the view; the sky in England was rarely as clear, nor did it provide the view and meteors so common in Aden.

# Chapter 64

After Jack had been in Aden for about four weeks, he was allocated to the HQ MEC Duty Clerk Roster, a rare honour for someone with such short service in Aden. It provided relief from the aggro and boredom of 24-hour guards—as it happened it was two days before he was to see the little shit who had pinched Sylva from him for the first time. He was short, about 5 ft 7 ins, certainly overweight by army standards, had bottle bottom glasses, and most hurtful of all, he was in the RAF. Gradually, Jack picked up bits and pieces of information about him. He was doing a short commission working on aircraft engines, mainly Beverleys and its successors, the Andover and Argosy. Apparently, his father owned an aircraft-servicing company in the UK, and he was getting a thorough grounding not only in how to service the engines fitted to these transports but also to gain a familiarity with the way the RAF did things whilst being paid handsomely for it. So, in a way, he was a little rich boy incognito, and having failed the RCB, Jack was a poor prospect and thus had been rapidly dumped. What a pity he could not have been dumped by letter, he thought, so that he could have stayed in the UK but now, two or so months later, he was adjusting to it, and life really did go on, as the platitudes said.

The Duty Clerk Roster was made up of eight Clerks in total out of the 350 or so in the HQ. They were regarded as the best eight in the HQ and all had to have security clearance of Top Secret UK Eyes Only. Their duties involved going on duty in the duty room at 1300 hrs when everyone else knocked off, except the Duty Officer, always a Major, and a Duty Driver. Because the army operated worldwide, there were always units operating around the clock. And signals, passed by coded tele-printer, were always coming in. Many were of the highest security rating thus requiring the highest security clearance of the Duty Clerk. Some of them had to be dealt with immediately even though it might be the middle of the night in Aden. The Clerk's job was to collect messages from the Message Centre and deliver them to the Duty Officer. Those requiring an answer had to be typed and replied to, but as sometimes the answer could only be provided by a particular officer to whom it was addressed, the Duty Driver, who also had to have top-security clearance, would have to find out where that Officer was and deliver the message to him. He would then wait for the necessary reply which the Duty Clerk would type up and, signed off by the Duty Officer, would be delivered to the Message Centre.

If you were lucky, no messages would need action and could simply be recorded and passed to the relevant department pigeon hole. If you weren't, you could be working all night and unable to put up the canvas bed for a few hours kip. Jack was to have one major, major night in the future when, fortunately, he had bedded in as a fully competent clerk.

With eight clerks on the roster and seven days in the week, it meant that your duty day progressed through the week as the weeks passed. With Saturday being a normal working day, it was only Sunday which could be a long pain as duty started at 0700 hrs as the Saturday Duty Clerk finished. With no one working in the HQ apart from someone catching up on work, it meant that the duty was for a full 24 hours. Generally, it was very quiet because no one was working in the rest of the world either, but occasional flaps did occur to break the monotony.

After Jack had been in Aden for about nine weeks, he was called to the office of a Captain in the Cheshire Regiment.

"As I know, you are foot loose and fancy free; how would you like a chance of meeting a few unattached young ladies?" Jack was a bit thrown. He had been in the army long enough to know that such offers did not come without a catch. True, he was a bit over Sylva, but there were very few females, about 80 WRAF and 40 WRAC—there were a few WRNS but they were almost never seen—and as Jack met very few of the WRAC girls in the offices with which he had dealings, and feeling that he had a big 'loser' board around his neck, allied with the fact that it was still so close to being dumped that he had not attempted to select one to ask out, the question was interesting but full of what's the catch? He did not want to say no in case there was an advantage here, but he didn't want to say yes either as there might be, probably would be, a catch of some kind.

Stalling for time, he said, "Well, quite honestly, sir, I am not sure that I want to get involved with a girl just yet."

Smiling, the Captain said, "Once you've fallen off a horse, the best thing is to get back on again straight away and I know just the bunch of fillies for you. I am the Deputy Director of the Pirates of Penzance Operetta being put on by the Aden Amateur Operatic Society in a few of weeks' time. I need someone to drive me, in the General's car, to rehearsals every Wednesday and Friday night. You would have to be armed to guard me in transit, and it would mean waiting around for a couple of hours and then running me back again. You could, of course, join in rather than just sitting around and get to know a few of the girls, daughters of families here, a few from the civvy organisations and all single." There were something like 17,000 troops in Aden at that time and less than 200 free females, the difficulty for the troops being how to get to meet them. And here was Jack being offered, for Aden, pretty much the opportunity of a life time. But where was the catch? He pointed out to the Captain that, as a Clerk on the Specialist Roster, there would be nights he could not do the job because he would be on duty.

"No problem, I've already spoken to Captain Robertson, and he will adjust the roster so that you are not on duty on Wednesdays and Fridays for the next few weeks. So, what do you say?" It was quite clear that it had already been decided that Jack would chauffeur and guard the Captain so there was very little point in continuing to resist, besides Jack quite fancied a drive of the General's motor, a brand new Ford Zephyr Mk 111 only just on the market, so Jack said, "Okay, sir, I'll give it a try."

"Right decision, Private Hughes, I'm pleased you made it. Draw a Stirling SMG and 20 rounds from the Armoury at 1300 hrs—you'll have to guard it until you collect the General's car at 1400 hrs from his house. Collect me from the Officer's Mess at 1800 hours and I'll sign the ticket there." By ticket he meant the document that accompanied every army vehicle which acted as a record of all the trips the vehicle had made.

As ordered, Jack collected an SMG and ammunition. An SLR rifle would be more effective as a weapon over ranges greater than 50 yards or more, but as they were travelling on crowded roads with high traffic densities and as the SLR was hugely bigger and more cumbersome to handle inside a vehicle, especially as Jack had a bloody big steering wheel immediately in front of him, the decision to use a Stirling, much smaller and fitted with a collapsible butt to make it smaller still, was clearly the right decision. It was dark as Jack pulled into the Officers' Mess at 1755 hrs. Being so close to the equator, the days were pretty much twelve of daylight and twelve of darkness varying by about only one hour summer to winter. Jack only waited a few minutes, and the Captain emerged. Known as the singing sod by the soldiers, Jack was a trifle worried about him. However, as Jack was doing him a big favour which he militarily was not required to do, Jack thought he would be all right. Indeed, he was chatting affably as they set off with basic directions coming from him as they headed for the school in Khormaksar where the operetta was to take place.

The journey was pretty much the length of the isthmus, about eight miles. As Jack was driving along the straight in Maala, a district of shops with flats over them, most five or six stories high, where most of the Brit families were housed, there was a flash of light accompanied by the most God almighty bang, smoke and the sounds of metal hitting the front of the car. Jack slammed on the brakes and skidded to a stop. Jumping out of the car, he grabbed the Stirling and looked around. As was common when attacks were made on the Brits, the native population had conveniently disappeared before it happened, something that came to be recognised as a clear warning signal, but this time, there was one man who was legging it down the street on the same side of the road as them. With no one else in view and sure that that individual was the one who had thrown the grenade, Jack shouted quickly, "Halt or I fire," three times. At the same time, he cocked the SMG, released the safety catch and fired a burst of four rounds. Not having had time to extend the butt, he simply had to clasp the gun firmly to his hip and fire. Just like in the John Wayne films, a row of bullet hits splattered against the wall just missing the terrorist as he ran around the corner.

The one thing Jack had been trained not to do in such circumstances was to go and look around the corner! Someone might have a weapon trained on that corner waiting for some daft sod to stick his head round it! But the terrorist had not had Jack's training and just as Jack turned back to the car, the terrorist stuck his head back around the corner to take a gander at Jack. Pivoting as fast as he could, he fired another burst, this time of three rounds, with the exactly the same result—a row of bullet holes in the wall and a disappeared terrorist.

Jack returned to the car extending the butt of the SMG as he did so; he wasn't going to be caught out a third time. Armed servicemen in civvies were starting to emerge from the flats, and sirens could be heard in the distance. The singing sod was sitting in the front passenger seat, rocking backwards and forwards bleating out, "They tried to kill me; they tried to kill me." This continued on even though Jack tried to speak to him. It was obvious that he was very shocked. Jack was extremely annoyed, there he was, a Marksman, and he had missed a target only 30 or 40 yards away, twice—twice! It was an absolute disgrace, and Jack was sure he was going to get into trouble for it.

The first vehicle to appear was a Military Police Land Rover with a WO2 in command of it. Instantly taking charge, he ordered the servicemen milling about to form a cordon about 40 yards out and set another half dozen to search for the pin from the grenade, any pieces of shrapnel they could find plus the empty cases ejected from the SMG. Although it was dark, the shop's lighting created a strip along the road almost as bright as day. He approached the Captain, in civvies, but could get no sense out of him; he kept repeating over and over, "They tried to kill me. Why did they try to kill me?" Leaving him and approaching Jack, his first question was, "Who are you, sir?"

Jack told him, "412 Private Hughes, sir."

"Well, I will forego the sir, Private, but you won't. Who is he?" pointing to the Captain. Jack told him. "Right," he said, "what happened from the start?"

Jack said, "We were on our way to rehearsals for the Pirates of Penzance at the school in Khormaksar; I had been volunteered to drive him when there was this almighty flash and bang in front of the car. I jumped out, taking the SMG with me and could see the sod who I thought had thrown the grenade at us running away. I called out for him to stop, but he kept running so I shot at him as he ran around the corner but then he looked back. I fired at him a second time but missed again. That's it."

"What was—say, that's not the Singing Sod, is it?" said the Sergeant Major.

"Yes, it is," said Jack with a grin.

"What did he do?"

"Sat there in the car singing to himself," said Jack, taking a little liberty.

"Would you recognise the terr again?" asked the Sergeant Major.

"Well, it was only a quick look and as you can see, it's a bit dark, but I think so," said Jack.

"Right," said the Sergeant Major, "tomorrow morning, 0900 hrs, report to our HQ in Khormaksar. I'm sure a bright lad like you with the GOC in C's car at his personal disposal will have no trouble getting there and ask for me, WO2 Stevens, and I'll show you some pictures. For now, I'm going to take your statement. Listen very carefully to what I ask and answer accordingly. Any questions?"

Jack knew that in a situation like this if he said the wrong thing, it would be used to hang him—literally. He also felt sure that he had the right to have someone with him, an officer who would represent him, but he was a bit confused and wasn't sure if that applied to Courts Martial only or other situations. He was to learn later in his time in Aden when he shared a room with a Corporal from the MPs just how dangerous answering questions could be, but that was in the future; now he had to decide what to do. He decided that he would start answering questions and then if they started to get a bit hairy, he would play the dumb soldier and clam up. So he said, "No, sir," and waited.

"Right," said the WO2. "Let's sit in the back of a comfortable car," and at that he headed for the General's Ford. "Corporal Foxfield, escort this Captain," pointing to the Singing Sod, "up and down inside the perimeter and get him some fresh air; he's had a bit of a shock, poor thing." The last said without the least trace of sincerity.

"Yes, sir," said Cpl Foxfield practically dragging the Singing Sod out of the front seat. Getting in the back, the WO2 took a pad out of a pocket and commenced with the formality of setting out Jack's full rank and number and commencing with Statement and the time and date.

"Right, I'll set out your statement, and you stop me if I get any wrong, but I won't, will I?"

"No, sir," said Jack, with a smile on his face; this was going to be all right.

"I had been asked to drive Captain Smiley to rehearsals for the Pirates of Penzance at the Middle School located in Khormaksar Airfield. I was driving along the Maala Straight at just under the limit of 40 mph when I saw a man throw something at the car. He was located on the left-hand side of the road about 30 yards in front of me. There was a flash and a loud bang. I knew it was a hand grenade from my basic training. I braked the car to a halt as quickly as I could, consistent with safety. I emerged from the car as quickly as I could, taking the SMG I had previously been issued with as part of my guarding duties. I loaded it with a magazine containing twenty." At that, he looked at Jack quizzically, and Jack quickly nodded his head. "I called out in a loud and clear manner such that the runner could not misunderstand what I was saying, to stop or I shoot three times, before cocking my weapon and aiming four separate shots at him. As he was running very fast, I missed him. He ran around the corner of a street which I do not know the name of. I did not follow, because we had been taught not to do so during training. As I turned away, I suddenly saw him looking back around the corner. I fired three aimed shots at him as I thought he was going to throw another grenade at me. I do not know the result of those shots as he ducked back, and I have not looked around the corner. That would seem to be it. I haven't missed anything, have I?" Jack simply answered, "No, sir."

"Right, sign this, and you can get on your way now and take the Singing Sod with you; he's not going to be any good until tomorrow at the best. Bring him along with you tomorrow. If he starts to be funny, tell him that's on the orders of the Provost Marshall himself."

"Thank you very much, sir," said Jack, having realised how the WO11 had dealt with every dodgy bit of Jack's actions.

Jack asked the Singing Sod if he wanted to go back to the Mess or to carry on to the rehearsals but did not get a coherent answer. As he was very much enjoying driving the General's car and it was further to Khormaksar than it was to return to the Mess, he drove to Khormaksar. They arrived in time at the break. Obviously, the school did not have a bar but with a little bit of organisation and a waiter's trolley, some liquid refreshments appeared during the break. Having calmed down a bit by now, the Singing Sod, clasping a glass of alcoholic reviver in each hand, was staggering around telling anyone he could button hole that he had just been the target of a terrorist incident and was only just lucky enough to be alive. He made no mention of Jack or his attempt to shoot the terrorists; the numbers were steadily rising with each person he corralled. By the time the break was over, he was in no fit state to carry out his role so Jack decided to drive him back to the Mess. Fortunately, the Singing Sod quickly fell asleep in the back of the car and Jack could enjoy driving it. Jack was a little pissed off that the terrorists did not know enough about British military procedures to realise that the star plate on the front of the car was covered over, indicating that the General, or any other Senior Officer, was not travelling in it. Still, they had put a few chips in the paintwork, only spotted the next morning in daylight, and they had put the shits up quite properly an army Captain and a little less so, an Army Private.

Jack left the Mess servants to get the Singing Sod out of the car and into bed. Jack gave them a message that the Provost Marshall had ordered them both to attend his HQ at Khormaksar at 0900 hrs and that Jack would collect him at 0830 hrs. The last thing he did was to phone the Corporals' Club and leave a message for the General's Driver that the General's car could be collected at the Officers' Mess. He did not meet the Corporal again for several weeks by which time the world had moved on and no words of complaint came from him for the damage done.

Jack collected Captain Smiley, who looked very much the worse for wear, at 0830 hrs and drove them both to Khormaksar. Smiley was whisked away by a clearly unsympathetic Snow Drop Corporal, the policing system being a unified one between the Army and RAF. The Navy only had a miniscule presence which only became obvious when a Navy ship was in the harbour. Jack was dealt with by the same WO11 as the previous night.

He greeted Jack with, "You're 'I'll blow your bleeding 'ead off, sir,' aren't you?"

"Yes, sir," said Jack—there wasn't much else he could say.

"I knew you were a good lad last night," said the Sergeant Major. He reminded Jack of the Official Secrets Act, which Jack had signed on joining the army and several times since and now he had to sign it yet again. The army certainly intended that you would have no defence if you were daft enough to speak out of turn. In fact, the longer he worked in the HQ, the more he became aware that it was the officers who were more likely to let slip security information. Junior ranks almost never did speak out of turn, fearing what would happen to them if they did, but the bloody officers never seemed to worry about it.

Having gone through the rigmaroles, Jack had a pile of photographs, of varying degrees of clarity, plonked in front of him.

"Take your time. Look at each one very carefully, and tell me if the little bastard that was chucking grenades about the place is in any of that lot."

Some were full frontals, clear and easy to see. Others had been taken surreptitiously from a distance in poor light and were much harder to make out. But after about ten minutes, one appeared that caught Jack's attention. He put it to the side and kept on looking at the other photos but kept coming back to the one. Eventually, Jack looked up at the Sergeant Major who had been sitting there quietly and said, "That's him."

"How sure are you?" asked the Sergeant Major.

"98%," said Jack. Looking at the back of the photo, the Sergeant Major read out,

"Mohammed Mohammed. What a pity you couldn't have aimed a little straighter, Private Hughes, the world would be a lot better place without that one. Remember the Official Secrets Act and forget everything you have seen and done here and get on your way. I expect you'll get a letter from someone sometime about last night's little lot. On your way."

"Sir, I need to wait for Captain Smiley."

"No, you don't. He has some answering to do as to why the only coherent person who had any idea of what was going on last night was a Private soldier and why he, a Captain, had to be put to bed by three Mess servants." Jack quickly left.

Word had quickly spread about Jack's adventures and he had to withstand a fair amount of good-natured ribbing including from the General's 2nd Driver, on leave the night before, who wasn't too pleased at having to get the chips, caused by the grenade, on the front of the Zephyr touched up. Jack did indeed receive a letter from the GOC in C commending him on his actions and which finished with a witty comment that on this occasion, he would not be charged for the repairs to the paintwork but if he made a habit of it, he would.

# Chapter 65

Life went by in a pleasant enough way for Jack. He enjoyed driving to pick up visitors from the airport at Khormaksar and driving them around Aden as their visits required. He particularly enjoyed driving them to Little Aden. Little Aden was at the other mouth to Aden Harbour and involved a drive there of just over 20 miles. The road was tarmacked in good condition and passed through basically sand dunes with a few palm and date palms here and there. Odd patches of scrub with bits of wild life littered the journey but his favourite bit was where the road cut across, on a man-made causeway, the north east corner of the harbour. In the shallow lagoon created by the causeway, thousands of flamingos could be seen. From a distance, it looked like a pink cloud floating across the water. Daft as it seemed to Jack, the picture lifted his somewhat battered soul when he saw it. During the times the birds were not there or Jack wasn't travelling to Little Aden, he felt quite deprived and wondered why Reece had wanted to get out of the job—for Jack, it seemed ideal.

One day he was ordered to collect a civvy specialist and an Army Major from the FVRDE (Fighting Vehicles Research and Development Establishment) and take the civvy and the Major to their hotel and Mess respectively. Because the Mess was closer, he dropped the Major off first. As it was nearly 1300 hrs—normally the UK flights came in about 0700 hrs but this one was late, and Jack had spent the morning in the café at Khormaksar Airport drinking coffee and reading day old papers—the meetings for that morning had been cancelled and rescheduled for the following day. Jack was surprised when the guy, whose name Jack did not know, invited him to lunch. Normally, Jack ate in the Airmen's Restaurant where the food was very good but the chance to eat somewhere else was very appealing. He wasn't sure about the protocol of eating with a civilian who obviously out-ranked Jack, were they both in the army, but what the hell, he'd get the meal inside him and worry about whether he should have refused later.

The guy introduced himself as the Senior Development Manager for Alvis who had their new Stalwart High Mobility Load Carrier on trial currently in Aden and other sites around the world. His presence was due to high repair rates to the three vehicles they had on trial and he had come out, along with the Major from the FVRDE, to see if they could identify the cause(s). Jack did not know that they were suspicious of official reports, hence Jack was to be politely interrogated about the vehicle. Unfortunately, Jack knew almost nothing about them. They were regularly used taking loads up country from Khormaksar, and since that was at the far end of the Aden peninsula from the HQ, Jack had never even seen one. He knew that a preliminary report had been produced by G Tech, which was after all responsible for all trials in Aden and the Arabian Peninsula, but it had been typed by Reece before his arrival, and Jack had only seen it as a file among many in the filing cabinets. The conversation was therefore about everything other than the Stalwarts—the most detailed subject being the security situation and how to keep safe. Thanking the Manager for the meal, Jack arranged to collect him at 0645 hrs, a bit of a surprise for him at the hours they worked in Aden, and said his goodbyes.

Jack collected him and delivered him to the G Tech Major, Major Clasher, the following morning. At 0930 hrs Major Clasher appeared before Jack's desk and ordered him to drive himself and visitors to 2 Coy RASC, shortly to become The Royal Corps of Transport, at Seedaseer Lines inside Khormaksar Airfield. Jack was to get to know this unit very well as it officially 'owned' the G Tech Land Rover and the Hillman Husky staff car, G Tech not being a unit in its own right and thus entitled to hold vehicles on strength.

At 2 Coy, the two visitors and Major Clasher had a meeting with the 2 Coy Officer Commanding and then with all the drivers who had driven the Stalwart. Because of the numbers, the only room big enough to hold them all was the NAAFI. As Jack was already sitting in the NAAFI, he got up to go but was told to stay where he was by Major Brown. Major Clasher introduced himself and the visitors, and they then conducted a question and answer session regarding the drivers' experiences with the new vehicle. In the main, they described the convoys up country, the loads they carried, about three tons, well under the nominal maximum of five tons, but this was in line with normal army practice in Aden, to drive vehicles with less-than-their-maximum loads because of the roughness of the desert, rock roads outside of Aden State. The convoy speeds were described as between 15 and 20 miles per hour because of that roughness. The general consensus was that the Stalwart was not a bad bit of kit, comfortable and easy to drive on most roads but it did need a lot of maintenance and it was a bit fragile; bits kept breaking, some of them serious like wheels coming off even if they could carry on with one less.

The FVRDE people thanked the drivers and made their way to the Officers' Mess along with the OC of 2 Coy leaving Jack in the NAAFI. In the way of soldiers' conversations asking who are you then and what are you doing with that lot were aimed at Jack. Jack was careful with his answers, explaining only that he was driving them around and knew nothing of what they were doing; the first he knew of it was when he heard them being questioned about the convoys. At that, they started laughing among themselves, clearly sharing a secret that only they knew. Jack carefully did not ask any direct questions about the secret but just let the conversation flow. Gradually, he built up a picture quite different to the one they had told their inquisitors.

Apparently, when the convoys formed up, the three Stalwarts were placed at the front and once they had left Aden State proper and had arrived at the unmade roads, the Stalwarts would use their much superior speed to the Bedford RLs and disappear off into the distance, generally maintaining about 50 mph over the rough ground. Because of the six-wheel structure, a row of three each side, the ride was generally quite smooth inside the cab but very hard on the suspension, hence the frequent damage. The drivers of the Stalwarts were quite happy to clear off on their own, even at the risk of their being ambushed, confident in their speed to outrun it quickly and safely.

Jack ventured the view that if they continued to wreck the Stalwarts by their high speed in unsuitable conditions, the army would regard them as unsuitable and not buy them. This simply generated jeers and laughter so Jack shut up. Soon after that, a messenger told Jack that his party was ready for collection from the Officers' Mess and that ended the conversations.

All the way back to the HQ at Steamer Point, Jack was in a quandary as to what he should do. Should he drop his fellow soldiers in the shit, or should he just keep quiet? Once they reached the HQ, the visitors went to see the Lt Colonel SD/Tech, leaving Jack with Major Clasher and Cpl Pectin. Pectin looked at him peculiarly as he walked into the Majors' office and closed the door. Major Clasher looked at him quizzically,

"Yes, Private Hughes, what do you want?" It burst from Jack in a flood. He had only been in the army for a short time and had been in Aden for even less. He was a Private speaking to a Major and the matter, to Jack, seemed extremely important.

"Sir, all that stuff you were told about the Stalwarts was a pack of lies." At that, Clasher seemed somewhat startled.

"Go on." Very incoherently, the story burst from Jack, and it took some little time to get the details sorted out and a coherent picture developed.

"Stay here," said the Major as he departed. Shortly he returned bringing with him the Colonel and the visitors. Clasher said to Jack, "Now there is nothing for you to worry about, but I am going to repeat the story you just told me about the Stalwarts and the way they are being driven, and I want you to correct me if I get anything wrong. Clear?"

"Yes, sir." Clasher then clearly and succinctly described what Jack had heard in the NAAFI.

"Anything to add or alter?"

"No, sir," Jack hesitated.

"What is it, Hughes?" asked the Colonel. Jack paused; he was clearly bothered and being addressed by a Lt Colonel was quite frightening for a young Private only a few months in the army. He had never even met one in the Army Cadet Force, only the one at the Training Battalion in Buller Barracks, and they were still a high and mighty figure to a mere Private.

The FVRDE civvy manager spoke up saying, "I don't know if you realise it, young man, but you have just saved Alvis's contract and the army's new, best ever vehicle purchase by what you have done, and we all here will be eternally grateful for what you have had the courage to do."

"Well, sir, I was all of a dither as to whether I should speak up especially as I will have to go back to 2 Coy for the routine checks and if the drivers find out I have grassed them up, I'll be right in the," Jack quickly changed shit to the doo-doo to complete his sentence.

"You have no worries on that score," said the Colonel,

"No one here will reveal what you have said and anyway, you will type up the report once it's written and if there is anything in it that concerns you, come and see me, and we will sort it out. I fully understand the courage it has taken for you to speak up, but it was vital that you did so, and I am very glad that you did." At that, the meeting broke up and indeed, Jack had no concerns when he typed the final report. The army did sign a contract with Alvis and they started appearing in the army about a year later. Whenever Jack saw one, he had a little smile to himself even years later when he had left the army and the 'retired' ones started appearing in re-enactors shows.

# Chapter 66

One day, Jack received a call to go up to the Colonel's office. When he arrived, the Colonel handed him a telex message and told him to read it. The text heading was Travellers' Diarrhoea Trial. The army was developing a policy where troops would be stationed as much as possible in the UK, Germany and relatively few base areas around the world, so if trouble developed somewhere in their region, they could be flown to the trouble spot at short notice. Heavy kit, artillery, tanks etc. would be stored in depots in friendly countries around the world, so that it too could be air- or ground-lifted quickly. Ironically, Aden had five infantry battalions located there as standby 'firefighters' and, as is common with bureaucracy, because they were reserved for fly away roles, they could not be used for the insurrection which had arisen in Aden; other troops had to be flown in from Germany, the closest reserve station to HQ MEC for that.

The problem that had arisen with the policy had various names, Montezuma's Revenge, Delhi Belly and in Aden, Aden Gut, whereby troops were being stricken by reactions to the local food and water causing quite severe illnesses and weaknesses such that they were unable to perform at 100% and in some severe cases, required hospitalisation. Whilst it generally appeared to be more severe in locations where hygiene was not high on the locals' list of priorities, the army had set up a worldwide trial to look into the causes and cures for travellers' diarrhoea. Jack knew that the trial was to start in the near future because he had typed memos on the subject.

So when he was called up, it was to discover that the Colonel had written on the tele-text with what looked like a brown chinagraph pencil. The writing said, 'Here's the names of the two officers who expect to run the trial; do you think they are winding us up? Sorry about the pencil colour; it was the only one to hand, and it seemed appropriate somehow!' The names were Major P Bucket and Captain S House. Jack laughed and said, "We'll know when I stand up at Khormaksar with the board with Major P Bucket and Captain S House on, and no one comes forward. Especially if I write the names in brown."

The Colonel laughed and said, "Take that down to Major Lovewell, whose auspices the trial come under, and give it to him, please." Jack could hear him laughing halfway down the stairs. The Major took it from Jack, read it and, laughing, gestured that it should be given to Maj Clasher who, in turn, read it and laughed. Maj Lovewell picked up a brown chinagraph pencil from his desk and wrote on the tele-text, 'Let's just hope Bucket doesn't get taken short, because he'll not know where to go for relief because none of them are labelled with his name!' (Shit houses were labelled but buckets weren't.) As is so often the case in the army, this tele-text was to be passed around with added puns for many months.

In due course, the two officers arrived at Khormaksar and responded to their name boards. They were a very taciturn pair, at least to Jack, and they spoke not at all during the eight miles to HQ MEC. The trial involved feeding and watering one company, A Coy of the Lancaster Regiment, who were due to arrive in Aden in a few weeks' time, entirely with food and water brought out from the UK. B Company were to be fed entirely by local produce and C Coy was to eat food sourced from the UK and to drink locally sourced products. In the event, all three companies were afflicted by Aden Gut to the same degree much to the puzzlement of the medics, Bucket and House. The final report, typed by Jack, speculated that A Coy personnel must have cheated by eating and drinking local products and thus caught Aden Gut.

There were other food trials that Jack became familiar with, the chief one being the 24-hr Ration Pack trials. Normally, when in the field, the British Army ate tinned product. One box of tinned food was designed to feed a Section of men for 24 hours. Breakfasts, dinners and teas were all tinned as were biscuits, jam, cheese, tea, in loose leaf form, and boiled sweets. The problem with it was it was heavy, and if troops were to be flown to trouble spots, every last bit of weight counted. So someone had come up with the idea that dehydrated ration packs, still sorted into packs to feed a Section of troops (actually eight men rather than the 10 nominally to make up a Section) for 24 hours would be much lighter and easier to pack for travel, especially as the dehydrated weight and the plastic wrappings would be considerably lighter than the tinned product currently used and referred to universally as 'compo'. The trial rapidly threw up the problem with the idea; water, which was needed in copious amounts to rehydrate the dehydrated ration packs, was simply unavailable in the desert, unlike in the jungles of Borneo where it was in overwhelming supply! The trial was rapidly wound up although Jack was to encounter the ration packs in the UK and Germany in future.

He was to encounter a problem with the tinned rations, 'compo', which, copiously containing baked beans, was notoriously responsible for 'wind' of an extremely smelly and explosive nature.

# Chapter 67

Jack had just stripped off his uniform one afternoon when the Duty Driver arrived to collect him. A Ferret Scout Car had been blown up by a mine in one of the wadis up country, and he was to accompany Major Clasher to operate the Polaroid camera as was his duty as the Command Photographer! He was to take kit for 24 hrs as they were unlikely to be able to fly back that night. Jack put on a long-sleeved uniform shirt, long trousers and slipped a jumper into his kit along with the other necessities he would need. He collected the camera and a couple of film packs from the office and an SMG from the armoury—an SLR would be too big and clumsy in the De Havilland Beaver in which they would be flying. The Beaver was a five-seater, short take-off and landing, single engine, high wing monoplane and not very fast. It was the first time Jack had flown in such a plane and he did have some, well, quite a lot of, reservations as to whether it could fly with the weight of the four passengers and all their kit plus some other kit carried aboard. Along with Major Clasher there was a CSM for the Coy whose position they were flying into, a Private returning to the position they were flying into and Jack, as well, of course, as the Pilot, a Warrant Officer from the Army Air Corp. As it turned out, they were all big men and Jack knew, from a report he had typed about Scout Helicopters, that obtaining lift in Aden was difficult because of the heat generating a thinner air than say, Europe. Consequently, most light aircraft flying was done in the early morning when possible when the air was densest. They were about to fly in the heat of the day—a necessity due to having to get to the vehicle and photograph it before it could be plundered by the local Arabs that night.

They were flying to a site codenamed Cap Badge. It was a small knoll in the middle of a large wadi. The position was ideally placed to block and police any traffic passing up or down the wadi. The tops of the walls of the wadi were irregular but were several hundred feet, on average, above the wadi floor. Consequently, they had to drop down a considerable height as they had been flying several thousand feet above the plateau to avoid the occasional shot fired by a bored shepherd or goatherd. The rough runway, scraped out and roughly levelled by the Royal Engineers, was no more than a hundred yards from the barbed wire surrounding the position but to Jack, it felt like ten miles knowing that insurgents in the hills could be lining him up in their sights and his relief when he reached the position was palpable.

Besides the trenches for the Company and units stationed there, more sangers than trenches since it was almost impossible to dig trenches by hand in the rocky floor, there was a tent set up in the middle of the position, used to draw enemy fire and not for use by the troops; there were a few, camouflaged bivouacs set up for visitors, one of which was allocated to Jack and one to Major Clasher; Jack was so glad he would not be sharing a tent with a Major. As for the other two passengers, the Private was claimed by his Platoon sergeant who had been waiting to claim him and the CSM, who was straight out from the UK, white knees and all, was taken off by a Sergeant.

Also inside the position was stationed a 105-mm pack howitzer, a 3-inch mortar team of two mortars and a squadron of armoured cars. With such a force, the British Army felt a full-scale insurgent army could be stopped in its tracks by the Cap Badge unit. But Jack was still glad he had his SMG until the Major commanding the site told him and Major Clasher, who was armed with a six-shot Enfield revolver, that, if it did look like they would be overwhelmed, they should save their last bullet for themselves, so appallingly did the National Liberation Front treat prisoners!

Jack attended a small 'O' group, held only 10 minutes after they had arrived, it getting dark down in the wadi bottom shortly after 1600 hrs, and it was 1500 hrs already. The OC decided that they would send a patrol of three Saladin Armoured Cars, armed with 76 mm quick firing canons, and three Ferret Scout Cars armed with .30 inch Browning machine guns to form a perimeter a quarter of a mile or so beyond the mined Ferret. Major Clasher, Jack and two riflemen would follow in a Land Rover and three more Saladins and Ferrets would follow them and set up a perimeter a quarter of a mile behind them.

In the event, everything proceeded smoothly, and Jack's Polaroids showed clearly the information required. Tea that night was much better than Jack had expected. An Army Catering Corps (ACC) Corporal was seconded to the position and that evening, he produced Lancashire Hot Pot, tinned, powdered mash potato, beans, roly-poly pudding, custard, biscuits, cheese and jam, or both, swilled down with buckets of tea, all from the tinned ration packs. It wasn't as good as the Airmen's Restaurant, but it was a lot better than some of the meals Jack had had to eat in Army Cookhouses. Breakfast was again from tins, bacon, scrambled eggs from egg powder, served up in square lumps, fried fresh bread, brought up with the last convoy to pass through, baked beans, lots of baked beans, biscuits, marmalade and tea. It was a comfort for Jack, not just the food, but the fact that he had survived to eat it. The night before, everyone settled down for the night just after dark—lights tended to attract bullets rather than moths in Cap Badge. Jack's bivouac was surrounded by a stone wall which reached halfway up the tent so that there was some cover which served to keep bullets out and a rest to fire bullets back!

Just after 2100 hrs, when Jack had just drifted off, he was woken by the sound of bullets hitting the joint wall, shared with Major Clasher's tent, and the very faint echo of shots. He could hear the Major swearing away, which given his rather strong Scott's accent and Jack's awaking from sleep haze, meant that it was a few moments before Jack could make out what he was saying. Jack eventually discerned that he was shouting, "None of you poxy bastards are going to take pot shots at me for free." It was taking time because he had carefully unloaded the Enfield pistol of its six rounds and replaced them in the box of twelve which he carried with him, but in the dark, he could not find the box! Jack gradually took in that the shots were coming from high up on one of the wadi walls about 800 yds away. Jack, whilst all this was going on, had loaded his magazine, containing 20 rounds, onto the SMG and had taken aim at the sparkles of light up on the wadi. Just then, one of the Saladins, which was kept manned overnight on a 2 hrs on, 4 hrs off with the other 5 Saladins, let fly with its 76-mm gun. This was closely followed by the 3-inch mortars and the 105-mm howitzer. Jack could make out the Major's swearing amongst the noise of all the riflemen and machine gunners opening up. The pop of the Enfield firing was almost lost in the general noise but was sufficiently audible for Jack to feel that it was authorisation for him to open fire as well. The insurgents were hopelessly out of range for the pistol and SMG, but it was considerably comforting to let fly. The distance was outside the effective accuracy range of the SLRs being fired by the riflemen, but you never knew; you might just get one of the bastards. The only really effective weapons were the Saladin's main armament, the 105-mm howitzer, the 3-inch mortar and the machine guns. Jack was to discover, when it quietened down after only two or three minutes, that the firing had come from half a dozen or so insurgents who fired a few rounds in the general direction of the position and then scarpered before the return fire could land on them. It happened twice again during the night to give them a disturbed night. By morning, Jack was faced with a smiling Major Clasher proudly showing off his one round left. Unfortunately for him no .38-inch ammunition was held at the position, the few officers there all being armed with 9-mm Browning Semi-Automatic Pistols. Jack was, however, able to replenish the 19 rounds he fired, but he did not feel it appropriate to tell Clasher. Breakfast was, therefore, welcomed with a hearty appetite tinned beans or no.

The Beaver was scheduled to collect them at 0900 hrs. Stand-to was just after 0600 hrs so with little packing to do, Jack just wandered around the position once they were stood down. One of the bags brought up with them yesterday was a bag of mail. One of the soldiers was sitting a little way from anyone holding a letter in his hands but not looking at it. As Jack strolled past, he spoke out and started a conversation. When Jack said that he was a Staff Clerk back at HQ MEC, the guy said, "You must be a clever bugger then, able to read and write and all that rubbish."

Jack could only laugh at that and say, "If you say so!"

At that, the guy handed him the letter he was holding and said, "What's that word then?" The word was 'when' and it was clearly written, so when the guy asked him about another one, Jack suspected that the guy could not read or write adequately so Jack said, "Why don't I read the whole letter for you?" and proceeded to do so. It was just a short, one-page letter from his mum saying little more than what was a standing joke in the army for letters saying 'All right. Love, Mum.' The paper was torn from something like a Reporter's Notebook. Jack asked him, "I just happen to have a notebook with me; would you like a couple of pages?"

The guy squirmed a bit and looked down at the ground. "I was quite good at the drawing and that at school, but the writing was a bit of a problem." At that, Jack said, "Why don't you let me do the writing? I'm not going just yet, and you could fill up the rest of the pages with some drawings of this place?" And that's what they did; Jack wrote nothing much more than a note and handed the letter to him.

"My name's Jack, by the way."

"Colin." Jack left him with the note paper and walked away to join Major Clasher who was shortly joined by the Major commanding Cap Badge. Before anything could be said, the just-arrived CSM came walking past and the Major called out to him, "Sarn't Major, while I take out this patrol, do something about the latrines would you; the smell could shave my corns." The CSM's face was a picture, how do you stop latrines, which were only clefts in the lava, from smelling in desert heat. But the Major carried on, "Pour some petrol down there or something and burn it."

The CSM's face lit up,

"Yes, sir, straight away, sir." And at that he scurried off.

What the Major did not know was that the CSM was something of a pyromaniac. What the CSM did not know was that the troops had been using the long, deep cleft in the rock for a purpose other than the obvious one. It was just comfortably wide enough to stretch a crude plank with legs with a hole in it across and as the cleft had filled up, so the plank had been moved along it. It had been in use for a long time, more than decades probably, as different events occurred necessitating use of the position and latrine, and it was, therefore, not surprising that the stench was powerful. It could even have had Alexander the Great's ossified turds down there!

The CSM ordered two of the soldiers to obtain two jerry cans each full of petrol from the dump for the armoured cars, a total of 20 gallons in all. He took the cans from the soldiers and proceeded to pour the petrol down the fissure. The two soldiers, eyeing one another surreptitiously, backed away from the fissure. Striking a match, the CSM dropped it down the crack. It flared up nicely and proceeded to create a huge fire. He then discovered the illicit use to which the latrine had been put. Over the years, there had been a fair number of misfires in the artillery pieces, the Saladins, mortars and anything else heavy based there. Army regulations made it clear that dud rounds should be taken out to a safe open space and there be detonated by attaching some gun cotton and a detonator. The problem was that a single soldier staggering out into the open desert with a 105-mm shell was a welcome target for the insurgents up on the wadi tops. Consequently, it had become common practice to drop the dud shell down the latrine; after all, who would go looking for one there? As the fire burned, so the rounds started to cook off. Being down in the fissure with solid rock walls, the only way for the explosive force to escape was upwards.

The OC had driven off, about half a mile, when he heard the first of the explosions behind him. Looking back, all he could see were god-almighty explosions, one after the other with clouds of 'dust' shooting upwards—his camp appeared to be being blown to bits. Turning around immediately, he sped back to his camp which he was sure was under major attack. He was just in time to drive into a pitter patter of falling shit and fluttering toilet paper, which decorated the area for a huge distance around the camp. Staggering out of the inferno came the CSM, covered from head to foot in shit and toilet paper with his uniform in shreds and loose wet turds dripping from his head; some even appeared solid—Alexander's perhaps! He was trying to say something, but no one wanted to go near enough to hear him. Eventually, he could be made out to be saying, "It must have been the compo!" which sent everyone into paroxysms of laughter even though they themselves had had a delicate sprinkling of doo-doo over themselves. The only one not covered was Jack who had gone into his bivouac to collect his kit as the explosions started. Jack laughed and laughed until he saw Major Clasher decorated with turds and decorations of twirly soiled paper; he stopped suddenly and nearly burst himself, trying not to add to the moist secretions decorating the place!

The Beaver arrived on time, and Jack and a heavily pomaded Major Clasher climbed aboard. Just as they were boarding, Colin rushed up and handed Jack the letter he had written for Colin and asked him to post it once he got back to Aden. He called out, "You can look at the pictures if you want."

The take-off was nothing less than hair raising. The walls of the wadi were too high for the Beaver to simply take off and fly up over them, so instead, it had to fly in circles within the wadi, gradually getting higher until it was able to scrape over the top of the wadi by a few feet; it had been bad enough flying round and round tipped over at an almost perpendicular angle but seeing wheel marks running off the edge of the wadi was terrifying. Gradually, the Beaver climbed away from the wadi with locals only just below them popping off at them with their rifles—they were close enough for Jack to clearly make out the mix of weapons being used from centuries old jezail muzzle loaders to Lee Enfield .303s that the army was only just giving up. The pilot explained that this was the norm for locals to have fun; they were supposedly on our side, but the opportunity to shoot down a plane and loot it was just too great to resist. Jack considered that he should be giving up the job of Command Photographer but never quite got around to it as his nerves calmed the higher and further they flew from Cap Badge which remained splattered in poo for many months as it did not rain in Aden to wash it away. Eventually though, enough soldiers had been caught misbehaving and punished by poo picking that the site was eventually sanitised by collecting and throwing it back down the abyss, neatly cleaned out by high explosives. Little did Jack know that he would be returning to Cap Badge in a far more dangerous role to the insurgents than throwing shit at them.

# Chapter 68

Christmas 1964 was a revelation to Jack. The previous Christmas Jack had been stuck on guard at Houndstone Camp in Yeovil with no heating and here he was, a year later in Arabia in temperatures of 80 °F or so during the day. Night time, it dropped to as low as 60 °F—like a glorious English summer to Jack. He found other soldiers putting on jumpers in the evening; funny because he was so hot but by the time he had passed through the hot season, there were really only two seasons, hot and cold, the transference periods of spring and autumn being very short and almost unnoticeable.

Christmas Day was a Sunday. Not very much work was done on the Saturday. About 10.00 hrs, spreads of light bites were being laid out on tables set out on the veranda at the front of the HQ building with more tables of drinks laid out at each end.

Invitations had been passed out to all the Private soldiers and junior NCOs to a cocktail party to be given by the Brigadier General Staff (BGS), the number limited to 20 for each one, spread out over the Christmas period, something quite unheard of in the UK or Germany but common in smallish garrisons around the world. Jack's was for the Monday, and he was not much looking forward to it.

On the Saturday as the numbers on the balcony increased, so the drinks and eats diminished. One of the Lt Colonels was going around dispensing drinks to any of the WRAC girls whose glass was only half empty. He made sure that the drink he handed them was not the same as the one they were drinking so that they were, in fact, mixing their drinks even if that was not their intention. It was not long before numbers of them were showing signs of being the worse for wear because of his antics. Jack merely saw that as being a strange way to behave but once Major Lovewell took him aside and asked, asked as in ordered him, to run the worst ones down to the WRAC in the Hillman, he wasn't so pleased as it took him from the free eats and drinks.

LCpl Taylor, who worked in the Registry Office in which Jack was also based, was Duty NCO at the entrance to the WRAC block. She took him aside after his third delivery and asked if he could spare her a few minutes when she came off duty at 1800 hrs. She had been on leave in Kenya when Jack arrived in Aden, and he didn't meet her until she walked through the door on Monday morning a few days after Jack's arrival. She was blonde, slim, sun tanned and a podium place in any beauty contest. Jack, still reeling from being dumped, would have viewed her as someone to ask out in different times and the fact that she wore a diamond engagement ring definitely said hands off. During the two months or so that they had worked in the same room, but not department, they had had a few conversations in all of which references to her fiancée had occurred, thus enforcing that she was unavailable even had Jack been that way inclined. Now, two months down the line and still alive, Jack was intrigued. What could she possibly want to talk to him about? So, being a sensible sort of bloke, he said, "Yes, sure. Where would you like to meet?" She suggested the seat in the Groundsman's shed where Sylva had given him the ring back, which was even more intriguing.

Jack turned up at the appointed time with all sorts of theories wiggle waggling through his mind. What she said came as a complete shock and was not any of the ideas Jack had considered. She took, from a small handbag, a letter, handed it to him and said,

"Read that." It was still just light enough to make out that it was a letter written to her and was clearly private.

Jack said, "I don't think I should be reading this."

She insisted, saying, "I need you to read it because I want your advice as to what to do about it." Jack read the letter; *this is becoming a habit*, he thought, *reading other people's letters*; it was only one page and was what was known to all troops in Aden, and around the world, as a 'Dear John'. It was a letter dumping her. Receiving such letters was a common occurrence for male soldiers, caused mainly by the physical separation of the two love birds, so much so that the letters had gained the generic title of a 'Dear John'; in Aden, such letters ended up on a notice board in the male accommodation block for all and sundry to see, attracting comments like '9 out of 10 for that one', 'I've never heard that one before' to 'No effort to let down gracefully, 3 out of 10'. Jack had not been able to pin his dumping letter up because there wasn't one; she had simply told him to his face and walked off.

Now Jack was looking at a Dear John, or more correctly, a Dear Janet, but the letter matched many other male soldiers had received; he had no idea if the women even did the same by using notice boards for their letters.

"Look," said Jack. "Would you not be better speaking to one of your female friends rather than someone, a male that you hardly know?"

"No, I want to talk to you, because you have just been through being dumped, and I want to know how you did it and I don't want any of the girls to know because I couldn't trust any of them to keep it a secret—you will keep it secret, won't you?"

"Yes," said Jack, committing himself by so saying. "Look," he said, "with all that's been going on, I haven't had my tea and I bet you haven't eaten properly either, so would you like to go to that Chinese restaurant in Maala, and we can talk there, away from prying eyes?"

Janet thought about it for a moment and then said, "Yes, alright, but we go Dutch." That suited Jack because he only had a couple of 100 EA shilling notes in his wallet anyway—about two pounds in proper money.

Very little was said during the five-minute walk. Janet said that she had never been there before but some of the girls had talked about it and some had liked it, and some had not. Jack, with all his experience of the two visits to the Chinese in Kingston, had loftily said the ones who hadn't liked it had probably chosen the wrong dishes and if she were to let him choose, he was sure she would enjoy it!

There were a lot of items on the menu which Jack hadn't a clue what they were but he ordered some that he did and, despite the circumstances, they both enjoyed it. During the meal, the quality was excellent, especially the ultra-fresh sea food items; it became clear that Janet had viewed Jack across the office and had been impressed by his conduct which did not appear as though he had been too upset by being dumped even though he was now stuck in Aden for two years, nor had he expressed derogatory terms about Sylva. Jack explained that he had been very upset and still was, but he had hidden it as much as he could to stop other squaddies from taking the piss or teasing him too much. He told her that he had considered shooting Sylva and her paramour, but he didn't have a weapon, he didn't know who the bloke was, and he couldn't think of a way of doing it without suspicion falling immediately on him! Janet laughed at that but did not realise how seriously he meant it at the time. Now, two months later, the ache and anger had diminished somewhat, which he did tell her. The old cliché that time heals was true, and he was sure it would work in her case too. They discovered that, in both their cases, their fiancées had been their first loves and so their sense of loss was greater since they didn't have the loss of previous dumpings and the getting over them to fall back on. This sense of great loss was to stay with them both for the rest of their lives; it did lessen and dull with time, but it was always there and characterised their relationship.

Jack walked Janet back to the WRAC and they said goodnight at the gate. Jack made no attempt to kiss her, but she did say she had enjoyed the evening despite the reason as to why it had come about and thanked him for his advice.

The following day was Christmas Day and at lunchtime, the tables in the Airmen's Restaurant had been laid out in long rows for the army. The RAF had their meal in the evening, so lunchtime was an all-army affair. Settings were laid out with crackers, beers, napkins and other goodies. The soldiers sat at the tables and were waited on by the officers of HQ MEC; it was a surreal experience being served his Christmas pudding by a Brigadier General. The ration was three bottles of beer each, but with several abstainers sitting around Jack, he drank much more than that. The WRAC girls generally were spread out amongst the male soldiers. With no previous experience of Aden, Jack had ended up sitting with almost complete strangers around him. He had, therefore, concentrated on putting as many beers away as he could. He did catch a glimpse of Janet a few tables away but had not felt it appropriate to approach her.

Once the meal was over, groups made their way to the NAAFI, and Jack went with them. It was a convivial evening and by the time Jack turned in, his brain was floating in an ocean of beer and brandy—not a good mix. By three o'clock in the morning, he was feeling very ill, projectile vomiting and filling the WC pan with oceans of liquefied horrors. He also felt really unwell. Jack had had nights before when he had drunk too much but although the symptoms were familiar, there was something not quite the same. After several visits to the loo and feeling very weak, Jack's brain connected his brain to the symptoms he had typed up for Aden Gut in the Traveller's Diarrhoea trials only a few weeks before. He persuaded one of his roommates to call an ambulance and in the early hours of Boxing Day morning, he ended up in hospital being treated by a very pretty and sympathetic WRN doctor who confirmed the diagnosis.

Jack was kept in the hospital for 10 days and then on light duties for a further five. Light duties meant very little as his work was hardly strenuous anyway and drill and PT didn't come into it. He did, however, make an enemy of the RSM who knew that Jack had imbibed far too much and, in his view, as a result was simply suffering from a hangover of monumental proportions. However, the RSM could not do anything because of the diagnosis by the WRN doctor.

The operating structure in HQ MEC was quite peculiar. The daily working of the Clerks came under the control and command of the Superintending Clerk, Captain Robertson. However, as a unit they came under the command of the Camp Commandant, a Lt Col of one of the Rifle Regiments. The RSM was his right-hand man, and more, and indeed mostly ran the camp, since after about 0800 hrs, the Colonel had imbibed sufficient alcohol to impair his regime. But as was typical in the army, his behaviour, resultant from a horrifyingly bad time as a prisoner of the Koreans as a result of a heroic defence of a pass where all but three of his unit of 350 men had been destroyed but which had delayed the Koreans long enough to allow a mixed refugee and admin column to escape, caused a particularly bad treatment of him by the Koreans. When he was eventually captured, wounded in three places and incapable of any further defence, the Koreans treated him abominably and kept him barely alive because, as a Major then, he represented a valuable prize. Such a man deserved that a blind eye be turned to his cure in a bottle for all the demons carried in his mind. The RSM had been especially selected to the position and had particular instructions as to how the Colonel and the camp should be run. Indeed, with the Clerks allocated to their positions by the Superintending Clerk and their day-to-day working observed by very senior officers, there was very little else to be done, the occasional inspections of quarters and the annual admin inspection sat mainly on the RSM's shoulders and the Colonel only really appeared for the annual admin inspection, the start of which was timed for 0600 hrs and the finish just before 0700 hrs so that the soldiers could be at work on time and the Colonel still be sober at the end of the inspection. There would be occasional Orders where soldiers had to appear in front of the Colonel for promotions, disciplinary actions and welfare requests, normally associated with problems back home, and for all of these, the RSM would handle the admin to such an extent that the Colonel had hardly any role at all and with all meetings set for first thing in the morning, the Colonel was more than capable of handling the duties required. A drunken Private on his own was of little regard—only if he caused trouble would action be taken.

Jack was visited in the hospital by Corporal Pectin, twice, and much to his surprise, once by Janet who brought a bag of apples and pears. Their conversation was stilted, as hospital visit ones always are, but the kindness of it registered strongly with Jack. He had said to her, when they went to the Chinese, that the biggest problem dealing with his dumping was having no one close he could trust to talk to and that if she felt the need in the future, she could always talk to him. The hospital visit lasted no longer than 10 minutes and nothing about her dumping was discussed. Jack was pleased to have seen her, but he wasn't planning on asking her, or indeed any female, out and as far as he was concerned, that was an end to the matter unless she came to him again for advice, although what that might be he could not guess.

# Chapter 69

Jack returned to work and life carried on pretty much as normal until one morning; both Majors had been driven to a meeting at RAF Khormaksar by Cpl Pectin, and Jack had been left to man the fort. When the phone rang, Jack answered it to find himself speaking to an agitated Commanding Officer of one of the Regiments at Little Aden. The Col wished to speak to either of the Majors and was somewhat upset to find that all was available was a Private soldier. He set the problem out to Jack which boiled down to the salesman from Honda had demonstrated to him a portable generator which was vastly superior to the standard army issue, and he wanted authority to spend £190 to buy one. The salesman was flying out in an hour's time, and he needed an answer now as to whether the G Tech Trial Fund would pay for it. Jack was horrified. He tried to head the Colonel off that he was only a Private and did not have the authority to give permission for such a purchase. The Col wanted his new generator and no Private soldier was going to stand in his way. Shortly, Jack found himself checking the Trial Fund file and was terrified hearing himself say, "Well, I cannot see any reason why you should not buy it, sir. Normally, the paperwork would be done in advance of such a purchase, but given the circumstances, I am sure you will not mind signing it later?"

"Good chap, send it direct to me, and I'll sign it immediately. Goodbye." Jack sat there trembling; he had just authorised the expenditure of a sum of money just greater than his annual pay.

He gathered himself together and looked at the paperwork in the file. It was clear from that that there was a set of documentation relating to requests to spend money on in-Command trials. It started with a request form from the unit making the request, a standard assessment form for the request and an authorisation or denial form. Jack knew the unit, why they wanted to buy it, the cost and the pros and cons for the new charger compared to the existing standard issue piece of kit because the Colonel had spelled them out in great detail, so filling in the application form was simple. The assessment form was a little more difficult but reading previous, completed forms in the file, he was able to cobble together a reasonable assessment form. He made no attempt to complete a rejection form!

It seemed like years before Major Clasher returned but when he did, Jack followed him into his office and started rushing, almost babbling, out what had happened. The Major said, "Whoa, slow down there, Private Hughes, tell me that all over again from the beginning and slowly this time." So Jack did, pointing out on the forms he had completed the information he had been given by the Colonel and making sure he made it clear that the Colonel would not take no for an answer. Clasher said nothing at all during this narrative and he even paused for what seemed like centuries before pronouncing sentence.

Clearing his throat, he said, "When faced with a problem, Private Hughes, any problem at all, one is always faced with two options, do nothing, do something. If one does nothing, then one never has any defence if something goes wrong and no claim to credit if it goes right; if one does something and it works thereby lies credit and even the route to promotion; if it goes wrong, then one at least has the defence that one tried to put it right. Your decision to do something and approve the purchase was absolutely the right one. Well done. Now if you leave me for a few minutes, I have a few telephone calls to make and then I will deal with these forms." Jack started for the door. "Oh and close the door please," which Jack did.

Quite a few minutes later, Jack heard the Major calling him to come in. On doing so, he handed the forms to Jack, entirely unaltered, except for a signature on each with the instruction, "Process these as usual please, Private Hughes. And I have spoken to that Colonel, and you will not find yourself under unfair pressure from him again. And if you are wondering how a Major can influence a Colonel, our respective reporting trees give me the seniority of an HQ General as opposed to a field command one, and by the way, he was very impressed with the way you conducted yourself when talking to him. Well done, again." Jack floated out of the office with his feet seemingly six feet above the floor. He had learned a valuable lesson in, do something, do nothing which was to stand him in good stead for the rest of his life as well as a lesson in power politics in Command HQs.

# Chapter 70

Part of the duties of G Tech was the identification and evaluation of captured enemy weapons. There was a steel cupboard, resembling a wardrobe, which had all sorts of weaponry on the top shelf and standing upright in the lower section. British weaponry was very carefully guarded with weapons stored in the Armoury and having to be authorised by an officer before issue or receipt. No one had ever considered what should be done with captured weaponry which gradually accumulated until it overflowed the cupboard. Then the run-of-the-mill weapons, which were well known to the MOD, were just taken out of the harbour in an RASC landing craft and dropped overboard in deep water well off shore, even then the bolts and/or firing mechanisms were removed and dumped elsewhere. That which was of further interest was packaged up and returned to the UK.

Some of the weapons thrown into the sea were beautiful antiques which Jack would have loved to have owned or, at least, fired. Beautiful, literally beautiful, engraved, gold and silver lettering in Arabic, possibly centuries old muzzle loaders which would probably have been worth thousands to collectors all went the same way to the bottom of the Red Sea. There was no official inventory of the weapons other than a basic typed list which could easily have been altered, especially as Jack typed it of his own accord, there never having been one before, but Jack could think of no way he could stuff three or four four-feet long muzzle-loading firearms under his coat without someone noticing when he passed through customs!

One day, a rifle, appearing very much like an SLR, was brought in. Fed up with being shot at every night and having their sleep disturbed, the OC had led a fighting patrol out as soon as it got dark and had crept up to within 50 or so yards of the position the insurgents were using. Sure enough, shots were fired from the estimated position at which the OC had shouted, "Charge," and off they went. They found a small tent complete with fire and cooking utensils, so they could make themselves comfortable whilst enjoying themselves attacking the hated English. They found no one or any bodies. The insurgents were always much faster going away from a fight than towards it. But the SLR lookalike was lying there on the ground with a small smear of blood on it indicating perhaps that the owner had been hit and unable to carry it away. The attackers had been into the position so quickly that no insurgent, owner or someone desirous of owning it, as many would have been, had had time to pick it up and carry it away.

Thus, Major Lovewell dumped it on Jack's desk as he walked past saying, "Be very careful with that; it might be loaded; it might be cocked, so it might go off if handled incorrectly," the last said quite faintly as he disappeared into the inner office. Before Jack could take it all in, he was back with an enormously thick manual which he also dumped on Jack's desk.

"Have a look in there—it should be in there somewhere, and when you've found it, come and tell me what it is." Thereby starting another aspect of his job in G Tech which he just loved, being a complete gun freak.

The manual had an index of weapons by name, but if you didn't know what the weapon was called, using the index was impossible—something Jack was to find, as his army career progressed, was absolutely typical. It took him about 15 minutes to find it. Surprise, surprise, it was a Hakim, an Egyptian copy of the Belgian FN FAL rifle which was issued to the British Army as the L1A1 SLR. The main difference between the Belgian and British versions was the British version could not fire in automatic mode—it would fire too much ammunition in the Mucky Mucks opinion—those who would be far away from where the bullets would be flying. Jack could not tell from the marks by the various levers but did determine from the identification manual that it had an automatic ability.

Major Lovewell called out from the inner office to leave that and pop upstairs to the Colonel's office and collect a message he had for Lovewell. Just as Jack returned to the office, it was to see Major Elias, RAOC Senior Ammunition Technical Officer, with the Hakim in the shoulder, pointing it out the window and saying, "What do we have here?" and squeezing the trigger, he fired a burst of six or eight rounds straight through it. Fortunately, the office faced out to the Red Sea, so the bullets would have dropped into the ocean about a mile out with no apparent harm done. Without a pause, he just carried on, "A loaded, cocked and functioning automatic weapon then," he said.

"Well, that answers whether it was loaded or cocked, but it doesn't answer whether it is still loaded," said Major Lovewell with utter aplomb, considering all of the rounds must have passed no more than a foot in front of his face,

"Perhaps Private Hughes, you would take it away and see if your manual tells you how to unload it and at the same time, will you have a word with the buildings chappie and see if he can get someone around to repair a window broken whilst furniture was being moved." Jack did as he was ordered regarding the window; after all, who was going to argue with the word of three Majors.

The Hakim proved more than troublesome. The manual talked about pushing the magazine clip forward, exactly the same as an SLR, but this was impossible as it was hard up against the magazine. It was either damaged or a design fault; if the latter, it might explain why the Egyptian troops in the recent conflict with the Israelis had only fired a few rounds and then scarpered—they were unable to reload their rifles!

Jack, having looked closely at the Hakim, favoured the damaged theory. He was eventually able to prise the magazine release catch away from the body of the magazine, allowing him to push the magazine release catch further forward which released the magazine which proved, on further examination, to have four rounds still left in it. There was probably a round left in the chamber, but Jack could not tell just by looking. Consequently, making sure the rifle was pointing down into the floor, he didn't think a hole in the roof would be appreciated, he cocked the weapon by pulling back the cocking lever and a live round flew out onto the floor. Job done, weapon identified and made safe. The rifle plus the five rounds of remaining ammunition were sent back to the UK, with a short note attached re the work done on the magazine catch to enable it to be pushed forward, and that the rifle definitely fired well in automatic mode. It was returned for further research to

235

see if anything on the weapon could be beneficially applied to the British Army SLR and whether their ammunition was superior to ours.

Jack was to have regular meetings with Major Elias; he frequently popped in claiming the G Tech coffee was superior to that in his office and to see what had come in since his last visit. He did not blow out the windows ever again, but he did nearly acquire a second fundamental orifice on one occasion. An anti-personnel mine had been, very carefully, sent in to G Tech. It was round, about an inch and a half in diameter, about a quarter of an inch thick with a rusty large screw head in the middle; in fact, it looked very much like the round, grey rubbers that many of the clerks bought for themselves, being vastly superior to the army issue ones when correcting typing errors.

The reason that it was being handled very carefully, or not at all if possible, was that it was armed! The plastic explosive-type material of which it was made was designed to be used against troops waking over the ground in which had been buried and therefore, did not need very much pressure to set it off. To arm one, the loader simply pushed the screw detonator into the hole in the centre of the mine and turned it a quarter turn clockwise which secured the detonator in place and set it ready for detonation at the same time. They weren't really designed to be unloaded. To do so, one had to push the detonator into the body of the mine and twist it a quarter twist anti-clockwise and, in theory, the detonator would just drop out. However, this theory did not take into account that lying in the dirt the mine gradually seized up with dirt, moisture etc. preventing an easy removal of the detonator. Given that the pressure required to detonate it was not much more than a couple of pounds at most and that pressure could easily be exceeded by a thumb pushing down on the detonator, and given that this mine was in a rubbishy state, no one down the line had been prepared to attempt to disarm it and consequently, it had arrived at G Tech armed and dangerous. No one in G Tech was prepared to disarm it either! So a telephone call was made to SATO to come and take it away and detonate it safely, it being of known design and therefore not worth evaluating further. In the meantime, the mine was placed safely on the table just inside the door to the Majors' office.

Unfortunately, when Major Elias arrived, two other officers were occupying the two seats in front of the respective G Tech Majors so Major Elias went to park his bum, weighing considerably more than a couple of pounds, by sitting on the table—just where the mine was placed! Luckily, Jack was following Major Elias into the room, saw what was about to happen, dropped the file he was carrying and grabbed Major Elias, pushing him away from the table at the same time. Elias went flying onto the floor. Jack started to help him up when Elias let rip with a good deal of Anglo Saxon, threatening Jack with all sorts of devilish tortures and only stopped when he took in what Jack was pointing at—the mine, on the table, exactly where Major Elias was about to park his not-inconsiderable arse. That, too, created a mini story and clip of fame which was building up for Jack in Aden; having threatened to blow the fucking 'ead off the Duty Officer, he was now famous for saving SATO's arse—literally!

# Chapter 71

One day, Janet asked Jack if he would escort her into Tawahi as there was a shop there in the back streets that sold a shawl that she wished to purchase for her mother but she was frightened, as a woman, to venture into the back streets as the atmosphere towards the Brits was definitely deteriorating and especially to a white woman on her own. Jack was glad to do so. Jack, also, could feel the atmosphere had changed. Several times with other lads from his room he had ventured into the back streets to a particular café to eat a Tawahi Wak. Jack had heard people talking of these curries with high praise, so he was glad when one of his roommates, Johnny Hodgson, invited him to join the other two members of the room to have a Tawahi Wak. They sat at a table and without ordering, plates and dishes started arriving, so well established had having a Tawahi Wak become. A large, segmented metal plate containing salad vegetables appeared in the centre of the table and then they were brought china plates with a tiny portion of curry in the centre. *Christ*, thought Jack, *I'll have to eat an awful lot of that lettuce, tomatoes and stuff to fill me up*—and proceeded to do so. He complained to the others that this was a bloody small portion but did not recognise that the reactions of his companions to these comments were suspiciously wrong. Waiters appeared and removed the plates and then other waiters appeared with what appeared to be twin copies of the first plates. Tucking in, Jack thought, *that's better*. He did notice that the second curry was a bit hotter than the first. That plate was taken away and another identical one took its place. This was hotter still. This progression of plates continued until Jack had to cry enough; this last one was as hot as he could stand. And that was the secret of a Tawahi Wak—the meat, goat, would keep coming until the diner was beaten.

Jack escorted Janet, she bought the shawl, and they left the back streets without incidence. Just a few weeks later, the back streets would be put out of bounds to unarmed troops. It was a vicious circle situation. Because the people made the Brits feel unwelcome, the Brits did not come; because the Brits did not come, the sales of the shops went down; because the sales went down, the more people, Arabs, in the main, suffered and the more their antagonism towards the Brits increased. And all this was precisely what the terrorists wanted.

Janet and Jack had a drink in the Seaman's Mission on their way back from purchasing the shawl, which was situated on the harbour side and, somehow, collected cooling breezes on its patio. This was the first of many meetings where their relationship slowly developed. Both of them, seriously hurt by their respective dumpings, were more cautious in their next relationships, and it took a long time for their friendship to develop fully.

Khaki, the tea, coffeemaker who was ensconced on the end of the veranda of the hut in which they both worked, noticed that they were more frequently seen walking, or sometimes driving, to work together and leaving together. One day,

Khaki, bringing a coffee to Jack, said what a fine Memsahib Janet was and how he wished he could get one like her for himself. Jack didn't immediately respond, partly because he was so surprised at the comment and partly because he didn't know what to say. He let it go for a couple of days and then he raised the issue with Khaki, saying that maybe he could sell the Memsahib to Khaki if they could agree a price; Jack had got used to bargaining with the local shopkeepers where a fixed price, like it was in the UK, was unheard of. After several days of bargaining, they agreed on a price of 500 EA (East African) shillings. The equivalent of £5—not very much at first glance but about three or four weeks' wages in local values. Unfortunately, Janet refused to go when Khaki arrived with the 500 shillings, and life became awkward for Jack as Khaki refused to make coffee or tea for him, nor would Janet speak to him for selling her for such a small price! Eventually things settled back to normal, but Janet never really forgave Jack for selling her for so little money, and Khaki was probably spitting in Jack's coffee until the day he left Aden.

# Chapter 71

Gradually, things started changing in the office. There were quite frequently times when the two Majors and Cpl Pectin were out of the office, leaving Jack alone and in charge. He would much rather have been out driving and spectating at whatever the Majors were up to, but as the junior, he got the shitty jobs. The first thing Jack had to do when mail arrived was to enter it into the mail book, listing which file the letter had been filed in. If the letter referred to earlier letters, then Jack had to mark the latest letter with A,B,C etc. and flag those letters in the file with a tag in the top corner A,B,C, as appropriate, enabling the reader to easily and quickly find the earlier correspondence. Rarely did this take more than an hour or so. If no other work had been left for him, then Jack had nothing to do for the rest of the day—boring.

Often, the response to the incoming mail was an outgoing letter with some updating of information in it from the file. Jack knew what these were because he typed them once the relevant Major had written them. Both of them had almost illiterate scrawls, and Jack would often have to go into the file himself to obtain the information or to ask the Major concerned who would not often be able to decipher what it was that he had written.

Consequently, one day, faced with nothing to do, he typed what he thought the answers would be and left them in each of the Majors In Files. Nothing whatsoever was said to Jack, but the letters came out signed, so Jack then routinely typed the answers and the Majors signed them. In this manner, Jack took over the running of the office during the course of which he bypassed Cpl Pectin who, idle sod that he was, was only too glad to let Jack do so.

One day, a captured rocket launcher and seven rockets were brought into the office. Jack immediately went through the weapons book to identify it. It was a standard Belgian weapon, but the rockets were about one third longer than they should have been. Taking the lot into Major Lovewell's office, Jack was greeted with, "So that's how the little buggers are doing it." Slowly it became clear, mainly from listening to the telephone conversation, that the Major had straightaway with the Colonel SD/Tech, that the terrorists had been firing the rockets outside the security boundaries patrolled by Army and RAF patrols around the airfield and Army camps. The patrols all patrolled about 600 yards out around the guarded establishments, knowing that the rockets had a maximum 500-yard range and therefore, anyone firing them had to be inside, in theory, the security cordon and be liable to capture. However, the increased rocket motor almost certainly extended the range but by how much was not known. An increase in motor of one third probably meant an increase in range of one third, but it was not as simple as that. It became clear from listening to the conversations that Major Lovewell intended taking the rockets and tube out to a field firing range and finding out just how great the range was, at which Jack immediately volunteered to take part. In fact, it needed the Major and Cpl Pectin as well as Jack. The range was booked for the following morning first thing for two hours before it became too hot in the open desert terrain making up the field firing range referred to as Bir Fukum.

The following morning, they set off in the Land Rover with Jack bouncing around in the back and desperately hoping that they would not hit a mine as the back of the vehicle was not protected, nor did it have seats for that very reason.

Arriving at one of the firing points, Major Lovewell gave Cpl Pectin a quick lesson in how the weapon system worked. It was exactly the same as the famous American Bazooka except it was slightly larger in diameter. The rocket was slid in from the back end and a copper wire dangling from the rocket was twisted around a screw thread and the cap screwed down to secure it—no electrical, contact no fire!

Cpl Pectin got to fire the first round, and Jack had to load it. Major Lovewell was to observe with the two of them operating the rocket launcher to observe as much as they were able to, given the expected smoke firing would give off. There was a weapon's pit ready dug from a previous user, so it was just a question of Pectin jumping into the pit and Jack handing the tube down to him. He then jumped down and Major Lovewell handed Jack a rocket. At the moment of firing, Jack had to be at the side of the weapon as did Major Lovewell. This was standard practice for anything like a rocket launcher or recoilless rifle as the blast exiting the back of the tube was deadly enough to kill anyone caught in the blast. On this occasion, it was just as well they were following correct practice. Normally, the rocket would ignite, blast backwards and then the rocket motor would cease to burn just as it exited the muzzle, leaving the rocket to simply free fly to its target. In this case, the rocket motor was still firing as it exited the muzzle and Pectin, and to a lesser extent, Jack received the full blast! There was also an incredible amount of dust blown up so that Jack and Pectin had been able to see precisely nothing of where the rocket went. Major Lovewell had escaped any injury from the blast as he was far enough off to the side to avoid the blast, but the dust had also blocked his view. After the first few stunned seconds and taking in the view of one another, the laughter started. Besides being covered in dust and dirt, Pectin, more so than Jack, was covered in 'shaving nicks'—that is, they both looked as though they had had a very bad day shaving with cuts all over any patch of exposed skin. They used water from one of the Jerry cans on the Land Rover to wash off most of the dirt but the nicks continued to bleed for a few minutes longer.

Winding down their sleeves and turning their collars up, they covered up any exposed skin as best they could. The rocket launcher had been aimed down range at a 45-degree angle to give the maximum range. It meant that they were aiming at the top of a mountain a few hundred yards away with the expectation that the explosion of the hit would be seen somewhere up the slope. Two more rockets were fired with Major Lovewell standing well off to the side and Jack and Pectin crouched right down in the trench. As before, Jack and Pectin could not see what happened to the rockets but Lovewell, well off to the side should have been able to but had not been able to see any strike.

As they had used three rockets for range, they had two for accuracy testing, and two to return to the MOD. They used a blown-up armoured car as the target. Pectin hit it with rockets fired from 200 and 700 yards, so it was clear that the accuracy had not been affected by the increase in motor size. It also showed that it could be fired at targets at least 700 yards away, i.e. 200 yards more than the safety perimeters currently operated. Jack was a bit pissed off that Pectin had got to fire all the rockets, but that was the reward of rank in the army.

Returning slowly down the track off the field firing range, they were met by a Federal Army Land Rover driving at some speed towards them before skidding to a stop and blocking the road. An FRA Major jumped out and started shouting at them. His English wasn't very good, and it took a while to become clear that he was looking for the terrorists who had been firing shells into his camp which was just over the mountain over there, pointing to the one they had fired the first three rockets at. Major Lovewell was able to assure him that if he saw any terrorists, he would contact him, but for now, he had a very important meeting at HQ MEC and couldn't be late! At that, they drove off quite quickly thankful that the rockets had hit the square and other pieces of hard ground—to have hit a building or FRA troops would have been exceedingly unfortunate. They, by the kind if not intended information from the FDR Major, had discovered that their rockets had a very long range indeed and security cordons were going to have to be extended by hundreds of yards. As for Cpl Pectin, he was sent off to have his photo taken which was distributed around the Command to assist security patrols to look for terrorists for similar nicks following an incident or for someone with heavy protective clothing which was not needed in hot weather. The last two rockets and the launcher were sent back to England, for a more professional estimate of the range to be carried out.

# Chapter 72

Shortly after the rocket launcher incident, Major Clasher approached Jack in a very friendly way, suspicious enough to make Jack wonder what he wanted. It did not take long. Clasher's little boy was to be christened the coming Sunday with a service at the Garrison Church followed by a bit of a party at the Officers' Mess afterwards. Jack could not see how this could involve him until Clasher said that recent changes to the security rules meant that an armed guard had to patrol the Mess whilst the party was going on. There had been a number of incidents of grenade throwing at military buildings and those where soldiers were likely to congregate, like the cinema and the NAAFI, so extra security was being introduced. The point was, was Jack prepared to guard the Mess for a couple of hours or so in return for a suitable payment, it not being possible for Jack to be ordered to cover a private event? Faced with a request from a Major, the only possible answer from a Private is a yes anyway so that, come Sunday, Jack found himself covering the Mess. Clasher had told him he could draw out an SLR or an SMG, whichever he preferred. Jack chose the SMG as it was a fair bit lighter to carry around and a lot easier to handle.

One side of the Mess faced the sea and was built almost up to the edge of the cliff that almost totally surrounded the fort, leaving Jack with three sides to patrol. To his surprise, Clasher appeared from time to time clasping a pint of lager, pretty much the only beer you could get in Aden, and, thrusting it at Jack, almost whispered, "Get that down you; if anyone asks, it's lemonade and to keep you hydrated." Jack took no second urging and very welcome it was.

The patrolling continued, quite unpleasant in the heat. He was just completing the leg from the cliff and turning the corner to the front of the Mess to be presented with a man just about to throw a grenade from which he had just pulled the pin—it was dangling from his right hand. Startled, they both just looked at one another for a split second before the terrorist dropped the grenade as Jack shouted. The Arab took off like a rocket running down the side of one of the wooden huts facing the Mess. Jack ran down the other side of the building shouting for him to stop. Behind them came the almighty bang of the grenade detonating, fortunately outside the Mess and causing no damage. Meanwhile, Jack was sprinting down the end of one row of the huts and the terrorist down the other. As the huts were laid out in a crescent formation, and as Jack was running down the shorter curve of the crescent, he was just able to get to the final alley between the huts before the terrorist did. He just had time to aim at the left-hand edge of the alley as the terrorists appeared at the right side, running like the clappers. Jack had only time to fire two shots before the terrorist had passed the alley. Running down the alley, Jack was determined that he would look around the corner this time and shoot the bugger if he could.

Reaching the corner, he peeked around it to see the terrorist sprawled on the ground. As Jack looked, he stopped moving. Jack, taking aim at the terrorist, walked over towards him, only a matter of three or four yards. As he got there, a siren started sounding from the Mess and men, carrying an assortment of weapons, erupted from the building in response to the explosion. Major Clasher was one of the first to reach Jack and, ordering Jack to make his weapon safe, felt for a pulse of the man on the ground. Finding none, he turned to Jack and asked, "What happened?" Jack told him.

Turning to one of the Mess Stewards, a Corporal, he ordered him to ring the RMPs and tell them that there had been a grenade attack and a shooting at the Officers' Mess and there was one fatality. He was to order one of the Mess servants to bring a bedspread out to cover the body and a pint of larger for Jack who was starting to shake a little. In a sotto voce voice only Jack could hear, he said, "Get the larger down you straight away and relax; you have just, possibly, saved the lives of many of my relatives and friends, including me, by your actions. The larger will cover your previous drinks and to be able to hit a running target like you did means you cannot have been under the influence. Very well done and thank you." By this time, there were many people milling around with the ones in the know happily stating that ten terrorists had been shot whilst attempting to destroy the Mess and all in it. The seven grenades that they had thrown before they were shot down had badly damaged the Mess, destroying the main door and vestibule, this last despite the evidence of their own eyes which clearly showed no damage whatsoever to it! The numbers of terrorists, grenades and shots expanded exponentially, and it was only when a short summary of events was printed in the Part One Orders Security News Section the next day that the hopelessly inexact events of the Sunday were corrected.

Jack, meantime, had had the SMG removed from him, after he had unloaded it and made it safe. Sitting comfortably in the Mess quaffing an ice-cold larger, he awaited the arrival of the Royal Military Police with some trepidation; after all, he was a Private soldier, and to the Monkeys, a Private was always guilty of something. Mrs Clasher came up to him, despite the protestations of her husband that he should not be approached until the MPs had spoken to him, and shook him firmly by the hand and then, saying, "What the hell, I owe you my life," kissed him smack on the lips. Jack's day improved immensely despite Major Clasher's somewhat taken aback look. Then appeared the BGS, Brigadier General Staff Brigadier Hackwell who, having been in the shower at the time, had taken a few minutes to dry and dress. He, too, approached Jack and shook him by the hand, but he did, at least, stop short of kissing him.

He also said, "What are you drinking," preparatory to buying him another when Major Clasher interrupting, pointed out to the BGS that as Jack had shot a man dead, albeit a terrorist bastard, he was, therefore, the key witness and should not be talking to all and sundry in case it should imperil his case in some way. The BGS, being a General and one of those who made the rules rather than followed them, opened his mouth to speak but was interrupted by a very loud and authoritative voice asking for permission to enter the Mess—this last request more of a statement that I am coming in regardless since it belonged to a Warrant Officer Class II in the Royal Military Police and who, in most circumstances surrounding a crime, could order almost anyone involved around.

Major Clasher described briefly what had happened and handed the WO11 the SMG. Looking at Jack, who was standing to attention and looking straight to his front, the best defensive position when faced with what might be very hostile authority; the WO11 walked over and looked him up and down several times. Clearing his throat, he said, "At least we won't have any trouble identifying the bugger this time, will we, Private Hughes?" It was the same WO11 as had interviewed and been so helpful to Jack when he had shot at Mohammed Mohammed when he had thrown the grenade at the GOC in C's car, which Jack had been driving. Given that he had actually hit the bugger and killed him, Jack thought it best to remain silent. "Right, I'll take a statement from you once I've had a look at the scene and taken some measurements. You may sit down if you wish, but do not drink any more of the free drinks you are about to be handed than you can handle." And at that he walked away, and proving his prophetic powers, Jack was handed two more drinks before he stopped; he had just killed someone, and he needed to keep his wits about him.

The WO11, Company Sergeant Major Stevens, reappeared shortly but before he could speak to Jack, the Aden police turned up. They should not have been able to get past the gate to the fort, and indeed, the Guard Commander who had let them through 'received some further training' after the event. The incident had taken place on army property and therefore came under the jurisdiction of the army according to CSM Stevens but the Policeman, a Detective Chief Inspector was of the opinion that the army base was on Adeni soil and therefore he had jurisdiction. Jack started to sweat. Incarceration in an Arab jail was not an attractive proposition, and since he had shot an Arab, he did not think the court would be unbiased. As an officer, and a Detective Chief Inspector at that, he did not expect to have any problems getting a mere Warrant Officer, an officer who was not really an officer at all as he saw it, to comply with his orders and it was, therefore, a somewhat surprised DCI who, two minutes later, found himself outside the shut gate of the fort and two very determined-looking sentries pointing rifles apparently the size of cannons, least that was how big they looked when they were pointing straight at him.

Jurisdiction indeed sniffed the CSM before turning to Major Clasher and saying, "As I am the only one who appears not to have a drink, I am sure you are about to remedy that, sir, are you not, sir?"

There followed loads of statements, paperwork and questioning by the RMP which was handed to the civilian police, but they were never allowed to interview Jack without a Special Branch Warrant Officer with him who always interrupted and advised Jack not to answer the question if they regarded it as irrelevant or dangerous ground for Jack to be treading on.

The post mortem showed that the terrorist had been hit by two bullets, the first just cutting across the chest skin deep which would not have been lethal and the second which had hit a couple of inches under the left armpit and passed through the body from side to side tumbling as it went and destroying pretty well everything in its path, including particularly the heart which was responsible for the immediate death—it was tumbling because it had just clipped the edge of the hut which sent it tumbling through the terrorist. WO11 Stevens, in the Sergeants' Mess, was often heard to claim, when he had drunk enough of the falling down water, that it was the bollocking he had given Jack for missing the first terrorist which had resulted in such good shooting in the second case.

Jack was the centre of attention for a while, the hero of the hour and an upstanding example of the British soldier. When the press picked up the story and wished to interview Jack, Jack asked for, and received, the help of the Army Press Organisation to keep the vultures away from him and to keep his name confidential to prevent him becoming a target of the terrorists.

# Chapter 73

Slowly, attention faded away as other incidents took more interest. There was set-up in one of the bedrooms on the ground floor of Jack's accommodation, an incident and ready room where a Section of soldiers, two Land Rovers and a radio and telephone were set-up to deal with any incidents. HQ MEC was only a hundred yards or so from the barrack block and troops based there were instantly available if there were to be an attack on it. Jack was surprised one day, shortly after it had been set-up, to be stopped by Colin whom he had last seen, and written a letter for, up at Cap Badge on the road to Dhala. Colin's Regiment, the Cameronians, had been brought back to Aden State to increase the number of troops immediately available, should they be needed. As they had been posted to Aden, some said thrown out of Germany, following a number of incidents involving fights between the Cameronians and German civilians, 6 feet or taller had been given a thorough going over by Cameronian soldiers who averaged 5 feet 2 or so in height. Recruited from the gutters of Glasgow, they had experienced very poor diets and upbringings where fights were daily occurrences—the police would only interfere when they were sure they had the troublemakers greatly outnumbered. Largely uneducated, hence Colin's approaches to Jack, many of their entrance papers were suspiciously similar, bearing as they did the writing of the Recruiting Sergeants, definitely illegal but they were hard men brought up in a hard life which made them excellent soldiers and fighting men. When they didn't have an enemy to fight, (the Germans were still definitely the enemy!) they would fight among themselves, something Jack was to witness on several occasions, his room being only two along from the Immediate Incident Room.

Colin must have talked about Jack and his letter-writing skill as a small but steady stream of Cameronians started appearing at his room's door clutching sad, badly written letters, usually from Mum, which they needed help to decipher and read and to reply to. If Jack was in the NAAFI, he would find a fresh pint on the table when he returned to it from the lavy with no indication of where it had come from. On one occasion, Jack had stopped for a quick, non-alcoholic drink in a bar in Maala, when four, drink-taken members of the Parachute Regiment started having a go at Jack. They started by stating in clear but drunken terms that this bar belonged to the Paras, the hardest Regiment in the British Army and no poncy puffter from another poncy Regiment of girl guides was going to come into it and drink soft drinks. They had only just arrived in Aden, and Jack had no idea that they regarded this bar as their territory. Jack was well familiar with this behaviour from other places he had been stationed, and in fact, he couldn't give a shit whether he came into this bar ever again, but he did care that he exited that bar all in one piece and so he moved quickly to the exit. Unfortunately, they followed him out and it looked very much like he was about to get a very good kicking in the street when a voice called out, "Are you having a problem with these pussies, Jack?" in a very strong Scott's accent. Colin was standing there, in uniform, with two more Cameronians. The Paras took in their Regimental badges and decided that they were going to return to their bar but that was not to be. What was to be was that the Cameronians decided the Paras needed showing where they stood in the pecking order so set about pecking them! Jack even had a close quarter guard to ensure that the Paras got nowhere near him. That left only two Cameronians to sort out the four Paras, but it was more than enough.

Colin later made it clear when he came across Jack in the barrack block that Jack was a very special friend to them and if he ever needed help of any kind, he was only to ask. Jack thought that was worth much more than reading and writing a few letters but, in this case, it wasn't his judgement that mattered; it was that of the soldiers he helped. Months later, a day or two before the Cameronians were posted elsewhere, Jack was surprised one afternoon to be interrupted by a Major in Cameronian accoutrements asking for him. Jack identified himself. The Major identified himself as the 2i/c of the Regiment and explained that he had come to officially thank Jack on behalf of the Regiment for his helping the soldiers who had felt unable to approach authority in the Regiment and ask for help. It was just a quick thank you and Jack much appreciated it. It was also an example that officers often knew a lot more of what was going on than they were given credit for. Whilst Jack hadn't minded helping originally, it had grown to be a bit of a task with 15–18 soldiers regularly coming for help so the fact that it would finish, he welcomed, but he would miss having heavies on hand!

The last incident, though, had not yet happened. One of the Privates, known for being short-tempered, had been steadily drinking in the ready room, illegally, and as his alcohol intake increased, so his ability to throw darts accurately and win darts matches diminished. Having been beaten for the fourth time in a row, costing him a fiver a time, he exited the room declaiming that, 'it was nae fair and he was going for a pish.' On his return, he was seen to be holding a Stirling SMG which he pointed at the darts board and fired a full magazine of 32 rounds in one burst. Everyone in the room dived for cover, the darts board disintegrated.

"Now try and beat me, youse bastards," were the last words he was heard to say as he was marched off by the MPs. All in all, Jack was quite glad to see the back of them.

# Chapter 74

Detail appeared on the Part 1 Orders that there was to be run a course for Second Class Education for those holding only a third-class pass. Jack read it and ignored it since he was exempt army education by virtue of his GCEs. A day or two later, Janet Taylor brought up the subject as they walked to work. It became clear that she had had a very poor education in an all-girls Secondary Modern in Newbury where the teachers were mainly ones brought back from retirement to help during the war and who were well past their best before date even before the war. Janet was subjected to their laziness and spite. As far as they were concerned, girls in a secondary modern, having failed the 11+ were only going to be housewives, have babies and cook meals. Janet had always resented their laziness and their failure to attempt to improve the education of the pupils. At a previous unit, she had worked hard and passed her third-class education exam. She wanted to take the second-class course but lacked the confidence to apply. She rather hoped that Jack would apply and they could attend the course together, with Jack providing the moral support she felt she needed. Jack had to explain he would not be allowed to attend the course even if he applied, and he had to explain why when she asked. Like Captain Robertson, she, too, was amazed at Jack's qualifications. She said that she would not therefore apply, lacking the confidence to do so, but Jack persuaded her that she should at least apply because if she were successful, there being more applicants than places, Jack would give her whatever help he could outside of the course.

So gradually developed a relationship built partly by their shared misery from being dumped, partly from a growing feeling of comfort in one another's presence and from Janet's insatiable thirst for knowledge. Although it was not that long since Jack had left school, he found himself having to dig deep to answer her questions. That having to dig deep was to last the rest of his life, although he was not to know it at that time!

One time, not long after the shooting, Jack was sent for one Saturday afternoon. He had planned to spend it with Janet at the beach but just as he was getting ready, the Duty Driver turned up with orders for him to get to the office tout de suite. He did manage to persuade the Driver to drop off a note at the WRAC for Janet explaining what had happened, and being an army girl herself, she understood and did not throw a wobbler like many civvy females would have done. In fact, many families broke up because of the inability of the wife to understand that the demands of the army come first; this also extended to police families where the marriage failed because of the female's wish to come first and not play second fiddle to husbands who could disappear at a moment's notice often with no explanation or information as to when they would return, which sometimes, of course, was never. It was a hard life for a service wife, with children to bring up alone for sometimes long periods at a time. Where the marriage did survive, it was most often where the wife was ex-service herself or was from a service family growing up with the experience of postings and family problems. Nothing as drastic as that on this occasion, simply a spoiled afternoon.

When Jack got to the office, he was immediately sent round to the POMEC office. This was a rather mysterious set-up, apparently nothing to do with the army, staffed by what appeared to be civilians, leastways they were never seen in uniform and their hair followed the fashion set-up by the Beatles and the Stones of long hair which would never have been tolerated by any Sergeant Major.

Once Jack got into the office, it was to discover all the Special Duty Clerks, bar the one currently on duty, were there present. They were addressed by an obviously senior person who explained, for those that did not know, that POMEC stood for Political Office Middle East Command and that they were all Civil Servants but employed by the Ministry of Defence. In fact, it became obvious as time passed that these were very strange creatures indeed. Of course, as in absolutely every situation in the army, the first thing this guy did was to remind them that they were governed by the Official Secrets Act and so serious was the work they were about to do that they had the relevant short version read to them and they each had to sign it.

The work they had to do was type. They were each allocated a civvy who started to read out in English a translation from pieces of paper which were written mainly in Arabic. Where it was written in English, they simply had to re-type it. One piece of the paper Jack's guy was trying to translate was actually in French and Jack contributed to the translation, the civvy having left school many years ago. The papers were a right old mish-mash of typed documents, handwritten scraps, some of the translations relating to military matters others mere shopping lists and mundane every day bits of lists. Gradually, it became clear that the army, acting on intelligence received, probably from these very POMEC people, had actually captured the leader of the National Liberation Front. The documents were all the pieces of paper in the house where he had been caught and had to be translated as soon as possible and, if possible, before news of his capture had got out. It was particularly important to identify significant addresses where other terrorist members might be living or hiding and squads of MPs and soldiers were on standby in the barracks at Khormaksar waiting for the intelligence as it was being translated and typed by the seven Duty Clerks. As they typed, it quickly became apparent as to whether the document was significant or not and a little shiver of excitement went through Jack as the meaning of the particular document he was typing was snatched from him the second he had finished typing it, and the civvy rushed off to a central desk where the bigwig sat and flashed out orders for certain addresses to be immediately raided. Jack loved being at the centre of such important work and reckoned it almost as good as an afternoon on the beach with Janet, almost!

The one thing that puzzled Jack was that news of the terrorist leader's capture never got out. Whilst it was understandable that the Brits would keep it quiet for a while, why did they not brag about it to the high heavens and embarrass and dispirit the NLF? Nor did the terrorists announce he had been caught and martyred. Whilst Jack enjoyed learning the snippets he did, he did not like working with the POMEC people, and they seemed a bit too superior and condescending towards

Jack and the other Clerks. They were not even thanked at the end of the day, 23.00 hrs, when they were dismissed with another warning about the Official Secrets Act.

The following Thursday, Jack was Duty Clerk, and all hell was let loose. He was reading a two-day old newspaper in the Duty Room when the telephone rang. Answering it, "Private Hughes, Duty Clerk speaking, sir," he was greeted with, "Private Hughes, come up to my office straight away please; this is the GOC in C." And the phone was put down. Jack was not slow in getting up there. To his surprise, sitting outside the General's office were the Commanders of the Army, Navy and Airforce. The door to the General's office was open and the General, espying Jack, called out, "Come in, Private Hughes, and close the door." Jack did so and stood to attention; after all, he was in the presence of a man who gave orders to God.

"Now I know you are familiar with the Official Secrets Act, Private Hughes, but what you are about to see is so top secret it involves politicians, and it doesn't get any higher than that. Nothing you see or hear in this office must ever be repeated without the express permission of a senior officer—is that clear?"

"Yes, sir," said Jack.

"Normally, what you are about to do would be done by my PA, but he is uncontactable and therefore it falls to you to do his work, but not, I am afraid, for his pay." Jack already knew the world and the army was unfair so this came as no surprise and he knew enough to laugh at the General's little joke. "I am going to need you to go down to the Message Centre and collect messages from them, return them to me, unopened and unread and then you will type any replies I might wish to send, delivering them in turn to the Message Centre. You will obviously become aware of everything I am sending because you will type an original and a copy for me. I want you to go and fetch a typewriter, message pads, carbons and envelopes and set yourself up on that table there," pointing to a large table normally used for meetings. "And before you go away, when I say you will tell no one what you see or hear, that includes the officers sitting outside my office." That did surprise Jack and drove home just how serious whatever it was that he was about to learn was.

Cheekily, Jack pinched the General's PA's typewriter off the desk amongst where the service Commanders were sitting as it was the nearest, newest and best in the Command—as you would expect of the Commander-in-Chief's PA. He also removed from his desk draws, message pads and lovely, lovely, new virgin sheets of carbon copying paper, something that an ordinary Clerk had to reuse and reuse until copies were almost illegible. Extraordinarily, each time Jack typed a message, the General took from him the brand new carbon used only once and burnt it in the metal waste bin by his desk. This was really tight security; only the General and Jack would ever know what the General had sent back to London. The General's messages were addressed to Harold Wilson personally, and you cannot get much more political than that, the Prime Minister himself.

It became clear that the fuss was all to do with Ian Smith, the Prime Minister of Rhodesia who had unilaterally declared the Independence of Rhodesia against the wishes of the British Government. The signals were all to do with this situation and the military readiness of the troops, Navy and Air Force in Middle East Command. Jack did not need retelling just how top secret, 'UK Eyes Only' this was; but he could not help a little quiet smirk to himself as he walked in and out past the

Commanders of the Army, Navy and Air Force that he, little old Private Jack Hughes, knew more than any of them.

The messages flew backwards and forwards most of the night. Aden being 4/5 hours ahead of the UK meant that in the UK, the Prime Minister was only working a bit late in the evening whereas in Aden it was getting on towards dawn before the messages stopped. Jack returned the super duper new typewriter to the PA's desk on the basis that as it was the only one in Aden, he probably couldn't get away with swapping it for his own, but the remainder of the carbon sheets went with him to his desk as those were not traceable, and the PA would not be able to tell from the pile of ash in the waste bin just how many had been used. Periodically, the Services Commanders had been called in to the General's office, and Jack had been excluded so they had obviously been discussing events but Jack could easily fathom just what had been discussed by what he then typed. Jack experienced yet again the invisibility of underlings shown by high-ups and when Jack did obtain a commission, it was fascinating to hear, when mixing socially in their company, these same high-ups talking of secret matters between themselves and revealing information to others that they should not, seemingly on an I know about this because I am important and to show off, where junior ranks revealing the same secrets would find themselves facing prosecutions under the Official Secrets Act. Jack was convinced that any leaks of security would have come from these senior officers discussing or talking about matters in front of the tea makers, cleaners and other domestics who were simply not recognised as being there.

Of course, on being stood down, Jack was again warned about the Official Secrets Act although the General did thank him nicely and the Army commander even gave him a, "Well done, Private Hughes," when he passed him—nice but somewhat worrying that a Major General knew his name.

# Chapter 75

Jack's relationship with Janet had slowly been developing until they were spending every afternoon and evening together. They spent the whole of Sundays together. Aden was not known as the arsehole of the empire for nothing; other than the cinema—films were shown for two nights so that one evening was spent at the cinema with a quick dash to the NAAFI for last orders and the NAAFI for the whole of the alternate evenings. The army did make pathetic efforts to provide other entertainments for the troops such as a chess club, bible classes and similar, run by the members with no input from the army; it was no wonder that drinking too much was a serious problem. Some of the societies were reasonably successful—the light operatic one putting on Pirates of Penzance got a full house for the three nights it ran but that was probably more because the audience had nothing else to do rather than any keen desire to watch Gilbert and Sullivan, and it went ahead without the services of the HQ MEC Captain, who had quietly been sent home in disgrace and forward posting to a lost-in-the-wilderness posting where his fright at a grenade attack would not matter. Neither did Jack attend, who did not fancy any of the females involved and who much preferred the company of Janet to would-be operatic divas. The Seamen's Mission on the harbour waterfront was a nice quiet sanctuary to read and have a drink, and Janet and Jack used it often, and Jack continued to use it after Janet had been posted back to the UK even though he wasn't a seaman.

The cinema was unusual in that it opened as soon as it got dark, usually about 1800 hrs; it had to get dark because it had four walls but no roof, and so the only way films could be shown was to wait until it had become dark. The films shown were all up to date films, suitable for a mainly male audience but some family films were shown, catering to the families when the male numbers in the audience reduced considerably. Most evenings, following the cinema, Jack and Janet would walk over to Abdullah's fish and chip lorry; it was an old, ex-army lorry that had a small cabin built on the back which dispensed fish and chips. As far as Jack thought, it was cod and chips and that was it, nothing else was offered, but it was always fresh and delicious. Jack's liking for it did suffer a slight knock back when one evening he casually remarked to Janet that, "This cod really is good, it's much firmer than the stuff we get at home and it's as fresh as can be."

"That's because it's shark," said Janet.

Jack was silenced. Janet just carried on eating her fish and chips. Eventually, in a small voice, he squeaked, "How do you know that?"

"I've seen him catching them when I went on a boat trip once."

Another long silence, then a small, "Oh," closed the issue which never arose again, and Jack kept eating it following the cinema most nights.

Janet did say to him, a few nights later when they had been diligently working on a maths paper, "See, I can teach you something for a change."

Relationships with Khaki were more or less back to normal, so much so that one day he appeared at Jack's desk with something in his hand. He was standing so that Janet could not see what he was doing as he held out to Jack a large grass hopper or similar; Jack never did discover what it actually was; it was about four inches long and the most beautiful bright green in colour, probably a grass hopper or similar; what was certain was that females did not like such things and Khaki was gesticulating that he should put it in Janet's hand. So Jack walked over to her; fortunately, she was looking intently at something on her desk and put her hand out without looking when Jack said, "Can this go to the MOD please?" He dropped it into the proffered hand and two seconds later, the forthcoming scream shattered the office.

It took a while for things to calm down and for Jack to catch the cricket/grasshopper and set it free outside. No sooner had it quietened down than Khaki appeared in front of Jack again, this time holding a locust. It was about eight inches long and a mottled sand and dark brown colour. Quite pretty in a monsterish way! Carefully holding it behind his back, Jack walked over to Janet and said, "I'm really sorry about that, and I have something to make amends. Please close your eyes and put your hand out." It took a few moments with promises of utmost good faith before Janet would do so, but do it she did! This time the scream lifted the roof; not only that, she threw the heavy date stamp used for stamping all incoming mail across the office at Jack. He ducked. The stamp then went straight through the dividing wall of the Majors' office. Everyone knew the building was old and falling down but this was quite unexpected. Silence shot across the office.

Major Lovewell appeared at the door, placed the date stamp on Jack's desk and simply said, "Enough," and walked back into his office. Janet never fully forgave Jack for that either.

Aden was generally quite free of creepy crawlies, the most common probably being the chit chat lizards which came in all colours and sizes. Generally, they moved around the ceilings and tops of walls catching anything they could. One night, Jack and Janet had gone to the cinema to see Too Hot to Handle with Jayne Mansfield. In one scene, she almost fills the screen wearing a very low cut black dress. It was filmed in black and white so that the chit chat, also black, which crawled down the light grey cinema screen stood out clearly as it appeared to crawl down the cleavage of her dress. The cinema, full of squaddies, erupted; the chit chat played his part to perfection, straight down the 'v' of the cleavage and into the black of the dress to 'disappear' completely. A night to remember!

Three weeks after that, Janet came out with a real bombshell. They were lying on the beach when she came out with, "I've received my posting today to the MOD at Mill Hill in London." Normally, soldiers received six months' notice of posting details but due to some cock-up a few months before, a cancellation of a posting order to Germany arrived three days before the posting order itself was received! Janet had, therefore, been waiting for a posting order and now, it had arrived. The problem was, the posting date was only 21 days away. Jack was stunned.

Again, all he could say for quite a few minutes was an initial, "Oh."

Jack knew that she still had some time to go in the army but he was not sure how much so he asked her and she said, "Six months." Their relationship had developed from the two injured souls taking comfort from each other to something far deeper and more meaningful without going through the like her/him; fancy her/him; lustful her/him to the comfortable companionship and trust relationship although they both retained deep within hurt and worry that if they revealed the true depth of their feelings for one another, they might be risking it. So Jack said nothing and talked about Mill Hill and how sure he was that she would enjoy it there as he knew it quite well, it being quite close to his home and how that would make it convenient for them to see one another.

The remaining time just flew by, and Jack just did not know how to say what he was just beginning to realise he felt. Jack managed to borrow the Hillman to drive her to the airport and they probably didn't exchange more than half a dozen words in the whole eight miles. They kissed, made promises to write and that was it—she was gone, walking out to the plane. Khormaksar did not boast such a luxury as a departure lounge, and the plane was gone.

Driving back to Steamer Point, Jack called himself a prat and a few other more Anglo Saxon based words; as soon as he got back to his room, without removing his revolver—G Tech staff had taken to arming themselves with the Enfield when in the car for its ease of use—he sat straight down and wrote on a huge card in large letters, 'Please marry me', folded it into an envelope and posted it in the box at the end of the barrack block. Feeling much better, he was whistling as he walked into his room where the Dhobi Wallah was just placing the clean laundry at the base of his bed.

Looking it over, Jack said, "Where the hell's my handkerchiefs, sunshine?" Jack had put one into his dhobi every few days, but none had ever been returned. He had had a go at the Dhobi Wallah several times but with no result. This time, probably caused by the mood he was in at losing Janet, he drew the revolver, held it up against the Dhobi Wallah's nose and said in the most menacing voice he could generate, "If I don't get my handkerchiefs, all 12 of them, immediately, I'm going to blow your bloody head orf." Although Jack normally spoke in a more educated and polished accent, he felt that a bit of sarth lundun might be more effective on this occasion. And it was. The Arab started shouting his head off and within moments, a sequence of underlings started appearing in the room, each bearing a handkerchief or two which they deposited in a neat pile making probably a pile of two dozen or so. Jack thanked him and with many apologies and salaams, the Dhobi Wallah backed out of the room and trotted away.

*What a nice end to the day*, thought Jack, a proposal and all his hankies, plus several others, silk at that and better than his own, returned from the Dhobi Wallah. Jack was to wonder for years why it was that the Dhobi Wallah could not see that the chambers of the revolver were empty, particularly as it was pressed so close to his nose!

Many years later, Jack attended a Spiritualist Church Service in Belfast and the Medium, coming to Jack, said, "I have a person here who knew you a long way from here; you were the only one he had respect for since you were prepared to enforce your rights by putting a gun against his nose to make your point, and he has respected you for that ever since and has followed your career with much interest and pride. And he says you still have much more to achieve!" Jack knew at once to whom she was referring and thought perhaps that's why he never reported me to the authorities. Arabs respected force; they didn't respect soft Western politicians who were all talk and no action. Jack was very aware that Arabic was very flowery and full of overstatement while English was very understated, so that the two sides normally did not really understand one another's positions too clearly.

Five days after posting his proposal to Janet, Jack received an enormous envelope, A2 in size, which contained a single piece of A2 paper with, written on it in letters reaching across the full extent of the paper, 'Yes', no name but he had his answer; he was now an engaged man, something he was to keep to himself for most of the rest of his time in Aden.

# Chapter 76

Mail started appearing in the office regarding a detector and intruder warning device. Following on from attacks on the airfield at Khormaksar, a site with such a huge perimeter, it was almost impossible to protect fully, and problems guarding other institutions worldwide, the MOD had put out a tender to civvy firms to produce something to protect sites of large areas. Eventually, Jack was ordered to collect two civilian visitors from Khormaksar airport and bring them to the office because they thought they had the answer to the problem.

At the office, Jack was a little surprised that he was included in the meeting. It became clear that Cpl Pectin would be posted before the kit arrived in Aden and, therefore, it made sense for Jack to know about it as he would still be in Aden. Indeed, Pectin's posting came through to a Field Park unit in Germany; it was not unheard of for an HQ Staff Clerk to go to a Field Park unit, but it was sufficient enough to cause some gossip and speculation amongst the Clerks that he was not material senior officers wanted around them. Pectin said his goodbyes on the Tuesday but it would be true to say not many were sorry to see him go; he was a bit arrogant, a minor public school boy who thought he was cleverer and better than he was and certainly better than the ordinary soldiers; Jack and he had rubbed one another up the wrong way frequently especially vis-a-vis the superiority of grammar schools versus public schools. Pectin, discovering Jack's abilities, had been only too happy to let Jack do all the work; something Jack was not to unhappy about because he enjoyed the new knowledge that came his way but he would have liked a thank you from Pectin occasionally and he certainly hated that Pectin often pinched the credit for something Jack had done.

Jack was surprised to see his name on Part 1 Orders for the day following Pectin's flight. Jack could think of no reason why he should be up before the Colonel, so it was with some trepidation that he found himself standing outside the Colonel's office at 07.30 hrs the following morning. As the RSM came out of the Colonel's office ready to march Jack in, Jack took off his belt and beret.

"Guilty conscience, have we, Private Hughes?" asked the RSM.

"No, sir," said Jack smartly.

"Put your belt and beret back on then and stand there," pointing to a spot outside the door. It was customary for soldiers facing disciplinary issues to have to remove their belts and berets which could be used as formidable weapons if the miscreant was so inclined, hence their removal. Jack let himself relax; at least he was not in the shit and so really did not worry too much as to what the meeting was to be about.

After a few minutes, the RSM reappeared and marched him into the Colonel's presence. Unlike when he first joined the Army, Lt Colonels were no big deal anymore, working as he did among many of them and indeed among many far more senior officers even including GOC in Cs. He was surprised to find himself outside the office again a few minutes later as a local, acting, unpaid Lance Corporal.

The RSM took him into his office and said, "Right, now, Lance Corporal Hughes, we did not get off too well on the right foot when you first arrived here, but I have watched you very closely since, and you have conducted yourself very well since then. If you will take my advice, you will put the first Private Soldier you see on leaving this office on a charge."

"But what if he hasn't done anything wrong?" asked Jack.

The RSM smiled and said, "If he's a Private Soldier, he will always have done something wrong so put him on a charge."

All Jack could say to that was a rather feeble, "Yes, sir."

The RSM reached into a draw and picked out a brass stripe of a Lance Corporal and said, "Here, put that on and wear it until you can get the tailor to sew stripes onto all your uniforms. I'll want it back, and here's the authority for the tailor to sew on the stripes. That's it; you'll have to complete the next cadre course to be confirmed in your rank and to be paid for it. Keep your eyes on Part 1 Orders for the details." In fact, there never was a course because the security situation got worse and no time could be spared for such frivolities as training, so Jack was never confirmed and, more importantly, never paid as a Lance Corporal. Something the army wasn't too bothered about, but Jack was!

As he was about to leave the office, the RSM said, "Hang on, are you going back to Steamer Point now?"

"Yes, sir," said Jack.

"Have you got a vehicle?"

"Yes, sir," said Jack.

"Good, you can give me a lift. Just hang on a minute while I sort the last of these papers." So Jack stood there for a few minutes until the RSM called in his Clerk and handed the papers to him with instructions as to what should be done with them. Jack looked at the Clerk whose face visibly brightened when the RSM said, "I'm going over to the HQ with Lance Corporal Hughes, and I will not be back today." Jack thought if I have the best job in Aden, and I have, that poor bastard must have the worst!

They both exited the door, the offices being situated at the edge of the square, to see a Private Soldier, fag on, beret off, hands in pockets strolling across the square. To the RSM, to any RSM, the most hallowed spot in all the world, much more hallowed than heaven even, was THE SQUARE. Turning to Jack, the RSM, visibly turning a beetroot red, said, "He's all yours, Lance Corporal Hughes." Jack had no choice other than to explode.

When Jack got back to his room after lunch and walked into it, the three in there immediately leapt to their feet and stood to attention. This was something Private Soldiers were supposed to do when an NCO entered the room but in reality, was not done unless the NCO himself called them to attention. It was evident that word had spread that Jack had already let his promotion go to his head and had already proved he was a bad bastard by putting his best mate, for that was who it was crossing the square, on a charge within five minutes of being promoted! Jack ordered them to be at ease and life carried on. His best mate was on Orders for the charge Jack had instigated and he received seven days' restriction of privileges as a result—not exactly a huge punishment since privileges were almost non-existent in Aden anyway.

Jack did wonder on occasions over the years, if the RSM hadn't been there, would he have put Ken on a charge? He wasn't sure, but the RSM's actions in advising him to charge the first Private Soldier he saw made sure that he had no choice when they exited the RSM's Office to be presented with the sight they did. The advice had obviously been given with knowledge and experience of how difficult a Lance Corporal's job was. As the first step up the ladder, a Lance Corporal was still the closest level to Private Soldier and, of course, many of them were friends who now had to be ordered around. Too close a relationship, and allowing laxity towards friends, was a sure way to disaster as a Lance Corporal. The Civil Service had a policy of moving an individual to a department of strangers on promotion to avoid that very problem, but the army did not do that, even to the extent of leaving Jack in a room with three Private Soldiers who only minutes before were drinking buddies but who now would drink in the NAAFI whilst Jack drank in the Corporals' club.

On balance, as time passed and Jack had a relatively easy task managing Private Soldiers, he appreciated that the RSM's advice had been sound in principle even if, on occasion, it meant slightly unfairly treating a Private Soldier for the greater good of a Lance Corporal. And it wouldn't hurt that about two years and a half later, Ken was the first soldier put on a charge by Jack when he was commissioned!

In his next letter to Janet, he wrote, 'and you can't order me around anymore because I am a Lance Corporal now just like you.' Janet wrote back, 'Oh yes I can, I'm a Corporal now!' Jack was just a smidgeon pissed off at that, but life went on anyway.

# Chapter 77

Life did go on, but it was getting harder. His position as a Private had not been filled, and he found himself doing a Reece, but with no Scott's accent and a little more politely when asking Captain Robertson for the third time, "Is there any sign of my replacement yet?" Perhaps because he was more polite, Robertson did explain that the problem getting a replacement was that it was rare to find an individual with two trade skills, i.e., clerical and driving. Reece had been luckier than Jack in this regard in that Jack just walked through the door!

The work kept coming in at a rate to keep two Clerks fully employed, so Jack, on his own, was operating with a 50% resource shortage. G SD upstairs in the main building had nearly 150 Clerks and could certainly have functioned pretty well if one of them had been diverted to work for Jack, but none of the bastards could drive!

Jack was having to come back after dinner and work the afternoon to try to keep up with the work. Every time he had to drive somewhere or attend a blown-up vehicle, he lost clerical time and reports and letters were not being processed on time even with him working almost double time. And a double sod's law, even when he was Duty Clerk, loads of work kept coming in from the Message Centre which required immediate answers preventing him from catching up on G Tech work during that time.

He then witnessed at first-hand what a Brigadier thought of a Major who couldn't get his work done in normal time. One of the Majors in G Ops had left instructions with the Duty Clerks that if the Brigadier came into the office after dinner, he was to be told immediately. When this happened, he would immediately come into work and make sure that the Brigadier knew he was in—presumably to create a good impression.

Jack was on duty and had contacted the Major as per orders because the Brigadier was in the office. Fifteen minutes later, the Major arrived and started working at his desk. Jack went down to the Message Centre to collect a message, as it happened, for the Brigadier, so he took it straight to the Brigadier's office. He was followed through the door by the Major, who Jack let speak to the Brigadier first because of his rank. The Major asked the Brigadier if he would like a coffee or tea. All the tea makers in the HQ finished at dinner time, so if you were on duty in the afternoon you made your own if you wanted one. The Brigadier said, "Major, you are always here working in the afternoons; is that because you have too much work or are you simply incompetent?" at which Jack started to back out of the office—a Brigadier's office with the Brigadier in full bollocking mode on a Major was no place for a brand-new Lance Corporal to be.

"Stay there," thundered the Brigadier as soon as Jack started sidling out. Jack did and witnessed why the Brigadier was a Brigadier and well able to spot a crawling Major keen to fool a Brigadier into thinking he, the Major, was a jolly good chap.

Once a very chastened Major had left the Brigadier's office and gone home, the Brigadier took the message from Jack, and with a large grin on his face said, "I'd love a coffee if you could rustle one up, Corporal Hughes." Jack grinned back and enjoyed making one with the kit on the Major's side table.

Jack's hut was divided into three, with an office at each end and a large centre space that was divided up 2/3rds Registry and 1/3 G Tech. G Tech consisted of two desks behind a row of filing cabinets almost cutting them off from the Registry. Captain Robertson had moved into the office at the far end from Jack as his little office attached to theirs had fallen apart. All of them were made of wood, were years past their use-by date but no one was prepared to spend any money on the HQ. It wasn't, therefore, a complete surprise to see Sylva walk through the Registry and into Robertson's office; he was, after all, the Superintending Clerk. What was a devastating surprise was to be called in and told that until a proper replacement arrived, Sylva would do typing, filing and telephone answering, in other words, general clerical work to help Jack. The army could do some stupid things and it proved it with this move. Jack could not now stand the sight of her; he loathed her so deeply that the bottom of the Pacific Trench could not describe the depth. Although Jack had seen her around in Aden, it was after all not a very big place, but he had not spoken to her since the night he arrived in Aden and under normal circumstances, he would not have done so—now she was to work for him and how the hell could he avoid speaking or having anything to do with her. He answered Robertson by asking if there was any indication of a proper replacement arriving and was answered with a straight no.

Jack left their office without speaking to Sylva and went and sat down at his desk. He was utterly distraught; he certainly didn't want to talk to her—the only thing he did want to do was shoot her. In the funny way of the world, that reminded him he was supposed to have taken the Enfield pistol to the Armoury so that an Armourer's check could be done on it. He went into the Majors' office and told Major Lovewell where he was going. He took the revolver out of the safe and strapped it to his waist, looping the lanyard over his wrist. He stopped by his desk and picked up a pile of 'to type' memos and replies to letters that he had sorted into a pile to do the next time he was Duty Clerk and took them through to Sylva. He said, "These need a top copy plus one," and placed the pile on the corner of her desk and said, "I'm off to Fort Morbut to the Armoury." He felt so bad that he considered whether he should shoot her now and solve his problem with her and his work overload, but he couldn't be sure that he wouldn't be hanged here in Aden, so he just walked out. The beauty of the army was that NCOs gave orders to Private Soldiers, so he did not need to say 'please' to her—something he would probably have done if speaking to any other soldier.

The Armoury Sergeant took the Enfield from Jack and immediately started sucking his teeth in an obviously well-practiced manner. After about five minutes of examining the pistol, he said, "This is unsafe, the catch which closes the barrel to the body is insecure, the cylinders do not line up properly with the barrel, so a round is likely to knock it off, in fact, it's scrap metal." Jack's jaw dropped, as far as he could tell the pistol had been in excellent condition and it had certainly fired all right when Major Clasher fired it up at Cap Badge. He had not noticed the smile on the Armourer's face as he spoke. He went on, "I'd better replace it, hadn't I?" He reached into one of the safes and withdrew a brand-new Browning Hi-Power Semi-Automatic 9 mm pistol. These were only slowly being introduced in the Army to replace a miscellanea of pistols which had been used throughout the Army from before the Second World War. It was a very welcome addition and replacement of a lot of the pistols that existed, such as the Enfield, which was double action and hopelessly inaccurate as a result. It only held six, .38 in rounds against the Browning's 13, 9mm, and could really only kill a man if you stuck it right against him—much as Jack had done to the Dhobi Wallah, perhaps he knew something Jack didn't, after all! In skilled hands, a Browning was much more accurate, had greater hitting and killing power and was easily lethal up to 50 yds.

G Tech, if it was on the list at all, would have been miles towards the bottom, almost every other unit in the entire British Army would have been ahead of it to be issued with one, but the Armourer Sergeant, who had been a Corporal when Jack shot the terrorist and who had been the one who had had to clean and keep the SMG Jack used and keep it especially secure in case it was needed for a trial or Court Martial, was an admirer of Jack and his actions, which explained why Jack found himself walking out of the Armoury armed with a spanking brand-new Browning Hi-Power a few minutes later. The Armourer had offered to show Jack the ropes on handling and dismantling the Browning, but Jack was certain he could remember the training he had had at Folkestone in the Cadets so he declined with thanks. He left the Armourer with, "You'll be able to shoot a lot more of the bastards with that little baby," ringing in his ears.

His elated feelings disappeared within five minutes of entering the Corporal's section of the NAAFI. He wanted to stay away as long as possible so nipping in for a mug of chai seemed just the thing. He met there two other Clerks from Army Legal Services, a Corporal and a Lance Corporal. They were clearly celebrating something and when it became clear what it was, Jack was horrified. They were celebrating getting rid of Sylva. She had, apparently, been allocated to them about four months previously; in fact, when she had arrived in Aden, and they had done everything possible to get rid of her since. Her work was poor, slipshod and full of inaccuracies—something deadly serious in documents that were going to be used in legal actions. Captain Robertson had been approached on numerous occasions to have her moved but he had always said there were no other positions to move her to. Jack knew this was untrue because both G Ops and G SD were short of staff. Jack hazarded a guess that she was left in Army Legal Services because it was only a Major in charge and all the others were commanded by at least Lt Colonels who therefore carried more clout. But something must have happened because she simply disappeared from their office, and Jack knew where she had gone! He was not prepared to put sub-standard work in front of his two Majors so it was with a dull heart that he drove back to Steamer Point.

When Jack entered the office and showed the two Majors the Browning, their faces went off the beaming scale. Jack had to tell them twice what the Armourer Sergeant had said, and they recognised far more than did Jack just why they had received it. Jack was ordered not to overtly display it anywhere, when wearing it, if he could possibly avoid it because of the jealousy it would cause. He was to indent for a new holster, the old one being for a pistol which was a much smaller pistol and did not sufficiently hold or hide the contents. Unlike westerns, and especially

261

American war films, British Army Officers kept their hand guns in a webbing material holster with a flap to cover the mouth of the holster which was secured by, in most cases, a press stud. In addition, most hand guns had a lanyard attached to the base of the butt which would slip over the wrist or waist belt of the wearer. The flap kept the weapon from falling out and the dirt and dust from getting in; the lanyard prevented the weapon from being snatched away or dropped at a critical moment. In most cases, the weapon was carried on the left hip, right hip for left-handed people, so that it could quickly be seized if sitting in a vehicle; carrying it on the right hip for a 'quick draw' was frowned upon as usually the driver sat too close to the door of the vehicle to be able to draw a weapon from a right-hip holster.

Having had a good look at the pistol, Major Lovewell said, "Right, Corporal Hughes, you need to book us a lesson with the Armoury Sergeant on how to handle this little beauty and book the pistol range at Bir Fukum for us to have some practice with it."

Jack looked at him for a few moments, deciding whether he should speak or not, and then, remembering the do something, do nothing conversation he had had months ago, he decided 'do something' was the correct thing and he said, "I can teach you the weapon, sir." Both Majors looked at him, astounded again.

"How in God's name do you know about it?" and Jack had to explain. Having done so, the two Majors looked at one another and then Major Clasher said, "Okay, show us." It was a very unusual situation, a Lance Corporal teaching Majors but events like this did happen, especially where the junior rank was an expert specialist in the subject and the senior one was not—the situation here.

Jack took them through checking the weapon was safe when first handed it, how to strip it, clean it and reassemble it, how to load and unload it safely. At the end of the session, he was thanked, and the Browning was locked in the safe.

A few days later, they all piled into the Land Rover and drove out to Bir Fukum, Jack having drawn an SLR from the Armoury since if any shooting were to take place on the way to, or back from the range, it would be at longer range for which the Browning, especially as it would have been one weapon between three, would have been useless.

Taking it in turns, they each fired six rounds at a man-sized target at five yards. At that range, the target looked quite big and impossible to miss. But miss they did. Both Majors missed the target completely with all six rounds. Jack hit the target once with a round through the knee! Clearly, this Browning was a bit of a beast and it took many magazines of six rounds before they were all putting all six rounds into the target, but by the end of the morning they were, and they drove away from the range feeling far more comfortable with the weapon and their ability to use it. Despite the instruction to Jack to conceal the Browning as much as possible, both Majors made sure that contemporaries discovered they were carrying it every time out, so great were the bragging rights!

Jack had managed to avoid Sylva quite a lot. Anything for typing he left on her desk before she arrived at work, often late, but since she answered direct to Captain Robertson he felt that was for him to deal with. Finished work would appear on Jack's desk following his absence from his desk for whatever reason. Initially, the work was short letters, memos etc. Even though it was simple work, it did contain numbers of errors meaning that it had to be sent back for correction quite often.

Suspecting that the situation would come to a head, Jack kept a detail of all her work; in fact, the record showed that she had never sent him a piece of work that did not have to be corrected.

Even though Jack had this part resource, he was still not keeping up with the work. Events like the half day on the range with the Browning, enjoyable as they were, were putting Jack further and further behind. There was a report which would be about five pages of A4 when typed up and a major report of some 60 or so pages which had to be done. Logic said that Sylva should type the longer one, thus releasing Jack to do other things, but Jack was certain that she would make a complete bollocks of it; so he gave her the short one and explained that it was going to the GOC in C in Germany and would be copied to the MOD in London. A top copy plus three was, therefore, required and it was to be headed Top Secret. Jack gave her the instructions when Captain Robertson was in the office and could hear the instructions and the manner in which he gave them. He gave it to her shortly before dinner and did not expect to get it back before mid-morning on the next day, a Saturday. He returned from taking visitors to the airport to find the report on his desk. He could not believe the state of it when he checked it. The layout was wrong, she had typed it as though it were a letter rather than a report, even though Major Clasher had written the draft in report format; as he read it, he found at least 16 typos on each page. Paragraphs had been mixed up together with wrong punctuation marks used e.g. commas instead of full stops. And finally, she had headed the 'letter' 'Restricted', the lowest level of classification, rather than the 'Top Secret' the Major had written. Jack could not believe it; he was utterly dismayed. He was also very, very angry. He still retained some small feelings for her, and he was very upset at what he was seeing—how could she produce such rubbish?

He sat there unable to think what he should do. It was clear now why the ALS people were celebrating getting rid of her; his problem, now, was how he could achieve the same aim; she was, after all, a member of a different department and only providing some assistance to him whilst he was overloaded. There was also the problem of getting the report re-typed. It had to go in the mail that day; that was imperative. When there was a small typo, the signing officer would often correct it by pen but this 'letter' would look like it had small pox if that was done to it. To erase the typo and re-type accurately in place, on the top copy and all the carbon copies, would take a long time and would have to be very carefully done, almost impossible, to ensure the correction would not show. That clearly was not an option; the only one was to type the report again accurately with no or only the odd typo and all the other layout and punctuation errors corrected. The question was, who should correct it? Sylva was out, there was no way she could be trusted to do it, especially as the clock was ticking. Even if he, Jack, were to type it, he was probably not going to be able to do it before Major Clasher knocked off for the day; but there wasn't anyone else.

Jack considered his options, the standard procedure for him now i.e. do something, do nothing? There really was no choice—what he had to do was to get the report typed properly, signed, placed in a classified envelope and then in a plain envelope with just the address typed on it and then get it into the post.

Order to do it? Major Clasher was going to leave the office before Jack could get it typed so where would he be later on so that he could sign it there? Easy, Jack asked him, and he was going home and not expecting to go out. Jack explained what had happened with the report and how he proposed to solve the situation. Jack had learned long ago that bosses did not want to be told about problems, they wanted to be told what the solution to the problem was!

Jack sorted out with Janet's replacement three properly addressed Top Secret envelopes, had them listed in the register, along with a plain addressed envelope for each. By the time Jack had typed the report, everyone had gone. He placed the reports in a locked briefcase, strapped on the Browning pistol and drove to Major Clasher's home and got the covering letters signed with no problems or alterations. He sealed the top copy, plus two, into the Top Secret envelopes. The file copy went into the file when he got back to the office but first, he had to get the three Germany/UK bound reports into the post. Luckily, Jack knew the system and more importantly, the people in Khormaksar post handling room, having met them with Janet socially on a number of occasions. It was a simple matter to put Jack's three reports into the UK mail bag and drive back to the office to replace the Browning in the safe and the file copy in the file. Job done!

However, the problem of Sylva remained. On Monday morning, he went in to speak to Sylva and asked her why she had produced such an appalling piece of work. She stuttered and stammered and then tried to justify herself by saying she was so upset at the manner in which he had given the report to her that she had been quite unable to type it, and anyway, it wasn't really bad. Jack was exaggerating when he said it was unfit to be put before the Major; he was always picking on her by sending work back for correction which was perfectly alright. It was probably because she had dumped him. Jack could not believe what he was hearing.

He turned to Captain Robertson and said, "Sir, I must ask you to take disciplinary action against Private Brodhead for the appalling standard of her work." At that, she erupted and shouted her way through the same allegations again that she had made only moments before.

"What do you have to say to that, Lance Corporal Hughes?" asked Robertson.

"Sir," said Jack, "you were present when I asked Private Brodhead on Saturday and therefore heard the manner in which I spoke to her." He brought his left hand which had been behind his back clutching a pile of paper around to the front. He handed it to Captain Robertson and said, "The report on the top of the pile is the one she typed as a result of that instruction which you heard. You will see it is terrible; would you give that to Major Clasher and ask him to sign it? You can see it is typed as 'Restricted' when it should be 'Top Secret' and each page goes from bad to worse." Jack went through each page making sure that the excruciatingly bad quality of the letter was really brought home. He then explained how he had had to type it himself and get it signed and despatched. He then finished by pointing out that the other documents in the pile were all ones typed by her and all contained numerous errors; she had failed to produce even one correctly typed document during the entire time she had been working for Jack. "And for the record, I deny I have been picking on her because she dumped me." As he spoke, another thought occurred to him and he finished his defence with, "And I would ask you to compare this work to the work she did in ALS which caused her to be moved here. I cannot, and will not, put such poor-quality work in front of the two

Majors I work for. I am sure if you showed any of that pile to them and asked them if they would find it acceptable, you would be stung by the answer you received."

Robertson said, "Thank you for bringing this to my attention, Corporal Hughes; leave it with me and I will deal with it."

Jack left the office knowing he was all right. He knew because Robertson called him 'Corporal' although his rank was Lance Corporal. Some ranks were a bit of a mouthful, Lance Corporal being one, so it was quite common for the shortened form to be used, but if he was in trouble, the full title would always be used.

The following day when he arrived at work, it was to find that Sylva was gone. He discovered that she had been moved to do duplicating. The most copies of a letter a typist could produce was the top copy plus possibly five carbon copies if the carbons were still reasonably new and the typist hit the keys hard enough when typing. Where a report needed 60 copies of a 200-page report, a duplicator had to be used. The typing would be done on a wax skin with the ribbon of the typewriter clicked up out of the way so that the naked key hit the wax sheet cut the letter through it so that the ink from the roller onto which it was wound could seep through the cut letters and leave their imprint on the white sheet of duplicating paper. It required little training and was hated by all the Clerks since the operator invariably ended up covered in ink. It was also terribly boring. Jack thought this was a wonderful job for Sylva and had a quiet chuckle whenever he had to give her major reports to be duplicated. He didn't think that she agreed with him.

# Chapter 78

Shortly after this incident, Captain Robertson called Jack into his office. Also, there was a moonie, the nick name for someone new to Aden who had round white knee caps peeping below their shorts and above their tube tops. Robertson said,

"I have had a word with your two Majors who have expressed concern that you have too much work, and they insist that you have a full-time Clerk allocated to assist you. Private Wide, here, will be joining you. He can't drive but the two Majors believe you will be able to manage." At that, they shook hands and Jack took him off to the office.

Wide took a deal of teasing, with a name like Wide and with a skeletal frame to match, it was inevitable, and he had learned to take it long before he met Jack. They took a few minutes talking about their respective careers to date in the Army, Johnny Wide having already served for the best part of six years. That fact and the fact he was still a Private told Jack nearly all he needed to know about Johnny. Jack's paramount rule was, if you don't know, ask—ask was the rule and he impressed this on Wide as strongly as he could. Jack saved the do something, do nothing mantra for later when he had had chance to measure his abilities a bit more.

They were now well into the hot season; Aden really only had two seasons, hot and cold. Spring and autumn each lasted only a few weeks or so. The hot season was very unpleasant, daily temperatures into the high 90s, hot enough to cook an egg on the bonnet of a Land Rover and a great trick for pulling birds from the liners; and night time down to about 60 in December, but the killer was the humidity. You were never dry; as you stepped out of the shower and started drying yourself, so the sweat started pouring out of you. A few miles inland into the desert and the aridity was wonderful. It was possible to carry out quite physical activities without struggling with the listlessness caused by the humidity.

Johnny Wide had only been in Aden a day when he reported sick. Astonishingly, he was on the UK-bound plane that night. Jack was told that Johnny was one of these rare people who cannot sweat and therefore, his body temperature was climbing way above normal. There really was no cure other than to immediately return him to a temperate climate. Thus, it didn't matter that he could not drive; he couldn't bloody clerk either!

Two days later, a WRAC girl, who had been in Aden for some months, was posted to G Tech to help Jack and she could not drive either, but by God, she got through the clerical work at a rate of knots. But the difference this time was that the Government had announced that we were to pull out of Aden and, in effect, leave them to it. Clearly, this changed the situation and there was no hope of getting a replacement who could drive as well as clerk since everything was to be run down.

It put a lot of pressure onto G Tech, and the Army as a whole, to complete desert trials of all sorts of new or proposed new equipment before the pull out.

The trial of the mortar to replace the ageing, but still effective, three-inch mortar with the NATO standard 81 mm mortar had to be pushed ahead, ironically injuring Jack in the process. A new, pressurised cooling system had been fitted to the G Tech Land Rover instead of going to an infantry battalion one, to get it done quickly. Up until that time, the radiator cap would leak steam if the engine got too hot (all vehicles did this) and would boil over if it exceeded 112 F, which they quite often did when grinding along at high revs in low gears in soft sand.

Someone came up with the idea that if the cooling system was sealed so that it could function at a higher temperature, then the boiling over problem would be solved. Fitting the system to the Land Rover only took the REME workshop less than an hour; it involved checking all the water hoses had tight clips with no leaks and fitting a new, more precision-made radiator cap that fitted tightly and would not allow pressure to escape.

The first trial of the system was when Major Lovewell and Jack drove out to the Bir Fukum firing range to observe the new mortars being fired. The trip involved four or five miles through very soft sand. Major Lovewell insisted on driving to test out his theory that you should drive on soft sand the same as soft snow. He thus drove in the highest gear possible at the lowest revs. Consequently, they kept bogging down as it is impossible to change down quick enough before the vehicle loses all speed and bogs down. Jack hated it as he was the one who had to keep getting the sand channels off the side of the vehicle and shovelling away sand to get them as close to the wheels as possible; and they weren't bloody light. Consequently, they arrived late at the range when there were only a few rounds to be fired at maximum range, so far that Jack could not see the detonations although Major Lovewell could because he had binoculars.

Jack was ordered to take a note of the temperature gauges, oil and water, before making his way to the char wagon. As was usual, Jack propped the bonnet up to let the engine cool off more easily and, as he had been told about the new system, he turned the radiator cap halfway, very carefully, until he heard the hiss of escaping steam and pressure, then in accordance with instructions, he opened it fully at which the still trapped steam and pressure burst out, scalding Jack's right arm from wrist to elbow. He could not prevent a scream of pain escaping. Major Lovewell heard and came rushing over. Taking in immediately what had happened, he took his handkerchief from his pocket, soaked it in water from one of the front Jerry cans and wrapped it around Jack's arm. As he did so, he said, "Sorry this isn't silk, Corporal Hughes, all my silk ones have disappeared in the dhobi." Jack could feel the silk handkerchief in his pocket burning almost as much as his arm!

Major Lovell disappeared away and came back a few minutes later with a Private from the Federal Regular Army and said, "Go with this chap, Corporal Hughes, he's going to take you to the Medical Centre at 24 Brigade in Little Aden, the closest point to where they were where you can get attention. They will be expecting you." Jack looked at the FRA Private and thought, *I'm going to be crossing the desert on my own with him with no protection, through an area known to be mined on occasions and to be open to ambushes and not least by the bloody FRA*; by this time, they were totally not trusted by the British troops, something that was to happen again years in the future with the Afghan Army troops, and he thought, *shit* and, *I don't think much of that bloody high pressure system either*. He was in a lot of pain and had lost his normal politeness when he said, "Will you cock my SLR for me, sir?" He had drawn an SLR because the desert was open, and engagements took place at long ranges. Even so, Lovewell had the Browning on his hip; *fat lot of use that will be*, thought Jack. He now wished he had drawn an SMG which could be handled easily and reasonably well inside a vehicle, but an SLR was a pain. Nevertheless, Lovewell cocked the SLR, which had 20 rounds in the magazine, applied the safety catch and handed it to Jack who took it in his left hand. He got into the unarmoured FRA Land Rover, thinking *if I don't get shot by this bastard or ambushed by insurgents, I can still have my arse blown off by a mine*. Anyway, he got into the Land Rover with the Major holding the door for him in such a manner that the SLR was pointing at the driver and with a bit of a smile, he said, "Come on then sunshine, let's go."

As the driver did not speak English, it was a quiet journey but at least he knew how to drive, and they did not bog down once. Watching his driving very carefully, even though he had a much lighter vehicle than the G Tech Land Rover, he stayed in the lowest gear possible at the highest revs possible, and they never once even looked like bogging down. It didn't help that they just sailed by the disturbances in the sand caused by Jack's digging on the way out.

Delivered safely to the Medical Centre, about half an hour after the accident, Jack was surprised that they were expecting him. Lovewell had had a message passed by radio to the Medical Centre and thus, they knew all about Jack's accident. Taken into the Doctor's room, a Major in the RAMC, the Major said to him, "You might not think so, being in pain as you are, but you are a lucky chap." Pointing to an opened parcel on his desk, he said, "This has come in this morning from the UK. It's a new wonder treatment, so they say, for scalds and burns. It's an aerosol that you just spray onto the damaged area, and it behaves like a plastic skin, keeping the air, and anything else, from the injured area whilst it heals. Don't get it wet for the next three days, and if you get any problems with it at all, report sick to the Medics in Steamer Point." At that, he removed the handkerchief and dropped it in the bin; *Lovewell will be happy at that*, thought Jack, *he's even lost a cotton handkerchief now*. The spray was beautifully cooling and five minutes later, he went looking for the Arab driver, who he found at a chai stall a few yards away and pointed to Steamer Point.

As they set off, Jack thought the MO told me to take it easy and protect the arm for a few days, so that ruled out escort on an armoured Land Rover and digging it out every few yards. *Fuck him*, thought Jack, *he can dig his fucking self out*.

Jack never did find out if Major Lovewell had to dig himself out, but he did discover that the wrong radiator cap had been fitted, hence the failure to reduce all the pressure when turned to the halfway position. It did seem a bit unfair that he typed the report on the effectiveness of the system which gradually spread to all vehicle users throughout the world.

# Chapter 79

Some trials were cancelled as they could not be completed in the nine months or so before the pull out. The two Majors disappeared about a week apart and were replaced by Major Walliams, mainly vehicles and allied subjects, and Major Scagg for weapons. They both settled in quite quickly and Major Scagg surprised Jack by bringing his family out. Jack drove Mrs Scagg frequently on various errands and got to know her quite well. They had a boy of about five and a girl of three. When Jack's second Christmas arrived, he and Jenny Whaleman, his new clerk, were invited to lunch on Boxing Day. It was actually held in the family's enclosure on the families' beach. Jack and Jenny enjoyed it immensely; Mrs Scagg had really pushed the boat out and the lunch was quite a picnic as a result. Jenny spent a lot of time playing in the sea with the two children while Jack was quizzed about his family and aspirations. During this time, Jack revealed that he was engaged to be married on his return. It ended with Jack carrying the little girl, fast asleep in his arms and Jenny carrying the boy to the Hillman for the Scaggs to go home. The previous two Majors had been nice enough but there had never been this degree of closeness and Major Walliams was okay too, but he kept a degree of separation.

The trial of the new Chieftain tank came and went with nothing to show but a long report.

The trial of the Hovercraft was a bit more traumatic. It arrived by freighter that had to anchor out in the harbour; it drew too much water to come alongside and be unloaded by crane. This was the first problem; the Arabs worked out a price for offloading onto a lighter and then transporting it to the shore and then offloading onto the quay. Arguments went on for three days with, not least, the freighter Captain complaining at the time he was being held in port. In the end, he was the solution to the problem; not liking the Arabs very much and hating the holdup, he suggested why not drop the bloody thing over the side and 'fly' it ashore in Little Aden. And that's what the Army did. The Arab port people were apoplectic but there was nothing they could do. However, they did have the final laugh.

The hovercraft was prepared and tested in a number of ways, bringing troops ashore and cargo and reloading it all again. The depot was a short distance into the desert, serviced by a metal road and someone had the idea to drive the hovercraft from the Navy support ship off shore straight to the depot without offloading on the beach. This worked well, with the Hovercraft 'driving' on the metalled road. Then the final test, could the Hovercraft cross the desert sand? They looked for the worst possible area, all such soft sand that virtually no vehicle could cross it. And then they drove across it; well, they did for about half an hour until the engine, with a high-pitched screech, just up and died on them. The closest they could get to it by vehicle was about two miles. Struggling across some of the softest and deepest sand you could find was extremely tiring and in the full sun, temperatures around

120°F, was not funny. The problem was quickly identified—the sand had got into the engine and, a technical term everyone understood, fucked it. It could not be left there unguarded while they sorted out what could be done to rescue it.

A full company of the Royal Anglicans was brought out to guard it. Even if a breakdown vehicle could get to the Hovercraft, it could not lift it back to firm ground because it was too heavy. It was not repairable in the sense that it could be made to start or run in any fashion.

The following day, Major Walliams handed Jack a short report to Jack for typing. It was about the trial of the Hovercraft and could be summed up as, 'fucking useless in the desert'. Jack felt emboldened to ask have they got a plan to rescue it yet. Walliams glumly looked at him and said that they hadn't but the blame was sure to land on G Tech and him in particular. Jack, obeying his do nothing, do something, said, "I've got an idea, sir."

Walliams looked at him and then said, "And?"

"We could use a Scammell, the heavy break down truck which could not lift the Hovercraft, to lay sand channels across the soft sand up to the Hovercraft. It will take a lot of channels, but we've got loads in the RASC depot, and then, having laid the road, the Scammell could carry the spare Hovercraft engine, which is somewhere in Little Aden, out to the Hovercraft and the REME people could fit it into it. They could then 'fly it out' along the sand track road to firmer sand or the road and load it onto a tank transporter or something similar. It might even have enough life left in it to make it to the harbour under its own power. It will probably knacker the second engine as well but that would be cheaper than leaving the Hovercraft to be looted by the Arabs."

Major Walliams looked at him for a few moments and then said, "Bloody good idea." And that is what they did. Unfortunately, it could only get to the quayside, so the Arabs had the last laugh and charged double to load it onto a freighter.

# Chapter 80

Jack was at 2 Coy RASC filling up with petrol when, in the distance, he saw a familiar figure. There, dressed in a 2nd Lieutenant's uniform was Charlie Wilson, last seen disappearing from the POC Wing at Buller Barracks, on his way to Sandhurst. Jack was not keen to talk to him, be seen by him or especially to have to salute him, so turning to the Corporal at the pumps and hiding behind them Jack said, "How are you getting on with Charlie Wilson?"

"He's only been here three days, and he's proved himself to be a right cunt on all three of them." *Figures,* thought Jack. Replacing the petrol cap and quickly signing for the petrol, Jack drove off. In his mirror, he could see Wilson gesticulating which looked like he wanted Jack to stop. Jack kept going and prepared his 'sorry, sir, didn't see you' ready for when Wilson did eventually catch up with him.

Two days later and the detector and intruder warning kit arrived from the UK. Jack, rather than Corporal Pectin, had been taught about it a month or so previously. Major Scagg consequently made arrangements to demonstrate it at 24 Brigade in Little Aden. The camp at Little Aden was a mixture of mainly wooden huts and a large number of tents for the infantry units who were posted in for six-month tours in Aden. Those there for the cool season were reasonably comfortable in the tents but those poor bastards there for the hot season really suffered in the heat and humidity. But hey, when did the suffering of troops ever receive any consideration and care from senior officers hell bent on obtaining their OBEs (the troops understood OBE to stand for Other Buggers Efforts) or even knighthoods. Due to its irregular growth, the camp had no recognisable, or defensible, perimeter.

Jack thought it typical that the area to be defended was chosen to be the area immediately adjoining the Officers' Mess and sleeping quarters. The kit was very simple; contained in a metal box were the controls. Basically, there were four small dials, a switch which could select which dial to monitor or all four at once and a volume control. With the kit were four geophones, basically microphones which could be buried in the ground with a huge length of wire attached to each. The ground around the area to be guarded was carefully assessed to identify spots for the geophones to be buried. If it was to be a permanent installation, then the cables to the geophones had to be buried too, but if a temporary installation, the cables were left lying on the ground. In such circumstances, the cables and geophones would have to be laid after dark to prevent their being discovered by the insurgents. Each cable was connected to a separate dial, or they could all be connected to one dial but that seemed pointless to Jack, thus the location of the intruder could be determined by which dial was reacting. Switching to that channel allowed the operator to hear whether the intruder was walking, running or crawling etc. but more importantly where the intruder was.

Once everything had been set up, Jack switched on the kit and nodded to Major Scagg. He then walked towards one of the geophones and his footsteps could clearly be heard in the head set and the instrument attached to that geophone started a needle twitching for each footstep. He then ran back, and the running footsteps could easily be identified as those of a runner. Looking at the watching group, Major Scagg selected a 2nd lieutenant and had him 'volunteer' to crawl slowly towards the geophone and that crawling could also easily be identified. Having him tiptoe next showed that even that could be picked up, so sensitive were the geophones, although they did not pick them up quite as far out as the running steps.

The onlookers were very impressed and wanted the kit immediately. The kit they had seen demonstrated was the only one in the Command and could not be left with them as a series of demonstrations had been planned for other units who might have a use for it. Attacks had been happening nightly and large numbers of troops were tied up just guarding their own camp. Critically, they were, therefore, not available for operations which desperately had to be carried out against the insurgents with only small numbers of troops.

Much to their dismay, the Brigadier pulled rank and decided that it would be a good idea if Major Scagg and Jack stayed there and used it that night in case possible insurgents attacked the camp. Perhaps, as some consolation, they were both well looked after. They spent a lot of time examining the ground around the camp with binoculars; they did not want to give the insurgents a clue to what they were doing by walking the ground to identify locations for the geophones.

Some shots on previous nights had been fired from a group of date palms about 400 yards from the perimeter and that was consequently chosen as Site One. Site Two was where the ground came to a dried-up wadi bed meaning people crossing it had to jump down creating a clearly identifiable 'thump' for the geophone to pick up. The other two sites were just where experience and intuition said the insurgents might hunker down to shoot at the camp.

Various weapons, GPMGs, mortars, Wombat anti-tank recoilless rifles, and 76 mm guns from three Saladin Armoured Cars were all surreptitiously sighted on the four geophone sites. Jack, with two infanteers to help him, laid the geophones just after dark, about 1900 hrs, and then it was a question of wait. It wasn't until 0300 hrs that any activity showed. Multiple footsteps could be heard and seen by needle reaction in the instruments for the geophones at Sites One and Two. Fire was returned instantaneously at the two sites from the pre-aimed heavy weapons when shots started coming in from them. Jack would much rather have been situated in one of the huts in a nice little 'nest' of full filing cabinets than the tent the equipment had been set-up in; he didn't think much of the protection offered by the canvas! The return fire was heavy, accurate and prolonged; in fact, everyone enjoyed banging away at the two sites—so much better to know where the fire was coming from than blasting into the dark at shadows. Cease fire was ordered after five minutes or so, two or three minutes after the last incoming fire was experienced. It was then just a question of waiting again, this time until dawn.

Jack went out with the first patrol; he borrowed a rifle just in case. Both sites showed signs of blood and body tissue but no actual bodies. The Brigadier was delighted with the results and made one further attempt to keep the kit, but a swift telephone call to the BGS back in Steamer Point soon sorted that out. Although clearly disappointed that he couldn't keep the kit, the Brigadier thanked Major Scagg profusely, saying he had not had such fun in ages; he had been on the line banging away with his own personal SLR. He even had a word with Jack, seeing if he would transfer to 24 Brigade as a full Corporal when the kit came through. Jack thanked him for the offer but said he would prefer to stay where he was.

Jack was to discover a few days later in the Intel briefing attached to Part One Orders that monitoring of the insurgent radio had revealed that three fighters had been 'martyred' in 'a huge attack' on an enemy base during which 'hundreds of infidels had been sent to hell'. This was taken to be the attack Jack had been involved in and so the enemy was telling them that three of the insurgents had been killed—their casualty figures were generally regarded as being accurate as they had no mechanism to hide casualties—the numbers being so small in the insurgent groups that the ones who had been killed were too well known for their families to not notice they were missing.

Jack had a massive breakfast in the 24 Brigade Cookhouse, Major Scagg had a better one in the Officers' Mess and then they set off back to Steamer Point. Jack had to stop at 2 Coy in Khormaksar to refuel the Husky. While he did so, Major Scagg went off to make a telephone call in the office. Then he heard the dreaded voice, "What a state you are in, soldier, and your vehicle, what have you got to say for yourself, and stand to attention and salute an officer when you see one." It was Charlie Wilson, determined to belittle Jack. Jack withdrew the hose from the car, slowly and turned and faced him. Jack did not salute, making much of the fuel pump he was holding.

"Firstly, sir, I am not a soldier, I am a Lance Corporal and entitled to be addressed as such. I did not salute you because you were behind me and I did not see you. As to the state of the vehicle and myself..." Major Scagg appeared from nowhere.

"Corporal Hughes has been up all night fighting insurgents at 24 Brigade, the vehicle has been driven there and back in a strong wind blowing sand and dirt all over it; and why have I not been saluted, 2nd Lieutenant, and where were you at 0300 hrs this morning when Corporal Hughes and myself were involved in a fire fight with insurgents?" Major Scagg, who had heard all the conversation through the open window of the pumps' office, had appeared silently behind Charlie and proceeded to dish out the same treatment as Charlie had intended to hand to Jack. He didn't like it, but as his OC had joined them and was standing next to Major Scagg, and clearly supporting this unknown Major, he didn't feel that he was in a good position to argue with two of them, both clearly angry, Majors.

"Well, I asked you a question, where were you at 0300 hrs this morning?"

"Asleep in bed, sir."

"Hm, not very impressive, 2nd Lieutenant. Do you still think you are justified in complaining about either the state of Corporal Hughes or his vehicle or indeed myself?"

"No, sir."

"Right answer. Now don't you think it would be a good idea to send a couple of your soldiers up to Steamer Point in an hour's time to clean this vehicle for a soldier who has just been in combat? Incidentally, Corporal Hughes is quite right to complain at being referred to as 'soldier'—he is a Lance Corporal and his rank is clearly visible; he should be referred to as such. So, what is your answer to be?"

"Yes, sir."

"Good answer again, that's two in a row; easy, isn't it?" Charlie didn't think this last was really a question, so he kept quiet. At that, the two Majors shook hands and Jack drove Major Scagg home before parking the Hillman at the Barrack Block for the 2 Coy men to clean it when they arrived—and a jolly good job they did too.

# Chapter 81

Charlie Wilson wasn't very wise. He was determined to 'get' Jack, not yet having realised that a Lance Corporal who works for a Staff Major can always call on rank to protect him, or, if the circumstances require it, an even higher rank. A few days later, Jack was at his desk when his phone rang. Answering it, "G Tech, Lance Corporal Hughes speaking, sir," he was greeted with, "This is the General upstairs; pop up as soon as you can please, Corporal Hughes." His 'can' was very quick— when the GOC in C calls you, you come running. Unusually, his PA was not in the outer office so Jack knocked and entered the GOC in C's office when directed to do so.

"Ah Corporal Hughes, I have a bit of a problem. My driver, Sergeant White, and my PA have been involved in an accident at somewhere down at 2 Coy in Khormaksar. Sgt White has been carted off to hospital, not too seriously hurt but he does need hospital treatment, and my PA has broken his right wrist and can't drive even if my staff car was driveable. I want you to get down there as quick as you can and bring my PA back here. Collect a weapon on the way; a Browning pistol will do," with a smile on his face—he obviously knew that G Tech had one—"and come back and see me the minute you get back. I have a job for you to do which may take a couple of days so grab some kit as well. Any questions?"

"No, sir."

"Good, good, chop, chop on your way." Jack was on his way!

Jack shifted to get to 2 Coy and covered the eight miles in 12 minutes. Pulling up at the petrol pumps with a bit of a flourish, he explained that he was in a hurry and could the Corporal in the Pump Office please phone the company office to tell the injured WOII there that he was here, and Jack would be filling up with petrol while waiting for him. Jack was just finishing filling up the car when he heard that voice—the one he just knew was dripping with vengeance to get him. Turning around, he stood to attention but kept hold of the petrol pump thus managing to avoid saluting the stuck-up little shit again. As Charlie started in on Jack, the GOC in C's PA arrived with his right arm in a sling thus he, too, was able to avoid saluting Charlie.

"Excuse me, sir, but this corporal has been sent to collect me, and we are in a bit of a hurry…" Charlie said,

"Well, I suggest you sit down in the office, Warrant Officer, while I speak to this Lance Corporal. I will not detain you long, just long enough for me to explain certain things to him vis-a-vis commissioned officers and Lance Corporals, the lowest non-commissioned rank in the army." The PA looked as if he was going to argue; after all, wise 2nd Lieutenants listened when WOIIs spoke, but seeing the look on Charlie's face, he turned and went into the office. Poor old Charlie had only just started on Jack when the office window opened, and the PA stuck his head out, "Excuse me, sir, you are wanted on the telephone…"

Charlie interrupted him, "Unless it's the GOC in C, I am not to be interrupted."

"Sir, it is the GOC in C." Charlie looked at the PA. Surely, he's joking—what if he's not? Charlie walked over to the window and took the proffered telephone as though it was covered inch deep in shit.

"2nd Lieutenant Wilson, sir."

"2nd Lieutenant Wilson, I am the GOC in C. I assume you know who I am?" Charlie's suntan disappeared instantly.

"Ye… ye… yes, sir."

"Good. You will accompany my PA and Corporal Hughes to my office where I want a word with you," and rang off. Charlie handed the phone back to the PA with a shaking hand and said, "I am to return to Steamer Point with you two," in a very quavering and little boy voice.

Jack drove to his barrack block first and said to the PA, "The General told me to pick up some kit for a few days and a weapon while I collect you." The PA nodded and said make sure you've got a cleaning kit, weapon and personal, with you. Jack nodded and got out of the car; he said nothing to Charlie. He was tempted to take a long time and leave him sweltering in the car but that would have meant doing it to the PA as well, and he was a decent bloke. He collected kit for a few days and then drove to the office and collected the Browning Semi-Automatic pistol. Knowing the effect he thought it would have on Charlie, he made a great show of placing it in the holster and attaching the lanyard to his wrist while standing by the car. He then drove to the GOC in C's parking space and parked in it. The PA led the way with Charlie trailing well behind. When the PA walked straight into the General's Office, it dawned on Charlie who he must be. The WOII was in there for a moment or two and he then beckoned both of them in. By this time, Charlie was in such a state that he failed to salute, but Jack did not.

"If a Lance Corporal salutes a General and a 2nd lieutenant does not, what does that tell you about the 2nd Lieutenant, 2nd Lieutenant?" By this time, Charlie was dying on his feet and saluting with his left hand, he mumbled something quite incoherent. The General let him struggle on and then, probably taking pity on him, thought Jack, he said, "This Lance Corporal is about to carry out extremely important work for me and the Command; you, on the other hand, are utterly dispensable. Do I have to repeat the words and threats you made to the Corporal to show you what I've been told, or will you take that as read?"

"As read, sir," said Charlie in a remarkably clear voice.

"Right," said the General, "I think it would be a jolly good idea if you were to take some time, about the length of time it is going to take you to walk back to Khormaksar, to consider whether your behaviour towards this excellent young NCO is commensurate with an officer in this modern day, volunteer Army. What do you say to that, eh?"

"I agree, sir."

"Dismissed." Charlie ran for the door, remembered where he was, stopped, flashed up a salute and left the office running. The General beamed a wicked smile at Jack and then started to tell him what he was to do.

Again, he started with reminding Jack that he was subject to the Official Secrets Act; *this is getting to be a habit*, thought Jack and then he said, "The new

GOC in C who is due to take over from me in a few weeks' time is arriving at Khormaksar at 1200 hrs, that is to say, in 15 minutes' time today. My driver and PA were on their way to meet him; he is arriving incognito and is not to be identified to anyone, when they had their little run in with a lorry which managed to do even more damage to my lovely new staff car than you did by getting a grenade thrown at it. Consequently, you are now going to Khormaksar at a rate of knots; he's an Admiral, you know." Jack laughed; he knew to laugh when a General cracked a pun. "Hold up this notice at the Reception area, and he will identify himself to you, it's not his real name, but it is the name he will be using while he's here. You are to take him wherever he wants to go; this may mean staying away for a few nights. No one is to know about this unless either he or I authorise it. Clear?"

"Yes, sir." Jack took the notice, saluted and walked out.

Looking at his watch as he got into the car, he saw that he only had eight minutes to travel the eight miles—he was certainly going to have to travel at a rate of knots. Some of the journey was in a 30-mph limit and some at 40 mph. Nowhere in Aden state was there a faster limit than 40 mph so as he set off, his thoughts about Generals and their impossible orders grew and grew.

He was lucky, threading his way through the traffic just outside the HQ, that there always seemed to be a gap just when he needed it. Traffic lights turned green as he got to them and gaps opened in the traffic going around the roundabouts so that he was able to infiltrate on and then overtake whatever vehicle was in front of him. At one roundabout on the outskirts of Tawahi, he nipped in front of an Alfa Romeo Giulietta Sprint GT Veloce—*nice car*, thought Jack—and then through a gap between a slow-moving ex-Army three tonner and a school bus. The driver of the Alfa was not happy judging by the length of time he blew his oh-so-wonderful Italian horn. In fact, he seemed to be coming after Jack or at least going the same way. Jack was able to keep comfortably ahead of him, by luck in gaps opening for him overtaking and closing for the Alfa and as the miles passed, it was obvious that the Alfa driver was getting increasingly irate, something that would be called road rage in later years, judging by his none-too-safe overtakes, head light flashing and horn blowing. But Jack, in an Army Hillman Husky, a fraction of the cost of the Alfa, and with nowhere near the performance, managed to stay ahead of the Alfa quite easily—the traffic being for Jack and against the Alfa.

But it was too good to last, the Alfa drove past him on the dual carriageway roundabout at the entrance to Khormaksar of all places, by driving up the inside lane and then in front of the Hillman, blocking any further travel. The man who jumped out ran around to the front of the Hillman, pulled the driver's door open and ordered Jack out in no uncertain terms. As he was wearing a Major's uniform and that of the Royal Military Police to boot, Jack complied. It was obvious from his high red colour and the steam coming from his ears, at least it looked like steam to Jack, that he was not a happy bunny.

He marched Jack at the double across the roundabout and into the Guardroom of Khormaksar and ordered the Snowdrop, (RAF) Flight Sergeant there to lock Jack up straight away. When the Flight Sergeant started to ask about charges, the Provost Major, for that was who he was, i.e. the Officer in Command of all the Military Police in Aden, the Major said, "Lock him up now or you'll be in there with him." The Flight Sergeant complied.

Staring at the cell walls, Jack thought, *well the shit can't be much deeper than this*. After a few minutes, the flap in the door opened and the same Flight Sergeant asked him his name and number and the flap slammed shut without Jack getting the chance to say anything at all. A few minutes after that, the flap opened again, and a pair of eyes perused the cell. The door opened and in walked Jack's favourite RMP WOII Stevens.

"I thought I recognised the name when Flight was spelling it out to the Provost and lo and behold, look who it isn't."

Jack smiled and said, "Well, I don't think he'll be the Provost for much longer if I am not released pretty damn quick." The WOII looked at Jack for at least a minute without saying anything; then on the basis that his experience with Jack had indicated that Jack was a bright lad for a private soldier, and now a Lance Corporal, that he might not be joking.

"Tell me more," he said. Jack was not sure how much he could tell WOII Stevens; he thought for a moment and then said, "Someone should ring the GOC in C's office and ask for his PA. If he is not there, it's possible because he was injured in the accident here earlier this morning; then they should ask to speak to the GOC in C and tell him where I am. I believe things then might happen," and at that, Jack shut up. The Sergeant Major looked at him again for what seemed like hours but probably was only seconds before turning and starting to walk out. Jack stopped him with a, "You might like to take this with you; it is unloaded," and handed him the Browning pistol. The Sergeant Major looked at him, smiled, took the pistol and magazine that Jack had removed from the pistol and walked out.

Only a few moments later, the cell door slammed open and the Provost Major shouted at him, "Come with me." Jack was taken into an office where a telephone was lying on the desk. The Provost picked it up as though it were red hot and said, "He's here now, sir."

He immediately handed the phone to Jack who said, "Lance Corporal Hughes speaking, sir."

The GOC in C asked, "Are you on your own?"

"No, sir, the Provost is here."

"Send him out, no one is to hear our conversation."

Jack turned to the Provost and said, "The General wishes to speak to me alone, sir." Looking daggers at Jack, the Provost left his own office.

"How much have you told them?" the General was pretty curt.

"I simply asked for someone to telephone your PA or in his absence, you, and tell him or you of where I was. Absolutely nothing more."

"Good, well done. They will release you now and escort you to the Arrivals at the airport. Have they given you your weapon back yet?"

"No, sir."

"Did they really lock you up and then you disarmed yourself?"

"Yes, sir."

"And how far did it take the Provost to catch you?"

"About six and a half miles, sir."

"How fast did you go?"

"Not much more than 50 in places, sir; the Hillman won't do much more than 60 anyway, and it takes an age to get up there." *Oops*, thought Jack, *I probably shouldn't have said that last bit.* There was a strange noise coming out of the phone and it took Jack a moment to realise that the General was laughing.

"He's been bragging for weeks about how he's got the fastest car in Aden and it took him almost seven miles to catch a clapped-out old Hillman. Ho, ho ho." The General took a little while to gather himself then, realising he had probably said too much to a junior rank, he said, "Right, Corporal Hughes. That's twice today I've had to get your nuts out of the nutcracker; don't let there be a third. Now get your skates on, we'll forget about knots, and, obeying all the speed limits, go and get our VIP."

"Yes, sir," said Jack and he put the phone down.

There was no sign of the Provost when he came out of the Provost's Office but Warrant Officer Stevens was there. Looking at Jack he said, "I do hope that you will be in Aden for the rest of my tour because I've never seen anyone with the ability to cause shit heaps seven miles high and then walk away from them smelling of roses! You're the best entertainment I've ever had in this shithole, and I do so hope it carries on."

"I fucking don't," said Jack very quietly.

"I suppose you'd like your vehicle and your pistol back?"

"Yes please, sir." Stevens handed Jack the Browning almost reverently—he didn't seem to care much for the .38 in revolver in his holster. Outside, Jack was relieved to find the Husky in front of the Guardhouse; after all, he had been ordered out of it on a roundabout and he had no idea what could have happened to it. Also, there was an MP Land Rover which proceeded to lead him to Arrivals with blue lights flashing and a siren shrieking. *Pretty incognito*, thought Jack, as he followed at 20mph, the speed limit for the airport. His last view of Warrant Officer Stevens was him offering a mock salute with a big smile on his face!

At Arrivals, the Land Rover drove into the area reserved for VIPs. Jack thought, *fuck that for a game of soldiers and drove past them into the normal peoples' area*. With a wave to the Land Rover, Jack trotted into the Arrivals hall. Looking desperately around for a lost and angry Admiral, Jack was relieved to see other people waiting by Arrivals. The board, with handwritten messages, indicated that the flight was late and due in fifteen minutes for which Jack was eternally grateful as it enabled him to get a cold drink from a trolley while he waited. He thought it was probably too much to expect that he would have been given one in the nick, given how mad the provost was.

But it wasn't the last time Jack was to come across Charlie Wilson.

# Chapter 82

The VIP came striding up to Jack and said, "It's me you're waiting for. Let's go." Jack had been torn between whether he should salute or not, but the Admiral solved that by moving so quickly. He looked around when they approached the vehicle and Jack thought, he doesn't know about the PA and the General's driver, so Jack explained what had happened and proffered the General's apologies that only a Lance Corporal was meeting him.

"No problem," said the Admiral, "about what one would expect from the Army." *Oh right, you pompous little shit*, thought Jack, *I'll get you for that.*

Once they were installed in the car, Jack asked, "Where to, sir?"

"Twenty-four Brigade, if you know where they are." Jack thought, *you really are a little shit, in fact you're a bigger little shit than Charlie Wilson speaking to a junior NCO like that.* Jack drove off. He was careful to observe all the speed limits. The Admiral only glanced once at the flocks of flamingos and then ignored a truly remarkable natural sight for the next few hundreds of yards while they drove past thousands of the birds. As they approached the entrance to 24 Brigade, the Admiral spoke for the first time.

"Take me to the Command Workshop REME, if you know where that is."

"I do, sir, it's back in Aden, in fact Khormaksar, where we have just come from." The Admiral looked at Jack for interminable seconds and then said, "Take me there, then."

Not a word was said between them for the whole journey, but Jack did smile for most of it. Jack was left to wait while the Admiral entered the Command Workshops. Fortunately, there was a char wallah with his char trolley from whom Jack was able to purchase three glasses of char while waiting. Eventually, the Admiral appeared after about an hour and a half, took a list out of his pocket and said, "Take me to 1st Queens Dragoon Guards, please." The please caused Jack to pause. Was this indicating a truce? Jack was about to drive off when his mantra, do something, do nothing reached out to him.

"Sir, they are out at Falaise Camp in Little Aden where we have just come from. May I respectfully look at your list and point out the best routing with the least travelling?" Saying nothing, the Admiral handed him the list. "The Independent Armoured Brigade Workshop REME are at Bir Fukum and as the road is all soft sand, we cannot get there in this vehicle. I can get an anti-mine armoured Land Rover for the trip tomorrow morning, but we would need an escort as the route is frequently ambushed and one vehicle on its own would be easy meat. The Radar Troop 1st Regiment Royal Horse Artillery are at Dhala, about 70 miles away, and all sand roads with ambushes. If you are hoping to see the Green Archer Radar in operation, I think I should tell you that when it was being towed up-country the day before yesterday, it was blown up on a mine and severely damaged.

The 2nd Coldstream are in Salerno Lines in Little Aden. As I said, the Queen's Dragoon Guards are out at Little Aden as well. The 5th Inniskillings are out there too..." The Admiral took the list from him and went back into the Command Workshops.

When he returned, he handed the list to Jack, and Jack saw that the locations had been numbered such that the minimum of travel between them had been sorted out.

"Take me to the main Officers' Mess at 24 Brigade and we will start with their units in the morning." Jack drove him there. He had no idea where he, himself, could sleep that night so he ended up going to the Guardroom and begging a bed there for the night. He had thus been in the nick twice that day and neither of the occasions did he enjoy it.

The rest of the time went reasonably quickly, although somewhat unpleasantly. The Admiral made no attempt to have Jack looked after and left him to his own devices for meals, drinks and a bed to sleep. One of the units, the 5th Inniskilling Dragoon Guards, looked after him with their Colonel telling the Squadron Sergeant Major to arrange a bed for him—he didn't know that he was to end up in another prison cell with two of their soldiers in a few weeks' time.

At the airport, the Admiral turned to Jack and said, "Thank you for looking after me. I did not look after you deliberately to see how you would manage. I need a driver with his wits about him and an ability to look after himself if necessary. You passed with flying colours, and I liked your courage as a Lance Corporal to correct my programme and save me wasting both our times. The reason for me speaking is that I would like you to become my driver when I return to Aden as the GOC in C. It will mean three stripes and a bit better car than the heap we have been travelling in. What do you say?"

Jack wanted to say, my Hillman Husky is not a heap, it's a match for an Alfa Romeo any time, but found himself saying, "I appreciate the explanation, sir, but I shall be tour expired fairly soon and I will be getting married when I return to the UK so there is no chance of me extending my tour."

The Admiral looked at him, "All the arrangements and that made?"

"Yes, sir."

"No chance of changing that little lot then?"

"No, sir."

"I understand," and at that, he shook Jack's hand and walked into the airport. Jack did see him again when he returned to Aden to officially take command shortly before Jack left to return home but that is for later.

# Chapter 83

One day, Jack was told to prepare to demonstrate the detector and intruder warning device for a visitation of Air Force personnel. He set out the four geophones on the waste ground at the back of the HQ, utilising as many features as possible to demonstrate how setting the geophones out carefully could tell the operator where the intruders were in the landscape. The area was quite small so could not compare with the perimeter of an airfield, but it could show very well how the airfield buildings could be protected.

Major Scagg called out from his office that they are here, and Jack was sent to the entrance to the HQ to bring the group around to the wooden hut at the back where G Tech was situated. Jack wasn't too familiar with senior officer badging in the RAF. He knew that a single, thin, stripe around the sleeve was a Pilot Officer, that a Flight Lieutenant, equivalent to a Captain in the Army, had two thicker bands but after that, he was lost. This lot had so many fat bands that they needed careful watching and a lot of 'sirs'. There was one Pilot Officer, and it rapidly became apparent that he was everyone else's gopher. It was also obvious that he saw Jack as so junior that he was going to be the group's gopher. Jack had already had trouble with one PO and he wondered if this one knew about the 'I'll blow your bleedin' 'ead off, sir.'

They had a number of security checks to pass through, and the PO kept rushing ahead to demand to pass through the gates but the MPs who guarded the gates were singularly unimpressed by a PO and only reacted once Jack produced the security pass. Arriving at the G Tech offices, the RAF senior ranks went first through the door with the PO penultimate who turned to Jack as he was about to follow them in and said, "There's no need for you now, Lance Corporal," and proceeded to shut the door in Jack's face. Before it was totally closed, Jack caught a glimpse of Major Skaggs's face and with a grin on his face, he winked at Jack.

Jack returned to his desk and sat down to listen to what was being said through the wall. After the introductions Major Scagg then said, to the PO, "I cannot explain the finer working points of this piece of kit but the Lance Corporal, who you shut out of the office, can; in fact he's the only man in the Command who can. I wonder if you would ask him to come in and not order my staff about in the future."

Hearing this, Jack picked up the telephone and said, "G Tech Lance Corporal Hughes speaking, sir." He then proceeded to carry on a conversation with, he put his hand over the mouthpiece of the phone and whispered to the PO, "It's the BGS, sir." The PO obviously didn't have the balls to interrupt the BGS, so Jack carried on the mythical conversation for as long as he could with a multiplicity of Yes, sirs, and No, sirs until he rang off. He said, cheerily to the PO, "Sorry about that, sir, but the phone rang and of course I answered it; if I had been in with you, as I should have been, then the phone would have been answered by Private Whaleman here."

Entering the office, Jack said, "The BGS sends his apologies, sir, but he cannot now attend and wishes me to go ahead with the demonstration anyway." Major Scagg was quick enough on the uptake to keep a straight face as he knew the BGS wasn't coming, having been told the day before.

"Right, Corporal Hughes, what have you to show us?"

Jack proceeded to give a concise explanation of how the kit worked and what the various switches did. Having done that and answered various questions on the way, he said, "I have set-out a practical demonstration outside if you would like to follow me." Jack picked up the control box and made his way outside to the back of the hut. There, balanced on a small table, were four cable ends. Jack pointed roughly to where the geophones were buried and explained that, because of the limitations of the site, they were only 30 to 40 yards away. They could, if necessary, be hundreds of yards away and he explained the advantages and disadvantages of that. For the purposes of the demonstration, he asked them to believe that one cable had been run out to a perimeter fence of the airfield at a point where a track came out of a small wood. He pointed out that they could have had heavy weapons zeroed at that site, but it would be better to let them come much closer where accuracy would be better and where there was a chance of capturing them, if that was an option they wished to pursue. At any rate, it would be their kit and they could lay it out any way that suited them.

He, facing them, said, "I would now like a volunteer to walk over to that gateway and walk around." It was, of course, obvious who the volunteer would be because, unfortunately for him, Jack was the equipment operator and couldn't be the volunteer. So, casually, he walked over to the gateway and started walking around. The table had been set up under the eaves at the back of the hut and was consequently in the shade. The gateway wasn't, and it was therefore very hot in the open. Jack showed how the footsteps registered as a flick on the number one needle in the gauges and he passed around the earphones so that each officer could hear the crunching sound the footsteps made. Because this took some time, Jack had to keep calling out to the PO to keep walking around and to try to do it on tiptoe or by treading heavily. Each step registered clearly on the needle and the earphones.

Once they had all had a listen, Jack called out for the PO to run towards a dustbin about 30 yards away and he had him do it time and again so that the group could hear the difference in the sound of the steps. Enjoying himself, Jack had him walk over to a small wall and bank and had him stepping off of it so that the loud thump could clearly be heard. Jack pointed out that it was possible to pinpoint clearly where someone was jumping down from a feature in the landscape. So that everyone could hear, Jack had the poor sod of a PO, who was by now really hot and bothered, climbing up and jumping down four or five times.

"Now finally, sir, I would like you to go over to where the fence is and start crawling up to it as though you were trying to creep up on a sentry."

The RAF boss man, probably a Wing Commander, interrupted at that point and said, "Oh I think you have demonstrated well enough that the crawling sounds would be clearly picked up and save Mr Sweetcorn more of the considerable stress he appears to be suffering. Perhaps you could arrange for a cold drink for him, Corporal Hughes." Jack gestured to Khaki, who had been hiding by the corner of the hut who then appeared pushing his chai trolley to the group. Major Scagg was delighted, as was PO Sweetcorn, although only for the drink. Jack was a bit sorry he hadn't got the PO crawling around to start with, but you can't have everything in this world.

# Chapter 84

Jack was to have two more adventures with the detector and intruder warning device. He was sent back to the Company position at Cap Badge in the Dhala route Wadi because the nuisance shooting at the position in the night had developed into something much more serious and damaging. Besides the rifles, the insurgents were now using Rocket-Propelled Grenades (RPGs) and machine guns, including one which had been identified as an old Vicars Medium Machine Gun—old or not, it was able to pour a huge number of rounds into the position without the position it was being fired from being easily identified so that return fire was proving to be pretty ineffective.

This time, Jack had to travel by road convoy, taking the best part of four hot, sweaty, dusty and rough hours. He spent most of the rest of the day trying, with the commanding Major's assistance, to pin down the rough areas the shooting was coming from, with, it must be said, little real success.

Some fighting patrols had been sent out following previous incidents with little to show for it. Jack asked if a patrol could be set up for the following morning so that he could more closely examine the ground, it being very difficult to spy out the lay of the land on top of the wadi walls from the bottom of the wadi. Arrangements were made for this, and Jack hoped that it would be a quiet night. It wasn't. Incoming fire started at 0100 hrs and continued for the best part of 20 minutes. Even with the powerful binoculars he had been issued, it was difficult to spot where the fire was coming from when it was something like 7-800 yards away. A machine gun was certainly being used, easy to be identified by the rhythmic sound of the bullets hitting the position. Distance helped the Brits in this respect as it was impossible for the insurgents to know where their rounds were striking. It was not known quite why they didn't use tracer rounds. Was it as simple as they didn't have any or were they shrewd enough to know that whilst tracer rounds showed the firer where the bullets were going, they also showed the targeted troops from where they were coming. Either way, they weren't firing any so no help there.

Several soldiers did catch the flash of two RPG rounds that were fired at them. Jack thought it was ironic that a captured RPG 2 had been brought into the office for identification a few weeks before. Now they knew that there were at least two of them in Aden. The RPG 1 had been a bit of a failure, but the RPG 2 was reputed to be much better. The maximum range was about 200 yards, with effective accurate range being half that.

The rockets fell well short of their position; even with the advantage of being fired from the top of the wadi walls, they were falling a good 400 yards short. Presumably, the insurgents could see the detonations and would see that they would have to come a lot closer to hit the position. They could easily do this in the dark; it just needed someone to think of it. Jack just hoped that would happen after he had gone!

Jack had a long conversation with the OC. It was clear that they would have to mount a patrol which would have to climb the wadi wall at the point where there was a small path up and down it—the point they had shot at when Jack had been there the last time. They would then have to scout the edge of the cliff edges both to the left and right of the path to see if they could identify any obvious firing positions, especially any with a helpful terrain like a small ledge the firers would have to jump down to approach it. Their second major problem was to see how they could run out and place the geophones when it got dark and how they could reclaim them before dawn—none of it easy in broken ground, high cliffs and the possibility of the enemy being around.

Climbing the path up the cliff, about 300 feet high, was physically demanding but not impossible. There were no signs of occupation at the top as there had been before – perhaps this was now a voodoo place where too many of their people had been killed. Jack had spent some time briefing the Sergeant who was to lead the team to the left on what to look for, not just evidence of a firing position but also the geographical features of the ground which might provide help in identifying the position of the firer. The geophones could, in ideal conditions, pick up footsteps a hundred yards away; fine to let you know they were in the area but not good enough to target precisely, that's where the surface of the ground came in.

Jack led off to the right. A narrow pathway led along the cliff edge. There were no obvious sites which had been used such as empty bullets cases; such cases were valuable as they could be reloaded so were normally picked up by the firer. The RPG rockets came in wooden boxes which were valuable to re-use as boxes or for firewood so there were no discarded piles to indicate firing positions. All there was were areas of scuffed ground which could have been caused by men or goats lying down. The Army position was in view for almost all of the 800 yards each patrol covered; there was no point traversing further as they would be outside the range of most of the insurgents' weapons. Some of the Lee Enfields they had were sighted to 2000 yards, i.e. over a mile, but no one fired at those ranges as the chance of hitting someone, even the entire camp, was so remote as to be totally unlikely.

When they returned and gathered to discuss their findings, it was to find that both patrols had had the same experience with no concrete firing points having been identified. Given the rough nature of the ground, it had not even been possible to identify a jumping point with any certainty. The path up and down the wadi was the only absolute certainty with two others being strong possibilities. The positions of these two had been indicated to the camp by Jack and the Sergeant stopping, taking off their hats and wiping their brow as an indicator that here was a good point. The camp had been watching through binoculars and had set down the range and bearing to that point.

The other problem for them was how to reel out cables to those three points and to recover them in the morning before dawn. The distance was huge, at least 800 yards for each cable and with the ground being as rough as it was, almost vertical for the last 20 yards or so, Jack just did not think they could do it. Jack then experienced a eureka moment that was to come to him on a few occasions in his life. They did not have to run out 800 yards if they set their operating position up only a hundred yards or so from the base of the cliffs. That way, the task of laying the cables would be so much less that it was eminently doable. With troops stationed at intervals as the cable was reeled out, they would be able to help 'grab it in' on reclamation—winding it around and around a drum would take far too long to recover and leaving the cable in place simply invited it to be stolen. Burying it for the whole distance in the hope it would not be discovered was a task that could only be carried out in daylight and therefore, an invitation for the locals to investigate what we had been doing. Such an investigation would reveal the cable in no time at all and, even if they could not exactly determine what it did, they'd steal it just for its value even if they did not work out what it was for.

Virtually, the entire Company was involved in the exercise, either reeling out cable, providing fighting patrols or guarding the camp. Jack set up his operating position about 100 yards back from the path up the wadi wall, and about 50 yards off to the side, with one cable run out to the side of the path with the last 20 yards shallowly buried to the side of the path by just scuffing over it and the two other cables run up to the possible stumbling points. Jack decided not to use the fourth cable as the effort to run it out and then recover it when they did not have a good position for it was using too much resource when they were not plentifully supplied with troops anyway was just not worth it.

As per Sod's Law, nothing happened that night. Whether their patrolling the day before had frightened them off or what, they did not know, but Jack did know just how pissed off he felt. Still, he and the troops did learn from the exercise so that the second night went a lot more smoothly. Again nothing. Jack was sure that what they were doing was not known to the enemy; but they were very sensitive to changes in the Brit troop's activities; they had, for example, been sleeping in the day for the last two days and normally they would sleep at night and patrol during the day.

With some misgivings at what he was about to suggest, Jack approached the OC.

"Sir, is it possible because…" and Jack set out his theory. "I am reluctant to ask but can we get the troops working during the day so that the insurgents think there is no night time activity going on and then put the kit out for one last time tonight? I know I won't be popular but I will be gone tomorrow on the convoy, so the blame can come with me."

"Oh, the blame can go with you anyway," said the OC with a big smile. He thought about it for a moment and then said, "A night's lost sleep is not the end of the world; that will happen anyway if the buggers shoot at us, and I think there might be something in what you say about them watching us and our pattern of working. They obviously do watch us, but it hadn't occurred to me that we might be signalling our actions in that way—that's useful for the future, anyway. Yes, we'll give it a try."

So they did and at 0130 hours, Jack saw the dial covering the top of the path up and down the wadi wall started to flick. Switching to the earphones, Jack could hear numerous faint footsteps. He spoke to the signaller accompanying him and said, "Warning Site 2." The three Sites had been numbered 1, 2, and 3 from the left. The warning passed, Jack knew that the guns of the Saladins, their machine guns, the GPMGs of the entire Company, the 3-inch mortar and the Wombat anti-tank gun would all be aimed at Site 2 awaiting his order to fire.

The crunch of the footsteps were getting louder but Jack had to wait until bullets from that position were fired at the camp—he couldn't just fire at someone walking in the dark for a slash and ending up getting his dick and everything else blown off. Jack could hear a mix of sounds, difficult to identify precisely but they could be people lying down and getting comfortable to fire. Jack suddenly saw the needle for Site 3 was flicking. Switching to that geophone, he could hear multiple feet seemingly hurrying; they were still faint but if they were supposed to be opening fire at the same time as Site 2 and they were late, that would explain the hurrying. Switching to Site 1 he could see no activity on the needle nor could he hear any sounds whatsoever. Speaking to the Signaller he said, "Send 'Activity at Site 3 as well divide fire between sites two and three.'" In the planning, they had discussed multi-site firing and how the firepower would be divided up. By the time the message had been sent and acknowledged, the activity at Site 3 had settled down to fussing around rather than fast walking.

"Send, 'believe fire on your position imminent.'" Before the message had been acknowledged, all hell let loose.

As soon as shots were fired at the camp, the camp returned fire at the two predetermined sites. The firing from the wadi top stopped almost instantly but the OC let the return fire go on for two or three minutes longer before ordering cease fire. No more fire was returned that night. Jack and his team went out, protected by a fighting patrol, to recover the cables just before first light and once it was light, two patrols were sent out to inspect the three sites. Nothing of any indisputable evidence could be found to indicate the presence of the insurgents at the two sites but the geophone at Site 2 had been smashed and severed from its cable indicating, if nothing else, that the fire had been accurate in hitting it.

The OC Cap Badge attempted to persuade Jack to leave the warning device with them for a few more days but as Jack was due at another site in two days' time, he couldn't leave it; he wouldn't have left it anyway since he had been in the Army long enough to know that it was highly unlikely that he would ever have seen it again.

No further insurgent attacks took place for another week and then only one brief firefight took place. Gradually, they increased in intensity as the positions were not immediately subjected to accurate return fire. Probably the insurgents had not been able to determine how they were being shot at initially, but they were able to tell when they were not. As the Army was to pull out, it served the higher command's interests that the insurgents should not get the opportunity to determine how it had been done but the fact that the poor bloody squaddies were being shot at again and losing their sleep did not register at all in Steamer Point—they couldn't even hear the firing from there.

# Chapter 85

Jack's final outing with the warning kit was to South Africa. Major Scagg was booked to go but at the last minute, Jack saw himself boarding an RAF flight in Khormaksar whilst Major Scagg boarded a brand-new BOAC VC 10 on his way to an urgent meeting at the MOD in London. Jack, however, was on his way to South Africa by way of just about everywhere else on an RAF flight that flew a route stopping in many places in Kenya, Tanzania, Mozambique and finally South Africa, he thought! He had not been allowed to disembark from the Argosy even to stretch his legs just by the steps from the plane. At each stop, various people disembarked or embarked, all of whom were extremely taciturn, unwilling to respond to any overtures from Jack. He could only suppose that they were from an outfit like the SAS, who wandered around the HQ in Steamer Point incognito. They were so incognito, not wearing berets or hats of any kind, with no regimental badges displayed or even rank that it had to be the SAS as they were the only ones who dressed or perhaps more accurately undressed like that.

Arriving at a dirt strip bulldozed out of the bush, Jack was told he had the time it would take them manually to refuel the plane for him to complete his business.

Fortunately, the detector kit was not complicated to operate, and it was only a matter of minutes for the Corporals, two of them, to pick it up. They were from a Platoon of the Lancaster Regiment who were guarding a radio station broadcasting the BBC into Rhodesia. They were only a couple of hundred yards from the border and over the border, about the same distance was a Rhodesian Brigade, a brigade against a platoon was not a serious battle if it all went ape!

They had been experiencing nuisance raids from the Rhodesians where kit was being pinched or damaged or insulting messages left in their camp. With the bush being quite thick and the area to be guarded quite big for just a Platoon, life was difficult and unpleasant and with the advantage lying with the aggressor in that they could attack whenever they wanted stopping or catching them was impossible. The Rhodesians were very experienced in the bush whereas the Lancs were not.

Jack was very careful not to physically do anything that might arouse any watching Rhodesians' curiosity but with the two Corporals, they identified where the best places would be to place the geophones after it got dark. In addition, Jack had another gift for them. He brought with him the first Night Sight Scope for trial which could see in the dark. It did so by multiplying existing light up and down a tube until a picture could be seen. Looking through the scope, it was possible to see in almost pitch dark. It showed a blueish screen, later versions were to be green, but this was the first one for trial which had been received. Unlike infra-red night lights which required an infra-red light source to he used and which could therefore be seen by any one equipped with infra-red viewers, the Phillips one Jack had brought with him was completely undetectable but it could see in the dark!

Jack was under orders to leave the kit with the Lancs which was to be returned later. Jack did receive the reports on the use of the two pieces of kit to type and very much enjoyed doing so. The very first night, one of the geophones picked up feet and examination of the area with the night sight showed three men approaching their site. Forewarned is forearmed, and the Lancaster's fighting patrol was easily able to scoop them up.

There was then the problem of what to do with them. Officially they had crossed the border illegally into South Africa and should have been handed over to their Customs and Border regime. However, the Lancasters were not officially in South Africa and their 'arrest' of the Rhodesians could prove diplomatically sensitive. The three men were handcuffed and placed in the largest tent so that they could not be seen by the Rhodesians who were well able to scan the Lanc's site with binoculars.

No instructions were received during the day to say what should happen to them. That night, the Rhodesians sent another patrol of three men from a different direction and again, they were easily scooped up. The third night they tried again, this time approaching from behind the Lancs position, but a geophone had been placed that side as 'a just in case' scenario and this time, the single soldier was simply grabbed. Their tent was now starting to get a bit full and they were running out of handcuffs, so it was fortunate that instructions arrived to release them back across the border with a note to say next time we'll start shooting.

The Captain in command, with a strong patrol to escort the prisoners, stopped them about 30 yards from the border, it wasn't exactly marked in the bush, and called out to the Rhodesians. Eventually, an officer appeared but the distance was just a bit too far to make out his rank as he, too was about 30 yards back from his side of the border. The Captain called out, "It should be obvious that none of your troops are good enough to come up against my men. This time we are going to release them back to you, sans weapons, with a warning that we have had enough of your little games and the next time someone approaches in the dark, they will be shot." At that, the seven sheepish soldiers were released.

The following day, a flag on a pole appeared on the border line. Examination through binoculars showed that there were a couple of cardboard boxes at the base of it. One of the Lancs went forward and retrieved the boxes which, on examination, were shown to contain fresh fruit of all kinds—something the Lancs were missing with their boxes of compo rations being their only supplied food. Attached to the box was a single word, 'Thanks'. Jack enjoyed reading the report and couldn't help feeling a measure of delight at the success of his training.

# Chapter 86

Jack received notice of posting to SHAPE which stood for Supreme Headquarters Allied Powers Europe and they were based in Paris. Not only was this a top-dog posting but he was going to Paris on his honeymoon, staying with an 'aunt' of his mum, who was married to one of France's leading architects, and Jack was sure he would be able to find a little flat for him and Janet. He wrote straight away to Janet with the good news. The next day, the French government, under the auspices of the Brit hating De Gaulle ordered that the SHAPE HQ be shut down and all NATO troops were ordered out of France.

Watching this happen in day-old newspapers was horrifying for Jack. Especially when he read that Mons in Belgium was to be the new base for SHAPE; he did not want to go there; it was known to be a thoroughly depressing town with inhabitants well suited to the place. Who would want to go there when Paris had been the alternative? It would turn out to be difficult to criticise De Gaulle as his 'uncle' loved the man. It was therefore no surprise when he received a posting order a week or two later, but it wasn't to SHAPE; it was to G Air in HQ 1BR Corps in Bielefeld in Germany, the command HQ of the British Army of the Rhine (BAOR).

Jack felt that was probably even worse; at least the Belgians were reasonably friendly towards the Brits, the Germans weren't. Reports in the papers and on the BBC said the Germans welcomed being saved from the Nazis—in Jack's experience, he was to find the opposite was true. A few days after that, a notice appeared on Part I Orders that volunteers were invited for the Army Air Corps (AAC) which was to be considerably expanded and needed many more helicopter pilots; helicopters were flown generally by NCOs and fixed wing aeroplanes by officers, probably so they could play at Spitfire pilots. Three stripes would be awarded to all those successfully passing the course and rank, or lack of it, was not a factor affecting those who could volunteer. *That's it*, thought Jack, *I fancy that*. The training would be at the AAC site at Middle Wallop, so he would be in the UK not bloody Germany. Applications were to be submitted on the application form shown in a manual used by every department in the Army; all Jack had to do was type out the form and then fill it in. It would have to be approved by the signature of one of the Majors, or possibly the Lt Col SD/Tech. Jack was fairly certain he could get it signed by the BGS or even the GOC in C if he went about it the right way! But that was for the future, first he had to type up and fill in the form. The lead time for submittance was months away, so he had plenty of time. He did not want anyone to know that he was about to apply to become a pilot until the form was fully completed and ready for signature, so he had to type the form during times when no one could look over his shoulder and spot it.

He had no sooner started on the form, he had only typed the first line heading, when Capt Robertson sent for him.

"I've not got good news I'm afraid, Corporal Hughes. I submitted a request for your acting rank to be confirmed, and it has been refused. Apparently, although you are certainly excused Army education, Map Reading isn't included, so you cannot become substantive until you have at least a 3rd class pass. Even worse news is that there will not be any further map reading courses run in this command because of the pull out." Jack stood there stunned, not because his rank could not be confirmed, but because he had to have a 1st class pass to be accepted for the pilot training. Robertson continued, "If only I'd known sooner, you could have been placed on the course which takes its exams tomorrow." Jack's ears pricked up.

"Sir, can I ask a question?"

"Yes, of course you can."

"I have done a lot of map reading over the years; I've even taught it in the ACF and to recruits when I was in the POC Wing at Buller Barracks. Is there any way I could take the exam tomorrow—I'm sure I could pass?" Robertson looked at him for what appeared a century.

"The problem is, if I can pull some strings, call in some favours to arrange that and you do badly, then we are both in the shit." He looked at Jack for a few more minutes and then he got up and walked over to one of the filing cabinets, reached in and pulled out a folder and returned to his desk with it.

"Sit down at that desk over there,"—the one which Sylva had used, such is life! And he took a paper out of the folder. It was headed to be a 'Map Reading First Class Examination Paper'.

"You have one hour to answer all the questions. Read the paper through first and then answer the questions. Good luck."

Jack read it through. It was all straight forward and he felt he would have no trouble completing it apart from one question which involved calculating the steepness of hills, up and down, and whether 3 tonners could ascend/descend them safely. Information was provided about the capabilities of the lorries; it was the slope angles that had to be calculated and that was really only a question of simple maths.

Jack finished the exam in 45 minutes and handed the paper to Capt Robertson. Robertson cast a quick eye over it and then said, "Leave it with me, I'll mark it later and let you know." Jack was a bundle of nerves for the rest of the morning. To make it worse, Robertson disappeared just before 1300 hrs and didn't return until the following morning. Jack was expecting to be called and told where to attend the exam. As time passed, he became more and more worried. Eventually he could wait no longer, and he knocked on Robertson's door and entered.

"Yes," said Robertson.

"Sir, am I going to be allowed to take the exam?"

"No, Corporal Hughes, you are not."

Jack's face must have been a picture because Robertson, who had intended to prolong the agony a little further, started laughing and said, "Congratulations, you scored 98% and passed."

"I don't understand, sir."

"No, Corporal Hughes, I don't suppose you do. The paper you completed yesterday was in fact the exam paper for today, and, as I said, you scored 98%

which is so remarkable, given you have received no tuition and just sat down and did it, that I took it over to the RAEC centre, explained the situation there and the Lt Col in command kept the paper and notice of your score and the pass will be published in due course."

Jack was delighted but there was further bad news to come about his rank being confirmed, but he wasn't to find that out for a while.

# Chapter 87

The week before Jack was due to return to the UK, he was given two pieces of work which were to prove the most awful of his life—they were to affect him with occasional nightmares for the rest of his life. Both Majors were called on to conduct enquiries into two separate incidents. The first involved producing a report into the torturing and death of a pregnant Arab woman accused of being a spy for the British and the second was an enquiry into the death of a Guardsman.

Major Walliams produced the pregnant spy report; quite why he was ordered to do it and not POMEC or the Intelligence Section of the Military Police, Jack never did discover. The woman had been tortured in the most abominable manner, her abdomen sliced open and the foetus destroyed before her eyes. Despite the most horrendous torture, she had been unable to answer any of their questions because she was not a spy for the British and, therefore, had no worthwhile knowledge. The physical description of what had been done to her and the colour photographs accompanying the report were simply shocking. That one human being could treat another, especially one who was pregnant, was unbelievable. Torture by the NLF was routine; by the British, it was not.

The insurgents often spread stories of torture by the British such that Dennis Healey, at the time Minister of Defence and gullibility personified, had flown out to Aden to meet a delegation of Arabs concerned about this alleged behaviour by the British. That the concerned Arabs were mouthpieces of the insurgents was obvious to everyone except, of course, Healey who took it all in as gospel. Jack had been at Khormaksar meeting visitors travelling on the same flight as Healey, so he knew from his own knowledge that Healey had only met the delegation, had refreshments and returned to the UK on the same plane so that his later statement that he had conducted a thorough enquiry rang hollow in Jack's and every serviceman's mind. The troops, better than anyone, knew that there had been no torture of captured insurgents, they knew how quickly they would have been thrown to the wolves if they did, especially by the Socialist politicians who were totally despised by all the servicemen who had been sent on to the streets unarmed by those same loathsome Labour politicians. It was to be a couple of years before he was to discover that the Tories were just as murderous.

The report wasn't terribly long but the details and the photos were to give Jack the heebie-jeebies for the rest of his life. The second investigation, by Major Scagg, involved the death of a Guardsman.

The Guardsman concerned had been one of a team operating a Wombat Anti-Tank Gun. In fact, the gun was more properly called a Conbat Anti-Tank Gun. It was a more modern version of the Wombat (and Mobat) because it had been fitted with a .5-inch spotting rifle to aid ranging. Being a recoilless rifle, when it fired, half the force drove the shell out of the tube and half was ejected out of the back, causing an enormous cloud of dirt and smoke to fly up into the air. This made the weapon very vulnerable because it could be easily spotted after it had fired only one round. The blast could also seriously injure or kill anyone immediately within its blast zone. Consequently, the crews needed to achieve a first-round kill; if they didn't, the tank at which they were firing would kill them. Unfortunately, unless they had got the range and the point of aim exactly right, their life expectancy on the battlefield was very short, it being particularly difficult to get the range right when the enemy tank was a long way away and moving. An attempt to correct this problem had been made to help range finding by the fitting of a spotting rifle—a half an inch in diameter round, carrying a tracer tail and a small explosive head giving of a cloud of white smoke when it hit. Firing bursts of three rounds with adjustments to range, if necessary, meant that ranges could be accurately calculated before a tank could spot them and fire at them. Leastways, that was the theory. They would still leave a heavy smoke signature as to where they were for the second tank to find them, but no one talked too much about this. Just coming out was a laser range finder but its trial in Aden had been cancelled so whether it was better than the spotting rifle was unknown, and it still left the problem of the smoke when the weapon fired!

The crews of three had all been trained during their training never to stand behind the recoilless rifle when it was firing. Not to stand in the front of the weapon was so obvious that no training had been attached to it. And this was where the problem arose. A team were wheeling the gun, on its two wheels, from the back of the Land Rover by which it had been towed, to the areas designated for cleaning the weapons. Arriving at the cleaning area, one of the team took up the firing position and pretended to fire. One of the Guardsmen was pushing the gun by the muzzle. Instead of there being just a dull click, there was the sound and judder of three rounds being fired by the spotting rifle. The Guardsman stood no chance and the three rounds blew a large hole straight through him. Not content with that, the rounds flew on and wounded two more Guardsmen in the Coy Office.

Major Scagg led a team of three officers investigating the death and wounding, the circumstances how it had come about, lessons and training to be learned and whether disciplinary action should be taken against anyone involved. Jack's job was to take notes of what each witness said, had to search out all the various training manuals and directions and type up the marked bits by Scagg, the final report written by Scagg and from the two junior officers' notes.

The photographs accompanying the report were just as horrendous, albeit in a distinctly different way from the 'spy' report and they, too, were to bother Jack for many years. It also bothered Jack that none of the blame landed on the Guards' Lt Colonel's desk; after all, didn't the buck stop there? Instead, most of it landed on the dead Guardsman—he couldn't complain, could he.

# Chapter 88

Two days before he was due to leave, Jack was told the BGS wanted him. Jack knew he wasn't in trouble, so he entered the office in a comfortable mode. Motioning him over, the BGS pointed to a piece of paper on the front of his desk and said, "Sign that." Jack picked the paper up and started to read it. "I said sign it, not read it." Jack had read enough to be shocked. It was a recommendation that he, Jack, be considered for Officer Cadet training.

He started to stammer, "Sir, if what I know is right, as soon as that form is signed I come, potentially, under the orders of the Commandant at Mons or Sandhurst…"

"Mons," said the Brigadier.

"And I would need to seek his permission to get married next week." Just at that moment, the GOC in G walked into the room.

"Well, has he signed it?" Jack's heart sank still further. Here he was, being recommended for a commission by, he was to discover later, two Majors, a Lt Col, a Brigadier and a full Admiral. And he was refusing an instruction. Fortunately, the Admiral was not an Admiral for nothing.

"What date are you getting married?"

"The 12th of November, sir." Picking up the form, the Admiral signed it and dated it the 13th November.

"Now sign the bloody form."

"Aye aye, sir," said Jack.

"And good luck to you at Mons and in your marriage, you won't find doing those two things together very easy, but they will be easier than driving an incognito Admiral."

Moments later, Jack was standing in front of his two Majors and stammering his thanks. This recommendation had come totally out of the blue. He hadn't noticed initially that Mrs Scagg was sitting in the office. She, too, congratulated Jack and handed him a paper-wrapped parcel.

"We all wish you a long and happy marriage, and this is a small token of our appreciation. You mustn't open it before the wedding but just in case Customs are awkward, it's a carving tray and carving knife and fork." And at that, she gave Jack another smacker on the lips. *I could grow to like this,* thought Jack, but he was wise enough just to thank them all.

Jack did not know what to do with the Application form to be a pilot in the AAC. Truth be told he probably preferred that now to a commission. Then he thought, why not both? He did not think it would be politic to ask either of the Majors, or indeed, any of the ones above them who had signed the recommendation for the commission. He puzzled on this for a while until Capt Robertson asked him to come to his office. It was only an admin issue to do with the closing down of the office when the Army pulled out of Aden. During the conversation, Robertson let out that he would be staying to the end. Jack thought, that's funny, Robertson was in Aden when Jack arrived, so his two years should have been up by now, and he should be winging his way somewhere else. So Jack asked, "Sir, if I may, how come you are still here in Aden, shouldn't you have been posted, the closure isn't for another three months or so, so how come you are still here?" Robertson looked at him and smiled.

"Here you are, Corporal Hughes, at the start of your Army career and now with a recommendation for a commission. And here am I, at the end of mine. My termination date for time served in the Army is just a few days after we pull out. It seemed a bit pointless to me to be posted somewhere else just for few day, not long enough to settle in and be useful whereas staying on here, I have a lot to contribute so I spoke to the mighty ones and they agreed, so I will see my time out here and then return to the UK for demob." Jack looked at him and thought, *I will almost certainly know within three months whether I have passed the RCB or not. If I haven't, I can then submit the application, it would still be in time, and that would be fine.* So he explained the situation to Robertson and asked him if he could leave the application form with him to sign and forward in the event that he failed the RCB. Robertson agreed immediately, he said, "Quite honestly, Corporal Hughes, I couldn't really see you in G Air at 1BR Corps so it surprises me not at all that you should go for the AAC, but remember, a commission somewhere, is always going to be better than a failed pilot somewhere else." And at that they parted never to meet again.

There was one more incident to amuse Jack before he left. He had been making his way around on the first floor of the main building of the HQ when he heard shots being fired from one of the offices up on the top floor. The air conditioners were being cleaned; this happened every week because the air filters became clogged. About three feet square, they looked like sheets of metal filled with holes. To remove them from the front of the air conditioners involved undoing lots of little catches. Apparently the GSO1 Ops became impatient with the time the Arab cleaning it was taking and started having a go at him to hurry up. The Arab attached the filter to the front of the air conditioner as quickly as he could but as he was standing on a ladder, working something like eight feet in the air, it wasn't easy as one hand was needed to hold on to the ladder and two were needed for the filter—a problem for most people. Eventually, the job was done, and the Arab left the office, slamming the door as he did so. Consequently, the front fell off the air conditioner and hit the Colonel on the head. Dazed for a moment, the Colonel seized his Colt .45 revolver from the drawer of his desk and set off in search for the air conditioner guy. Spying him from the veranda of his office, the Colonel let fly with all six shots. All missed. The Arab took off as fast as he could, which was pretty fast as bullets were being fired at him, and the Colonel was rushing to reload when the Brigadier came in and 'had a quiet word' with the Colonel who was taken off to the sick bay to have a cut on his scalp seen to and the Arab was never seen again. Jack hoped that Colonels in 1BR Corps did not have loaded revolvers in their desk drawers. What a way to finish a posting.

Parting in a Corps was always different to parting in a Regiment—a Regiment was a family that you joined on joining the Army and you stayed with it for the whole of your Army service, barring the odd secondment, but you always returned.

In a Corps, you were posted to a unit and at the end of your posting you moved to another unit within the Corps so the attachment to one posting or another never really had any force to it, unlike in a Regiment. But Jack did leave Aden with a sense of sadness, he had done a lot of growing up there and had created a bit of name for himself which he hoped would prove of use in the future. However strong the regret at leaving was, the future prospects seemed stronger.

He checked in at Khormaksar, an airport he had visited so often, and it felt a bit peculiar leaving himself rather than meeting or saying goodbye to visitors. He had flown out to Aden in a Britannia, the Whispering Giant, in just over 12 hours. Going back, he flew in a VC10 in just over five hours—things were definitely improving.

# Chapter 89

His time on leave just flew by. All the preparations for the wedding to be checked and cleared, confirming the setting up of a joint bank account, something so rare that the bank had to ask Head Office how to do it, collecting the posh suit, shirt and tie for the wedding itself, paying for the flight tickets to Paris and obtaining francs to the value of fifty pounds each—the limit the Government allowed—and what seemed like a million and one things of no importance whatsoever. He had to do a lot of placating of his mother who only one day before the wedding was still trying to add distant relatives, of whom Jack had never heard, to the list. Jack and Janet were paying for the wedding themselves, Janet's parents being in no position to pay for anything. Because it was the bride's parents' job to pay, Jack's parents were off the hook although they did pay for the wedding meal and the hire of the Working Men's Club of which they were members.

The day passed in a flash and everything went to plan. Jack got a little pissed off that his father had placed pennies in the hub caps of the wheels of his car and decorated it with 'Just Married' signs. Words had to be spoken to get them all removed as Jack was a singularly private individual and drawing all that attention to themselves was definitely not on. The fact that the last flight out of Gatwick on the Saturday night was the cheapest and known as the 'Honeymoon Special'—the passengers most of them in pairs and obvious going away clothes—rather gave the game away, but, what the hell, by that time they were well away from anyone who knew them.

Collected at the airport by 'Aunty Lois' and Uncle Danny, they were treated to a fantastic honeymoon in what were still rather economically restrained times. Danny had been a Free French Pilot and had courted Lois in the last 18 months or so of the war. They had met regularly at Jack's parents' house, somewhat scandalously but allowed discreetly during the war. Lois was the sister of Meg who had gone into service with Jack's mum when they both were sent from home at the age of 14. This was their chance to return the favour and they did, indeed, provide an excellent time. Danny had become one of France's leading architects and was a very wealthy man. Jack was allowed to drive his Facel Vega 111 and even to take the controls of his light aeroplane for a short while. Danny was a leading light in the RAF Club and Jack was introduced as 'serving now'! Jack knew enough from the joint services command in Aden and the fact that the Army lads fed in the Airmen's Restaurant to head off any awkward questions when they were asked.

The honeymoon passed very quickly, and he was even shown a flat that Danny had picked out for them before De Gaulle threw a hissy fit at NATO. Jack had never had a high opinion of De Gaulle and had had to be very careful what he said about him as, to Danny, he was a hero and demi god, but he was able to express considerable disappointment that the flat was not to be. All too soon he was boarding a BAC 111 at Gatwick for Gutersloh.

# Chapter 90

There were a fair number of servicemen on the clapped-out Bedford coach driven by a mentally challenged RAF driver. For long distances, he drove on the wrong side of the road causing most aboard the coach to wonder if he knew they drove on the right in Germany. It was freezing cold and if the coach had any heating, it had long given up the ghost or the idiot driving did not know how to work it. Jack was glad he had elected to travel in uniform, SD uniform and even his Great Coat, and even then he was cold. The countryside was grey and dull except where there were patches of snow and to Jack, back from two years in the Middle East, it was thoroughly unpleasant. And, of course, Jack was the last to be dropped off.

It was to get worse. Jack had no sooner reported to the office and sirens started sounding everywhere. Jack had no idea what it was about, but people started scurrying about with voices shouting, 'Crash out get moving.' Jack was grabbed by a Corporal who announced that Jack would be working with him in G Air, pointed him at a Land Rover and told him to get in the back of that. Over the next 20 minutes or so, he was joined in the back by a Major, a Flight Lieutenant and the Corporal who sat in the driver's seat. None of them spoke. Last to appear was a Wing commander who handed the Corporal a piece of paper and said, "That's where we're going," and at that, the Corporal took off as though someone had lit a fire under his balls. He exceeded speed limits willy nilly. Jack thought, *what a pity the Provost is not here!* It took about 25 minutes to reach wherever it was in the back of beyond and then nothing happened. *Typical bloody Army*, thought Jack, *hurry up and wait*. There were other vehicles around them in the forest and more kept arriving by the minute. Once a large tent had been erected by Pioneers, the officers disappeared into it. Office type equipment arrived and was unloaded into the tent and set up.

The Corporal came over and sat in the back of the Land Rover with Jack. Introducing himself as Graham Plover, he explained that Jack would be working with him in G Air. What he had just experienced was a 'crash out'. Although HQ 1BR Corps was the commanding unit of the British Army in Germany and was normally based in Bielefeld, it had to be ready to disappear into the woods at a moment's notice so that it would not be an easy target for the Russian Air Force. The whole HQ had to be out of its headquarters and in position at a specified spot, different every crash out, ready to control the Army units under its command within one hour—this despite the fact that they were only a few minutes' flying time from the Russian bases. The extra time was allowed for an intelligence warning, the RAF stopping the incoming bombers and a huge element of hope.

Jack, although in uniform, was hopelessly wrongly dressed and whilst he had some combat kit in his suitcase and kitbag, there was nowhere near the amount of right stuff that he needed, and he was decidedly unhappy at the thought he would have to dig trenches etc. in his best uniform. A Great Coat and his SD uniform took up all the space in the Army-issue suitcase and kitbag so wearing those two items gave much more space for civvy clothes, wash bag and other necessary items of uniform—except for a crash out where he was decidedly in the wrong kit. Still, if he had travelled in civvies, he would have been in an even worse state since he would have been freezing his balls off; not that he wasn't bloody cold, the way he was dressed.

So he asked Plover how long these crash-outs lasted.

"Well, if it is for real we would probably be dead by now, so it is almost certainly a practice in which case it can be for a few minutes to a few days. As it's a Friday, and the brass are likely to want to get away for the weekend, it's likely that we will get the all clear pretty soon now." As he was speaking there was activity spreading through the site with vehicles being packed and moving off. Sure enough, the Major reappeared, followed by the Wing Co and the Flight Lieutenant and announced that the exercise was over. If anything, Corporal Plover drove even faster on the way back.

Once back, Plover took Jack to the QM's and told him to get settled in; they'd go through the official welcome stuff on Monday morning at 0830 hours and with that, he was gone. The QM's people were not too keen to be landed with the work for a new comer at 1600 hours on a Friday when they had been hoping to sidle off about 1615 hours. Still, Jack found himself handing in kit he had only just been issued with in the UK but the most important bit, as far as Jack was concerned, was that he was issued a bed space and all the bedding necessary.

The barracks were enormous, with the living quarters mixed in with the HQ admin blocks. The rumour was that they had been built just before the war for the SS and no expense had been spared in the building of them. Certainly, they were vastly better than any Brit barracks Jack had been in. Shaped pretty much like all barrack blocks, the accommodation ones were two stories tall with the ablution areas around the central stairwell. But best of all, they were centrally heated, something the Germans had started before the war and which the British Army were only just getting around to some 23 years later. Instead of being open rooms for 16 soldiers or so, they had been divided up into two-man rooms, and in Jack's case, he had the two-man room to himself. It deprived him a bit of companionship but it gave him peace and quiet and freedom from farts and gases—right on!

Feeding was in a typical cookhouse, but it was plentiful, hot and well cooked. Queuing in the queue for tea, he was greeted by a Lance Corporal he had known in Aden who offered to show him around that evening. Jack was happy to accompany him to the Junior NCO's club which was warm, welcoming and well run. Jack was to discover that there were many displaced persons (DPs) around the HQ who were waiting to be officially identified and issued with identity cards. Ever anxious to please and very fearful of upsetting someone in authority, they worked far harder than any of the NAAFI staff which was the only other place on camp providing pub-like facilities. Jack knew that he should not be there officially as he was pretty certain that he had lost his acting rank leaving Aden and no confirmation of this permanent promotion to Lance Corporal had come through. In fact, he was to officially lose his acting rank on the Part One Orders on Monday and the permanent rank never did catch him up as he kept moving units.

Still, he enjoyed that Friday night, but he did not enjoy much else in Germany. Going into any bar and ordering a beer, in German, normally resulted in a boorish response and an obvious hatred of the Brits. On Sunday morning, Jack witnessed an Oompah band coming up the road which was creating a militaristic response in all the German civilians it passed. Jack thought, witnessing that, that it would only take a military band to come up the road and World War Three would start immediately! And as for the, 'I was not a Nazi and nor did I support them,' it was discredited by the numbers who had voted for them, in excess of 95% in some areas, but Jack could only find that 100% of those he came into touch with were in the 5% who didn't vote for Hitler!

Again, there was little for the off-duty troops to do and the Brass were always surprised when surveys showed the troops hated Germany, their posting there, the Germans and the fact that there was bugger all to do off duty but drink and sort out the Krauts. The comparisons between the Yanks and the Brits was a disgrace. The truth was that for senior British officers and Civil Servants, life was very good, and for the squaddies, it was crap and no senior officer gave a damn. The lowest ranked Yanks, by comparison, lived like kings. The Brits did, however, have a splendid Library and Jack, as an avid reader, was in absolute heaven.

G Air was situated in the next block to Jack's, on the top floor, easy to get to and home from. The work was mind-numbingly boring. Their main duty related to co-ordinating RAF and Army needs in the form of air support, whether this was in the form of reconnaissance flights, passenger flights or bombing or fighter patrols. His job was purely clerical plus, as the most junior rank, gopher when the task could not be carried out by one of the DPs, and he was the official coffee maker! As the kitchen facilities were on the ground floor, this meant a bit of a trek up and down three floors. The biggest problem was the swing doors at the end of the corridors. Placed adjoining the central stairwell, they were meant to keep the heat in the building, and they did this very well. The problem was the width of the doors and the very strong return springs attached to them. The only way to get through them carrying a tray with five full cups of coffee was to back through them to the furthest possible extent and then to step smartly back whilst at the same time turning sideways so that the doors swinging shut did not catch the tray. The coffee stains on the wall and floor were a clear indicator that this was not always accomplished successfully.

Jack had been doing this for about three weeks when the accident occurred. Jack did not know what it was about senior ranks that he had to have so much trouble with them. Like in Aden, a junior General would not do, it had to be the commander of 1BR Corps himself, General Sir John Magrill. Stepping backwards smartly, as was the norm, Jack swung to the right, collided with the General and emptied the boiling hot coffee, from five mugs, all over him. For a second, nothing happened, then, swearing vociferously, the General started ripping of his trousers where his private parts were being boiled by the finest instant Nescafe money could buy.

The noise attracted all sorts of spectators who were instantly despatched by a bad tempered and hugely loud command to get back to work from the General. Jack did not know what to do. To offer to wipe the coffee off the General's balls did not seem wise. So he picked up the mugs, none of which had fortunately broken, and took them back to the kitchen from where he grabbed several dishcloths and returned and started mopping up the spilt coffee. This took a few trips back to the kitchen to squeeze out the coffee. By the time he had finished, the General had disappeared along with his Aide, who had brought a Crombie, an officer's overcoat, to restore a modicum of modesty. Jack made five more coffees and took them back to the office with no further problems.

Jack had only been in the office, open plan, for five minutes when the Wing Co's phone rang. He called out across to Jack,

"Did you, by any chance, empty coffee over the General and scald his balls?"

Jack had no other option other than to answer, "Yes, sir."

At which the Wing Co answered down the phone, "Yes, he's here." Putting the phone down, he said, "The General wants to see you immediately, and it's been nice knowing you for the short time you've been here." Jack was not amused but he did make his way to the General's office quite quickly.

"Now listen here," said the General once Jack had been marched in in front of him to announce his number, rank and name. "It occurs to me that you might be a bit worried that you were in trouble for boiling the GOC's balls. Well, you're not. It was entirely my fault. I came up behind you; I could see quite clearly that you were trying to get through those bloody swing doors with a tray of coffee and I stood much too close to you for safety. My fault entirely. You will no doubt enjoy the soubriquet, 'the General's balls boiler' but that is not your fault, it's mine. So get back to work and don't worry about it. Dismissed." At that, Jack smartly about turned and returned to his office where he was subjected to intense pressure to reveal all. He was the hero of the hour for a few days but gradually, it was forgotten about, but the General was not to forget him.

Jack woke one Saturday morning with intense toothache. Being a Saturday, he couldn't report sick to see a dentist; he had to suffer it for the weekend. On Monday, he was driven to the medical facilities about three miles away where he saw a male dentist. The experience was nowhere near as pleasant as when he had reported sick in Aden with a problem with the same tooth. There he had been eating a soft bread roll, a roti, when a filling came out of one of his upper right molars. Before he realised it, he had bitten down on the bread which had squeezed into the now available hole and split the tooth. Painful.

He was seen by a young, attractive WRNS dentist who, to work on his tooth, had to rest a rather large boob on his shoulder. Jack had always hated dentists but this one could have pulled out all his teeth with no anaesthetic if she had wanted to. She finished much too quickly as far as Jack was concerned but now, here he was, only three or four months later, suffering pain again from the same tooth.

The RAMC Dentist was not a happy chappy. He did not need Jack to point out which tooth it was, prodding it with one of their pointy instruments of torture, produced the reaction he expected in the form of a grunted 'Aaargh' from Jack.

"This tooth has only a temporary filling in it. Why have you not had a permanent one fitted?"

Jack said, "Because I didn't know it was a temporary one and I wasn't told to do so, sir."

"But surely you were told by the Dentist. He must have told you and you are in serious trouble for not having it done." Jack repeated that he had not been told, that the woman WRNS dentist had not told him, that having had the experience of her breast on his shoulder, it was so pleasant that he would have been delighted to have more treatment from her. The Dentist paused. Jack's details sounded convincing—especially the boobs bit! Believing that a Navy dentist had cocked up was not hard to do, inter-service rivalry being what it was and a woman at that was the only detail needed to convince him that Jack was telling the truth. There would not have been any real way to check Jack's story with HQ MEC closing down so he let it go. What he didn't let go was Jack's tooth.

"This will have to come out; there's not enough left to repair," and at that, he started sticking needles into Jack's gum to numb it. Jack only discovered years later that his four wisdom teeth had erupted from his gums horizontally, thus pushing all the other teeth tightly against one another meaning that the damaged tooth was held as in a vice. He didn't know that at the time and the Dentist, an officer, dealing with a Private, the lowest of the low, would never have deigned to explain. Having failed with the first two pairs of pliers, he reached for the giant killers. To Jack, sitting laid back in the chair and only partly able to see what was going on, the situation was dreadful. He was being pulled about all over the place and, despite the anaesthetic, it bloody hurt. This, as it turned out, last pair not only dragged the tooth out but it splintered it into many pieces in doing so—the last of which pushed itself out of the gum two years later during which time he was totally unable to bite down on the right hand side of his mouth. The hole bled profusely for the rest of the day, so much so, that at 1100 hrs, the Major took pity on him and told him to take the rest of the day off—something he was delighted to do.

Corporal Plover, in conversation in the queue in the cookhouse a week later, asked him if he felt fully recovered because the Wing Co was flying the following week and, as it was a dual seat Hawker Hunter, was offering to take anyone from the office with him. Jack thought about it for a moment and said that he didn't think that he felt better enough.

"Good answer," said Plover, "whoever goes up with him comes back with all the sick bags full up so the Major and the Flight Lieutenant, a non-flying type, had both been very ill and no one from the office now wanted to fly with him."

Although Jack had not given up on the idea of joining the AAC, he did not want to experience the delights of air sickness just yet. A week later, just before Christmas, Jack's posting back to the Depot for attendance at the RCB came through. He was posted on the 2nd January. Now why couldn't he have been sent back to the UK before Xmas where he could have surely wangled some time at home; but no, the Army always did things the worst way possible. He was due back in the UK on the 2nd January but was not due to go to the RCB until the middle of February, so he would be hanging around the Depot for the best part of two months plus and waiting to go to Mons time after that. In the event, he did experience Christmas in BAOR. To be fair, the Army did its best to make it an enjoyable time for the troops. The highlight was undoubtedly the Christmas Lunch when all the other ranks were served by the officers. Being the commanding HQ for the whole of the BAOR, there were a lot of very senior officers around the place and to be waited on by them generated a lot of banter between the ranks. Jack's favourite was being served coffee by the GOC who, since no coffee was being served to anyone else, must have arranged that especially for Jack. It was funny and indicative of the General's sense of humour and Jack was to remember it for many years, particularly when the coffee incident came back again nearly a year later.

Jack left BAOR on the 2nd of January as planned and returned to the depot which was now at Deepcut, Jack having been transferred to the RAOC on the disbandment of the RASC. All the RAOC units were concentrated there, the Depot for passing through soldiers, the Officers Training School, the Junior Leaders Regiment (for boy soldiers) and the Training Regiment for recruits joining the Army.

# Chapter 91

Jack was posted to the Depot. It handled soldiers passing through from the UK to abroad or other units in the UK, issuing them jungle kit, desert kit or whatever as appropriate; welcoming (in the loosest sense of the word) back soldiers from abroad and issuing them with kit as necessary for their next posting, handling the discharge of time served soldiers and holding any soldiers who were, for whatever reason between postings and did not, as yet, have a 'home' to go to.

Jack was in this latter category. It was a déjà-vu situation; directly applicable to the old POC Wing. These soldiers were spare bodies and 'available' for any odd jobs that needed doing. Jack was not a happy bunny as he could foresee what the next couple of months held for him. But he was too gloomy too quickly. As he marched towards the Company Office, he was spotted by WOI Dasanayaka; Jack had known him in Aden and Dasanayaka knew Jack's abilities. Asking where Jack was headed, Jack told him he was reporting to the Company Office for work allocation. Dasanayaka said, "Oh that's easy to sort out, go and change out of your fatigues, and put on your SD and report to me in that office over there. Do you know anything about issuing travel warrants?" Jack's face lit up as did Dasanayaka's when he told him about his experience moving the families out of Cyprus a couple of years before. It was only a matter of minutes before Jack was changed and ensconced behind a desk issuing train and plane tickets. But Jack was right to be gloomy; on the second day, a WOII, the nominal Company Sergeant Major, appeared, demanding of Jack why he was working there. Dasanayaka, a rank higher, interrupted and pointed out that he, seeing Hughes on the way to the Office, as ordered, had changed his orders and allocated him to work in the office for him using his expertise in issuing travel warrants etc. The CSM could thus not officially have a go at Jack, but he was not a happy bunny. Jack was not to know but there had already been problems between the two Warrant Officers. The CSM simply left the office, and Jack hoped that was the end of it. However, it was not to be. On Part I Orders that night, specific orders were published for Jack to be attached to the CSM's Team for 'special training'.

When Jack asked the CSM if he could have a copy of the 'special training' programme, he was brusquely told, "I'll tell you the bloody programme when I'm ready to do so." Life then became really unpleasant. First thing in the morning, before breakfast, Jack was sent with two or three other soldiers in transit to the stables and was ordered to muck them out. The RAOC still taught new officers to ride and had a Mule Company for use in inhospitable countryside. Breakfast had to be snatched as best they could before they were sent to the Officers' Mess to act as servants and waiters for the midday and evening meals. In-between, when they were released after washing up after lunch, they were given all sorts of unpleasant tasks, digging ditches for drains, digging out clogged up drains and anything else the CSM could conjure up.

One morning, Jack saw one of the 2Coy RASC boys from Aden, the Petrol Pump NCO, passing through. They only had a brief conversation but the Corporal, knowing Jack's history with Charlie Wilson, told him his latest adventure. Apparently, he was overseeing the loading of some of 2 Coy's vehicles onto lighters in the port. It was a time-consuming business as each lighter, nothing more than a flat platform with two out board motors at the back, had to be secured to the landing stage by a number of ropes to prevent it drifting away and leaving the vehicle being loaded to drop through the gap into the harbour. It was well past dinner time, but the vehicles had to be loaded before they could knock off. Charlie Wilson, looking at the last vehicle, an Engineer's Recovery Vehicle costing a small fortune, was dismayed when the Corporal in charge of the raft said to him that given the size and weight he would use the ropes as usual but in addition would want to assemble a mobile bridge structure, a bit like sand channels welded together to cover the gap to make sure it wouldn't strain the ropes, open up a gap, and drop the Scammell into the harbour. No, Charlie knew better. He was already late for his lunch, (officers had lunch, other ranks had dinner) and he was dammed if he was going to be any later. Consequently, he told the Royal Engineer's Corporal in charge of the ferry to simply drive it up against the harbour wall and keep the engines running to hold it there whilst the Scammell was driven on board. The Corporal was horrified.

"But, sir, that is unsafe. The Scammell is heavier than the power of the outboards can hold, and it will simply fall into the harbour."

"Do as you are told, Corporal, it will be quite all right."

"But, sir…"

"That is an order, Corporal. Do it."

Just then, the RE Sergeant turned up to be told to put the Corporal on a charge for disobeying an order. The Sergeant looked at the Corporal and asked him why he was disobeying an order. The Corporal explained. The Sergeant turned to Charlie Wilson and said, "Corporal Johnston will, of course, obey your order, sir but as, in his view, driving the Scammell in such a manner is very dangerous, who do you expect to drive it?" Charlie was now stuck. After a short pause he said, "I will, of course." And he did, straight to the bottom of Aden Harbour. The soldiers simply stood there watching to see if Charlie made it to the surface; no one made any real attempt at a rescue, but they did laugh heartily as he climbed up one of the ladders extending down into the harbour. Nor did anyone remember hearing the ferry outboard engines being throttled back just as the Scammell drove aboard. The Sergeant was heard to say to Charlie, "I hope you have a very rich daddy, sir, otherwise you are going to take a very long time to pay for that very expensive piece of Army property you have just driven into the harbour." Jack loved the story and hoped he would meet Charlie again to be able to wind him up about it, but he never did.

Jack gradually learned that the CSM had a pathological hatred of any soldiers who were considered as potentially officer material. Apparently, he had applied to be considered for a Quarter Master Commission, which would not involve having to pass an Officer Cadet School course but would simply mean being promoted to a commission based on experience and good performance. The rumour was that three separate Commanding Officers had turned his request for promotion down and the last time it had been made very clear that he should not waste his and more particularly the CO's time by applying again. As Jack hadn't even passed the RCB, and thus his attendance at Mons OCS was, therefore, totally in doubt, being picked on in such a manner seemed especially hard.

It seemed to Jack that some of the work they were doing wasn't quite kosher. Things like mucking out the stables and working in the Officers' Mess were obviously military in nature but digging pipe trenches for civilian projects, although good for strengthening muscles etc. were not of a military nature— builders were coming along and laying pipes in them and that didn't seem quite right. These doubts lingered with him, but he couldn't place them in a manner which would attract attention and expose just what exactly? So Jack just left it at the back of his mind to be dealt with later.

In February, he went to the RCB, almost hoping that he would fail to get that bastard CSM off his back, but it was equally possible that Jack was extra-determined to pass so that he could pay the bastard back in spades.

Rather than go on the train as he had the last time and be just one of a number turning up, Jack decided to hire a car, in the event, a brand new Ford Cortina, and make an entrance. He had talked to as many people as he could about the dos and don'ts which would get him through or fail him instantly. None of them were insider secrets and therefore to be relied on, so he decided to just be himself but this time, instead of remaining in the background, he would be there at the front leading and commanding. Quite how he would do this, he didn't know, but that was the plan!

The format was exactly the same as the first time. The athletic tests were a doddle as before. The written tests were hard, and he had no idea what he had scored. The personality assessments weren't hard, but some of the answers would cause problems. He knew from the reports he had typed up in Aden on the Parachute Battalion assessments when they were being assessed to fire the Vigilant Anti-tank Missiles that certain answers in combination could lead to failure or success although quite why that was, was a mystery. He, therefore, made sure he avoided them as far as he could. There was a current affairs question paper, most of which was straight forward. One question made him think a bit. The question was, 'Why has Sir Richard Turnbull been in the news recently?' The name sort of rang a bell but it was one of those where it is somehow running around the back of your mind so that it was difficult to pin down. He, therefore, left the question and carried on with the rest of the paper. He finished it within the time allowed and so had some time to rack his brain. And then it came to him. Turnbull had been the High Commissioner in Aden and he had recently commuted the death sentence on a Guardsman Gabriel to life imprisonment. Gabriel had been one of a group of soldiers who had attempted to cheat a taxi driver out of the taxi fare by running away at their destination. Unfortunately, the taxi driver had caught Gabriel and in the ensuing fight to escape, Gabriel had killed the taxi driver. He had subsequently been tried, convicted and sentenced to death by an Arab court. By commuting the sentence, Turnbull had done Gabriel no favours since life imprisonment in an Arab jail in Aden would have been hell on earth for a British soldier, but that was why he had been in the news. And Jack just had time to write it in before the bell for time up rang.

He was interviewed by a Lt Col in the RAEC who asked a wide range of education-testing questions, but he also gave Jack some praise. He said he had been much amused by Jack's clever allegory to soldiers drinking too much alcohol and seeing pink elephants. At first, Jack had no idea what he was talking about as he certainly hadn't intended any allegories—he didn't even know what they were. Then it came to him. A part of the testing involved writing an essay. Various subject headings were offered as options, none of which appealed, so he chose, 'I well remember…' to describe a trip to Tsavo Game Park in Kenya when he had gone there on leave from Aden. When serving in Aden for two years. Troops were entitled to either one trip back to the UK for four weeks and one to Mombasa, or two trips of two weeks each to Mombasa. Like most troops, Jack had chosen one trip home to the UK and one to Kenya. The UK one had been great, spending the month with Janet and his family but the Mombasa one had been a bit of a disaster.

It started with having to carry his seat out to the Argosy aircraft in which he was to fly from Aden to Mombasa. The plane had been stripped out of all home comforts from previous flights, hence a string of soldiers carrying out their seats to the plane. They were at least fitted by RAF personnel who made it clear they didn't much like doing this for army types. The few families that were on the flight at least had theirs fitted by the RAF, and it was noticeable that there was a considerable gap between the two groups.

Jack was seated between two troopers of the 5th Inniskilling Dragoon Guards. With Jack in the middle, it was not long before he was included in the conversations of the two troopers which were taking part across him. The Argosy wasn't pressurised, so it could not fly high in the less turbulent air. It was noisy, uncomfortable, and entirely lacking in creature comforts. Refreshments in the long flight were dried up cheese sandwiches, obviously leftovers from British Rail, and lukewarm orange juice. No toilet facilities had been pointed out to them although a canvas doored corner reeking of sick and crap advertised its own existence.

Staggering off the flight in Mombasa was a strange experience. It was July and boiling hot in Aden. Landing in Mombasa, they had crossed the equator and in just a few hours, they had gone from the height of the hot season to the height of the cold season so the natives hanging around the airport were amused by white men arriving in Africa and putting on jumpers!

The families were guided towards a ubiquitous Bedford coach in good condition and the troops were ordered to board a beaten-up old wreck. On their way to the Silversands Leave Centre, they were first told of the official rules regarding out-of-bounds areas, things to watch out for as there was developing in Kenya, which was basically self-ruling, a whites out campaign and there were certain basic precautions it was wise to take. They were also unofficially advised on behaviour with the local women and in the bars which abounded the dock area, some of which provided very dubious entertainments indeed.

On arrival at the camp, first class huts for the families and tents for the troops, their passports were collected from them—broke soldiers were known to have sold them and then claimed they had lost them—and allocated bed spaces, they were told to watch the post boards for Part I Orders for return flight times etc. and that was that, their time was their own. Having agreed to go for a drink that evening, Jack took a stroll around the camp which was inhabited by more Vervet monkeys than people, monkeys that were very tame and expert thieves at stealing anything edible or not tied down. The beach was magnificent, beautiful white sand stretching for miles—hence the title Silversands. Just offshore, visible at low tide, was a coral reef with a small line of black seaweed indicating the high water mark on the beach. There was nothing in the way of beach beds or parasols, but it truly was a magnificent site, just crying out to be overdeveloped for tourist multitudes.

After a short, refreshing kip, Jack met up with Padraig and Paddy (Jack always thought it was funny that an Irishman should actually have the name Paddy as a given name) and serious drinking began for them but Jack, careful of alcohol since his experience of ending up in hospital in Aden, was very efficient at masking how little he was drinking. They were astonished that the bar they were in started closing up just before 2400 hrs. Padraig, grabbing hold of a passing waiter, demanded to know why they were closing when they had been told you could drink all night. The waiter answered that they would have to go to a nightclub if they wanted to continue drinking.

So they did exactly that. The place didn't open until 0030 hrs so they had a few minutes' wait to get in and when they did, they were lucky to grab a booth right at the edge of the dance floor. They sat down with Jack in the middle and the two troopers either side of him. As they were ordering their Tusker beers, two easy, but expensive, ladies of the night attached themselves to the two Irishmen. When Jack looked around the club, there were quite a few women in pairs making up to pairs of men. Jack being in a trio was therefore a little unusual. Just as well, as it turned out.

A girl approached Padraig, who by this time had a girl already sitting on his lap and in a loud and strident voice demanded to know, "Why you with this girl tonight when you with me last night?" Padraig had no idea what she was talking about, having only arrived in Kenya that day. He rapidly discovered that among the working girls men who moved from one girl to another were referred to as 'butterflies' and they didn't like it because of the loss of trade and the chance of a disease being spread across lots of women.

Trying to explain that he had only arrived that day and could not have been with her the night before did not go down well, so convinced was she of his identity. Her mate, even less convinced, picked up one of the bottles of beer and laid Padraig out with one blow. Paddy, seeing this, simply punched her and laid her out at Padraig's feet. At this, the first girl grabbed one of the other bottles and laid Paddy out. Not content with that, she then headed for Jack, clearly intent on serving out the same treatment to him. Jack was trapped in the middle of the booth with two unconscious Irishmen on either side of him and one woman, unconscious, draped over both of them and no way to escape a bottling. Well, one way did occur to Jack and he took it—a straight right to her solar plexus sat her down in the middle of two Irishmen and the other working girl with Jack half standing half sitting in the booth just as the Kenyan police burst in. Looking at the four recumbent bodies and a half way up Jack, the Sergeant, who was the biggest man Jack had ever seen, he must have been at least 6' 9" and 25 stone and wearing a uniform so heavily starched and pressed, you could have shaved with the creases, this man mountain carefully surveyed the scene and then said, "You come with me, white man," and Jack did. Various waiters and Constables were used to dump the other four bodies in the back of the police wagon, was it called a Black Maria here in Mombasa, Jack wondered, and they were all carted off to the nick. Thrown into the holding tank, no effort was made to revive any of the four, although the female 'leader' was puffing, moaning and being sick. Gradually, they all came around with little more to show than a few bruises and bumps between them.

It was a good hour before the three lads were interviewed by the same Sergeant who had brought them in. It was clear he had spoken to the girls and gave every appearance of accepting their story although quite what crime they had committed by acting as butterflies was unclear. Once Padraig had explained they had only arrived in the country that day and they had been attacked by the women, not as the women alleged, seemed only to confuse the issue. Proof that they had arrived the previous day, it now being well past midnight and their not being in the country the day before, which took some working out. The demand for proof could not be met until Paddy announced that he had not handed his passport in to the office and if someone would only run him back to the camp, he could prove it. So that's what the police did.

Whilst Padraig and Jack waited in the holding tank until Paddy returned, their education was completed. There were a few ladies of the night incarcerated, including the two in involved in the lad's case, and they continued to carry on their business in the tank—quite extraordinary. The police allowing this to go on was even more extraordinary until one of the Constables explained that in this way they could afford to pay their fines (including bribes to the police!) and everyone was happy, girl, customer and police.

How life changed once Paddy arrived back. With absolute evidence that he had not been in Kenya and could not have been a butterfly, the police were all full of apologies; Padraig's loud protests that they had been illegally arrested obviously struck home. The police even took them back to the night club, entered them without the necessity of a second entrance fee and even ensconced them into 'their' table at the front of the rows. Three bottles of Tusker beer even magically appeared before them and although there wasn't much of the show left, it being nearly dawn by this time, they did manage to enjoy what was left of it.

# Chapter 92

Jack decided to stay away from the two Irish Troopers as much as possible—they got him into too much trouble—and so he planned a couple of trips, one a full day to the Tsavo Game Park, quite a way inland and up on the plateau, and a ride on the little narrow-gauge railway. He also arranged to hire a Morris Traveller for the day to explore the coast. The Tsavo visit, on a coach with loads of other people, left extremely early in the morning, before dawn.

In the essay, he filled it with what he felt was soppy comments. He wrote, 'the musical dawn chorus of many birds, most of them unknown to him were in full song, and similar extravagant phraseology. At one stage, when the sun was way above the horizon, the guide started getting excited about elephants. Shouting it out loudly and gesticulating out of the coach, he was clearly enraptured at seeing them. Jack was baffled. No matter how hard he looked, he couldn't see them. For Christ's sake, elephants are bloody big grey things; how was it possible that he couldn't see the bloody things? Then he could. They weren't bloody big grey things at all—they were bloody big pinky red things. The soil in that area was a reddish pink and the elephants' habit of throwing dust up over themselves meant they adopted the colour of the countryside. It didn't help that the area was populated with huge numbers of termite mounds, fifteen to twenty feet high, made of the reddish pink soil so it was no wonder Jack couldn't see the elephants! He didn't know a Lt Col in the RAEC would be delighted by this.

Returning to the camp was to discover that he and Padraig had been designated to accept the kind invitation of Mr and Mrs Patel to take tea with them the following day. Neither of the lads were pleased, but it was made clear to them that they had no choice in the matter. Most of the officer families had received similar invitations but from up-country white farmers. Officers got the good invitations from the planters and the other ranks had to make do with the rest.

Arriving spot on 1600 hours, Jack and Padraig found themselves ringing the doorbell of a quite palatial house. The door was opened by a uniformed butler who ushered them into a drawing room where tea had been laid out. Waiting to greet them were Mr and Mrs Patel and two sons; if there were any daughters in the family they were not on view. Introducing themselves as Sergeants, it had been made clear that the Patels would be expecting NCOs, not other ranks, they were invited to sit. There then took place tea as per the finest days of the Raj. Sandwiches with the crusts cut off, tiny tea cups and loads of cakes were slowly consumed. Fresh pots of hot tea were brought in by a young black girl who could not have been more than 11 or 12 and for whom the tea pots were very heavy. The accident waiting to happen did; she knocked over one of the stands piled high with cakes and broke one of the plates. Mrs Patel went berserk. She started slapping and punching the girl around the face and neck all the way out of the door. Returning, completely composed with the Butler who proceeded to tidy up the mess, Mrs Patel said, "These damn blacks, they're only just down from the trees; one does one's best to civilise them, but it really is just a waste of time."

Jack was to discover several times during the rest of his life that racial prejudice between Asians and blacks was far worse than anything between whites and blacks. Jack and Padraig soon made their excuses and left. It was the only time in his life that Jack was to experience 'high tea' and very glad of that he was. The rest of his leave passed quickly and uneventfully, and he was almost glad to return to Aden.

Writing his essay at the RCB, he, of course, left out the interesting bits of his leave and only made reference to the reddish pink elephants because that was true and the Colonel had thought he had made a clever reference to soldiers seeing pink elephants because of their drinking. Jack was about to put him right when he heard the Colonel saying, "I thought it was so good that I've given you an A minus and I've never given an A before." Jack shut up. The Colonel went on to say, "And you were the only one here who knew why Sir Richard Turnbull had been in the news recently. Well done. How did you know?"

"Saw it in the newspapers, sir."

"But what made you remember him?"

"Served in Aden, sir."

"Ah, so that's it, but very well done anyway."

There was no gang of hooray henrys on this course which was just as well as Jack had decided that he would not be shut out this time by a bunch of public-school nonentities who made bloody awful officers in Jack's quite considerable, by now, experience of the Army. In conversations, Jack had let it out that he was a serving soldier recently returned from Aden. He was able to entertain his team with stories such as the CSM and the exploding shit and the exposure of the "I'll blow your bleedin' 'ead off, sir."

As it happened, Jack was the one selected to be the Team Leader for the command task that introduced the team to the way such tasks were to be carried out. Jack was given three minutes to make his plan and then he described it to the Major. Calling the team over, who had been deliberately kept out of earshot, Jack explained his plan to them. He then allocated tasks to each of the team and away they went. It did not go to plan. Jack knew that there would be problems and he was able to keep control until they did just complete the task in the time allotted.

Jack was again the first one chosen for the individual command tasks where how he did mattered. Looking at the task as the Major described it, he was looking at two platforms, about four feet square each with their tops about three feet off the ground. They were about seven or eight feet apart, and it was obvious that the timber planks available to him, should he want to use them, were all much too short to span the gap, the longest being about 5-6 feet. There were also scaffolding poles available, all about ten feet long, but they were very flexible, wet and slippery. Although there was some rope available, Jack could see no use for it. Whilst the team members were all fit young men and could be relied on to jump gaps of reasonable size the real problem was the burden they were required to take with them. It was a 40-gallon oil drum, half full of water, and a devil to handle. It meant that the 'bridge' that they built would have to be sturdy and that ruled out the scaffolding poles. In the five minutes he was given to formulate a plan, Jack

314

walked round and round the site desperately trying to work out what to do. The tops of the platforms were painted green and thus could be touched. Anything painted red could not. Jack's eyes were drawn to two 'A' shaped pieces of wood which were sticking out from the front edge of the platform from which they were starting. Similar 'A' frames stuck out towards them from the other platform. Examining them closely, they were painted mainly red, but the inside of the 'A' was painted green. There must be a reason for that he thought. Looking around, he could see some logs which were available to him but which were painted red apart from two bands of green around them. Offering one of them up to the 'A' shapes the log would just fit in the space between the two legs of the 'A's. Having spotted that it was easy to see that a plank could be hooked under the top of the platform and resting on the green part of the log could project halfway across the gap. Someone walking out on it could drop a plank onto the other platform and carefully cross. The one across could then place a log through the 'A' frames on the other side, place the plank on top of the log and under the top of the platform and the bridge thus created would enable the team and the barrel to be rolled over. They could then disassemble the starting 'bridge' and carry the log and planks used over. Describing his plan to the Major produced a smile and the team completed the task well under the 15 minutes allowed for it. The Major quietly said, "Well done. When I saw that you had seen the logs fitted into the 'A' frame I knew you would do it." He probably shouldn't have spoken to Jack that way, but Jack did appreciate it.

The second task was again to get across from one platform to another, but this time in between was a small stream. The burden was again a 40-gallon drum and to assist them were several long ropes, scaffold poles and no planks at all. Jack was only half listening to the plan, which seemed highly unlikely to succeed, but was giving the area a good looking over. The almost hidden green paint on the 'A' frames had taught him to look carefully at everything. There was a huge oak tree growing on the other bank of the stream and the trunk was painted red up to about eight feet.

The team started on the task by trying to tie together scaffold poles which were supposed to form a bridge. The first problem was immediately apparent—they were too short to reach across the gap once they had overlapped lengths to tie together. They tied more poles together and then attached them to the first set of poles to form a longer bridge. Dropping it over formed a bridge all right but it was nowhere near strong or secure enough to support the first volunteer to attempt the crossing who discovered just how cold water is in February when he was deposited into it by the collapse of the bridge.

The leader did manage to keep control but persevering at the same system which failed time and again did not get them very far, with Jack worrying that he would need to volunteer for a soaking pretty soon or be marked down as a shirker. Looking around, he, in a different position to the one he had originally surveyed the site from, had a better view of the oak tree and what he could now see was a narrow green band around one of the red painted branches. *Now why should that be,* he thought. *It must be there for a means to cross the stream, but how?* Then it came to him; if a rope was thrown up and over the branch hard enough and long enough to swing back so that it could be caught by the thrower, they could then swing people across a la Tarzan and then swing the barrel across to be followed by the whole team. The rope could then be pulled across and taken with them as the task required. It was a matter of moments to interrupt—they only had five minutes left—and get the rope thrown over. The first couple of attempts failed miserably, either not swinging back far enough to be caught or landing on the red paint on the branch. The one the Major allowed was a bit of a cheat because it did land a bit on the red, but he allowed it to pass so away they went to finish bang on the time allowed.

Thereafter, Jack had them eating out of his hand; anything he suggested was seized upon with alacrity even though it didn't work more often than it did. Jack was convinced that some of them were impossible so that the problem threw up the natural leader of the group for the others to follow. Whether they succeeded or not, Jack undoubtedly remained the leader of that group.

He left with all the others on the Thursday lunchtime but whilst they went by train, he drove the hired Cortina back to his parent's house in Crowthorne. He had booked a day's leave for Friday and was due to return to the Depot, about 11 miles away, for 0859 hours on the Monday morning. Janet had also booked a day's leave to make it a long weekend. On Saturday, a letter arrived in the post. When he first opened it, out fell a brochure about Mons Officer Cadet School and nothing else. It was only when he looked inside the envelope that he saw a squashed up A5 piece of paper informing him that he had been successful at the RCB and would be offered a place at Mons Officer Cadet School in due course; he was posted to the Depot at Deepcut in the meantime. Everyone in his family went mad. His mother rang one of the aunts in Maesteg to brag, twenty minutes on the phone, very costly long distance, describing her heroic son who had been recommended for a commission by three generals in Aden, in the war, and all of a sudden, Jack was back in her good books.

# Chapter 93

Arriving back at the Depot on Monday, Jack said nothing of his success. He wanted to keep it quiet for as long as possible and himself as far away from the CSM as possible. He had been a bastard when there was only a chance of Jack being selected for Officer Cadet training and now Jack thought he was likely to be an even bigger bastard once he knew Jack had passed the RCB. And he was. Jack had an early start every day in the stables, including Saturdays and Sundays; horses don't stop for the weekend; working in the Cookhouse peeling potatoes and other vegetables for dinner; he was not sent to waiter in the Officers' Mess this time— that would put him too close to officer country and the CSM didn't want any relationships striking up—he was back to the Cookhouse for washing up after dinner and tea and was very often employed in digging channels for pipes. It was this last that struck Jack's mind as being odd. Once he had dug them, civilian contractors laid the pipes, then Jack was set to covering them over. Surely digging the trenches and filling them in afterwards was the contractor's responsibility rather than the Army's?

It was only the day before he was due to go to Mons on the 11th May that he heard a possible explanation from one of the other soldiers who had also fallen foul of the CSM. He claimed to have seen the CSM in a pub in Aldershot with the contractor and a brown envelope had been seen to change hands. *That's it*, thought Jack. If soldiers, free labour, dug the trenches and filled them in again afterwards, the contractor would be saved those labour costs, and so the CSM was certainly getting a kick back. It was too late for Jack to do anything about that now, especially as a Private Soldier's word, albeit now of an Officer Cadet, would carry no weight against that of a CSM. So it would have to wait until he came back.

On the morning of 11th May, Jack handed in kit and said his goodbyes to those it was politic to do so but he left the CSM to last. Jack walked into his office without knocking nor did he slam to attention. Looking up, the CSM said, "What do you want?"

"What do you want, sir," said Jack. The CSM looked at him dumbfounded. "With effect from 0001 hours this morning, I am an Officer Cadet and thus entitled to be addressed as sir by anyone in a more junior rank to me, so 'What do you want, sir.'" Jack had no idea if he was talking bollocks or not but the look on the CSM's face whilst he tried to work out whether what Jack said was true or not was worth a million pounds and showed he didn't either. The one thing he was absolutely certain about was that the CSM was not going to call him sir, rules or not. So he carried on, "In any case, when I return, you will both call me sir and salute me, and I fully intend to make your life hell, I'm going to get my own back on you, you bastard and you'll wish you had never set eyes on me."

The CSM was on safer ground here and he replied, "In your dreams. CSMs eat 2nd Lieutenants for breakfast, and I will enjoy eating you, you stupid stuck up little cunt. Now fuck off." Jack looked at him for what must have been a minute—he had been told by several people that he had an intense and unnerving stare, which he used to best effect and he then said, "It's us cunts that make you pricks stand to attention, and stand to attention you will." Jack then turned and walked away.

On the Saturday before, Jack had been to a local garage and bought a car. Mons OCS was only about 14 miles from Crowthorne where Janet was temporarily living with Jack's sister, having now been demobbed from the Army, and he wanted to be able to nip off over there whenever the chance offered to see her. Little was he to know how few chances there would be and how hard they would be worked. He bought a Morris Isis, a luxury version of the Oxford, fitted with a straight six cylinder, 2,600 ccs engine and slightly past its best days; after all, he did not know where he would be posted to post-Mons and he did not want to be in the position of having to sell an expensive car at a loss because he was posted abroad and could not take it with him. Therefore, for just £80, he had wheels and off he set in plenty of time to be there by midday.

The sign said 'Welcome'…

# Epilogue

Aden was a very small place. The stories, on the whole, are true – I don't propose to identify how true, that is the liberty an author has to create his own characters, places and times, and if you think you can identify yourself, you can't – you're not in it – my Aden, my characters!